"I keep telling myself that she just can't get much better, but with every book she amazes and surprises me!" —*The Best Reviews*

Praise for the futuristic fantasy of
Robin D. Owens

Heart Search

"Will have readers on the edge of their seats . . . Another terrific tale from the brilliant mind of Robin D. Owens. Don't miss it."
—*Romance Reviews Today*

"A taut mixture of suspense and action . . . that leaves you stunned."
—*Smexy Books*

"Thank you, Ms. Owens, for this wonderful series."
—*Night Owl Reviews*

Heart Journey

"Sexy, emotionally intense, and laced with humor . . . Draws readers into one of the more imaginative otherworldly cultures."
—*Library Journal*

"[A] skillfully crafted read for any lover of futuristic or light paranormal romance."
—*Fresh Fiction*

"It is no secret that I love Ms. Owens's Heart series . . . [A] wonderful piece of fantasy, science fiction, romance, and a dash of mystery. *Heart Journey* is no different, a delight to read." —*Night Owl Reviews*

Heart Change

"The story accelerates as new dangers to Avellana crop up, and the relationship between Signet and Cratag develops, making for a satisfying read." —*Booklist*

"Each story is as fresh and new as the first one was. I am always delighted when a new Heart book is published!" —*Fresh Fiction*

"A satisfying return to an intriguing world. Cratag and Signet will leave you wanting more." —*The Romance Reader*

Heart Fate

"A true delight to read, and it should garner new fans for this unique and enjoyable series." —*Booklist*

"[This] emotionally rich tale blends paranormal abilities, family dynamics, and politics; adds a serious dash of violence; and dusts it all with humor and whimsy." —*Library Journal*

"A wonderfully delightful story . . . The author's creativity shines." —*Darque Reviews*

Heart Dance

"[A] superior series." —*The Best Reviews*

"I look forward to my yearly holiday in Celta, always a dangerous and fascinating trip." —*Fresh Fiction*

"Sensual, riveting, and filled with the wonderful cast of characters from previous books, as well as some new ones, *Heart Dance* is exquisite in its presentation." —*Romance Reviews Today*

Heart Choice

"The romance is passionate, the characters engaging, and the society and setting exquisitely crafted." —*Booklist*

"Maintaining the 'world building' for science fiction and character driven plot for romance is near impossible. Owens does it brilliantly." —*The Romance Readers Connection*

"Well-written, humor-laced, intellectually and emotionally involving story, which explores the true meaning of family and love." —*Library Journal*

Heart Secret

Robin D. Owens

BERKLEY SENSATION, NEW YORK

THE BERKLEY PUBLISHING GROUP
Published by the Penguin Group
Penguin Group (USA) Inc.
375 Hudson Street, New York, New York 10014, USA

Penguin Group (Canada), 90 Eglinton Avenue East, Suite 700, Toronto, Ontario M4P 2Y3, Canada (a division of Pearson Penguin Canada Inc.) • Penguin Books Ltd., 80 Strand, London WC2R 0RL, England • Penguin Group Ireland, 25 St. Stephen's Green, Dublin 2, Ireland (a division of Penguin Books Ltd.) • Penguin Group (Australia), 250 Camberwell Road, Camberwell, Victoria 3124, Australia (a division of Pearson Australia Group Pty. Ltd.) • Penguin Books India Pvt. Ltd., 11 Community Centre, Panchsheel Park, New Delhi—110 017, India • Penguin Group (NZ), 67 Apollo Drive, Rosedale, Auckland 0632, New Zealand (a division of Pearson New Zealand Ltd.) • Penguin Books (South Africa) (Pty.) Ltd., 24 Sturdee Avenue, Rosebank, Johannesburg 2196, South Africa

Penguin Books Ltd., Registered Offices: 80 Strand, London WC2R 0RL, England

This book is an original publication of The Berkley Publishing Group.

This is a work of fiction. Names, characters, places, and incidents either are the product of the author's imagination or are used fictitiously, and any resemblance to actual persons, living or dead, business establishments, events, or locales is entirely coincidental. The publisher does not have any control over and does not assume any responsibility for author or third-party websites or their content.

Copyright © 2012 by Robin D. Owens.
Cover illustration by Tony Mauro.
Cover design by George Long.
Cover handlettering by Ron Zinn.
Interior text design by Kristin del Rosario.

PUBLISHING HISTORY
Berkley Sensation trade paperback edition / August 2012

Library of Congress Cataloging-in-Publication Data

Owens, Robin D.
Heart secret / Robin D. Owens.—Berkley Sensation trade paperback ed.
        p.   cm .
      ISBN 978-0-425-25314-4 (pbk.)
      1. Life on other planets—Fiction.   1. Title.
PS3615.W478H475   2012   2012015839
          813'.6—dc23

PRINTED IN THE UNITED STATES OF AMERICA

10   9   8   7   6   5   4   3   2   1

ALWAYS LEARNING

PEARSON

To those who enjoy visiting Celta.
Thank you.

Characters

The Mugworts:

Artemisia Mugwort: SecondLevel Healer assigned temporarily to Primary HealingHall, who caretakes and lives in the secret sanctuary of Druida City that only lets in the desperate, BalmHeal estate.

Tiana Mugwort: Younger sister of Artemisia and good friend of Camellia Darjeeling D'Hawthorn (heroine of *Heart Search*), a FirstLevel Priestess at GreatCircle Temple.

Sinjin Mugwort: Artemisia's father, ex–GraceLord Mugwort, ex-judge, author of legal treatises, caretaker of BalmHeal estate/FirstGrove.

Quina Mugwort: Artemisia's mother, a SecondLevel Healer and caretaker of BalmHeal estate/FirstGrove.

Randa: Artemisia's Fam.

Garrett Primross: Private investigator and owner of Prime Investigations. Sole survivor of the first people infected with the dreaded Iasc sickness.

Rusby: Garrett's Fam.

Note: Garrett's feral Fam informants are not listed here by name since their numbers are always in flux, but include a gang of cats, at least two dogs, foxes, and the occasional housefluff (rabbit).

The Hawthorns, Garrett's Friends:

GreatLord Huathe Laev T'Hawthorn: Entrepreneur and Garrett's best friend. Laev is nephew to Lark Hawthorn Holly, a FirstLevel Healer (*Heart Search*).

Camellia Darjeeling D'Hawthorn: Wife of Laev, friend of Tiana and Artemisia. Owner of Darjeeling's Teahouse and Darjeeling's HouseHeart. (*Heart Search*)

Brazos: Laev's Familiar Companion, a young long-haired black cat.

The Healers:

FirstLevel Healer Ura Heather: Head of the Primary HealingHall.

FirstLevel Healer Lark Hawthorn Holly: Works at Primary HealingHall and All Class HealingHall, niece to Ura Heather (*Heart Duel*).

GrandLord T'Heather: Retired head of Primary HealingHall, patriarch, father of Ura, MotherSire (grandfather) of Lark Hawthorn Holly.

The Guards:

Captain Black Ilex Winterberry: Captain of the Druida City guards, liaison with the FirstFamilies, wed to Trif Clover Winterberry (*Heart Quest*). He handled the original investigation of the Black Magic Cult.

Fol Berberis: A guard who investigated the original Black Magic Cult.

Rosa Milkweed: A guard who investigated the original Black Magic Cult.

Others/Suspects:

GreatLord Muin T'Vine (Vinni): The prophet of Celta, who has a Fam (Flora) who was nearly sacrificed by the Black Magic Cult.

Avellana Hazel: Mural artist and prodigy. She has a Fam (Rhyz) who was nearly sacrificed by the Black Magic Cult.

GreatLady Danith Mallow D'Ash: HeartMate of T'Ash, an animal Healer. (*HeartMate*)

A. Gwydion Ash: Second son of GreatLord T'Ash and D'Ash, an animal Healer.

Straif T'Blackthorn: GrandLord T'Blackthorn, FirstFamilies Grand-Lord, best tracker on Celta, married to Mitchella Clover D'Blackthorn. (*Heart Choice*)

Trif Clover Winterberry: Wife of Captain Black Ilex Winterberry, surviving victim of the Black Magic Cult. (*Heart Quest*)

Dufleur D'Thyme D'Willow: Wife of GreatLord Saille T'Willow, surviving victim of the Black Magic Cult (*Heart Dance*), cousin to Captain Black Ilex Winterberry.

Sedwy Grove D'Clover: Wife of GrandLord Walker Clover ("Noble Heart" in *Hearts and Swords*), dupe of the Black Magic Cult.

Barton Clover: Brother of GrandLord Walker Clover, head of security of Clover Compound.

One

Nightmares and a sense of foreboding woke him, so Garrett Primross walked to work as dawn broke hoping the infrequent uneasy feeling of doom was wrong for the first time in his life. In his career as a private investigator, he felt in control. He knew what he was doing. And at work he might be able to avoid or mitigate any disaster that might be looming today.

As he approached the back entrance of his shabby office building located in a lower-middle-class neighborhood, a cat hissed and a group of seven intelligent feral cats slipped from the shadows within the alley. Animals that Garrett used as observers and informants, they were able to become Familiar Companions to people if they'd wanted. Most didn't. They preferred the wild and free life—with regular meals and occasional petting.

Garrett had contacts within the fox dens and with the rare wild dog.

Gar-rett! the current leader of the ragtag band of ferals shouted loudly in Garrett's mind.

I hear you, he broadcast to the group. Their milling around slightly decreased.

You promised first thing at office, We get FOOD! Black-and-White tom insisted.

I haven't broken that promise, Garrett said.

There is a MAN on OUR front stoop. He has big magic-Flair. He looks like he belongs around here, but he wears clothes that don't smell of him. He wants to talk to YOU.

At a little after dawn, septhours before WorkBell? Not a good sign. *How do you know?* Garrett asked telepathically.

He said your name to the door, but the door was quiet. Then he looked at Us and told Us, but We ignored him. You can talk to him, but We get Our FOOD first!

That's the deal, Garrett agreed, though his curiosity was ruffled. So were the hairs on the nape of his neck that warned of trouble.

The young and slinky short-furred black cat slipped around the corner of the building at the end of the alley. *I got close. He did not see Me.*

Maybe not, but if the man had great psi power—Flair—Garrett would have bet that the guy had sensed the intelligent animal.

He did NOT sense Me with any of his Flair, the cat, also a tom, insisted. *He smells like rich.*

Garrett grunted. Probably a Nobleman. A spot between his shoulder blades twitched and the damn foreboding increased. Sounded like a man with a problem. A high-class client usually meant a tough problem. The last one had included theft, kidnapping, and murder.

And he smells like a long-eared, ball-tailed housefluff Familiar Companion, the black cat that Garrett called Sleek Black continued.

More interesting, but still not enough data for Garrett to figure out who the guy might be.

And he smells like RESIDENCE.

Only the greatest Nobles on the planet lived in Residences—Houses as intelligent as these animals, and a lot longer lived. Interested, Garrett asked, *What do Residences smell like?*

Cats would sometimes answer, but usually not unless they wanted something from him. He made it a point to always be in the credit column with intelligent cats, giving them information without expecting payment. It had irked him at first, then he'd shrugged and accepted it as a cost of doing business.

This time, again, there were many replies.

Special housekeeping spells for pee, said the brindled tom.

And for puke, said the fat brown tabby female.

Thick, rich, nose-stop smoke smells for rituals, said the leader, sniffing lustily, as if proving he could.

Expensive incense, Garrett translated. The twenty-five First-Families—descendants of the colonists who had funded the trip from Earth—all resided in sentient Houses. Garrett ran through the lords mentally, but didn't come up with any reason why a person so powerful would want to hire him.

A yowl went up, followed by more. *We get Our FOOD!*

Garrett winced. *FINE!* he yelled back at them telepathically. *Stop that caterwauling, NOW.*

They did, having learned by experience that when he gave such an order, the consequences of disobedience could be major. Like a delay in being fed.

Now they ringed his feet, staring up at him, narrow-eyed.

He said, *I will feed you in the back courtyard.* Then he'd see if he could come up from behind the Nobleman and check him out—begin the conversation on his terms. And whip his inner dread into shape, get control of the problem from the start.

Quiet, the cats trotted after his own soft-footed prowl to the back entrance of the office building. The area was paved with flagstones as old as the building in the optimistic hope that the tenants would have gliders to park. No one who rented in the building was wealthy enough to do so.

He murmured the spellshields down and the locked door open with a few Words. Once inside he tilted his head but sensed no one else was there.

So he went to the small spellshielded storeroom off the one long main corridor. There he kept cat food, treats, a few toys, and a small canister of catnip. He'd left the back door open and returned to the courtyard with the bag of kibble and poured the daily amount into the trough.

As if they'd unconsciously expected him to renege on the deal, they all hurried up to the trough with minimal jostling for position and crunched up the food. The cats were his informers and observers, but he knew that more than one of them had gone hungry before they'd become his secret eyes and ears around the city.

Sleek Black finished first and sat back on his haunches, staring at Garrett. He'd only joined the band in the spring. Garrett got the impression that the tom might be considering becoming a Fam . . . if Garrett, as an example of a human, impressed the young cat. Garrett figured that the youngster would want a home and a warm hearth when winter came.

The black cat burped discreetly, flicked his whiskers. *What do you want Us to do for the food?*

Garrett shrugged. He'd find out who the Nobleman was soon enough. After that, if he felt he needed more information, he could have the cats check the guy out.

Ears swiveled in his direction. *As always, keep your eyes open and listen.* He continued to speak mentally. He didn't know what the man might be able to hear; his psi power Flair might have gifted him with augmented hearing.

Sleek Black nodded and vanished into the deep shadows of the morning. The rest left the food trough, some stopping to clean themselves, some shooting away like they had their own business or something that might bring them an extra treat from Garrett. Dogs and the other ferals would come to eat now.

Going back inside, he closed and locked the door with a Flaired Word and padded softly along the dingy corridor with offices on either side toward the front door. His sword was heavy on one hip, his blazer on the other. They were emotionally comforting, but they'd never been much use in the three events that had come after the warning dread had hit.

He stopped at the front door and used Flair to make the small window panel in the door transparent on his side.

The Nobleman in disguise was younger than he by about a decade. But his young face still had lines beginning to etch deeply in his skin, and his long dusty brown hair showed silver threads—careworn. His eyes were a muddy green. He was more even-featured, of course, than Garrett and held himself well. The man was nearly as tall as Garrett, who was a big man, but the guy wasn't as muscled.

Garrett yanked open the door. The Nobleman whirled, set into his balance, raised his arms ready to defend.

"Good reflexes." Garrett nodded to him. "I'm Primross." He gestured the Noble to proceed ahead of him down the hall.

"Vinni T'Vine," the man said as he stepped inside. He waved the door shut, but made no other move.

A great Noble, highest of the high. And *the* prophet of Celta. No one wanted Vinni T'Vine to show up on his doorstep with the knowledge of his future in his eyes.

Close up, Garrett noted strain on his face, his sunken eyes. A hint of darkness in the tender skin under them showed T'Vine hadn't gotten much sleep lately. Garrett really didn't want to contemplate what might keep a man who saw visions of the future up at night.

The Noble continued in a low voice that held more rough than smooth, "You must have figured out by now, Garrett Primross, that you are a point the fate of Celta circles around."

Garrett's mouth dried and his bowels went sloshier than he'd ever admit. "Haven't thought of that much," he lied. Ever since he'd lived through a sickness when everyone else around him had died, he'd been considered unique by most.

"I don't like to try and guide the future." An unamused smile from T'Vine. "Bites me in the ass more often than not." His gaze drilled into Garrett with nearly tangible force. T'Vine examined him, shook his head. "But sometimes I have to take the chance." His nobly sculpted mouth flattened, he dipped his head in what might be respect.

All of Garrett's nerves twined tight as he waited. The moment took on the glassy and acute atmosphere of danger.

"You should cooperate completely with the FirstLevel Healers," T'Vine said.

Healers. Hell. Garrett didn't like Healers, too much poking from them during the epidemic as he gave blood and Flair to help stop the sickness.

He and the prophet stared at each other for a full moment of silence, until Garrett dragged out words. "That all?"

Vinni inclined his head. More heavy silence. More matched stares. Breath stopped in Garrett's lungs until his ears rang from the lack and he knew from the hair rising on the back of his neck that he had to listen to the prophet. Probably follow T'Vine's advice. "I hear you."

The Nobleman's head tilted. Garrett felt his own eyes widen as he watched T'Vine's eyes change color from dull green to hazel, a better tint for the guy. The Noble's shoulders relaxed and Garrett heard the puff of relieved breath. Then he smiled and his gaze warmed. "You'll do." He paused and his grin spread. "You and your HeartMate." Another dip of his head and T'Vine teleported away.

Leaving Garrett to stagger and lean against a wall.

Healers. Hell.

He'd almost forgotten his HeartMate was a Healer, he'd avoided her for so long. He wasn't a good bet for a husband or father. Not to mention that he still mourned the woman he'd wanted as a wife.

Healers. HeartMate. Doom. Damn.

*A*rtemisia *Mugwort Panax* stood with two *FirstLevel Healers* in Primary HealingHall looking down at the sweaty and panting boy of six, Opul Cranberry.

The room was tinted a rich cream and furnished comfortably, but it was still in an institution and the faint odor of sickness underlaid even the cleansing herbs.

Her heart thudded hard as she waited for the verdict.

"Yes, it is the Iasc sickness. The first outbreak we've had in eighteen months," Ura Heather said flatly.

"We can't Heal him with our regular psi Healing, our Flair." Sympathy with a touch of fear laced Lark Holly's tones. No doubt she was thinking of her own children.

The middle-aged Ura Heather turned away. She was the best Healer on Celta since her father had retired, and was in charge of all Healers. "Get that guard guy. Primross? Only survivor when everyone in the first group hit by the virulent illness died. Maybe his blood and the Flair in it can help.

"No one except you two and the guard are allowed in this room. Lark, you and SecondLevel Healer Panax must take all care. We can't afford another epidemic." Ura Heather strode through the sterilization field Artemisia had erected, grunting as it affected her. Then her Flair spiked as she killed any lingering germs before she walked from the room.

Artemisia took the child's hand and stroked the back of it with her thumb. "Easy, Opul, we'll help you."

The child tossed and turned, whimpering.

Lark sighed. "I'll contact Garrett Primross and let you know when you should meet with FirstLevel Healer Heather and me."

That was moving in circles Artemisia had only dreamt of. "Why do you need me?"

Lark blinked lavender eyes. "Because Opul Cranberry is your patient."

"I was manning Private Intake Room Six a septhour ago when he was brought in," Artemisia agreed. "But I work for the HealingHall." And glad she was that she'd been accepted temporarily on the Primary HealingHall staff. "I don't have him as a private patient."

"Now you do," Lark said. "All his fees will be paid to you by the council." Lark met Artemisia's eyes and smiled. "Since you don't get a NobleGilt salary."

Not since Artemisia's Family, the Mugworts, had been smeared with scandal. Her father had lost his title and judgeship, her mother, her Healing practice. Everyone knew Artemisia was a Mugwort, but since she went by a distant Family name on her mother's side, everyone could pretend she wasn't touched by the ruin of her Family.

Lark glanced at her wrist timer. "I must put this in motion; Ura Heather isn't a patient woman. If she hasn't spoken with the boy's parents, I'll talk with them, too."

If it had been Artemisia's son, she'd want the more sympathetic Lark Holly rather than Ura Heather to brief her.

"I'll see you later," Lark said.

"Yes," Artemisia agreed. She pulled up a chair and sat by the elevated bedsponge. Even as she wiped the boy's face with a tepid cloth, deep inside she experienced mixed emotions. A whisper of happiness that she was advancing in her career, along with the dread of every Healer, every Celtan, that the sickness that had claimed too many people was back.

Two

$\mathcal{M}$inutes later, standing outside Heather's office, Artemisia smoothed her tunic and said spell Words to tidy herself. She'd been through three sanitation and germ-sterilization procedures. The large windows on one wall of Opul's room were uncovered, with a staff member observing him until she or Lark Holly returned. Artemisia touched the monitoring bracelet that matched the one on Opul's wrist. All was fine with him.

Her pulse was fast and she was flushed. She was rising in the world, and though she didn't have great ambition, she wanted to find her place and keep it. This was another minor step, a consultation with the Healers because she had a patient with Iasc sickness.

She rapped on the door and Lark Holly opened it.

"GentleSir Primross doesn't seem as angry about being called as before," Lark murmured. "Yet."

"I haven't met him, but I've heard of him."

Lark gave an ironic half smile. "Every Healer has. He's mostly refused to let us . . ."

". . . Experiment with his blood?"

Now Lark's smile was full. "Yes."

"I've heard he's been difficult."

Lark's breath was audible. "Also true, but he helped us stop the sickness." She slanted Artemisia a glance and said, "FirstLevel Healer Ura Heather has a plan. I think we'll find out how difficult GentleSir Primross is. He's already here." She opened the door wider and stepped aside.

"Thank you." Artemisia straightened her shoulders. She wanted to be a solid, permanent member of the Primary HealingHall staff. If she followed Heather's instructions, she'd get that position and prove herself. She'd have allies who would look beyond her name and the scandal. She'd be set exactly where she wanted to be in her career for the rest of her life.

The paneled chamber was richly furnished with a large carved desk and several cushy chairs set on a thick rug of dark purple and gold. The scent of expensive herbal housekeeping spells permeated the room. Long curtains of gold gracing the Palladian windows were pulled aside to let in the sunlight. The torpid heat of summer didn't reach here.

Outside showed the lush green of the Healing Grove and Artemisia wished she were there. All she'd ever wanted was to be a Healer, and she disliked having to play politics to get what she wanted. She preferred to avoid confrontation and risk.

Lark Holly sank into a chair. Since the man was propped against a wall with crossed arms, and his scowl deepened as Artemisia came in, she decided he had no intention of taking a seat. So she angled a chair to see him and FirstLevel Healer Ura Heather.

He was not a handsome man, but there was something about him that made her catch her breath. He was tall and extremely well built—not slender nor thick bodied. His face wasn't well proportioned. He had heavy brows, amber eyes set deep, jutting cheekbones, and a nose and mouth wider than was considered good-looking. His natural skin tone was a couple of shades darker than the average Celtan and went well with his sandy brown hair.

His hair was tousled as if his fingers had plunged through it. He wore an air of supreme competence as well as sturdy brown work trous tucked into black boots and a top that appeared to be more like leather armor than a shirt. The masculine scent of him went straight to her core.

"GentleSir Primross, you know FirstLevel Healer Lark Holly; this is SecondLevel Healer Artemisia Panax, who is treating the patient with the sickness," Ura Heather said. She didn't rise from her seat behind her desk.

He hadn't been fidgeting but now went completely immobile. "It's back."

Ura Heather lifted her index finger. "One case."

His shoulders shifted, drawing Artemisia's attention to their broadness. "Not good."

"No," Lark said quietly.

"What do you want?" Primross asked, still not moving from the wall.

Heather smiled sharply. "Quite a bit. Please, take a seat."

His eyes narrowed and his face took on a lack of expression that was wary in itself. "One case. I'll donate my blood if it will help."

"Opul Cranberry, age six, will thank you for that," Artemisia said.

He winced. "Starting with kids again?"

"Maybe," Heather said. "We know how he was infected." She snorted. "Luckily the Cranberrys have stayed on their estate outside the city for the summer and didn't have much contact with anyone else, and none when they guessed what the sickness was. The three of them teleported here immediately. We think we can contain the malady."

Primross grunted, nodded. "You want to increase my blood production?"

"Much more." The gleam in Ura Heather's eyes was sharp.

"What?" Primross asked.

Heather glanced down at a papyrus file, then at Primross.

That scrutiny wasn't reassuring, either. Artemisia was shocked that the woman didn't cultivate a better bedside manner.

Primross pushed away from the wall, eyeing the premier Healer of Celta.

"I have the details of your history." Heather tapped the file. "But I'd like to hear them from you."

Pain flickered on his face, then was buried under impassivity. He jerked a nod at the folder. "I went over every fact many times, with many people, including your father, T'Heather himself."

Ura Heather's mouth turned sour. Artemisia realized the head of Primary HealingHall doubted whether her reputation would ever equal her father's, and that mattered to her. Artemisia shifted. Again, she didn't want to be here, taking part in a conflict.

The man's gaze switched to her and she flinched at the storm in his eyes. Then his glance seemed to soften as he stared at her.

"You're a private investigator," Ura Heather gritted out. "Surely you must prefer to talk to witnesses yourself and not rely on others' reports." She opened the file.

Lark Holly stood and walked to him, held out her hand. "Please. We need you."

He flinched. "That's pretty much what the Healer in Gael City said to me when all this started." His voice, too, was rough.

Lark gestured to her seat. As a shroud of dread enveloped her, Artemisia wondered if she could get out of hearing the tragedy. She knew Primross's story vaguely and was sure the details would be much worse. Everyone had died except him.

The skin on his face had tightened and he appeared haunted.

Ura Heather looked at Lark Holly, her niece. Lark was of greater status and had a more sympathetic outlook. Primross would be an individual to Lark, and only a case and an informant to Heather.

Primross stood on the balls of his feet, as if he might break away. Artemisia thought of Opul's suffering. "Please," she added.

Once again his dark and brooding gaze touched her; a corner of his mouth curled. He snorted and trod to the chair and sat straight in it, challenging Heather. "Yeah?"

She leaned forward over her desk. "We have new information. After three years of decontamination, we retrieved the locking mechanism of the door for the body storage in the back of the transport vehicle that you drove." She touched a hand-sized panel that

ran with the slight orange light of Flair tech along the curving lines
of spell algorithms. "Its recording mechanism of when and how
often the door was opened is intact. So we have better details of how
the sickness progressed that we would like you to confirm."

Garrett stared at the small piece of the bus he'd driven, and his
brain played back Old Grisc in the driver's seat when they'd smelled
the first scent of death. He'd reached over and pressed the red
button . . . setting the recorder as well as unlocking the door, Garrett now understood.

Beads of sweat formed along his spine, were absorbed by his padded and Flaired armor. Now he knew why he'd worn it. More for
emotional protection than physical. Primary HealingHall was in a
well-protected part of town—not to mention that many of the less
advantaged had died during the sickness that swept through the land
two to three years before.

"GentleSir Primross, can you give us more details about your
experience?" prompted Lark.

Nothing he enjoyed more than reviewing the worst days of his
life. He felt his impassive expression stiffen into a stone mask. He'd
made this report before . . . more times than he wanted. Doing so
now just hurt because he hadn't been expecting it. The scab had
been ripped off his inner wounds. He wouldn't let the tear or the
inner bleeding show.

"No." He stood and walked back to the door.

"Of course you do not need to help us," FirstLevel Healer Ura
Heather said. "We are only facing an epidemic again. One that you
can stop."

He slammed his hand against the door and muttered curse words
that should have singed the air with his frustration at having to fall
into line with someone else's plans.

"Yes," the Healer nearly purred, though he'd have expected more
of a satisfied snake hiss. "Anyone else who dies of this sickness could
be due to you."

"You shouldn't say such things," the SecondLevel Healer protested.

"Stop this, Aunt!" demanded Lark Holly.

"It's true." Heather's voice was smooth, like she was a fighter who knew she had him by the balls.

Guilt always gnawed. He'd start off as usual. "The Iasc sickness was traced to an unknown fish with an unknown infection that washed ashore on the beach of the Smallage estate near Gael City."

"We know that." Ura Heather's brows snapped down.

Garrett angled his thumb at the thick folder. "You know all that I have to tell you." He put his hand on the door latch.

"Please, stay, GentleSir Primross. We understand this is hard for you," Lark Holly said. "We'll take it in chronological order so you can settle before we ask about the new information."

His gut twisted. It was hard for him and he didn't want any of the women—especially his HeartMate—to pity him.

Yeah, he hadn't seen her for a while, a year maybe, since he avoided her. They'd never met. He didn't think that she knew they were destined mates, and he couldn't legally tell her and limit her choices. Not that he wanted to tell her anyway. Not that he wanted her.

Maybe his blood was humming because they were in the same room, but that was his body. His emotions were . . . Who the hell cared?

"The Iasc sickness was traced to the discovery of the large fish on the former Smallage estate," Ura Heather repeated.

There was no more Smallage estate. The house had been demolished, the land sterilized, remotely. There were no more Smallages.

Garrett stood where he was. He didn't want to be sucked back into that dark time. But words came from his mouth. "People from the estate got sick, a group went to a research HealingHall on the edge of Gael City for help. By that time, they were sick, too," he began in a monotone.

Rushing air pounded in his ears, matching an inward, rumbling shudder. Even if he left this office, memories would slice him. He might fall apart in bits before he left the HealingHall.

Someone made a soft noise of concern. Not someone. He knew

who, the SecondLevel Healer. She was there, standing beside him, her fingers light on him near his elbow, nudging him back to the chair. He picked up his feet carefully, let the pressure on his arm guide him since he was having trouble seeing. Seeing outside. Inside, his mind flashed vision after vision of those terrible days.

He bumped the edge of the chair, sat back down. His face felt cold. But the memories were fever hot. Like the sickness he'd survived.

Heather said, "The research HealingHall determined the sickness was unknown and virulent. They took samples and wanted the infected moved to a quarantine clinic in the hills. You were called in to guide the off-road quarantine vehicle."

"Me and the driver of that bus, Old Grisc," Garrett said. Old Grisc had been tough, but not tough enough. "We both knew the rough back trail to the clinic." Little used, and since one part of the shelf road had crumbled behind the heavy vehicle, never to be used again. The trip had been hazardous. More from the sickness than the rugged terrain.

"There were twenty-three who left on the journey. It was supposed to take six septhours?" Lark Holly asked in her calm voice. Not as pleasing to his ears as the younger woman's, who he didn't want to name.

Pain razored through him as he was back again in the Gael City HealingHall. He saw the fearful expression of Dinni, his childhood friend. They'd been each other's first lover. But Dinni was the girl who'd rejected him because he'd had a HeartMate somewhere and Dinni believed in that kind of love. She hadn't wanted to take a chance on him and the love between them.

Dinni had cradled her fretful and sick baby. Her son, no more than two months old, his father already dead of the sickness. She had begged Garrett to take the job, to go with them. Had the utmost faith he would save them.

His Dinni. More memories—sweet, laughing, as sunny in nature as her blonde hair, as a child, a girl. He'd have done anything for her. So he'd agreed.

"GentleSir Primross?" Healer Lark Holly prompted with an underlying command that greatly Flaired and greatly Noble people used to get results.

Something warm brushed against the back of one of his fists and he saw it was a steaming mug of caff. Strong and dark. He took the cup and drank and the bitterness of the caff was lost in that of his mouth.

He cast his mind back to what the woman had asked him. His voice came out like something old and rusty with edges flaking off, gone forever. "Yeah, the trip was supposed to take six septhours. Took eleven." Hideous trip. "Not many of us made it."

"Five," Ura Heather snapped.

As if he didn't recall every individual. Garrett couldn't prevent the shudder from showing this time, ripping through his body. Hot caff slopped on his thigh. He barely noticed.

More words spewed. "But your HealingHall in Gael City wasn't as good as you all thought it was. The sickness got out from there, didn't it? Despite all your warnings and all your sterilization procedures and everything." He didn't care if he sounded harsh. *No one* knew what had happened on that trip. "One of your own Healers spread it."

Heather's nostrils pinched. "A ThirdLevel Healer." A sneer from a woman who'd been born a highest Noble with best psi-magic, Flair.

"She died, too." Lark Holly sent an admonitory glance to Heather.

Blinking, Garrett recalled the two were aunt and niece.

Another concerned noise came from the beautiful SecondLevel Healer he tried to ignore. He made his eyes shift from a frozen stare; his glance swept the file again. How many times had he told this story? So many that the words were the same.

"The door was first unlocked at thirty-two minutes into the first seventy-minute septhour." Heather was pedantic. "Does that match your recollection?"

He leaned forward and glanced at the panel. "Sounds right. First three to die were Brev and Partha Sundew, HeartMates, then Avena

Blackoat. I don't remember after that." His mouth twisted. No. He would not go through this again. He'd already guaranteed himself more nightmares.

Plunking his caff down on a table, he set his feet and rose. "Don't have any more to tell you. You've got all the words about this that I have in that thick file. Either take me to the boy so I can give him a transfusion or tell me what you really want."

Frustration set on Ura Heather's face. Too fliggering bad.

As she met his gaze, her expression smoothed. "We've learned a lot about Iasc sickness, enough to enforce certain processes to keep it from becoming an epidemic. It's not enough. The herb NewBalm helps mitigate the sickness but doesn't have as good results as your blood."

Her words jarred him completely from the past and anchored him in the present and he was grateful. Maybe he would never go back there again.

A few deep breaths and he could answer her. "What do you want?"

She smiled and it was knifelike. "You survived the most deadly strain of the sickness, and"—her glance lowered to the now open folder and the sheets inside—"your case of Iasc is believed to have been the shortest on record."

He grunted. "Not many records from the quarantine clinic, I'm guessing." Everyone had perished save him.

Her lips thinned again. He didn't like her and he was sure he wouldn't like what she was going to say.

She snapped the folder shut, leaned forward. "We need more information on how you—your body, your Flair—combated the sickness. We want to reintroduce the Iasc into you."

"No," he said.

Lark Holly offered her hand to the young Healer, who looked at her but took it. Together they moved before Garrett. Two gazes to his one. Holly's violet and the other's emerald.

The SecondLevel Healer spoke. "We need your help. A little boy is sick."

He flinched and met her gaze. Soft, tender, deep. And he knew no matter how hard he fought, he would lose this battle. The past and the future demanded his blood.

Bile seared up his gullet, coated the back of his throat. His pulse hammered in his temples.

"Yes," he said thickly. Only then did he recall the prophet T'Vine's words: *You should cooperate completely with the First-Level Healers.*

He picked up his caff and drank, keeping his own gaze hard. "Lay it out for me."

Three

We'll do our best to ensure your survival," FirstLevel Healer Ura Heather said.

He believed her. His blood was too valuable an asset to lose.

Heather pushed his file aside; again she leaned forward, a hint of concern shading her eyes. For the project more than him, he guessed.

"We don't anticipate the project will last longer than six days, but we want you available for a full week."

Six days of hell, descent into the very Cave of the Dark Goddess and a crawl back up.

"You will be monitored the entire time."

He looked outside at the green Healing Grove, knew he wouldn't be anywhere as pretty as that in reality or delirium. Here in Primary HealingHall, his body would be cradled in luxury. The rich chamber displayed more wealth than the den of his friend, FirstFamily Great-Lord Laev T'Hawthorn.

Garrett's brows rose. "Here?" he asked.

Heather looked startled. "No."

"Oh," Garrett said softly, "you won't risk this place, your domain, eh? Just like the HealingHall in Gael City."

Heather's eyes should have bored holes through him. Again he moved to the wall and lounged against it, drinking caff. He had the upper hand now and they all knew it.

"This place is very large and busy," the SecondLevel Healer murmured. He kept his gaze on Heather, lifted and dropped a shoulder.

"I live in MidClass Lodge." He smiled. "That building is even larger and busier than here."

"That won't work as a venue, then." Ura Heather turned her gaze toward Lark Holly. "Options?"

FirstLevel Healer Holly cleared her throat. "I've contacted the Turquoise House, the House becoming a sentient Residence. TQ is between occupants and has decided to redecorate, so it is empty of all furnishings. It is intrigued with the project." Her smile showed the pity that he hadn't wanted. "TQ is also interested in GentleSir Primross himself, as a private investigator."

"Huh," he said, but his curiosity was snagged, too. Not many people were allowed in the Turquoise House. It was more exclusive than the greatest Noble Residences that had huge staffs.

Heather's lips pursed, but she couldn't hide her interest, either. "When will it be available for us four to view it?"

The younger woman squeaked. As the words sank in, he stiffened. He opened his mouth to protest, then remembered T'Vine's words and the man's haunted eyes. Garrett shut his mouth.

"Surely you don't want me—" the lower-level Healer began.

"You've already been exposed to the sickness and have shown you're smart enough to call in better Healers when the diagnosis is beyond your skills," Heather said. "You've followed proper sterilization procedures. You're SecondLevel and will be an acceptable assistant to us on this. You will monitor GentleSir Primross."

Garrett carefully put his cup down on a table, retreated behind an expressionless mask again.

He didn't like this, but now T'Vine's prophecy replayed, echoing in his mind. He wouldn't stare at the woman, no matter how often his gaze wandered that way.

Lark Holly said, "Opul Cranberry is Healer Panax's patient, and needs her."

Heather waved that aside. "Panax will be of more service by tending to Primross. You, FirstLevel Healer Holly, can supervise the child's case. When can we see the Turquoise House?"

Lark Holly's sigh was faint. "I'll scry the House that we are on our way."

"Good." Heather snapped her fingers, then smiled in satisfaction. "The glider awaits us at the main entrance." She strode from the room.

The other two Healers fell in behind her, Lark Holly commenting quietly to the younger woman, "I'll make sure that you take no harm from this project, financially or otherwise."

"Thank you," the SecondLevel Healer said politely.

Garrett strolled behind them, thinking how he could broach the matter of losing several days' worth of work to Heather. Did she expect him to donate his time as well as his blood? He supposed so.

As he brooded, he realized his gaze was fixed to the SecondLevel Healer's ass. Nice and high and round, though he couldn't see much because she had on trous and a long tunic over that. He liked the way she moved, gracefully, elegantly.

Not at all like Dinni's bouncy step. The Healer had long dark brown black hair tied back in a severe braid. Her face was roundish and he preferred pointed chins. She had a creamy complexion that showed she didn't spend much time in the sun.

Not at all like Dinni.

But SecondLevel Healer Artemisia Panax was his HeartMate.

He didn't want her.

He'd never wanted her.

Now they'd be together for as long as his sickness ran again. She'd see him at his absolute worse.

That was good.

*Throughout the drive from Primary HealingHall to a mid-Noble-*class area, Artemisia's mind buzzed. From the glare he'd given her, Garrett Primross wasn't happy with the plan. Who would be? She must have made a terrible impression on him since he'd barely looked at her. His animosity sent a thorn of unexpected hurt into her she tried to shake off.

She wasn't pleased, either. Caring for a very sick person developed an intimacy, and her feelings toward him were mixed—attracted but wary. She wouldn't have trouble being professional but wasn't sure how he'd react toward her.

And she'd have to leave her home. She hadn't lived away from the hidden sanctuary in Druida City since she and her Family had been named caretakers years ago.

No lover had been strong enough to break those bonds. She didn't know if that was depressing or not.

They pulled into the glider drive and the courtyard of the Turquoise House and Artemisia understood why it was called that. The outside walls were a shiny blue green. The door of the sprawling one-floor House was an equally glossy oak with bright brass latch and fittings.

Lark Holly walked up to the entrance and Artemisia followed. Primross was behind her and FirstLevel Healer Ura Heather brought up the rear. The door swung open and they stood in a bare entryway.

"Greetyou," said the House in the mellow tones of a famous actor, lilting with satisfaction.

Primross stiffened. "You speak with Raz Cherry's voice?"

"Yes," said the House. It—he—chuckled. "We came to an agreement years ago, when I first became aware of myself and wanted a male voice. I am pleased you recognized it, Garrett Primross."

Garrett made a half bow and said, "Where would you prefer me to stand so you can scan me?"

"Very intelligent!" the Turquoise House said. "Very courteous. Please move to the mainspace fireplace, down the hall ahead and to your left, first door on your left."

The man took the lead, Lark Holly appeared amused, and Heather reluctant. Artemisia's shoulders relaxed. She lived in a Residence now, one who was like a crotchety old man who had to be catered to. This House seemed much more cheerful. That would be helpful in the trying days ahead.

"You and SecondLevel Artemisia Mugwort Panax will stay for a week?" the House asked as they stood around the empty main-space.

Artemisia tried not to wince. The Turquoise House had included her real surname. Her shoulders tensed, but a sliding gaze at the others showed they appeared focused on the bare House. A week seemed a long time to her, though the sickness had lingered and been fatal for as long as three weeks.

"Yes, a week," Heather said brusquely. Artemisia wondered if the woman was trying to ease her out of Primary HealingHall. Arte-misia straightened her spine. She was sticking. She wasn't flashy, but she was determined and knew how to do stubborn.

And she hoped she had a supporter in Lark Holly. Still, there were more detriments to this project than advantages.

"Ah," the Turquoise House said in a tone that had her listening closely. "I know of both individuals, Garrett Primross and Artemisia Panax."

Now it was being discreet. So Artemisia knew that her home, BalmHeal Residence, had been too chatty with the Turquoise House. How many of her—and her Family's—secrets did this House-becoming-a-Residence know? How would the House use what it knew? Would it? How ethical was it?

"You know of me, do you?" Primross said coolly as he stopped near the empty fireplace. He reached into his trous pocket and pulled out a gold coin, rolled it across his knuckles, made it disappear. "You know that?"

"Sleight of hand!" the Turquoise House said delightedly. "More!"

"Want to learn more secrets?" Primross shrugged. "Maybe, maybe not." He left the impression he'd established dominance in the relationship. Artemisia could only envy how quickly and easily he'd done that.

Ura Heather had stayed near the door. Did the older Healer won-der what her own ancient Residence might have said about her to the Turquoise House?

Even if Artemisia's home blabbed of her, it would have been complimentary. It loved her more than anyone else who lived in it, which had also kept her close.

Staring at the slick-looking walls, Heather said, "You have instituted sanitation, decontamination, and sterilization procedures, I see. Well done."

"Thank you," the Turquoise House said with an edge of irony. "It is very important that the human populace of Celta declines no further. If I can help in that endeavor, if I can save lives, I am well rewarded." There was a drop in the air pressure in the room as if the House gave a soft sigh. "Unlike any of the HealingHalls, I can monitor all the organisms within me, understand the slightest changes in my walls and beings."

"Residences are uniquely suited to do that," Lark Holly soothed. "Only one had the sickness within."

"T'Hawthorn Residence," Primross said. He leaned an elbow on the mantel as if he were already at home within the spare and sterile walls.

The emptiness would take Artemisia some getting used to. Her home was the most comfortable place she'd ever lived, including the Family estate they'd lost when she was a teen.

"Yes, T'Hawthorn Residence had a death," Lark said.

"I have spoken at length with T'Hawthorn Residence," said the House. "I need all records of the sickness from the Healers and HealingHalls transmitted to my Library."

Heather gasped. "We don't share confidential—"

"You want me for an experiment." Turquoise House's tone was harder. Artemisia was amazed at its range of expression. "I will not accept this project without sufficient data. Change the venue to a HealingHall, or your father's home, T'Heather Residence. Your Residence is interested in the sickness. We all are. Or use the starship *Nuada's Sword*. I know it has laboratories, sick bays, and sterile rooms."

"Not the starship," Artemisia said. "I don't work well there, not where Flair is diminished or suppressed." She couldn't offer her own home, BalmHeal Residence, the original HealingHall of the colonists, now a hidden sanctuary for the desperate of Celta.

Not many of those suffering from the sickness had made it to the old BalmHeal estate in time. She and her mother had had only two cases during the epidemic. Both casualties were buried in one of the sacred groves. Artemisia was sure the Turquoise House knew everything that BalmHeal Residence did. Their Residence had taken the deaths very hard.

"I'll transfer the information," Lark Holly said.

Ura Heather walked out.

"Thank you both." Lark Holly curtsied to them and swept from the room, leaving Artemisia with a man who still hadn't met her eyes. Awkward.

If she'd had regular clothes on, she'd have tucked her hands in the wide opposite sleeves, but she was wearing a work tunic with tight cuffs. She stood by the open door, but he didn't move.

"You aren't going to refuse our request?" she asked him.

"It's mostly the Heathers' request, isn't it? FirstLevel Healer Ura Heather and Lark Holly, whose mother was a Heather."

"The Heathers have always been the best Healers."

"That doesn't bother you? That no matter how hard you try, you'll never be their equal?"

Artemisia blinked. "Why should it? The Heathers are from the FirstFamilies, are descended from people who had psi power on ancient Earth. My Family isn't so old, our Flair isn't as evolved." She lifted her chin, held out her hands, and flexed her fingers. "I'm sure you've practiced your sleight of hand for a long time. If I began now, would I ever reach your level of competence? I doubt it." A corner of her mouth quirked. "Even if I had the natural dexterity you do."

He nodded. "I'm good with my hands." Then he swayed back, bumping against the mantel as if surprised at his own words. His heavy brows lowered. "I have a problem with the power of the entrenched Nobility. I also happen to agree with the Turquoise House. This situation is about saving lives, but with Heather it's all about status. The first epidemic happened on her watch as the highest Healer of Celta. Her father had to come out of retirement. I don't think she'll ever forget. If she could eradicate the disease, she'd be redeemed and go down in history as the savior."

Artemisia stared at him. Now that she looked more closely, an element of his natural intensity was anger. Another reason to be wary. "I get the impression that you don't want me to be with you in this project."

"I want you," said the Turquoise House.

"Thanks," she replied but didn't take her gaze off Primross.

He shook his head; his wide mouth thinned. "I don't, but I don't dare refuse you."

"Why not?"

"Vinni T'Vine, the prophet, visited me this morning and insisted I follow *all* the wishes of the FirstLevel Healers."

Her chest went tight. No one liked hearing a prophecy featuring himself or herself. She focused on what Primross previously said. "I don't agree that the Nobles are too powerful. I think they're doing their best."

His eyes widened. He shook his head. "You are naive."

"You're cynical. All the FirstFamily Nobles I've met have been decent people." It hadn't been the FirstFamilies who'd demanded the Mugworts' title be stripped from them, but other Nobles of their own rank, at the instigation of the newssheets.

He jutted his chin at the window facing the courtyard where the HealingHall glider was pulling away. "You think FirstLevel Healer Ura Heather is decent?"

Artemisia flushed. She'd had unkind thoughts about the lady but wouldn't admit them. "She's doing the best she can. If we're in this together, I don't want to talk politics."

He nodded slowly. "Done."

"I suggest you take a tour of my premises," the Turquoise House said. "SecondLevel Healer Panax can determine how things should be arranged best for this experiment."

"Fine," Artemisia said.

Primross's mouth twisted, but he said, "Sure."

"This is the mainspace," the House repeated. "I have a Master-

Suite and MistrysSuite and several bedrooms and waterfall rooms, a kitchen as well as many no-time food and drink storage units. I have a playspace and a den and a library."

"Give us the tour." Garrett's half bow to Artemisia held a mocking quality. "After you."

She sniffed and went into the hall, followed the House's instructions, and studied the rooms. Lovely proportions but all were set up to contain and destroy the sickness with sticky white walls and no furniture. Bare, bare, bare.

The more time she spent with Primross, the more it seemed as if she became sensitized to him. Her skin felt hot, and it wasn't the sickness. She was all too aware of his size, the way he moved, and his deeper and rougher tones that contrasted so well with the House's actor voice.

Time and again she had to yank her focus from the virile man to the stark House.

Garrett was too aware of the woman he didn't want to replace his lost love and tried to concentrate on his conversation with the slyly knowing Turquoise House. That entity hinted at more than one secret regarding itself, the woman, and Garrett.

The Turquoise House had figured out that riddles itched Garrett like a bad rash. The House dropped innuendos, ensuring Garrett was intrigued. Why, Garrett didn't know, but the House had an agenda.

So the obligatory tour wasn't over when a data stream came from Primary HealingHall, officially approving the project. Garrett's last trickle of hope that he'd be spared the whole terrible thing was squashed.

He and the SecondLevel Healer stood in a small bedroom that connected through a dressing and waterfall room to the bedroom of the MasterSuite. The view out the undraped windows was the only thing that made the place tolerable. The Healer had decided the chambers were right for the experiment. This would be her room.

Garrett glanced at his wrist timer. "I need to make arrangements for my business."

"You are a *private investigator*." The Turquoise House rolled the sentence. "A fascinating business."

Garrett grunted. "I like it well enough."

The Healer's delicately curving brows arched. "You wouldn't pursue a vocation if you didn't enjoy it."

She already sensed too much about him. Every instant he was with her, the innate bond between them grew from the wispy tendril they'd always had to a thin thread. It would only get worse.

"You will tell us of some of your cases?" the House asked. "Though that business with the Hawthorn jewels earlier this year was well publicized—a triumph for you!"

The woman blinked as if she didn't recall his greatest case, the juicy events of kidnapping, attempted murder, accidental death, jewel theft, and a goddess's curse. Garrett shouldn't have been irritated in the slightest, but he was. People were contrary.

"Maybe I'll tell some general stories. Nothing confidential." He wanted the woman to ask. But she stared around the place, frowning. She wasn't comfortable in the House and he wondered why.

No. He would *not* wonder about her. She presented no intriguing puzzle. "I'll go to Primary HealingHall and let them take my blood for the boy. Then pack my stuff," he said.

She sighed. "I must, too."

"Do you teleport?" he asked. She should be able to at her level of Flair.

"Yes," she said, not sounding offended as he would've been if she'd asked him. She didn't appear to be easily offended. Easygoing. Soft.

Not like Dinni, who'd been adamant in her refusal of him.

The Healer wet her lips and his reluctant gaze went to her wide, tender mouth. She said, "I must plan procedures with the FirstLevel Healers. We probably won't start the project until tomorrow morning. You'll be scried with the information."

"Fine." He gave her his briefest nod. Again no reaction from her at the slight. Garrett teleported away from the disturbing female and to Intake at Primary HealingHall.

Four

The irritating *Garrett* Primross *was gone.* Artemisia *relaxed her* shoulders.

"My HouseHeart is quiet and serene if you wish to rest," the Turquoise House said.

The offer to visit its most secret room surprised Artemisia so much that she stretched out a hand to steady herself. Her skin cringed at the tacky feel of the wall.

"All organisms deposited by human contact have been destroyed," said a flat voice.

The House rushed into speech. "My apologies, Healer. The decontamination and sterilization system came with med announcements that I have not yet programmed into my own voice."

Artemisia never recalled an apology from her own sentient home. "It's very brave of you to host us, Turquoise House."

"Please call me TQ. T'Hawthorn Residence said it took no harm. I want to be able to offer my humans the very best." Strong, solid, and determined tones.

"I can't understand why you'd let me in your HouseHeart." If the inner sanctum of the HouseHeart was destroyed, the Residence died.

"I trust you," said TQ. "BalmHeal Residence and I talk a lot."

There came a cacklelike sound Artemisia couldn't place, but she knew it as punctuation. "He is very old and I am very young, but I was there when he stirred from sleep. My inhabitants at the time were with us both. BalmHeal Residence speaks of you a lot." A short silence hung. "My HouseHeart needs maintenance," TQ said, embarrassed.

"You don't have permanent caregivers?"

"No. FirstFamily GrandLady Mitchella D'Blackthorn decorated me, and will help me later. Others who have helped have agreed to have their memories bespelled so they forget details."

Artemisia rocked toward the wall again, moved to the middle of the room. "No one knows how to reach your HouseHeart?"

"Not at this time," TQ whispered.

She wouldn't say that was foolish. "I'm extremely honored."

"I believe I need a failsafe human."

She let out a held breath. "So another Residence has information on how to reach your HouseHeart and about your House-Stones?"

"Yes."

"I'll be glad to help you, and agree to memory blurring."

"Would keeping your memory be acceptable until my true person comes?"

"Your true person?"

"I have had tenants, but am waiting for my Family."

She didn't suppress her curiosity. "Are you waiting for a destined person?"

"Like humans wait for HeartMates?" His voice lilted. "No, I know the Family I want."

"Oh."

A long creak came from a distant room. "My HouseHeart is very restful and you have had a difficult morning. I am sorry I mentioned your surname."

"I don't think that will be a problem." Though Garrett Primross seemed an observant man. But she hadn't hidden information about herself. If he checked, he'd know who she was and of the Family's scandal.

"And I am sorry about Opul Cranberry's illness," TQ said.

"How do you know of Opul?"

"T'Heather Residence heard Ura Heather speaking to her father about the child. The GrandLord cautiously approved the experiment. T'Heather Residence told me."

"Ah."

"Incoming scry from Lark Holly at Primary HealingHall. Visual on your bedroom wall."

A second later the whole wall rippled, then showed a huge image of Lark Holly.

"Greetyou, Artemisia. Opul Cranberry is being prepared for the blood transfusion from GentleSir Primross. We anticipate all will be well, but Opul is upset I'll be his primary Healer." Lark smiled. She probably wasn't often considered secondary to anyone else. Artemisia was glad Lark was amused. "Can you come say good-bye to Opul? It's essential he remains calm."

"Of course."

"You can give me your recommendations for contamination spellshields and such to keep you safe, as well as the rooms you chose for the project in the Turquoise House. We anticipate starting at WorkBell tomorrow morning."

Artemisia swallowed and kept her gaze steady. "I'll be ready."

"I know you will." A warmer smile from Lark. "Primary HealingHall is lucky to have you."

They signed off and the scry faded and the wall went back to blank white. Artemisia breathed deeply. "TQ, can you scry Balm-Heal Residence, please? I must talk to my parents." She was sure her younger sister, a priestess of the Lady and Lord, could set up a blessing ritual that evening.

"Of course," the House said.

"I promise I'll come this afternoon and help you with your HouseHeart."

"It can wait." His voice was soft. "We are patient beings."

"Thank you for your support in this endeavor, TQ. It will be a difficult process."

"The experiment will be fun and interesting!"

Artemisia was sure it would be fascinating . . . and terrible.

*A*t the *HealingHall, Garrett was met by a worn Lark Holly.* "Thank you for returning. Little Opul needs your help. He's responding very slowly to the new medicine." Lark's expression hardened into sheer resolve. "We *will* save him. We *will not* have another epidemic."

Garrett made a noncommittal noise.

Her lavender gaze lasered in on his. "I give you my personal word on that."

He held up a palm. "This situation is not under your control."

Her breath huffed. "You're right, but we know this sickness now. We will not let it win. Please follow me to the transfusion room."

He hardly needed to, he'd been here to donate his blood so often, but he was glad to stop talking and take action.

He was placed on a bedsponge near the sick child, a young boy who stared at him with bright blue eyes in a pale face. Even his red orange hair seemed subdued.

"You're not pretty Artemisia," the boy whispered, voice rougher than a child's should be.

"No, but he will help you." Lark Holly pulled up a stool between the two beds.

"He's big."

Garrett managed a smile. "Yeah, I am."

The boy turned his head and closed his eyes and Garrett saw pain roll through him. He engulfed Opul's hand in his own. It was small and hot and reminded him of Dinni and her baby. He didn't know how to avoid the past. How many times would he be expected to relive it?

Then the child looked at him again and tugged words from him. "I'm here to help. It will be all right."

Opul's chin trembled, his lips compressed, then words tumbled from him. "I was bad and opened the box that came from G'Uncle Hulten before he died."

"Sshh." Lark Holly held out a softleaf to the kid.

He grabbed it and scrubbed his face. "Now I'm sick and I'll make everyone else sick and more of my friends will die." The boy bit his lip bloody. Lark exclaimed and touched it, Healing the small wound.

"No," Garrett said and knew he'd make more promises that could be broken by death. He squeezed Opul's small and sweaty fingers. "I got the sickness and lived and so will you."

Slow blinks at him. "Yeah?"

"Yes." He struggled to think of something to help the boy. Struggle was right. He'd struggled all through the sickness to get the bus to the clinic. "What do you want to do most?"

"GentleSir Primross." Lark Holly's voice cooled with warning that he was not an expert in this area. Healers generally wanted Iasc patients to stay quiet, relax, and rest.

He met her eyes. "I survived," he said. That was the bottom line. He'd lived when others died.

"I like to run best." Another chin wobble. "I'm going to miss the southern district race because I did something stupid!"

An idea came to Garrett, dried his throat. His glance clashed with Holly's intense stare; she watched him closely, listening hard. For something he hadn't put on the record? Who knew what worked? He reached for the tube of water and swallowed fresh liquid. "Listen, Opul."

The child's pale blue eyes looked into his own. "When the fever and shakes come again, pretend you're running a race. Know that you *have* to reach the finish line, *must* win." Like he'd had to get through the mountains.

With a little quiver, Opul's fingers clamping on his hand, the boy said, "Hard, to be sick and in a race and try to win, not stumble or fall, make mistakes."

Hard to be driving a strange vehicle and know he *had* to get to the clinic. But he'd had a goal; everyone else had been giving in to their misery, even Old Grisc.

Garrett's teeth clenched on the tube of water, pierced through it, and liquid spurted everywhere. Cold and shocking.

With a ladylike snort, Lark Holly rhymed a spell couplet and the water evaporated, even from his clothes. An odd feeling he'd brought on himself. She took the split tube away to the disintegrator and gave him another.

"You think that would really work? Thinking I'm running a race?" Opul asked.

"Having a tough goal worked for me."

Eyes wide and with trust, the boy nodded. "I'll think of that."

"A good idea," Lark Holly said softly. "Now let's get some of GentleSir Primross's strong blood and Flair into you."

Another nod from the child.

"I'll come to your next race," Garrett said.

"I live in Toono Town," Opul said. "Sometimes adult work makes it difficult to attend races."

Garrett didn't like the excuse. "You're a priority for me." He didn't have any hot cases, could use more work. If something heated up, he'd still make the time. It was rare he had emergencies, life-and-death situations.

"You're a priority for all of us," Lark Holly said.

"Even pretty Artemisia?" Opul asked. "She's not here."

"Not her choice," Garrett said. "She was assigned away."

"She'll come say good-bye," Lark Holly said.

The boy pouted, then his fingers were twisting, growing hotter. "I don't feel good. How long will I be sick?"

He didn't seem to be thinking he'd die, at least. Not that that had helped many. No one Garrett had known with the sickness had thought they would die.

"Perhaps a week," Lark Holly said.

"Let's get this done," Garrett said.

Lark Holly said, "I doubt he'll have more lucid moments.

I helped clear his mind for the transfusion and now will put him into a trance. Can you self-trance and stay grounded?"

"Of course."

Holly counted down and Garrett sank into a meditative state. He was aware of hands on him. A Flaired suction tube was placed against an artery in his arm. Hurt flashed; his blood flowed. This wasn't the first time he'd had his blood and Flair sent into someone with the sickness.

He hoped it would be the last.

Opul's pain and heat and shudders reached him and he could only endure. And know they were a precursor of worse, but he didn't want to think of that.

*W*hen he came to, he wasn't in the same room but lying on a hard table in a sterile place, naked. "What the hell?"

"Preparation for your ordeal to come," a ThirdLevel Healer said, cheerful enough to irritate. "Decontamination and all physical, emotional, and Flair measured."

"I don't recall agreeing to this."

"Part of the procedure."

"Hell. How's Opul?"

The Healer's round face folded into serious lines. "The sickness has him. He's thrashing around a lot more than he was. That's your fault, I heard."

He sat up. "You're done."

Her lips pursed. "Just."

Ura Heather and Lark Holly walked in.

"Where're my clothes?" he asked. They were his favorite set of leathers.

"They'll be fine," Lark assured him.

"Being decontaminated, too?" Couldn't be good for them, especially the padded tunic or boots. Dammit.

"That's right," Heather said. "You're in excellent shape."

"Good to know. Gimme my clothes."

"Incoming scry from the Turquoise House on the wall screen."

The Healers turned to it. "My clothes?" Garrett prompted. With a dark look, the ThirdLevel Healer went to a wall handle and pulled. Garrett's breechcloth, leathers, liners, and boots were there along with his pocketed belt. They didn't look any worse, but how would they feel?

"I need today and tomorrow to set up," the Turquoise House announced arrogantly. "I received the specifications for the beds and bedsponges and linens and cabinets and medical equipment. I am upgrading them to luxury and ordering them from Clover Fine Furniture. I will send the bill to Primary HealingHall."

"You won't!" Heather exploded.

"This is your project. Pay for it or cancel," the House said.

The House was doing well, especially for an entity that had no backup Family.

"The All Councils will fund the project," Lark soothed.

Heather's expression set in furrows. It would take some of the shine off the project if it was funded by all the councils. Take some of her glory if she found how to beat the sickness through his blood.

"Primary HealingHall can handle the expenses," she said stiffly.

Lark Holly lifted a brow in his direction. "Including compensating GentleSir Primross for his time."

Garrett heard the grind of Heather's teeth. Without sparing him a glance, she said, "All right."

He'd dressed fast. "My thanks. Much to do, arrange. Gotta go."

"GentleSir Primross," the Turquoise House's tones were warmer. "Please come over tomorrow morning."

Garrett nodded. "Will do. Later."

He left and strode down the carpeted hall—spell cleansed every half septhour with fragrant herbs. Primary HealingHall could handle a load of expenses.

He turned the corner and saw his HeartMate leaning against the wall outside Opul Cranberry's room.

His body surged toward her, yearning. He feared for the boy and his gut twisted. "Is the kid okay?"

Five

*A*rtemisia *looked at him with anger and his chest hurt.* "*Little Opul has Iasc sickness. Of course he isn't all right.*" A second's pause. "The transfusion went well. Though he's more active than most patients, it appears your blood is mitigating his ordeal. We are hopeful."

"Hope is a terrible thing," Garrett said.

Her emerald eyes gleamed with understanding. "Yes."

He had to leave before more stuff fell out of his mouth. "TQ asked that I come by tomorrow morning."

"Me, too," she said with a smile—at the thought of the House and not Garrett. Damn, he was obsessing.

"See you later, then."

In the next day, he'd be using a lot of Flair teleporting and keeping his twitchy nerves in order, so he took the public carrier to his office. On the way he decided to have client scrys forwarded to the man he trusted most—FirstFamily GreatLord Laev T'Hawthorn.

The minute he stepped off the vehicle, the band of feral cats flowed toward him. Black-and-White tom said, *We have heard you will stay at Turquoise House. You will feed Us there?*

Garrett grunted. "I'll make sure you have food."

Good.

He and the cat scanned the street and alleys, much busier than that morning, which felt like years ago to Garrett.

A change of place is fun sometimes and the yard of Turquoise House is nice. We will spread the word.

"How did you hear?" Garrett asked.

The House told Us.

Garrett reached the few steps up to the building and glanced back. The cats sat at the bottom, all in a row, all looking up at him, tails curled around their paws.

He knew what they wanted. "I'll check your food trough."

It is too low; dogs and others ate.

"Since this isn't a regular feeding time, I'm checking my office, first."

More than one cat sniffed in disapproval. He ignored that.

Inside his office, the wall scry panel showed ripples of Hawthorn purple. No doubt Laev T'Hawthorn had already heard of the experiment. Garrett grimaced. He'd have to talk, and explain or something. At least the Noble lord hadn't called his personal scry pebble.

No other messages flashed so no clients had called.

Garrett took a bucket of dry kibble from storage and proceeded to the back door. More than seven animals were in the courtyard. Garrett sensed a raccoon in the bushes, which meant he must set a spell to clean the water after it left. Raccoons weren't as communicative as cats and were scarcer. Garrett was cultivating the raccoons. He didn't know of any FamRaccoons. He might get goodwill from Nobles and others if he introduced another Fam animal.

He looked at the beady eyes a few meters distant and sent, *Greetyou.*

The raccoon ran away in a hunched lope.

The cats yowled for food.

Garrett dumped the kibble along a trough and hearty slurps began. The cats wouldn't finish it all and the raccoon would return.

Back in his office, after he'd squared away for his absence, he called Laev T'Hawthorn.

The man answered immediately, with a gleam of curiosity in his eyes. "Merrily met," Laev said.

"Yeah, yeah," Garrett said.

Laev laughed, then sobered. No matter that he loved and cherished his HeartMate, his first wife had died of the Iasc sickness. The illness had also affected Laev's FatherSire's health and weakened him to die later. "I heard about a new case of Iasc and that you went to Primary HealingHall."

"Yes," Garrett said.

"And FirstLevel Healer Ura Heather has a project to clear her name of the smudge the epidemic left on it?"

"Also true. I gave Opul Cranberry, age six, a transfusion."

"You got good blood."

Garrett lifted and dropped a shoulder, sucked a breath to the bottom of his gut. "I agreed to an experiment to reintroduce the disease into me. FirstLevel Healers Ura Heather and Lark Holly will supervise the case and I'll be under constant observation by a SecondLevel Healer."

"What!"

"You heard me." The ramifications would run through that smart head fast.

"Then NewBalm isn't working as well as we all had hoped."

Hawthorn had a financial interest in the herb so his mind naturally went to that aspect first. Garrett flicked his hand. "Still early days for that medicine, young harvests. The Healers anticipate that I'll be unavailable for an eightday. I thought I'd forward any calls to you to hold."

"I don't like this idea."

"I don't much, either."

Laev tapped fingertips together. "If the Healers believe it will work . . ." A line dug across his brows. "Much to consider."

"Yeah."

"I value you."

The warmth of friendship welled through Garrett, easing his mind. He could trust Laev. "Thanks."

The man's face set into brooding Garrett didn't like to see. Laev asked, "Someone will care for you?"

"The SecondLevel Healer," Garrett said.

Laev frowned. "Who?"

Garrett realized he couldn't avoid it any longer. He'd have to say her name.

Eyes narrowed and keen, Laev asked, "Who is the Healer who will be on-site?"

Yeah, Laev had deduced Garrett wasn't telling him something about the woman. Usually the Noble wouldn't press, but there was payback. Garrett had pried a few secrets from Laev, so the guy wouldn't quit.

And, hell, he was a friend. Breath trapped inside Garrett's chest so that it ached, then he said, "SecondLevel Healer Artemisia Panax."

"I don't know her or of her," Laev said. Then his eyes widened, mouth opened, shut, and he cleared his throat. "I amend that. I know the lady."

Garrett stared, understanding that they both kept secrets that neither would reveal.

"You can trust her," Laev said.

"I know," Garrett said. The Lady and Lord wouldn't give him a HeartMate he couldn't trust. He didn't know all the ins and outs of HeartMates and didn't want to discover them, but he already knew enough of the SecondLevel Healer to respect her.

Her superiors trusted her and now he had an independent opinion from his good friend.

Laev's gaze angled past Garrett, a habit of the Nobleman's when he was thinking. "We have to beat this sickness. Ura Heather and my aunt are the main Healers on the case?"

Lord and Lady, Garrett had completely forgotten Laev was related to the Healers. That was the problem with the FirstFamilies. Each and every one of them had ties to others—by blood, alliances, or enmities.

"Lark Holly is your late father's sister," Garrett said.

"That's right." Laev's look was direct. "I love and trust her very much. You want me to call my G'Uncle T'Heather about this matter?"

"That would make everything worse."

"Very well." Laev inclined his head. "Know I will attend closely to this situation."

"It's a Healer deal."

Laev shrugged. "I have a business interest in the herb that mitigates the disease."

"I know."

"So the Healers will keep me informed. As for your business, I'll take care of anything that is forwarded to me," Laev said with relish.

"No investigating. Only rescheduling."

"Of course," Laev said blandly.

"Thanks, Laev." Garrett touched two fingers to his forehead in a short salute. "I'm leaving for home." His smile was more grimace. "The experiment takes place at the Turquoise House, day after tomorrow."

"Do you want me to come with you?"

Yeah, Garrett would like his friend near, a man in the whole mix that he could trust. But Garrett wasn't going to say so. "Thanks for the offer. No. Just keep track of the whole deal."

"I'll do that. Go with the Lady and Lord. Blessed be."

"Blessed be."

*A*fter the lovely Family ritual in a sacred grove of the sanctuary, Artemisia excused herself for bed. She didn't sleep.

Throughout the deeply touching ceremony, as she experienced the cycling energy of her parents and her sister, Artemisia realized a few things. One of the reasons she hadn't left this House for a home of her own was because of this loving acceptance. They'd all faced the hideous scandal of being accused of conspiring with the Black

Magic Cult murderers. They were innocent but tried in public opinion and found guilty. They'd gone through that time together; not many others would understand.

And her mother and father were HeartMates. She liked being around them, included in the circle of love with her sister. Both her sister and she had HeartMates and neither of them had looked for their loves.

Men tended to do that if they were older than their HeartMates and experienced the connection with a HeartMate first in the dreamquests that freed Flair—Passages. Artemisia and Tiana knew their fated mates were men, and were older than they.

The few times that she and Tiana had spoken of the matter, they'd come to the conclusion their HeartMates weren't interested in them, perhaps because of the scandal. Who needed men like that?

Tiana had focused on her goal to be the premier priestess of the Lady and Lord in all of Celta and used the Mugwort name. But her teachers and colleagues were supposed to be compassionate and forgiving.

Artemisia's peers were only supposed to be compassionate. Forgiving was a different matter.

So Artemisia went by the surname of Panax, a branch of her mother's Family of Healers who had distanced themselves from the Mugworts when the whole nasty mess had happened. She worked with an aunt, uncle, and cousin who completely ignored her.

She wondered if that would change if *she* became notable due to the experiment. If it helped her Family, that was good. Like most Families, they lived together in a large House. Unlike most Families who were not of the highest nobility, the Mugworts lived in a Residence, an intelligent House. The Residence loved her, too.

And her home was utterly unique. It was the first Healing Grove founded by the colonists and became the estate of the caretakers, the BalmHeals, who had all died out. Celta was still tough on its Earth transplants, as the Iasc sickness proved. Illness and sterility took a toll on the population—human and animal and plant. But Celtans had the length of their life and the increase of magic, psi powers, Flair, augmented. Not a fair trade as far as Artemisia was concerned. Like everyone else, she wanted it all—long life free of sickness and phenomenal Flair.

FirstGrove, BalmHeal estate, was a triangle in the northeast corner of Druida City, so two of the estate's walls were also the city walls. The concave triangular wall facing the city looked out onto only empty warehouses. The place was hidden from everyone except the desperate, the whispered secret sanctuary of Druida.

Like the rest of her Family, Artemisia was bound to the estate by blood and love. If she cut those bonds, she could never remember the location or return—unless she, herself, was desperate. She was bespelled to not tell anyone of the place.

Her Family had been stripped of their nobility and fortune and were running from Druida City when they'd been approached to be caretakers for the Residence. The best blessing of their lives.

No one knew what would happen when Artemisia and Tiana wed, if their men would be welcome at BalmHeal. If it was up to the Residence, he might be contrary and throw them all out, or grudgingly accept the new men.

Artemisia wanted a husband, but she wanted to stay in the sanctuary, too. She loved the old, crotchety Residence, her parents, the grounds that were a mixture of Earth and Celtan plants and hybrids. The sacred groves and the Healing pools were the best on Celta. No, she didn't want to leave. But she wanted a busier career outside the sanctuary.

She wanted a career, a mate—not necessarily a HeartMate—and to live in her home.

She couldn't see Garrett Primross accepting those modest goals. Like Tiana, ambition burned in him.

His image slid into her mind with the thought. Tall, muscular, powerful, with excellent Flair. Sexy. And he loved solving riddles, but he wouldn't be contemplating *her* secrets when he was infected with Iasc and wrapped in fever and nightmares.

She hoped it wouldn't be nightmares, but with his history, she suspected they'd torment him. Not that she should look at him with lust, enjoy the slow sensuality that ebbed through her in his presence. He was her patient, forbidden.

And she wasn't even sure she liked him.

*A*rtemisia *Mugwort Panax*. *Her name jerked Garrett from a doze* near dawn. He'd curled up on his bedsponge as if he were a kid, so he stretched long and hard, thinking.

He'd heard the name of Artemisia Mugwort during his investigation for Laev T'Hawthorn . . . and Artemisia's younger sister was the best friend of Camellia D'Hawthorn, Laev's HeartMate. A small mystery solved. There was something else, but his mind had alerted him to the new day. The last day before he was infected with the horrible sickness. His stomach tensed.

Better make the most of it. He'd hired someone to spellshield his office and was due to meet him in a septhour. He'd send that bill to Primary HealingHall. He wasn't sure who provided the Healing-Hall's budget; it wasn't funded totally by the councils of Celta. He thought Nobles who wanted to use the facilities paid an annual tithe and the Heather Family plowed gilt into it. Didn't matter much as long as he got reimbursed, but his curiosity encompassed everything.

He was glad that the Turquoise House had decided on luxurious linens and furnishings. Not that Garrett would appreciate them when he was thrashing around with the sickness.

He had other tasks: clearing space in his no-time food storage so he could add his fresh food, dragging out his oldest clothes to wear, finding a damn nightshirt. He didn't want to examine why he wasn't comfortable being nude with the SecondLevel Healer. Dozens of small errands he had to take care of, including updating his will.

Splat! Something soft and squishy hit his window. He glanced at

the long smear of blood and winced. Dead mouse head. The feral
cats were hungry.

Now he had to clean the window.

*A*rtemisia *arrived at the Turquoise House an hour before WorkBell,*
was greeted enthusiastically and informed she was the first to arrive.
Which had her relaxing; that was irritating because she'd told herself
she was perfectly calm.

"Come in!" TQ said. "I have camp chairs and a table in the mainspace by the window. My people like that window best. I also have
an old drink no-time ready to be deconstructed."

He sounded insistent, so she let her steps take her to the small
seating area and the window out onto the gardens. She halted when
she saw several cats chasing each other in the back grassyard. An
orange mother cat followed by a small kitten avoided the others and
paraded, tails up, to a cobbled space. Moving so she could see the
pair, Artemisia noticed an area complete with several bowls of food
and a small fountain.

TQ said, "My friend and your Residence, BalmHeal, says you
prefer warm half caff and half milk?" As it spoke, the no-time drink
unit extruded a shelf with a steaming china mug. Artemisia took it,
though she'd already had three cups that morning. "Thank you," she
murmured.

"I have received all furniture and equipment on our list. A holo
wall mural artist came yesterday afternoon. We practiced and I can
sterilize the entire room and not affect the art!"

"Wonderful. I like murals for my patients."

"I have heard Opul Cranberry progresses well through the sickness. It appears the duration will be significantly shorter than anticipated."

She'd already checked and was relieved. "Yes."

"Because of GentleSir Primross's potent Flair-imbued blood,"
TQ pointed out.

"Yes."

"He is a tough man and an interesting individual," TQ continued with admiration.

Easier to agree. "Yes."

"Here as requested, TQ," Garrett called.

Six

Artemisia tensed again at *Garrett's* voice, then forced her muscles to ease.

TQ broadcasted, "We are in the mainspace. Some of our cat friends have arrived to stay with us."

Artemisia said, "I don't have cat friends." Then she realized TQ spoke of himself and Garrett. The guy had cat friends. Yes, he was interesting. And when he walked into the room, his impact made her catch her breath. He had a very intense aura and too much of an effect on her. She'd hoped she'd been imagining that.

He wore standard trous and tunic of cotton in a deep brown that accented the light amber color of his eyes. The clothes didn't show his musculature, but Artemisia knew he had a good body.

TQ said, "Hot, strong black caff, GentleSir Primross, your preference. Please take the mug to the GentleSir, Artemisia."

"Call me Garrett, TQ." A corner of his mouth lifted.

Artemisia picked up the new mug with liquid hotter and darker than her own. His mug was thick, manly pottery of dark green. He looked at her pretty floral mug with light-colored caff, then his own. His lips quirked deeper but flattened into a line when their fingers brushed. "Thanks."

Did he feel the same sizzle of affinity that she did? She thought so, and he didn't welcome it. She didn't, either, though if he'd been at least nice the previous day, she might have. She'd noticed his slights but ignored them.

He was her patient, forbidden to act on any attraction, though a less vulnerable man she'd never seen. But that was now. Tomorrow he'd be at the mercy of the sickness . . . and her. She swallowed. She didn't want to watch him suffer.

"Artemisia, about that matter we discussed yesterday?" The House addressed the Healer in rich tones while Garrett sipped the best caff he'd had in days. He watched her over the rim of his cup; obviously she and the House had bonded more after he'd left. He shouldn't have been irritated that the House might prefer her, but was. Competitive and stupid.

"Yes?" she asked. She was aware of him; even though she turned and walked to the window, her body angled toward him.

"I have decided to offer Garrett an invitation. No doubt he has kept many secrets."

"Oh," she said, her glance sliding to him. He remained impassive, but curiosity began to itch along his skin.

"Yeah, no doubt I have secrets and keep them." Garrett was antsy enough to pull out a coin and run it between his fingers. Showy to others and fun for him, the action did double duty.

The Healer stared at Garrett with wide emerald eyes, studying him, measuring him for the first time. His body reacted to her scrutiny, his chest expanded, his abs tightened. His feet shifted to widen his balance a little—women could deliver the most awful blows. And his cock grew heavy. He didn't want that and was damn well going to keep her focus on his face. So he smiled.

Her eyes widened and her mouth curved, but she compressed her lips. As if she didn't believe that smile of his. Smart woman.

"Do you keep secrets?" she asked.

"Love secrets. I keep them if I think that's the right thing to do. And for the right person." He let his voice chill.

Her chin lifted. "Fine. TQ, you deal with this guy. I want to check on the furnishings."

"I will explain to Garrett." TQ's voice was smooth on top, with a warning underneath. The House had learned to use its actor's voice well. "Artemisia, the furnishings are fine, exactly as ordered, and Clover Fine Furniture delivered on schedule."

"Maybe I want my own pillow," the Healer said.

"It would have to go through decontamination often, I'd think," Garrett said. He continued to roll the coin. Occasionally it would flash and her gaze would go to it.

"My pillow won't be harmed, I don't think. It's a feather pillow." Artemisia walked from the room.

There was a slight hiss from TQ. "You have irritated your Heart-Mate."

Yes, that he knew Artemisia was his HeartMate was one of Garrett's secrets. He flinched. "How do you know?"

"Everything my inhabitants have whispered of, I know," TQ said.

Which made Garrett want a list of those who'd lived in TQ. Must be a record somewhere and he'd find it, later. But now he was stuck for a week with the Healer.

"I keep secrets, too," the House said. "And I know you're a discreet man."

"Don't suppose you'd give me a list of the people who've stayed with you?"

"No. And I have my own secrets, naturally." The House made a sound like clearing a throat—which he didn't have, and which the actor who'd given him the voice wouldn't have done at this moment. It showed weakness. TQ was definitely his own entity, and not a human male. "My HouseHeart chamber needs maintenance. I asked Artemisia to help. I want this done before the Healers' project."

"Which is why you aren't ready today." Garrett slipped the coin into his pocket. His lust had subsided. Good. He could still smell the woman in the room, though.

TQ said, "Correct. I had considered requesting your help, too."

Fascination blazed through Garrett. He nearly trembled with it. He'd never been in a HouseHeart, the most important place of a sentient House. The HouseHeart reflected the Family. But the Turquoise House had no Family, so Garrett himself might be able to infuse a bit of himself into the long-lived being. That would be a satisfying goal in itself, a tiny legacy of himself in stretching infinity.

After his loss of Dinni, he'd discovered that he'd needed to make a mark on the world. Something more than just surviving the disease. This could be a true contribution.

"You are reconsidering your offer?" His throat was hot with desire to learn, to see, to discover.

"You do not treat Artemisia well, though she is your HeartMate. Humans are very odd."

"HeartMate and HeartBonding is odd."

"I have seen HeartBonded people."

Garrett wondered if the House had actually had a HeartMate couple exchange the bond sexually within its walls. How much could the House sense? Garrett's mind veered to an image of a naked Artemisia screaming her passion. Shut that down!

"Why do you treat Artemisia as you do?"

"My business."

"How am I to help my people, help *you* during this time, if I don't understand you? How am I to learn?"

The plea socked Garrett's gut.

Dammit, now he couldn't speak because his throat had tightened. He coughed. "We're private here?"

"Artemisia is making arrangements to get her pillow." There was a slight pause as if TQ's attention focused elsewhere. The House wasn't omnipresent, then. "I do not think that her pillow will survive the decontamination processes. When the pillow arrives I will measure it in all ways. If the object does not last, I will replace it with an exact copy."

"Things aren't always interchangeable. The pillow you provide, no matter how it seems like a match, won't be *her* pillow."

The air around him pressed against him, TQ's attention sharp. "Did you lose someone dear and irreplaceable? A woman?"

Garrett didn't answer.

Silence throbbed. Garrett shook off the rough mood and went over to the window that looked out on the rear grassyard. Beautifully landscaped, of course. One or more of TQ's residents had been a gardener. Smooth green turf, colorful flowers shifting in the slight breeze before bushes staggered in front of small trees, then tall trees, keeping the yard private. All of the feral cats he knew, and others he didn't, snoozed in the sun.

The yard looked too manicured, as were the formal gardens and fountain of the inner courtyard of MidClass Lodge where he lived. He preferred a natural tangle of plant life like he'd found on his travels outside cities.

"The records of the Gael City HealingHall state a young woman with a baby asked you to accompany the driver of the quarantine vehicle to the isolation clinic in the mountains."

He jerked, remembering. Dinni had begged. Her husband had been one of the men to find the infected fish and had died. Her baby had been sick. She'd looked fine except for sorrow and worry.

Garrett's throat closed. He couldn't answer, pretend this didn't matter.

"*Her* records at that HealingHall state that she had told the Healers she would scry a friend—an old lover—who she was sure would help with the driving, and that you grew up together."

There wasn't even a sturdy chair he could sit on, only two little rickety ones. He hitched a hip on the wide windowsill. His chest hurt.

"I have lost people, too," TQ said softly. "One or two died here despite all I did to save them. You lost the woman, Dinni Spurge Flixweed."

"Yes," Garrett forced out. "I lost my first love, my first girl."

Footsteps echoed in the quiet and the Healer paused at the door, expression irritated. Then her head tilted as she picked up the atmosphere. The woman seemed more sensitive empathically than most.

Why would it take so long to get a pillow? A messenger service could 'port anywhere in moments if she gave them visual clues. Another thing for Garrett to figure out later.

She crossed her arms. "Have we considered the situation?"

Garrett's past swept away with the lure of seeing a forbidden place, a HouseHeart.

"I will allow GentleSir Garrett Primross into my HouseHeart with the usual proviso that a spell will be applied to his memory so it will fade, and if he gives us his Vow of Honor that he will record no details."

Not so easy an access as Garrett had expected. Disappointment shadowed his thoughts, but he would know that he'd been in a HouseHeart, had made a contribution that would live after him. He'd know it in his very bones, and that would be good. "I agree."

"This experiment will be stressful for all of us, but especially you two humans. I believe time in my HouseHeart will be good for you before we begin this process."

Artemisia's arms uncrossed and her shoulders lowered, a genuine smile lightened her eyes. "It's wonderful you will allow me in your HouseHeart. Thank you."

"You are welcome here, Artemisia. You will always be welcome," TQ responded. The House didn't add permission for Garrett. He shrugged the caring away.

A chuff of air came, followed by TQ's words. "There is a secret passageway from my southwest corner. At the end of that hallway, there is a trapdoor in the floor, under the carpet. I will tell you the secret poem. I am very good at telepathic communication, but my people must be better attuned to me than you currently are."

After all the information, the woman let out a long breath.

Garrett said, "Right." When they reached the first hallway, she turned the wrong direction.

Gritting his teeth, knowing it was a mistake, he took her elbow in his fingers. Pure desire flashed through him. Maybe the more he resisted temptation, the more his lust would mount, would rage within him. Too bad; he wasn't going to change. She wasn't the woman he wanted.

But three years had passed since Dinni's death and his grief and loss were waning, like bright moons coming from shadows that had been cast upon them.

Artemisia stopped and looked up at him.

"Wrong way."

"Oh." Her smile was quick and meaningless. She turned and Garrett had to force his hand to drop. Her elbow wasn't even that sexy.

He lied.

She hesitated at the cross corridor.

"Left," he said.

"Thank you."

There was a good-sized window at the end of the hall. No one would expect a hidden entrance to the HouseHeart to be there.

"The moles of Celta and Captain Ruis Elder of the starship *Nuada's Sword* helped me excavate a proper concealed passage and secret HouseHeart," TQ said. "Then Mitchella D'Blackthorn and I decorated it *ourselves*."

"Sounds wonderful," Artemisia said.

"It *is*!" TQ said.

The Healer caught sight of the change in the plush and patterned carpet before Garrett. He searched with his Flair and he found that the hole was narrow. "You have a problem with claustrophobia?" he asked.

"No, nor darkness or dankness."

"I am not dark or dank!" TQ objected.

"No. You aren't," she agreed absently, passing her hands over the area covered by the rug.

Garrett was struck with the idea that she knew about House-Hearts, this woman who was not one of the twenty-five FirstFamilies who had most of the intelligent Residences. From sheer curiosity, he'd made a list of sentient buildings and there weren't more than a dozen that didn't belong to the FirstFamilies, descendants of the colonists who had funded the trip to Celta. What did she know? And how?

Taking a moment to clear the desire from his senses, shutting down even the thin thread that pulsed with molecules between them, he used his Flair and caught tendrils of mystery wisping around her like fog.

"What's the spell and the password?" she whispered.

Following logic, he understood that TQ knew more about the woman than he did, and so must the Healers. He was being left out. Nearly intolerable.

On an inner breeze, TQ recited:

Home is where the Heart is
My HouseHeart is Home,
Is Me,
Home, Home, Home
For the right Family
Us

Garrett had expected a cheerful little jingle. "That doesn't make sense."

"I wrote it," TQ said with dignity. "I like it."

"It makes sense to him," the Healer murmured.

"Yes, Artemisia," TQ said.

Softly, repeating the emphasis exactly as TQ had, she said the spell.

The carpet and floor lifted straight up, the rectangle attached to the ceiling, then illusion covered it.

Illusion on the floor, too, as if the carpet remained. The spot rippled, and Garrett figured if TQ didn't want them to see that warning, he wouldn't have. "Good safety measures. Even if someone knows the words, they won't see the opening unless you allow them."

"That is correct," TQ said.

The Healer stepped forward, frowned as she peered down. Garrett came up until his body almost touched hers, looked to the floor— and beyond to a dark hole. "Light?" he prompted.

It shot in spears from the opening. The walls of the very steep stairway—large enough for a big man—were painted pale yellow.

"I should go first, in case you fall," Garrett said.

"I do not let anyone fall on *my* staircase," TQ said.

"By accident," Artemisia said.

"By accident," TQ agreed.

Without a glance at Garrett, the Healer began descending.

"These are my only stairs. I was very young when the House-Heart was made," TQ said.

"And that was?" Garrett asked. The stair treads were only a centimeter or so larger than his feet. The steps themselves angled around corners and he couldn't see Artemisia. That twanged his nerves, because they were HeartMates. But right now he didn't care that the bond between them was strengthening; he wanted her in sight. He picked up his pace.

"The HouseHeart was made fifteen years ago," TQ said. The House had actually given him information.

"Nice," she said, farther down.

"Thank you," TQ said.

Garrett jumped the last stairs and found himself in an oval natural cave with rocky ground ringed by stalagmites. A couple of huge stalactites descended from the ceiling that TQ could drop on unexpected visitors. Maybe use as missiles. "Excellent defense."

"Thank you. This space is such that people can teleport into it, as long as I don't change the light or my rocks."

"I don't see a door."

"Touch the point of the lowest stalagmite," TQ said.

"A challenge and a riddle." He scanned the room for the lowest upthrust rock. The smallest reached his shin and he touched the top. The point fell off; a grinding echoed. One of the large stalactites moved into the ceiling, the illusion of rock behind it shimmered, then dissipated. A turquoise pointed-arched door with black hardware and surrounded by dressed stone appeared.

"Lovely." The Healer strode to it, touched the latch. A spark arced and she yelped, shaking her fingers. "Don't you think this security is a little excessive?"

"No," TQ and Garrett said together.

"I am the best-known House-becoming-a-Residence and famous. I don't often have a greatly Flaired person living within my walls. I need all my shields."

"All right," she soothed.

Garrett eyed the door. "Good spellshields there."

"Yes, needing spell Words. Palms on the door," TQ instructed.

Garrett slapped his palms on a smooth surface that felt like metal. TQ could run electrical current through the door. "What're the spell Words?"

"Together we weather," TQ said.

A quick image of sleet hitting the windshield of the quarantine bus, the frigid cold around him, as he slogged through the storm to check on the vehicle flashed before Garrett. He shuddered.

Then there was the scent of summer and sweet woman and mysteries beside him. If he opened his lashes that he'd clenched shut, he could look down on her head. But it would be a dark head instead of blonde.

Lord and Lady, this whole situation stirred up grief at losing his Dinni.

"Together we weather," the woman said with a thickness to her voice indicating her own tough memories.

The door slid into the wall and the HouseHeart beckoned.

Seven

*W*onderful *smells and sounds wafted from the HouseHeart, teasing* Garrett—cocoa, vanilla, cinnamon, burning wood.

"I have flatsweets on the table by the fire," TQ said.

Garrett couldn't move. The woman was too close, the dim chamber beyond stirred a great yearning inside him, as if he knew once he set foot in it, the true essence of *home* would seep into his bones and he'd never get it out of them and forever miss it.

Ignore that.

Artemisia entered first. Keeping his steps light—he'd wanted to leave something of himself here in TQ's HouseHeart, not have something imprinted upon himself forever—Garrett walked into the room.

It had brackets near the top of the walls with spell-lights that looked like flames. The door slid shut. On this side it appeared to be a seamless wall covered with pale yellow paper with red and blue flourishes. Artemisia stooped. "What a lovely cat!"

"I made her and am making her and she is becoming. She can move her tail, look!"

The painting of the gray and black tabby cat—who also had red and blue flowers tinted on her—moved. The round tip of her gray and black tail extruded from the wall, flicked, then disappeared again.

Meewww. Tiny, as if it took great effort.

"How do we feed her?" Artemisia asked.

"I can draw the Flair and energy you naturally emit throughout the day, like body heat, to her," TQ said.

"Hmm." The woman sat with crossed legs, stroked the cat's painted forehead, then left her hand there. Closing her eyes, she stilled. Garrett sensed her gathering Flair.

Her full breasts rose as she took a deep breath, the cloth of her tunic shaping over them. As she exhaled, golden motes of Flair-magic spun around her.

"What's she doing?" Garrett asked.

"She's sending *love* to my cat!" whispered TQ.

Garrett wasn't sure how that worked.

"You know Fam animals," TQ said.

Garrett did. They were drawn to him, maybe because he could speak to them all, and sometimes they had plenty to say.

"Think how you feel about them," Artemisia said. "How you care, and send that feeling to them. When you do that, you send love. As I do to this cat who belongs to TQ and herself."

Garrett watched Artemisia breathe deeply a few more times. He should have been examining the first HouseHeart he'd ever been in but couldn't take his gaze off the woman.

MEEWWW. The sound was stronger and followed by a short and rumbling purr.

Artemisia smiled at the cat. A damned painted, mostly inanimate and unalive cat, and Garrett's heart wanted that smile for himself.

She rose smoothly and glanced around. "A truly lovely chamber."

"I am modern and have much Flair and have had many Flaired people giving me energy and I have the newest Flair tech," TQ boasted.

"Um-hmm," Artemisia said neutrally. She crossed to the mural on the north wall. It was a jungle scene with a small round turquoise pool. People moved through the tree shadows. With a little shock, Garrett recognized Tinne Holly and his wife.

Artemisia tilted her head. "These are your former inhabitants?"

"All of them," TQ said proudly. "Even the ones that I didn't like much and didn't allow to stay long. They remain mostly behind the trees."

Garrett's breath caught as he stared.

"Will we be there?" Artemisia asked.

"Perhaps you. Garrett has a home in MidClass Lodge," TQ said.

And it wasn't nearly as homey as this. This was a HouseHeart and special, but if this reflected how the House above had looked when it had been furnished, he'd never had a home like the one TQ had provided his tenants. The thought jolted that Garrett had never made a home for himself after Dinni had rejected him so long ago. He'd drifted and stayed in places, but he hadn't had or made a home.

Artemisia Mugwort Panax looked completely at ease in the surroundings, a woman who knew about offering comfort and making a home.

No, he wouldn't let himself yearn for her or what they could have together.

Garrett's throat was clogged but he wouldn't clear it. His voice rasped. "What do you need us to do, TQ?"

Flames in the huge fireplace faded and so did the scent of coal and wood burning, the crackle of fire, even the smoke and heat vanished. All fake.

"Helluva illusion," Garrett said.

The House chuckled like settling stone. "My kind of sleight of hand."

Artemisia went to the fireplace and sat on the high hearthstone, held her hands over the bottom of the fireplace. "It's cool."

There was the scrape of stone and inside the slab tilted up. "My HouseStones," the Turquoise House whispered.

Artemisia's breath was quick and hard.

Garrett couldn't keep himself from lunging to see the rare sight. In a small shallow depression were five glowing pebbles and a chunk of obsidian. How could something as large as a Residence have such a small brain? "Wow."

TQ said, "They need to be moved, rearranged. Also . . ."

Several heartbeats of tension strung silence no one broke.

Finally, hand stroking the fireplace wall as if she might calm TQ, Artemisia said, "Also?"

A shower of soot had them coughing. Garrett wiped his nose and mouth on his sleeve; Artemisia pulled softleaves from her long-sleeve pocket and handed one to Garrett.

One good cough to clear his lungs and Garrett said, "Not very good punctuation, House."

"Sorry," TQ mumbled. "I did not think. My HouseStones are bare and vulnerable."

"And we're torturing them so badly," Artemisia said with faint irritation. Soot smudged her light complexion.

"Sor-ry!" TQ repeated.

"Do you have a design you want us to put your stones in?" Artemisia asked.

"I want the obsidian one out of the center and to the northwest. It will catch better vibrations from the starship *Nuada's Sword*," TQ said.

The Ship was several kilometers away. Garrett would've denied feeling anything from it, but when TQ had mentioned vibrations, he'd felt a tiny pressure against his skin.

Artemisia lifted the pyramidical piece of obsidian from the center of the stones and it slipped from her grasp, slicing her hand, falling. She cried out. Garrett snatched at the rock, caught it, and swallowed a curse as a sharp edge cut him, too. With great precision he put the obsidian in the northwest point of the depression and withdrew his hand.

Blood from his fingers and from Artemisia's hands dripped on the HeartStones.

TQ gurgled.

"Eww," exclaimed Artemisia. She grasped his hand in hers and Healed his cuts.

Not before Garrett felt some of her blood invade his, whisk through him, strengthen their bond.

She wiped her hands on the softleaf, but blood welled from the fleshy side of her hand. Clasping her hands together, she Healed her own injury.

"Thank you!" TQ sang.

"Not sure that you're welcome," Garrett muttered.

Artemisia huffed. "What else, TQ?"

Garrett was tired of playing by the house rules. He stuck his hand into the depression and rolled the stones together, flicked and flipped them around until they felt right in a now-they're-here, now-they're-gone gesture, then rolled them out.

"Ooooh," TQ said. "Very nice. I never would have considered that arrangement." Then the House purred like its cat. "I like this. Well done, Garrett!"

"What else?" asked Artemisia.

"I request you bring me a stone or a rock from your homes."

"MidClass Lodge? They only have rock paths," Garrett said.

Artemisia rolled her eyes. "And native rock in the garden soil."

"Yeah." The woman was too close. He could smell her skin and her innate scent and blood and breath. Restless, he moved away. "You want me to get something from T'Hawthorn estate, too?" he asked sarcastically.

"I will scry that Residence immediately and ask it and T'Hawthorn himself!" TQ exclaimed.

Artemisia chuckled and stood. She waved her softleaf and the bloodstains and soot vanished, then picked up the one Garrett had dropped and tucked them into her sleeve pocket.

Foolish to have wanted to keep it because it was hers. Her nearness made him revert to a boy with a crush.

"T'Hawthorn Residence and GreatLord Laev T'Hawthorn say they would be honored to provide one of my HouseStones!" TQ announced. "They are choosing one *right now*."

"I will bring a stone from my home's oldest and most sacred grove," Artemisia said.

"Thank you! You can both teleport from here."

"All right." Garrett crossed to the west to examine the fountain. He wouldn't be the first to leave.

Artemisia stared at him. Then she tidied her clothes, counted down three teleportation beats, and vanished.

"This has been interesting," Garrett said, "but I don't like being manipulated."

"You like to do that yourself?" shot back TQ.

Garrett shrugged. TQ must have a scrystone here, maybe even a camera. "Maybe."

"Thank you for helping me, and for your blood. It will always be a part of my essence."

Garrett jerked. TQ was observant, had winnowed out something it had taken him a couple of years to understand. One thing he wanted deeply was to leave an important legacy. He'd lost so much in that mountain clinic—his lover, his hope, the identity of the man he'd been.

Even then, his parents had been long dead. He needed to know something would outlast him. Now the Turquoise House had given this to him and he'd been ungracious. But he'd been manipulated into giving himself.

"The blood must hold surprise at being shed," TQ said softly.

"Anything else?"

In that same tone, TQ said, "I want you to call Artemisia by her given name."

Garrett stiffened and his hand swept into the cool and jasmine-smelling water of the fountain. He grimaced. "Or else?"

"What?" asked TQ.

"Aren't you going to add a threat? You want me to call her by name, *or else*."

"You do not strike me as a man who responds well to threats."

"Got that right." Well, he'd already made his mark on TQ. And his case for Laev T'Hawthorn wouldn't be forgotten soon, and Garrett definitely had had a hand in an exceedingly strange death that Flair scholars were still discussing. So those were ways that he'd be remembered, too. Three stories with his name attached that would live on. Would that be sufficient?

Inner hollowness still echoed. He didn't think so. This project would do it. But he didn't want to be recalled for his blood, for the worst part of his life. Humans were definitely contrary creatures, himself included.

TQ said, "It strikes me that refusing to be courteous to Artemisia within my walls, something I deplore, will become more evident and rouse more questions than not."

Garrett flung up a hand as if a fencer had scored a hit against him. "All right."

"And as for the *or else* . . . if you aren't nice to her within my walls, your avatar will probably spend time hidden in the trees of my mural." Humor in the House's voice now.

"Like I care about an avatar."

"I will be disappointed in you. You will not be the man I thought you to be, the courageous and compassionate man who volunteered for this project."

"Like I care about that, either."

"I won't ever let you come back, especially here. Which I anticipate you might need after your ordeal."

"A bribe?"

"A reward. You live in a busy lodge and share your office building, yet I believe you are a man who treasures being alone. How often do you get to be completely private?"

"Anytime I take off out of Druida and spend some time in the countryside—on a beach or walking in woods." Never hiking in mountains. "You do have another point."

"The countryside is not as secure or as fascinating as my House-Heart. I will have my person, my couple who will be the start of my Family, within three years."

"An interesting notion." One that had Garrett's curiosity throbbing again.

"Will you treat Artemisia well? Like she is a partner?"

"She's a Healer," Garrett said drily. "And there will be other Healers. I doubt any want to interact with me other than professionally."

"Artemisia has a tender heart," TQ stated. The House knew her better than Garrett had thought. "Her blood pressure rises, her breath comes quicker, and she shows signs of sexual arousal when you and she are together. So do you."

"You keep track of such things?" Not hard to put *appalled* in his own voice.

"I got new medical spells and was shown how to use them as soon as I heard the Healers might need a venue. Be glad the T'Blackthorn garden shed isn't being readied."

"Thrilled." Garrett ran his coin through his fingers. "Believe me, House, neither your tenants nor your Family will welcome hearing such bits of information about themselves."

"You think not?" TQ asked in surprise.

"I'll be back in a while."

"T'Hawthorn Residence has agreed to return you here by one of the Family gliders."

"Thank you. Later." He went from the lush HouseHeart to his Spartan mainspace, landed hard—he'd been off-balance for the last couple of days—shook his head, and strode to a comfortchair to line up all the things said and unsaid that morning.

*B*ut the Turquoise House is your friend; you should <u>want</u> to gift him with a stone!" Artemisia protested to BalmHeal Residence. She sat on the window seat in her bedroom and looked in the direction of the first sacred grove made by the Earth colonists when they'd arrived on Celta. "Why don't you want to donate a rock for his HouseHeart?"

"Upstart," BalmHeal Residence sneered, deep in his grumpy-old-man persona. "We'd be tied together forever."

She raised her brows. "That assumes that every rock on this estate belongs to you."

"They do!"

"And you can feel each and every bit?"

"You want to take it from *my* best grove."

"That's right. A grove established several years before your walls and the oldest of your foundations. If anything defines this place, it's the groves and the Healing pools."

All the open doors of the Residence slammed shut. There was a short cry from Artemisia's mother.

"Be careful," Artemisia snapped.

"No one is careful of me or *my* feelings," the Residence rumbled.

"That is not at all true." Artemisia sighed in exasperation and donned patience. She'd had to learn it as a Healer, and it usually came in handy more with the Residence. "We love you. The Turquoise House deeply, *deeply* admires you. He is thrilled that you would so condescend to allow him to have a pebble for his House-Heart."

"A *pebble*! Who does he think he is? He believes he can store data and think in *pebbles*! Rude upstart." The shutters on the wall outside the window clacked shut, then open.

It wouldn't be wise to inform BalmHeal the upstart already worked with pebbles. "I suppose you could, perhaps, donate a large stone, then? Perhaps even a dressed one, like one of those in the outside storage area?" She put a wheedle in her voice. The Residence liked that.

"And you will be staying *away from me*." This time the shutters clapped over the window as if to hold her in. "A whole eightday."

Eight

*Y*es," *Artemisia said.* "*I'll be away from you and my Family and the* estate for a week. That's the term of the project. None of us anticipates the experiment will take that long." Her voice lowered. "The FirstLevel Healers think it will take Primross no more than five or six days to throw off the sickness." She heaved a sigh for the Residence. "Too bad we couldn't bring him here; *you* are the best HealingHall in all of Celta."

"Yes." The slats of the shutters opened and she could see the green of verdant summer outside the window, the swathes of lawn, the glitter of Healing pools, the tall tops of trees. Familiar, exquisite, beloved.

"That young House has no occupants?" BalmHeal asked.

"No. And it's empty, white walls. Pitiable."

A groan of the wood of the window seat under her was disconcerting.

"It is, perhaps, lonely?"

"Maybe," she agreed.

"It knows nothing of abandonment, of loneliness." Back to sneering. That was the issue. BalmHeal Residence had been abandoned for centuries, so long it had nearly died. The estate had welcomed the desperate, but few had gone to the House, even fewer passed its shields and inside.

Artemisia hauled up another sigh, let it out noisily. "I was not exactly asked." She rubbed the molding around the window up and down, shiny because of her habit.

"You could always stay here, always."

An old argument. "Outside I can meet a man and have children for you."

The Residence wanted children. Might not want the man. "Tiana will most likely live outside for several years." Artemisia pressed her palm on the window glass. "So my children are the ones who might tend to you."

Her door latch depressed and the door opened. BalmHeal Residence knew she hated that, but she said nothing.

"The new young House may have a rock from the summerhouse."

"Not from the oldest grove? *Ple-ease?*"

"Very well. A largish stone from the summerhouse. A *pebble* from the sacred grove."

"Thank you so much!"

"You will be back this evening?"

"For dinner, I promise." She raised a hand.

"Your pillow is on its way to the youngster," BalmHeal said.

"Not my favorite."

"No."

"Thank you." She ran through the door, closed it behind her, and patted it, then took off for the summerhouse that was not really on the way to the sacred grove, which was in the far southwestern corner of the estate. She was pleased with herself for cajoling the Residence and being able to fulfill TQ's dreams. And pleased with the Residence for being so generous. It, too, was Healing well, emotionally. But slowly.

*A*rranging *the four stones in* TQ's *HouseHeart had been an experi*ence Garrett prized: the welcoming ambiance of the place, TQ's comments, Artemisia's easy presence. This time there had been no blood or reason for her hands on him, a disappointment. He'd enjoyed the HouseHeart, held to that even after the details of its location had begun to fade as he went up the steps. There had been steps?

By the next morning, the conversations he'd had in the House-Heart were still clear, everything else was dim, superseded by the nightmares that had plagued him. His clenched gut was ample reminder that today he'd have the Iasc sickness introduced into his body again.

One small reassurance was that when he'd contacted Primary HealingHall to check on Opul, he'd been told the youngster had passed the danger point and was recovering.

Garrett's blood had kept the kid alive, had helped. Maybe Garrett's advice, too. If his blood and advice could help the child, they'd carry Garrett through. He dreaded the time between now and then.

The Healers would be studying him and maybe they'd find a cure for the sickness. That's what this whole damn thing was about.

He didn't say a shaving spell. Why bother?

This morning he arrived at TQ early. He preferred to be the first on the scene, especially if he might be ambushed. Though the ambush had taken place two days ago.

The front courtyard was shadowed, showing only a few patches of sun, yet still looked welcoming. TQ radiated cheer, but no pleasing atmosphere could chisel away Garrett's irritation and discomfort.

He prowled the courtyard, the curving irregular flower beds bright with colorful blooms, the verdant bushes, the staggered trees. All charming.

Cats streamed from the back grassyard to surround him for scritches and pets and rubs.

We like this very much, said the leader. *We are pleased to be back here.* He lifted his nose. *Though We had to show the three local cats who den here that We were tougher.* A twitch of whiskers. *They do not want to become part of Our gang. They wish to always stay here.*

One of the reasons that the cats were so useful to Garrett was that they ranged the whole city, saw and heard things that humans paid no attention to or missed.

TQ cracked open the front door. Only three crept close to the stoop. One was an orange tabby mother and her kitten, who was beige with the dark brown spots of a hunting cat.

The tom standing next to Garrett made a disgusted noise. *Smells bad and scary.*

And that was before the sickness.

No human smells, no Fam smells, no cloth or wood or metal smells, another cat said, waving her white tail.

The kitten, smaller than the front step, mewed a question that wasn't formed enough for Garrett to understand.

Not inside today, the mother said decisively. *Not soon.*

The kitten mewed defiance and his dam picked him up by his scruff and trotted away from the door. She studied Garrett with narrowed eyes and came over.

Treats? Treat for Momcat and Kit?

All the cats perked up. They could smell the jerky bites in Garrett's trous pockets. His feral mob moved into the pattern of status, a fluid thing that changed from day to day as to which had the best hunt in the night.

He passed treats out—left a small pile of three in front of the mother and kitten.

Like! the kitten said, seething with excitement. The mother snapped her paw on the treats and broke them into smaller bits. The kitten snarfed them up, then jumped onto Garrett's boots and looked up at him with wide yellow eyes, purring with enthusiasm.

"What if I had to run?" he asked the kitten.

With you!

There was a small creak as TQ's door opened wider. Cats scattered. The little one tumbled off Garrett's shoes and tried to catch up with the ferals, his dam behind him. A few seconds later, all indications of life were gone from the courtyard, though Garrett sensed where they watched in the bushes of the back grassyard. He had no doubt they'd crawl out to sleep in the sun as the morning drew on.

TQ remained quiet. At least the House was giving him a little privacy, now.

The realization that soon he wouldn't have any privacy crashed down on him, wiping out the lift the cats had given him.

When he strode into the House, his footfalls thudded softly. Too much emptiness to cover the noise, so he moved more carefully even though there was no one to hear. Good practice.

He glanced in the mainspace and saw the camp chairs he didn't think would hold his weight, and the table. He searched his memory for the way to TQ's HouseHeart. Nothing. He'd given his permission for his recollection to be dulled, but he didn't have to like it.

Only four rooms would be minimally furnished, and when done, TQ would raise the heat and incinerate the furniture.

Garrett would have the master bedroom, the attached sitting room would be an observation room, the opposite connecting room would be full of medical supplies and a waterfall, and Artemisia would have the far bedroom.

She should have had a suite and help, but he'd said nothing.

Just live through the fliggering time again. All the times of the sickness, the slow, the hot, the hurt. The shudders. Worse than the three dreamquests that freed Flair, Passages. At least with Passages you got an acceptable payoff, an increase in magic.

The last payoff he'd gotten with the sickness was the girl he loved dead.

"Greetyou, GentleSir Primross," Artemisia said. He tensed at her soft voice. She'd crept up on him when he was brooding, and that wasn't good for a man who was supposed to be offering observation and investigation services. But he was so used to blocking her from his life.

He turned, not bothering to smile. She appeared as if she hadn't slept well, either. She held herself tight, her arms close to her body.

The duffle that floated on an anti-grav spell beside her looked a lot like his own. Somehow he'd expected larger and less practical.

Her clothes were a dull brown. Probably masked vomit, urine, shit, and blood. His stomach pitched. As the damn Healers had instructed, he'd eaten a good breakfast. Actually, he'd eaten the meal Lark Holly had had sent to his apartment.

Artemisia shifted her feet, cleared her throat gently. "Shall we go to the bedrooms?"

That surprised a crack of laughter from him and she flushed.

He swept a hand toward her. "Lead on." On the way, he breathed deeply and rolled his dread and discomfort up into a tight ball, shoving it into a crevice in his gut. The sooner this was begun, lived through, survived, and done, the sooner he could get on with his life.

TQ opened the door. "Greetyou, Artemisia. Greetyou, Garrett." He sounded subdued.

"Greetyou, TQ," they said in unison, entering the sitting room where the other Healers would observe him. The decontamination shields and forcefields weren't raised yet.

Artemisia went through the bedroom and into the dressing room. Drawers opened and closed as if she checked her equipment. Garrett stripped and put on loose sparring pants. They were stained, gray tinged, and raggedy, and he didn't care if they were destroyed. He had three more pairs in the same shape.

Every fliggering person who would come to look at him, and he reckoned the great T'Heather would do that at least once, were Healers and used to nudity. In general, Garrett, like the rest of his culture, wasn't bothered by nakedness. But now being nude equated with being vulnerable—at the mercy of the Healers and the sickness. He'd start out clothed and in control, at least.

He folded his clothes into his duffle, unsure if he'd see them again, left out the other soft pants, then set the bag beside the bed. "TQ, I like my duffle. If you can decontaminate it without destroying it, I'd appreciate it."

"So noted," TQ said.

Garrett sank into a luxurious permamoss bedsponge set on a cheap wooden platform. His hand rubbed the soft cotton sheet.

"I have scanned Artemisia's pillow. It is of odd composition," TQ whispered.

"In what way?"

"The feathers inside are down from Earthan geese."

Garrett's brows rose. "There aren't many Earthan geese. The SecondLevel Healer doesn't seem wealthy enough to buy down from the starship."

TQ hesitated. "That is not what surprises me. The shell of the pillow is rough cotton and it has spots of different properties."

"Like what?"

"Mucus, a little blood, and more salt."

"Snot, nosebleed, and . . ." He could imagine her, the cool and calm Artemisia Mugwort Panax, crying into her pillow. The idea twisted his heart.

"And?" TQ prompted.

"Tears," Garrett said uncomfortably.

"Oh, of course."

"Surely your other occupants—"

"They preferred permamoss or foam or gel pillows with daily cleansing spells."

"Oh."

"It is interesting that Artemisia likes feathers."

Garrett shrugged.

She came to the doorway between the bedroom and the dressing room, frowning. "It's WorkBell."

"Time for the experiment to start, then." He stood.

"The FirstLevel Healers aren't here."

"Then they're late," Garrett growled. "Let's get on with this."

Nine

*A*rtemisia *looked at him with large green eyes, nodded, and disap-*
peared back into the small room. As usual, he watched her fine ass.

She returned, hands at her sides and hidden behind folds of her
tunic. He still knew she held a vial with a propel-spell top. She
walked close to him, and he scented her on a quick inhale that
fogged his mind. Her own sweat—she wasn't as calm as she
seemed—and the inherent fragrance of her, woodsy like deep green
forest shadows. And an herbal smell that he'd never scented before
teased his nose like hidden secrets.

"Focus on the mural," she said.

He blinked. "What?"

She gestured to the opposite wall.

His gaze went to the mural that had flickered on with her words,
showing a view of the Great Labyrinth's bowl in full, green summer.
The image cycled through the seasons, then the labyrinth faded to a
jagged-toothed view of the Hard Rock mountain range. He flinched.

"I haven't even touched you yet," Artemisia said.

His yearning body had noticed. "I don't like mountains." He
tensed again at the revealing words.

"I don't imagine you do," she murmured.

The wall blanked, flickered on to a rush of waves against a rocky beach, matching his inner turbulence more than the serene scenes. Then showed a great blue river. "Too fast," he said.

"Hmm?" she asked, glancing at the observation room door. Ura Heather and Lark Holly had teleported there and raised decontamination spellshields.

But TQ had figured out what Garrett had meant and the mural halted on a scene of an ancient grove. Looking at it relaxed him. The trees were tall and old, some gnarled. Some he didn't recognize and deduced the grove had a mixture of Celtan and Earthan and hybrid trees.

Had to be a sacred place.

Maybe even the first Healing Grove established by the colonists on Celta. There were rumors it was a secret sanctuary for the desperate, a hidden garden. He didn't know where that was. Hadn't spent time—much—looking for it.

He hadn't seen anything like the place and wondered how TQ got the holos. Slowly the shadows deepened from late afternoon to evening dusk.

Artemisia set the vial against his neck, said a Word, and plunged the fatal sickness into his body.

Artemisia saw Garrett's amber eyes widen, but he didn't flinch or yelp.

"Is it done?" asked FirstLevel Healer Heather from the sitting room.

"Yes."

"Good job," Lark Holly said.

Artemisia braced her hand below his elbow. "Lie down now."

He sent her an irritated glance. "Doesn't work that fast."

"This was a concentrated amount of the sickness," she said.

"I got a dose of the original, the most virulent." But he sat on the bedsponge. Artemisia threw the vial into a decontamination container, then moved to stack and arrange his pillows.

"How long did it take for you to feel the effects the first time?"

Lark Holly asked. Her voice hissed from being behind the Flair and tech forcefields.

Garrett scooted back. Artemisia began to lift his legs onto the bed when he frowned at her. "A few septhours."

"You can't narrow the time period down?" asked Heather.

"I had other things on my mind. Leave the sheet at the bedsponge foot. It's the hottest month of the year, and I'm going to be hotter still."

"I will monitor your status as well as the heat and humidity in each room and adjust the temperature accordingly," TQ said.

Artemisia had figured Garrett would be a terrible patient. She went to the dressing room and got a fluids belt that fastened low around a patient's hips and was bespelled to draw out toxins, urine, and digested food from his body to pockets.

He grimaced and held out a demanding hand. "I know how to put it on and start the spell."

"You're sure you don't want to take off your trous?" asked Lark Holly.

The tiny unprofessional note in her voice—amusement?—had Artemisia looking at her mentor. Lark winked and Artemisia's spirits sank. The older Healer had noticed Artemisia's attraction to Primross. Right now he was hale and virile, hard to consider a patient. It was the height of unprofessionalism to want to see his body.

His chest was wide and beautifully muscled, with no scars and sparse dark blond hair. His skin color was the same as his face, tanned and darker than her own paleness.

"No, I do not want to take off my trous." He angled his chin toward a stack of raggedy garments. "I have more when these go bad."

He meant when his body soaked through them with sweat.

Artemisia's gaze met Lark Holly's. The threat of failure hovered over them. If Garrett Primross died, the Healers participating in the project would be infamous for decades.

"How many sheets did we order?" asked Ura Heather, as if supremely sure that nothing would go wrong.

"Three sets per day," Lark Holly said.

Heather grumbled, "So many, so expensive, and all to be destroyed." Artemisia was sure the woman didn't notice any personal cost but knew to the last silver the expenditures of Primary HealingHall.

Primross slipped the belt under his trous and grunted. Artemisia knew the belt and spell didn't hurt but felt odd. With cool and steady fingers, she checked the belt. "Fine."

Garrett pulled the tab of his waistband snug, then stacked his hands behind his head. His stare fixed on the wall mural showing the Great Labyrinth.

"TQ has several vizes of walking the labyrinth, one in all four seasons." Artemisia waved. "Summer, please."

The rocky outcroppings of the labyrinth seen in early spring transformed until the bowl was covered by greenery.

"Too short," Primross muttered.

"What?"

"The person who vized this path is too short," Garrett said. His gaze cut to her. "You?"

"Yes, last year," she admitted.

"I have a viz in the autumn provided to me by Tinne Holly," TQ said.

"Closer, but still not my height," Garrett said. His muscles flexed. "I like the sacred grove better."

Of course he'd noticed the image of BalmHeal grove that Artemisia had provided the artist. "Not a place I've seen," Garrett said.

TQ showed the trees and the glen, the ancient pillar and small slab atop it.

"I don't know that grove," Ura Heather grumbled.

Artemisia saw understanding in Lark Holly's eyes, but she said, "One of the FirstFamilies estates, perhaps."

"Hah." Heather's brows stayed down.

TQ said, "Every FirstFamily Residence provided me with data, including pics and holos of their estates, when I became sentient, including T'Yew."

"No one's been on T'Yew's estate in years," Heather said.

"The starship *Nuada's Sword* gave me historical Earthan information as well as holos from its Great Greensward, both as it appeared in the past and currently."

"Fascinating," said Garrett, lounging on the pillows.

Artemisia wasn't sure if he meant that or not. She sensed he'd soon become impatient since he was an active man.

"Would you like stories?" she asked.

"What kind of stories?"

She swallowed. "I could tell them, or play vizes or read to you."

He stared at her, his eyes darkening to deep gold. Ancient gold like an Earthan coin in one of her home's display cases. "What would you read?"

"I'm rereading the Tabacin Diary. She was one of the colonists who came to Celta on the starship *Lugh's Spear*."

He nodded. "I know that one." His smile flashed. This was the first time she'd seen it aimed at her and her insides gave a happy twinge. Tilting his head, he considered her, like he could tell his effect on her and it pleased a part of him. "No vizes now." His smile fell away and his shoulders moved restlessly. "They can become part of my fever dreams." One side of his mouth quirked ironically. "Don't need that. Why don't I do magic tricks?" He reached into his bag and drew out some coins—a few silver slivers and a gold piece of gilt, a couple of softleaves, and a deck of two-dimensional cards. He arranged his tools on the side of the bed.

Artemisia got a folded camp chair from the dressing room.

"Before you start," Lark Holly said, "we'd like some health readings and a blood sample."

He shrugged.

Ura Heather's footsteps clicked as she removed herself to the end of the hall.

Lark Holly pushed through the decontamination shields and

forcefields, crossed to the dressing room, and got a vial and a Flaired blood-suction tool.

Garrett narrowed his eyes. "How often will you do this?"

"Every two septhours. We sent you info yesterday," Lark said.

Primross frowned. "It was sketchy."

"We decided only SecondLevel Healer Panax will tend you physically." Lark touched a vein in his arm, murmured a sterilization Word, pressed the blood-suction tool against it, pulled the blood into the vial, and stoppered the tube.

Garrett didn't react. "So you being here is an exception."

"You're not exhibiting sickness." Lark gave him a cool smile. "I can chance it. Though, of course, I must take care of my own health."

The man hooted laughter. "I can tell you're a real coward, marrying into the Holly fighting Family and working as a FirstLevel Healer."

Lark nodded. "Yes, I'm as weak and cowardly as Artemisia."

Garrett's eyelids lowered. "You have great faith in the Second-Level Healer."

"If I didn't, she wouldn't be here." Now Lark's smile was brilliant. "You're a very important project for us, GentleSir Primross." She paused. "You may be the solution to this horrible sickness. And . . ."

"And?" he asked.

"My nephew, Laev T'Hawthorn, would be very irate with me if anything happened to you," she ended. "So it won't."

Garrett snorted. "Like you can promise that."

"I can promise that all of the knowledge and skill of the Healers of Celta will be focused on keeping you alive."

Artemisia sat in the camp chair and watched the exchange.

"So the retired T'Heather himself will come tend me if necessary," Garrett said.

"If necessary. You're a valuable asset," Lark said.

"I know. Why don't you go away and do observations on my damn blood."

"No one thinks you're damned," Artemisia said.

Lark and Garrett looked at her for taking the comment seriously, but cross-folk like Artemisia's mother believed in damnation.

He focused his intense attention on her. "Maybe not, but I tell you I'm pretty *damned* sure that I'll be descending to the Cave of the Dark Goddess and crawling back up the pitted and rock-strewn path."

Artemisia touched his hand. "You won't be alone."

"Sure I will. Everyone's alone in their mind."

"Except HeartMates," Lark said.

"Don't know about that," Garrett said. He moved his hand from under Artemisia's and sent the two silver slivers rolling over his knuckles, into his palm, appearing and disappearing.

Lark smiled and left through the forcefields into a portable decontamination and waterfall chamber that had been erected in the MasterSuite sitting room.

Heather wasn't taking any chances with any of the observers' health, including her own. Lark stripped and put her clothes into a deconstructor, moved to a stingy sanitizing shower.

When the waterfall stopped, TQ said in a flat tone, "Healer Holly has no microbes of the Iasc sickness. No cells of the Iasc sickness were found in the deconstructor. That liner has been sent to a Noble Death Grove with such notations."

"Thank you, TQ." Lark Holly dressed and stopped by the doorway. "Take care. Artemisia, scry immediately if you need help."

Artemisia swallowed hard. Suddenly the project was all too real. She was the sole Healer on call. "Of course."

Garrett continued to roll the coins across both hands, fingers fast and steady.

"Merry meet, Artemisia and Garrett," Lark said.

"And merry part," Artemisia responded.

Garrett snorted.

"And merry meet again," Lark ended.

"That would be good," Garrett said, not looking at her. "Give our regards to FirstLevel Healer Heather. Doubt I'll see her until I'm on the mend."

Lark dipped her head, met Artemisia's eyes one last time, then teleported away.

Now there was only the two of them . . . and as if keeping her at a distance, Garrett ran through his sleight of hand tricks with an easy patter.

After the second septhour, his hands and voice had slowed. He met her eyes with a steady gaze.

Already she knew that look; he'd say something she wouldn't like.

"How does it feel to be expendable?"

She sucked in a breath; the chemicals in the air weren't as sharp as the hurt. She smiled brightly. "I'm not expendable." She faced his mocking lips and straightened her shoulders. "I was given some of your blood two days ago to help me stave off any infection. I've been drinking NewBalm tisanes, plenty of liquids, and I've participated in two blessing rituals."

His eyes narrowed. "I wasn't aware I gave blood to anyone other than Opul."

She was angry enough to put mockery in her gaze. "We Healers have our ways."

Moving impatiently, his coins dropping and his snatch at them too slow, he said thickly, "I guess you do."

She regretted snapping at him.

His breath came on a ragged cough.

"Here." She handed him a water tube with floating green bits.

"What is it?"

"NewBalm mixture and spearmint." Her smile was quick and compassionate. "It will soothe your throat."

He frowned at his trembling hand, wrapped all his fingers around the cylinder, and drank it all. She took the tube away.

He closed his eyes. "Yeah. The throat. I'd forgotten that." One of his shoulders lifted and fell. "It was minor. Nobody was talkin'."

"You don't have to talk, now, either."

"Good," he said. His eyelids cracked, too narrow for her to see the color of his pupils. "I ain't gonna." His fingers scrabbled, found the coins, fisted around them. "Gotta fight."

"No, relax . . ." she soothed.

He jerked upright, eyes open. "No! I. Must. Fight. That's wha', *what*, saved me before. Fighting to save . . ."

"I understand."

"No. You don't," he croaked, then flicked the coins and the rest of his magic paraphernalia into his bag, coughed, and grimaced, subsiding back onto his pillows. His dark amber gaze met hers, then he set his arm over his eyes. "You don't understand. But you will."

She was afraid of that.

Ten

As the minutes passed, his great strength faded and his eyes dulled as sickness marched through his body. She laid her fingers over one of his fists, compelled to reassure him. "You're safe. I won't let anything harm you."

That he was hurting now caused a twisting ache inside her. She was too close to this case, this patient, this man.

He jerked. "No!"

She flinched back. He grabbed her hand, hung on hard. "I didn't stop fighting the first time. I won't now." He blinked, as if trying to keep heavy lids from shuttering his vision. "Have to fight."

"All right."

He breathed unsteadily, his eyes glinted at her. "Aren't you afraid?"

"Yes, I don't want the Iasc to . . . I don't want you to succumb."

He barked a laugh. "Aren't you afraid for *yourself*? Bad sickness. Lot of people died." His face set into a mask covering deep hurt. "Epi . . . epi—"

"Epidemic," she finished for him.

"Tha's right. Afraid?"

She *could* die. Hurt her Family with her passing. Not do all the things she wanted—forge a family of her own, have a child or two. Despite their religion, despite her mother's cross-folk faith, no one knew what came after death, and death itself could be hard. She'd seen that.

"You are afraid," he whispered roughly.

She couldn't deny it when her body quivered. "Yes." Even with all the precautions, all the knowledge and Healing skill, even with TQ's help, she could die. As could he.

His eyes were wide now, bright amber. Feverish.

"You look hot," she said.

"Hot. Sweating." He shuddered. His lashes closed and his hand fell from hers as if he needed to fight alone.

Her breath trapped inside her chest, knowing she was losing him to fever dreams.

"Have to fight. Have to drive this bus," he said, grabbing the linens, thrashing, entangling himself in them.

She yanked with hands and Flair to free him. Sweat slid from his body, suffusing the room with sickness and his determination. His hands opened and closed, curving around an imaginary steering stick. "Have to fight. Have to get Dinni and the baby to the clinic."

Who was Dinni? Probably a woman that Primross cared for. Artemisia should think of him as *Primross* or *patient* now, not Garrett. He'd been healthy when they'd met and worked together in TQ's HouseHeart, but now he was sick and dependent on her. Put away any tendrils of attraction. Strictly forbidden to fall for a patient, to encourage any patient who might be aware of her as a woman instead of a Healer. So dishonorable. Until he walked from TQ, she'd be strictly professional.

Her hands had been checking his temperature, the fluids belt, wiping away his sweat, while she scolded herself. Time to draw blood again, make notations to her own report.

"I have the time of 10.29.46 as when the Iasc sickness overtook GentleSir Primross," TQ said softly.

"That's right."

* * *

*P*rickles of heat bloomed on his body, from scalp to soles. He moaned. No! He didn't want to experience this again! Too late. Sweat slicked, turned steamy, and tormenting visions began.

He walked toward the looming one-story medical clinic in Gael City that stretched tall and fearsome, made of sickly yellow blocks. All his muscles tightened in horror. This was how it started. He'd gotten an emergency call from Dinni on his perscry that she needed him.

Of course he'd gone.

No. He would *not* go into that clinic. He would not see Dinni holding her sick baby son and others from the Smallage estate where he'd grown up.

He dug in his heels before the double white doors. He would not press the latch. He would not open the door. He would not go in and agree to help Old Grisc drive the quarantine bus to the mountain clinic.

He refused to budge.

The world revolved around him in a slow swoop. He coughed, retched, spewed. Low and monstrous roaring pierced with garbled words hit his ears and he curled. Hands punched his sensitized skin and he yelled.

He flopped, spun, saw the clinic with an open door gaping at him and set to run *backward*. Again reality looped, narrowed into a pinpoint tunnel of darkness that squeezed him through. Blessed dimness and quiet enveloped him. As he drew in a breath, the room lightened and he sat once more in FirstLevel Healer Ura Heather's office.

She frowned at him; her writestick tapped on the desk like a hammer. "We must hear of every moment of your journey," she said in that priggish demanding voice of hers. *Tap-pound-tap-pound-tap-POUND!*

"No," he muttered. But she'd gotten him in her clutches, *forced* him into the past.

He was in the clinic with the Healers and Dinni and Old Grisc and the refugees from Smallage. Again. Nausea inundated him.

Ura Heather stared at him, writestick lifted, lip curled. Lark Holly's violet eyes were wide with compassion as she shook her head mournfully.

And the gorgeous woman, who was the HeartMate he'd avoided, had an expression full of pity. They watched.

Watched. Judged. Saw *everything* that he'd never told.

He fought, as he'd fought every moment, but memories tore into his brain . . . to rip him to pieces again.

Dinni cradled her crying two-month-old son. She begged Garrett to take the job, to go with them. In her eyes was the utmost faith that he would save her child, all of them.

He'd looked at Old Grisc, the others, and agreed.

The HealingHall loaded every one of those twenty-three into the vehicle, even the sickest. The first died only a half septhour into the journey. An old man who'd been hot but shivering. The first death smell. Even in the cab with doors closed to the main compartment, Garrett and Old Grisc could smell it. They shared a bleak glance, wondering if they'd fall ill.

The quarantine bus was separated into three parts: the drivers' cab, seats in the main compartment for the living, and the refrigerated back compartment with corpse shelves for the dead.

Garrett had moved the man to the chill dead area, cleansed in the sanitation tube, figured it wouldn't help.

People deteriorated and a lot of them died. The stench rose around him.

He moved bodies to the back, but there wasn't enough room for them all. He had to raise the shelves against the wall, stack bodies.

Old Grisc, the driver, succumbed to fever eight septhours in. Garrett had to stop. The road was bad, the weather got bad—sleet and mud. People were dying, and he'd never driven such a vehicle.

The very worst memory rose like a ghost. Vivid and horrifying. Icy pellets had battered the windshield. It was full dark, and the console in front of him was lit, but the timer was nothing but a blur. Night was deep and dark, no bright twinmoons or stars, but they were finally off the mountain.

An eternity of time had passed. He thought he'd been in the hell-box forever. He stopped the bus and rested his throbbing head on the steering bar, felt the cool press of padded metal against his hot forehead.

A time later he'd lifted his aching bones from the driver's chair and moved into the main compartment. No reason to keep the doors shut.

Old Grisc trembled and sweated in a front seat. Another old woman had died. Garrett picked her up and shuffled down the broad aisle. There were few enough now—eight? ten?—that everyone slumped across a row.

He glanced at Dinni. She was pale with a gleam of sweat. He nodded, but she didn't look at him or the woman he carried. He opened the door and put the shell of the person atop her husband. They'd been bonded HeartMates, so there'd been no hope for her. HeartBonded died within a year of each other. That hadn't helped the grief of loss. He'd known the pair. The little town he'd grown up in, Dinni had grown up in, was attached to the Smallage estate.

The dead section of the bus was colder than outside and a relief to Garrett. Cold to preserve the lost for study.

After a while he got his feet moving and went into the main compartment.

Dinni was crooning a little sleep song to the baby that mothers sang. He moved to her and everything in him simply stopped.

The baby was dead.

Dinni didn't seem to understand or acknowledge that.

Garrett's knees gave out and he fell into the seat next to her. "Dinni," he said and his lips cracked and he tasted blood-salt.

She lifted big blue eyes to him, smiled sweetly. "You'll get us to the safe place, Garrett." Her voice was barely a rasping whisper.

"I love you," he said.

"I know you do," she said.

He closed his fingers over her upper arm. "Don't leave me. Stay with me. Stay alive. Please. Please, Dinni."

She nodded solemnly. "We will." Her lips cracked, too. "When will we get there?"

He levered himself away from the horror, back into duty that would force him to the driver's seat, to the clinic, to more of this hell. He wanted to stay with her, hold her. But he couldn't face the dead child.

"Stay with me," he demanded as he had before.

Unlike when she'd left him, this time Dinni said she would.

"Stay alive."

"We will."

Didn't matter if he thought she lied. Didn't matter that she'd never love him as he loved her, would never be his wife. He only wanted her alive. If he could get her to the clinic, they would help her.

His steps back to the cab dragged as if chained weights were attached to his ankles. His hands whitened around the steering bar. He could set the autonav now. They were close enough for that. Nothing else on this road and only a couple of septhours to the HealingHall. He would make it. So would Dinni.

He had to. He *had* to save Dinni, so he couldn't give up.

And he didn't. He jolted from a daze as they pulled into the clinic yard. Healers rushed out, spellshields surrounding them in lovely colors, seeming to pick up the light of the dawn. He moved back into the bus. Old Grisc was dead. So were most of the others.

Dinni wasn't and Garrett prayed and prayed. "We're here. Stay with me."

"We will," she croaked.

He'd helped her out, and the other three.

Healers took her away, but after a moment he heard screams.

Then time passed as he fell into nightmares. Felt cool hands and sipped liquids. They took care of him. For a while.

He fought to stay alive for Dinni, passed out, revived, succumbed. His head finally cleared enough for him to smell his own filth days later.

He was the only one alive in the entire clinic. That had been another horror he'd dealt with, cleaned up.

He yelled, "Dinni!"

And the bright light of the mountain clinic glared on and on, revealing only death.

It dimmed and he was in Heather's office again. That FirstLevel Healer continued to tap her writestick and judge. Lark Holly was no longer there.

Artemisia Mugwort Panax held out her hands and wept.

He didn't want her; he turned away.

Garrett had quieted except for the fever tremors. Artemisia didn't know whether that was good or bad. She sensed he fought.

For the first time in two septhours, she took a deep breath, wiping her sleeve across her forehead. She was sticky with perspiration. TQ had adjusted the atmosphere of the room for Garrett's comfort and she'd suffered through the changes.

"He seems to be resting more easily," TQ said.

"For now," Artemisia agreed, standing and shaking out her limbs.

TQ creaked.

"Yes?" she asked.

"I reviewed my records. Dinni Spurge Flixweed and her two-month-old son died at the mountain clinic. She had recommended and requested Garrett be a driver for the quarantine bus. Dinni had a prior personal relationship with Garrett."

Artemisia's heart gave a large, dull thud. "The child wasn't Primross's?"

"No, the child's father was one of those who found the fish and contracted the disease first. He died and left Dinni Flixweed a widow."

Artemisia put a hand to her chest. How horrible that must have been for the woman, for her husband to die fast of an unknown sickness, for her baby to contract the same illness. To leave her home for sanctuary—and be turned away. What a terrible situation. Artemisia's throat closed at the pity of it. She swallowed tears.

No one at the mountain quarantine clinic had survived except Garrett. So Dinni and her baby had died.

So sad. Tragic.

"Shouldn't you take a blood sample?" TQ reminded gently.

Artemisia shook off the bleakness of the past. "Yes."

Again she automatically did what needed to be done. But Dinni's story haunted her, and after she took Garrett's blood and stored it, she found herself in the dressing room, shivering with effort to suppress fear. She could die. Worse, the epidemic could arise, mutate, kill off every single being of Earthan origin—human, Fam, and animal—on Celta. They could be a dead race.

She let the brain-numbing fear whirl through her, coat her skin in cold sweat, drip tears from her eyes as she trembled and gasped, visualized all that could go wrong. Not a technique she used to weather terrible events, but this time it worked. When she was on the far side of panic, she felt stronger, able to recapture serenity.

Once again she checked on Gar—GentleSir Primross, and he appeared to be as well as possible. "Can you monitor our patient while I take a quick waterfall and change my clothes?"

"Of course, Artemisia."

"Thank you."

After she'd washed her panic-sweat away, was cleansed and smelling of fresh herbs, dressed in shabby, loose clothes that she could sleep in, she felt steady. She *wouldn't* let the sickness win. Nor would any of the Healers.

Garrett wouldn't, either. Even now he fought, muttering, back in that terrible time.

This time they would all win.

She was hopeful until he began shouting again.

"Dinni! Dinni!" He called so desperately it squeezed her heart and brought more tears. She bent and covered his fist with her palm. His fingers turned, grabbed, his eyelids opened. "Not Dinni!" His

voice broke. He flung her hand aside and thrashed until he rolled
and his back displayed a purple-bruised rash.

She gasped and hurried to smooth ointment onto his skin. When
she touched him, he moaned and writhed . . . and pled for Dinni.
Artemisia forced emotions away. She could not fulfill the man's cry
for the woman. He was a patient who needed her help and that was
all she could provide.

By the time the cream was gone, he'd sweated through his trous
and sheets again. This she could deal with. And now he couldn't
mind if he were nude, and it was better for them both.

"Clothes off!" she ordered and the spell-melding seams disinte-
grated. "Cleanse!" Garrett's body lifted and clothes and linens
whipped from under him and rolled, dry sides out. The scent of fresh
herbs flooded the room. "Fit!" New sheets skimmed over the bedsponge, tucked themselves in, again adding fragrance—clover in
bloom.

She quickly replaced his fluids belt. He groaned again as she reac-
tivated the spell, then checked it, sighing when all was working
properly.

The FirstLevel Healers appeared and she listened to TQ's report.
She walked to the observation door and gave her own, handing over
the blood samples and fluid belts. Ura Heather seemed satisfied,
Lark Holly concerned. Lark said they'd come by in the evening, then
Artemisia and TQ would be on their own throughout the night.

Late in the afternoon she heard a bumping at the window and
looked over to see cats sitting outside it, staring at Garrett.

Their mouths opened and they yowled in chorus.

"Stop that!" she snapped, then, "Soundproof the room, TQ!"

Silence descended with only the sound of Garrett's harsh
breathing—and his joints cracking as he struggled to get out of bed.
"Feeding time," he gasped. "Must feed ferals. Cats on the bus? Do
we have food? Grisc?" He looked to the window, blinked around
crusty lashes. "I *hear* you already. What are cats doing on the front
of the bus?"

Artemisia was amazed to see Garrett stagger toward the window. She grasped his unsteady body, using Flair to get him back in bed.

He tussled with her. "Must feed feral Fams!"

"I'll take care of it! TQ, the cats must be speaking to him telepathically. Tell them I'll be right out!"

"I am repeating that announcement through an outside speaker," TQ said.

Garrett blinked again. "Dinni? You don't know the cats." His head shook ponderously. "Not Dinni."

"No, but I'll take care of the cats." She didn't want to send him into his tormenting past. "Time for a little break, isn't it?"

He sat against pillows as if they were a driving seat, his fingers curled like they held a steering stick.

"Rest, get your strength up," she said.

"To make the trip." He glanced along the wall. "Dinni is still there. Old Grisc is sick."

"We can do this."

Garrett's shoulders set, his jaw firmed. "*Will* do this. Don' like the looks of that shelf road. Might crumble behind us. Gotta go fast as we can . . ."

Artemisia shuddered, then counted every second as she was decontaminated and drew on new clothes. Once TQ told her that she was Iasc-microbe free, she teleported out to the back grassyard.

Cats circled her, staring.

Eleven

$\mathcal{T}Q$'s *actor's voice lilted indulgently. "The SecondLevel Healer is* coming to feed you, please wait."

"I'm here," Artemisia said.

A short growl and inimical glare from a black-and-white tom.

"He says you have no food in your hands," TQ said.

"You can speak with them telepathically?" she asked.

"Not quite," TQ said. "But I have had cat Fams within and can read their body language."

Artemisia glanced around until she spotted a series of scrystones that TQ must be using to view them, and a speaker.

A spotted kitten gamboled up. "Pppht, phht, fhhoot!"

"Food?" She frowned, glanced at TQ. "Isn't he too little for dry food?"

"He will eat a bit, but will also be fed by his mother."

"Oh." She stared at the line of bowls on the deck under the House's overhang but saw no food. Turning, she caught the glimmer of more eyes in the bushes.

"The cats who live here are hungry and want to eat before the dogs and others come."

"All right, all right. Where's the food?"

"In the small south-side porch," TQ said.

And Artemisia realized she was irritated. Instead of being annoyed, she should bless the distraction for getting her outside, letting her feel colorful comfort.

She moved to the window to check on Garrett. He was "driving." Sweat slid down his face.

"I must get back," she said.

"His vital signs have not changed," TQ reassured her.

A door clicked unlocked. As she walked to the south, spellshields vanished and a pale turquoise forceglass door opened.

Artemisia sighed and went into the porch made of the same tinted glass. She smiled. The House-becoming-a-Residence was optimistic in all its ways, including cheerful tinting.

There was a bin with a slanted top. Inside was a huge bag of dry "Multi-Fam Tasty Fooood!" She didn't think so. "Is this—" she began but stopped when she saw cats lining up near the door. "I guess it is." Using Flair, she lifted the bag and filled ten bowls to the rim.

Gobbling noises filled the air.

"GentleSir Primross does this every day?" she asked, looking at the motley sizes and shapes of the FamCats, the scruffiness of the dogs who'd appeared.

"Twice a day," TQ affirmed.

"He's more generous than I thought."

A thin black cat lifted his muzzle, stared at her, made sounds she couldn't decipher.

TQ chuckled. "The cats say this is payment for information."

"Hmm." Artemisia put the bag back and looked longingly at the late-afternoon summer sunlight. "How's he doing?"

"I would inform you if he had problems," TQ said.

As she nodded and left the porch, a plump calico trotted up and swished across her legs.

"The cats also get petting," TQ said.

"Oh." Artemisia crossed to a bench that was half in and half out of shade. The sun felt good, but she'd get hot soon if she stayed in it, and she didn't want to spare any Flair to shield herself from rays.

She was enjoying petting the cat when the black-and-white tom strolled up, growled at the calico, swatted her rear, and took her place. Other cats sauntered up in a raggedly spaced line, waiting their turn, and grooming.

Stroking the cats, rubbing the dogs—who were at the last of the line—helped Artemisia relax even more. And as she saw the cats arrange themselves in the sun or shade as they pleased, she thought of the small cat in TQ's HouseHeart.

"Feral Fams?" She projected her voice.

They all looked at her.

"GentleSir Primross must like you very much." A couple sniffed, most revved their purrs. The dog she was petting swiped her hand with his tongue. "If you like him, you might want to send him any energy you can spare during his sickness."

At that two of the cats jumped upon the wide sill outside the MasterSuite bedroom window and stared in. Artemisia could *feel* their support—mental, emotional, physical, even Flair—being transmuted to Garrett.

Which reminded her it was time to step back into his nightmares. She stood slowly, absorbing all she could of the peace in the grassyard. Then with a sigh, she teleported into her dressing room.

And saw the spotted kitten on the bed with Garrett.

"What are you doing here?" she demanded.

I am his Fam, the kitten insisted.

"TQ?" she asked.

"He teleported through the window. I think a Fam will be good for Garrett."

The kitten looked at the four cats on the windowsill and lifted his small brown nose. *I will give him MORE love, MORE energy, than They. Because I want to be FAM with him.* A loud sniff. *They come and They go and They eat and get little pettings from him, but I will give more and get more!*

She certainly heard him clearly and didn't know if that meant he was more Flaired than the others or he was more interested in telepathically speaking with her.

"What about your mother?"

She does not want to be a Fam. I do.

"Aren't you too young—"

No. This is MY FamMan. With a rough purr, he curled up in the curve between Garrett's shoulder and head and flicked a tongue out at Garrett's jaw, then sent her an accusing gaze.

He needs washing.

She supposed he did—and his fluids belt changed and his blood taken again. But the man appeared to have subsided into sleep, though his fingers fisted and released and he mumbled.

Narrowing her eyes, she thought she saw the aura of the small cat impinging on Garrett's, helping him.

All to the good.

"Animals don't get the Iasc sickness?" She knew that, but her voice raised in a question to TQ anyway.

"No, Artemisia," the House said.

After one last sigh, she got to work.

The next couple of septhours, she spent hands-on time with Garrett, wiping him down, rubbing ointments into his body, replenishing his fluids. The kitten watched her, and the Fams outside the window rotated.

Ura Heather and Lark Holly arrived after Artemisia had drunk her liquid meal and energizer, and they all discussed Garrett. Heather referred to him as *the case* or *the experiment.*

Opul Cranberry was continuing to do well.

Before the FirstLevel Healers left, Lark Holly said, "Get a few septhours' rest, Artemisia. The Turquoise House will monitor GentleSir Primross."

"Very well," Artemisia said.

"We will return at TransitionBell," Lark said.

"What!" Ura Heather exclaimed.

"Many of those with the Iasc sickness died during TransitionBell."

"As many folk do," Artemisia murmured.

"Exactly, that's why it's called TransitionBell," Lark said. "I will be here, at least."

"I will, too," Ura Heather gritted out, but Artemisia could tell that the woman's niece had forced her hand.

Without another word, they both teleported away.

"TQ, please wake me every two septhours to take GentleSir Primross's blood."

"You should call him Garrett," TQ said.

"Not when he's my patient, and he didn't give me leave to do so," she said primly.

"He thinks you are beautiful," the House said.

Artemisia snorted. "I doubt that." Once again she dabbed his face clean of sweat, then arranged his pillows.

The kitten hummed approval, then curled by Garrett's shoulder. After a deep sniff, the little cat raised his muzzle and smiled. *Smells nice. I like being in a warm, clean room, next to a nice-smelling man. My room, My FamMan.*

"I'm sure he'll appreciate you," she said. Whether the man knew it or not, he was making a family. If he appreciated the ferals for what they were—unique and uncivilized—it was another reason why he didn't care too much for overcivilized Noble humans and their rules.

Or was she making sense at all?

The long day of summer wasn't done, but she was exhausted. Two septhours of sleep sounded like the most wonderful thing in the world.

She trudged toward her own bedroom, using real effort to push through the decontamination shield. After showering, she slipped into bed. Long, soft summer shadows patterned the back grassyard with varying shades of green. At any other time, she'd have gone to the window or even to the garden. Not now. She could only hope for instant and deep sleep and no nightmares. Watching Garrett fight his own demons, relive the first time of his sickness, was nightmare itself.

And more would come.

Her eyes remained open; she continued to strain for sounds of Garrett. The sickness was progressing as if he'd received germs through second- or third-hand contagion, not a pure, virulent injection.

TQ said, "You need sleep. I will observe."

She was used to a sentient Residence, but one who knew how to use its atmosphere to Heal and when to alert humans. So she hesitated.

"Do you not trust me, Artemisia?" TQ asked softly.

"I'm just not accustomed to you." She bit her lip. She *did* need her sleep. "Contact me if his temperature rises, if he has convulsions or fever dreams."

"Yes, Artemisia."

"Fine." She shut her eyes. The insides of them hurt with dry strain. Rolling over, she buried her face in the familiar comfort of her pillow and let sleep take her away.

He was the main driver now—good thing he was a quick learner and had mastered the controls. Old Grisc had hack-coughed his way to the first row of the main compartment. Garrett hadn't bothered to shut the door of the cab. No reason. He'd started sweating and shivering like all the rest of them.

Night had fallen and sleet started. This was going to be bad.

For a while, he'd felt as if he'd already survived this; reality had been misty around the edges. He'd even caught a whiff of clean scent that lured him into thinking of hidden sacred spaces. And he'd thought he'd seen a well-kept road before him, leading to a special, wondrous grove.

But now rain and ice spattered and his breath shuddered from him, fogging the windshield. He'd have to go out and check the road and the vehicle.

Now there was only the trip and he was grimly determined to get this bus to help. Dinni was still alive, and so was the babe. They *would* live. So would he. If he fought hard.

So he did.

* * *

*A*rtemisia *woke before TransitionBell, made Garrett comfortable, did* all her tasks, and tidied before the FirstLevel Healers arrived.

Then she gave her report and handed over all the fluid belts and blood vials. The work was tedious, but she kept her goal in the forefront of her mind. She was participating in a project that might find a cure for the Iasc sickness. And she was ensuring her place on the staff of Primary HealingHall.

As minutes ticked to TransitionBell, they watched Garrett, and though his condition deteriorated, when the dawn came, he still lived.

The crises happened in the middle of the next day.

*T*he *trip would never end. He knew that now. He would be trapped,* forever driving the sick and dying.

His eyes hurt. Hell, all of him hurt. He gripped the steering stick hard, peering through the thick fog before him.

Had there been fog before?

There was now, and ever would be. He was stuck.

And Dinni stood before him, sad faced as she so rarely was, tears dribbling down her cheeks and dripping into the mist with the scent of sickness, death, despair. She cradled and rocked her child—her dead baby son. She was too pale. One last inclination of her head and she turned from him.

He knew she'd walk away, as she'd always walked away from him, and disappear into the mist. He didn't think he could bear it.

"Dinni! Stay with me!" he yelled with all his might. He reached for her.

But she didn't listen and vanished.

He gave up and let the sickness take him.

*A*rtemisia *had been napping—septhours had begun to seem like weeks* and she'd lost track of time—and awoke to thready mews and cold.

Too cold, especially for Garrett, who had been nearly steaming with fever.

She hopped from bed and flinched through the two decontamination shields to find a bare Garrett huddled in fetal position, face gray and sheened, shivering. His Fam was perched on his hip, also curled tightly.

"TQ, raise the heat, fifteen degrees *now*!" She yanked linens over him, found a blanket and a comforter, and piled them on him, but didn't think it would be enough. "What were you thinking to cool the room?"

"I was so ordered," grumbled TQ.

"And *your* orders are not necessary," said Ura Heather from the sitting room door. "The room was too warm for the patient."

"The temperature was fine! Now it's far too cold!" Artemisia repeated, warming a scarf and putting it on Garrett's head. Still not enough.

Her gaze focused on the machine next to the FirstLevel Healer, an experimental med-tech. It was a thin, meter-high domed metal construct with two spindly arms ending in tri-pincers, and an extruded antenna. A light blinked green. "Warning! This unit's previous recommendation to reduce the temperature in the patient's room is not being implemented! Cooling *must* take place. Waiting for confirmation from FirstLevel Healer to drop forcefields so unit can enter the Healing area. Warning, the room must be cooled," it said in a tinny voice.

"No!" Artemisia countermanded. "TQ, keep raising the temperature. Primross is too chilled."

Nothing for it, she'd resort to basic body heat and body-to-body warming spells. She stripped and flung her clothes on the floor. Crawled between the linens. They were cold.

Quickly, quickly *lift*! Garrett and the kitten floated. And *warm*! She warmed the bedsponge beneath. Nice, toasty.

She lowered the two and spooned around Garrett. His skin was clammy, but he felt like he belonged with her.

"TQ, follow the recommendations of the med-tech," Heather said. "It's not that cold in here."

"The temperature in the sitting room is twenty-two degrees Celsius," TQ said.

"You see!" Heather said. "Stop the heat!"

"Warning, the temperature in the adjoining room is too high for good health. Warning. Warning," the machine said.

"The temperature in the master bedroom is thirteen degrees Celsius," TQ said.

"What!" Ura Heather slapped her hand on the top of the small machine.

"Perhaps the med-tech's readings are wrong due to the force-fields," Artemisia mumbled. She shivered against Garrett, spending Flair profligately to heat him.

His breathing stuttered. Wrapping her arms around him, she squeezed. *I need you to fight!* she snapped, aloud and telepathically. *FIGHT!*

Twelve

Garrett heard the command. It wasn't Dinni, but he sensed the need came from someone with a claim on him. More sounds—a small animal whimpering, shivering. Another need he must fill.

But he was so cold.

Let the sleet take him. Follow Dinni down that foggy path.

FIGHT!

He was tired of fighting.

Something bit his ear. Ouch! Warm blood trickled down it, and then the cold faded and the rain and sleet and ice and fog stopped and bright primary colors swarmed behind his eyelids.

Warmth. He shuddered. His muscles were all bunched together and warm was becoming hot. Groaning, he straightened his legs. Sighed as they felt better, as a small furred shape snuggled near his chest, just right. Sighed again as the heat behind him lessened as a mass moved away.

Covers settled around him. He was on a bedsponge. He'd made it to the clinic. He'd need to wake soon to check on Dinni, but for now he'd take a little sleep. He could do that, set an alarm in his brain to wake him in a few septhours. Dinni was in good hands.

Doom hovered, and he knew when he woke he would face rending teeth, but darkness tugged at him, offering sweet relief, and he let it suck him into sleep.

*A*rtemisia *crawled from Garrett's bed, bent to pick up her clothes. She* let her hair fall over her face until she could control her seething anger so it wouldn't show in her expression. Her fingers trembled as she dressed. She knew why FirstLevel Healer Heather had brought the med-tech. To care for Garrett instead of Artemisia.

There had been talk of Flair-tech mechanical servers to replace Healer assistants and low-level Healers. No doubt the FirstLevel Healer thought she might combine two experiments in one, make more efficient use of funds.

A soulless consideration that might have had terrible consequences.

Self-preservation and confrontation avoidance warred with fury that the Healer would take such a risk at this time.

"I—" she began, but her throat was so clogged with ire that she barely heard herself. She pulled in a large breath and marshaled her wits.

"I've silenced the med-tech. Report on the patient, Turquoise House," Heather said.

"He is breathing well again," TQ said.

"What! He'd stopped?" the older Healer demanded.

"Yes." Artemisia's face was hot and tight, but expressionless, she hoped. Keeping her voice equally impassive, she continued, "Perhaps this isn't the right project with which to test a med-tech."

"I agree," TQ said austerely. "After I followed your insistent instructions to cool the room, GentleSir Primross stopped breathing. Since I have mitigated the chill in the room, GentleSir Primross's heartbeat is no longer slow and erratic, and his body temperature is acceptable."

Artemisia sucked in another cleansing breath. Her anger had made her alert. But what was done was done, and she was sure that the FirstLevel Healer wouldn't press the matter further. Nothing to be gained by pointing out her error.

"That's good to hear, TQ." Artemisia kept her tone mild. She looked at the med-tech machine. Its arms and antenna were down, its light off. Poor, stupid piece of junk.

"TQ, do you think that the decontamination and forcefields skewed the med-tech's readings?" she asked.

"I think the med-tech machine is not as close to completion as many believe. It is obviously a thing without true intellect. I was not informed that it might be used during this project and do not approve. Nor will I accept any further instructions based upon its recommendations. Not enough study has been done for the thing to be used in real-life trials," TQ said. "Especially one as delicate as this."

Ura Heather's roundish face flushed and she banged a fist on the machine. "Defective thing." She narrowed her eyes as if in warning when she met Artemisia's gaze. "I will leave you to your regular duties and teleport back to Primary HealingHall. I don't think this small incident needs to be reported to anyone else, does it, Second-Level Healer?"

Garrett kicked aside the covers, stretched, and rolled over. His color was healthy; Artemisia sensed he was in an almost natural sleep. The fever would return, but for now they had a respite. "No, FirstLevel Healer."

"I also expect you to be discreet, Turquoise House." Heather and the machine disappeared before TQ could respond.

"I'm sorry, Artemisia," TQ whispered. "I was interested in the med-tech machine. I should not have listened to it or obeyed the FirstLevel Healer's instructions."

Artemisia let her weak knees fold her onto the bedsponge. "No lasting harm done, TQ?"

"I will do a full scan."

Artemisia nodded and rearranged the covers again, then glanced at the timer and saw it was NoonBell. Three cats slept on the windowsill of the bedroom, and beyond in the grassyard lounged the rest of Garrett's ragtag band.

"No, Artemisia, no lasting harm was done to Garrett."

"That's good."

"From my studies of the Iasc sickness, it seems this might have been the main crisis for Garrett and the sickness will progress more smoothly?"

"Perhaps, but there could very well be more than one crisis."

"I will watch him very closely."

"I'm sure you will. So will we all." She stretched. "What you need to recall, TQ, is . . ."

"Yes?"

"You don't mind me giving you advice?"

"Please do, Artemisia."

"Many Nobles aren't accustomed to personal failure, so sometimes they ignore risks," she ended softly. She was all too aware that bad things could happen, that personal failure could be inflicted from outside forces.

"I will remember that, Artemisia."

"Our main goal is to keep Garrett Primross safe, our secondary goal is to observe him and study his blood to help find a cure for the Iasc sickness. Anything else is of minor importance."

"I will not allow anything to threaten him again," TQ said.

"Good."

"And I will not allow anything to threaten you, either."

Artemisia managed to curve her lips, but shrugged. That wasn't in TQ's power. She did know that she'd have to step carefully with regard to Ura Heather.

*A*gain the fragrance of hidden forests teased his nostrils. He was aware of floating free. Shouldn't he be doing something? Driving?

No, he'd made it to the clinic. Dinni was in good Healers' hands. This was a dream and he could go where he pleased.

With that thought he found himself liberated from the endless trip and struggle. No longer spring, it was full, hot summer and he was walking toward rusty iron gates that framed a secret garden. A cool turquoise pool beckoned, since he was beginning to get hot again.

Maybe if he reached it, the fever would not come.

Lovely thought.

He shifted his shoulders. He wore a fighting harness more appropriate for an arena sword bout—yeah, his longsword was angled across his back, and a blazer at his hip—than for traveling or guarding a merchant. Or being a private investigator, which he was now.

But hadn't someone demanded he fight?

Yeah, he remembered that.

And he remembered he'd have to.

But not until he got a peek at the garden.

The wonderful fragrance wrapped around him again and spun him away.

*N*ear *MidAfternoonBell during the third day, Garrett went com-*pletely still. It took a minute for Artemisia, nearly dozing in her chair, to realize his breathing had quieted, he no longer thrashed. She leapt up, papyrus medical records falling out of her lap, and lunged toward Garrett.

For an instant her breath stopped as she thought he'd died. A crushing sense of loss pervaded her. Worse than when she was a teenager and her Family had lost everything.

His face dribbled sweat, but when she put her hand on his cheek, it was cool. Breath fast, she moved her hand to his heart. The strong and steady thump reassured her.

Then his eyes opened and a piercing gaze pinned her. His hand covered hers. She said the first thing that came to mind. "I'm not Dinni."

"I know that." His voice was low and raspy. "The lovely Artemisia Panax, SecondLevel Healer."

"You are awake and aware!" TQ said joyfully. "You have survived the sickness once again."

Garrett grunted. "Guess so." He tried to lever himself up and Artemisia put her arm behind his back and helped. He was a big and muscular man and she used Flair.

"I have informed the FirstLevel Healers," TQ said. "GrandLord T'Heather and Ura Heather and Lark Holly are arriving."

"Great," Garrett muttered.

"And I will initiate the celebratory actions."

"Huh?" Once again Garrett looked Artemisia in the eyes. She shrugged.

His hands went to the fluid belt.

"Let me do that." Artemisia moved his fingers away.

"I don't want you—"

But she'd dispelled the suction and whisked it off him and into the container to be studied before he finished his sentence.

He drew in a long and uneven breath, seemed wobbly sitting up, but she wasn't going to say a thing.

"Want a waterfall," he grumbled. "Feel filthy."

"You had a full sponge bath a septhour ago," Artemisia said.

This time his gaze was hot and deadly. "Did you do it?"

"Of course."

His jaw flexed.

"You must be examined by the FirstLevel Healers," TQ admonished.

Garrett mumbled a curse.

The alarm from the decontamination field sounded loud and raucously and three people stepped into the bedroom. Artemisia withdrew to her chair as Lark Holly rounded the bed to take her place, and the Heathers stopped on the other side.

"Incredible." GrandLord T'Heather's shaggy eyebrows rose. "You're awake and sitting up. Look a little rough, though. I suppose it felt as if you crawled down to the Cave of the Dark Goddess and back."

"Exactly," Garrett said, and his shoulders relaxed. Artemisia wasn't sure whether it was having the greatest Healer on Celta in the room or having another man with him that changed his attitude.

"Don't need all these people in my bedroom right now," Garrett said. He stared at her, then switched to Lark Holly.

T'Heather rumbled a laugh, snagged a large water bottle, gave it to Garrett. "Must be dry; drink up, son."

"Thanks. My fluid belt is in the damn canister."

"Of course," said Ura Heather.

"TQ, can you report?" Lark Holly asked.

"Garrett Primross's levels of the microbes of the Iasc sickness are decreasing. If his recovery follows the same steep arc of his succumbing to the illness, he will be free of Iasc by NightBell and could leave here by NoonBell tomorrow."

Garrett made a satisfied noise.

TQ continued, "This room has a medium level of the Iasc sickness microbes. I will sterilize it after everyone leaves tomorrow. The sitting room has a very low level of Iasc, and the dressing room and Artemisia's bedroom has a low infestation of the microbes."

Everyone stared at Artemisia. She stood straight. "I followed all the procedures and am perfectly fine."

"That is correct," TQ said. "The levels of the sickness in the dressing room and adjacent bedroom are below our original projections. SecondLevel Healer Panax herself has no microbes of the virus within her."

"Success!" Ura Heather said.

"Yes, but the whole reason for this experiment was to study GentleSir Primross's blood and determine how he survived the most virulent sickness and whether we could develop a precautionary serum or cure," Lark said. "And Artemisia should be examined, too." Lark went toward the door of the sitting room and gestured to Artemisia. "Come along, I'll check you in here."

Garrett grinned at her with a certain amount of glee. Then he yelped and his expression turned to surprised horror as he stared at a small lump under the cover by his foot. "What is it? Get it off me!"

T'Heather yanked up the cover and roared with laughter at the beige kitten with brown spots sitting on Garrett's foot.

I am his Fam, the little cat said.

Glaring, Garrett said, "I don't recall agreeing to that."

The kitten ignored him. *I was very helpful, wasn't I?*

"Very," Artemisia murmured, returning Garrett's smile with an overly sweet one of her own as she entered the sitting room.

Stubby tail straight up, the kitten walked up Garrett's shin and to his thigh before T'Heather's hand engulfed him. "Why don't you sit on the table here."

"You can supervise," Lark Holly said, sounding as if she said those words often.

"Continuing my report," TQ said, "I have scanned all my space and have no cell of the illness beyond these rooms."

"Good job!" T'Heather said. "Now let's check you out, young man."

Lark gripped Artemisia's upper arm. "And I'll do your examination. You look weary."

"It wasn't an easy project," Artemisia said, and wondered when she could go home. And wondered why the idea of going home didn't bring a rush of joy.

"Strong, active men are rarely good patients," Lark murmured.

"Here, Ura," T'Heather said to his daughter. "You want all the blood and fluid samples and the reports. Take 'em home to one of T'Heather Residence's sterile rooms."

"I have sent you and T'Heather Residence all my raw data," TQ said.

"Thank you, Father." FirstLevel Healer Ura Heather gave a little cough. "Thank you, Turquoise House."

"You are welcome," TQ responded.

Ura Heather nodded, organized the various containers, and teleported away with the samples.

Artemisia admitted to herself that she was glad to see the head of Primary HealingHall go.

Lark's examination was quick and professional, the results what Artemisia expected. She was a little dehydrated and exhausted. She *didn't* show any signs of the sickness.

Lark shook her head. "I wish you had had relief, another Healer. The Turquoise House is wonderful at monitoring, and can manipulate the atmosphere in amazing ways, but it doesn't have hands, or physicality."

"I was fine." She wasn't about to mention the med-tech. Yesterday seemed like years gone, anyway.

"You certainly were. And you didn't get the disease. What I saw of the studies is promising. I really want to develop a prophylactic for the sickness from Primross's blood."

"Everyone wants that," Artemisia commented. "Him, too, or he wouldn't have suffered through this."

Lark stared at her sharply.

Artemisia raised her hands, palms up. "I have great admiration for him. I comported myself professionally," she said before she remembered the time during TransitionBell when she sat by his bed and stroked his forehead, bathed his face, held his hand.

"Hmm." Lark went to the no-time food storage and took out a large bowl of furrabeast stew, set it on an old table. "Eat."

"I smell good food. Furrabeast. I want some of that," Garrett called from the other room.

T'Heather said, "You get clucker soup."

Garrett groaned.

"Here, this is for you, a token of appreciation from me," Lark said. "It is free of any Iasc germs and has a decontamination spell woven in every fiber."

With wide eyes, Artemisia accepted the robe of silver-shot gray silkeen Lark had translocated into the room. "Thank you."

She hadn't had such a garment since her teens before her Family had been disgraced. She wrapped it around her, letting the soft fabric slide against her skin in comfort. She had risen to the task she'd been assigned and done well, had survived. Had accompanied a man down the path to the Cave of the Dark Goddess and helped him fight the disease and return.

Relief began to trickle through her and she welcomed it. As she picked up the spoon and sat to eat, her tiredness changed from struggling to give her best to a patient to the satisfied triumph of seeing a sickness beaten.

Furrabeast stew wasn't her favorite, but the smell tantalized and the big chunks of vegetables in it made her mouth water. Her fingers wanted to dip the spoon into the bowl faster and faster, taste the rich broth, so she controlled them. As she ate, she let the familiar sounds of Healers around her, the robe, and the simple meal reassure her down to her quietly pumping heart that she was safe, that she'd done well, and all would be well in the future. Her current trial was done.

And Lark Holly was pampering her. Lovely. Artemisia wanted to hope her job was secure, but couldn't forget the chill in Healer Ura Heather's eyes.

T'Heather's gaze was on Garrett as he ate his clucker soup. Garrett was full but hadn't given up because he'd eaten only a tiny amount. Odd how having nutrients transferred into his blood directly made a man's stomach shrink. He wouldn't be eating a large and thick steak for a while and that was perturbing. He liked his meat.

The kitten had eaten as much as he. Right next to him on his bed. Didn't look like he'd be getting rid of the thing anytime soon.

It was good spending time with a guy, listening to the older Healer. Garrett had figured he'd like T'Heather if he got to know the man.

"So," T'Heather said casually, "tell me why you wanted Second-Level Healer Artemisia Mugwort out of the room."

Garrett choked. On broth.

Thirteen

Garrett coughed until the Healer put a large hand on his chest and tweaked his insides and Garrett breathed easily again. "Nice trick," he gasped out.

The man shrugged heavy shoulders. "Simple." T'Heather's shrewd gaze seemed to look inside Garrett's head. He wasn't used to talking with older FirstFamily Lords with such great Flair. Then T'Heather raised a hand. "I know why you avoid Healer Mugwort. You are very attracted to her and don't want to be."

She is kind, said the kitten.

Grunting, Garrett picked up a small hunk of bread, sopped up the last of the clucker soup, and stuffed it in his mouth. When he was done chewing, he said, "Thanks for coming by."

The GrandLord's face was serious as he responded. "You're clear, son. You have done all of Celta a great service."

I know, said the kitten.

Garrett felt himself flush—with embarrassment this time, not fever, thank the Lord and Lady. "Anyone would have done the same."

"Maybe, maybe not. The FirstFamilies won't be forgetting this, I assure you."

"Good to know."

Lark Holly strolled in from the sitting room. "Nor will history. I am sure that with all the information this project provided us with, as well as your blood samples, we will be able to control the Iasc sickness." She curtseyed deeply to Garrett. "Thank you."

"Welcome," he said.

WELCOME, said his Fam.

She turned to T'Heather. "With your permission, I would like to return home."

"Go," the lord said.

A nod to Garrett, then she walked back through the decontamination spellshield and forcefield, and when TQ declared she was clean of any Iasc cells, she teleported away.

Before Artemisia could return, Garrett flung off the thin sheet and held out a hand to T'Heather. "Help me into that damn waterfall, will you?"

The Healer eyed him professionally. "Looks like you dropped some weight, still a good figure of a man, shouldn't worry about scaring the ladies." The lord yanked him up smoothly and set his thick arm under Garrett's. "Except for your face, of course. Grim, son, grim."

Garrett snorted.

T'Heather grinned. "I'll wait in the dressing room while you cleanse."

Me, too, said the little cat, trotting after them. The lord deftly kept them from tripping on the Fam.

Garrett scowled. "I don't need anyone."

T'Heather laughed. "Oh, son, you are so wrong."

"I don't need you, either." Garrett glared at the kitten.

The tiny spotted cat lifted his nose. I am Rusby. I named Myself with a Primrose name. My friend TQ listed Me names and I liked Rusby best.

"I'm a distant offshoot of the Primrose Family. I go by Primross," Garrett said.

The cat sniffed.

He stared into little yellow eyes. "I don't need a Fam."

The small white and spotted muzzle lifted. *I want a FamMan and you will do.*

T'Heather coughed. "I've found that young cats can be stubborn."

Yes, Rusby said.

Garrett had found that all cats could be stubborn and they all wanted their own way. Sometimes you could negotiate, sometimes bargain, sometimes cajole, often blackmail. Didn't make living with them any easier.

"Get in the waterfall and wash some sense into your hard head," T'Heather said.

*S*moothing her new robe, Artemisia stepped into the bedroom. Already it looked less of a sickroom. She moved quickly through the dressing room—overfull with Garrett in the waterfall, T'Heather examining her medical setup, and the cat on one of the cabinets.

TQ had new linens for her bedsponge and she dumped the old ones in one of his canisters.

While Garrett luxuriated under a strong and pulsing waterfall, she remade both beds. Soon everything in the rooms would be ash—a pity about the furniture, but Artemisia was glad she'd had the expensive bed. It had been so much better than a cot.

She and Garrett were exhausted, but TQ would watch them this last day and night, then they would leave at noon. Since the man was back to politely avoiding her, she didn't think she would see him again. Stupid to miss someone she'd known only a couple of days, and not much of that when he'd been healthy.

She hoped his nightmare memories had finally burned out. That his reliving the loss of his lover was a final ending to his grief. Oddly enough, Artemisia thought she'd sensed some of those dreams, they had been so intense . . . and she had been the only other person in the House, and caring for him.

Or would the experience have stirred the loss up for him again?

She didn't know. There had been grief in her life, but death had never claimed someone she'd loved. She'd been lucky in that. Her whole Family had. A blessing she hadn't realized.

Looking inside herself, she believed she'd changed, too, grown a little tougher. In the depths of the night, when she was weary and fearful, she'd had only herself to rely on. TQ was there, if she'd wanted to talk, but he had respected her aloneness. Not loneliness, exactly, but aloneness.

She'd been alone for the first time in her life. Her previous lovers had lived in a building with others, or in their Family homes. Being alone had been an odd feeling, but satisfying. She had come through the pressures of the experiment. And if those pressures hadn't been too difficult, they were still more than she'd ever faced. She would have to thank her Family for the blessing ritual again.

She heard the waterfall turn off and male voices. Before she could hurry to help, GrandLord T'Heather filled the doorway, thick finger pointing at her. "You," he said.

She squeezed her abused pillow tight. "Yes?"

"Good job, Mugwort. Leave the boy alone for now and go to sleep. That's an order."

She blinked, shrugged, glanced at her tempting bedsponge. "It's the middle of the day."

T'Heather chuckled. "I've been on round-the-clock jobs; surprised you know the time. You need sleep, girl; take some. You'll be busy enough once you get back to Primary HealingHall."

A little bump of the heart, of hope. "Yes, GrandLord."

He nodded, stepped back, and closed her door.

*G*arrett surfaced to clogged-hearing silence. Yawning, his ears popped and night bird tweets trilled.

Yes, too quiet. The quiet of no one in his room. His HeartMate was gone. He was alone in the dark. He uncurled from a fetal curl, groaned, and struggled to an elbow.

"You are awake again," said the smooth voice of the Turquoise House.

"Yeah. Light?" He coughed.

"Say when," TQ said as a glow began around the ceiling, banishing the night to dimness.

"When!" Garrett blinked stinging eyes. A little more than when. The lights faded.

"Don't—"

"You were blinking. For many sicknesses it is appropriate to press recovery, but not the Iasc, and not when you've fought the sickness every second of three days."

Garrett tried to sit up, couldn't, couldn't even get his elbow propped back under himself, and flopped back into the softness of the bedsponge. He'd thought he'd be stronger the second time he came around.

But the bedsponge was dry.

He sniffed. He didn't smell too bad. And he didn't recall any dreams. The fever must really be gone, and he hadn't sweated. Probably still had a grim face.

Though his nose might be as plugged as his ears had been.

"Three days . . . that makes this?" His mind was too sluggish; he should be sharper.

"Twinmoonsday."

"Uh." He looked at the very white ceiling. Yeah, that hurt his eyes, but he thought he'd pried against crust to open his lashes and he didn't want to close them again. He lifted his hand to rub his eyes and hit himself in the nose. "Dammit."

"Your muscles are weak," TQ said.

"Yeah, like I didn't notice."

"That is sarcasm."

"That is right."

"It is good that you are no longer in so much pain—"

"Who says I'm not?" Shifting on the sheet made every strand of muscle in his body ache in different ways. Some were too tight, some too lax, some cramped with outrageous strain.

"—and it is good that you are coherent."

Garrett grimaced and felt dried drool around his mouth flake off. Maybe snot, too. A little reminder of the sickness.

"Where's Artemisia? Isn't she supposed to be caring for me?"

"She is feeding the feral animals. They have gathered from all over Druida the last few days to . . . sit vigil for you."

"Huh." His pleasure at the attention of the Fams mixed with irritation that Artemisia was giving them food and winning some loyalty. That reminded him. "What of my self-appointed Fam?"

"The kitten is keeping Artemisia company. He likes her very much."

Garrett hissed out a breath as he straightened his cramped leg. "Yeah, well, of course. She's the only other human around."

"But your Fam loves you."

"Uh-huh." Damn that hurt, enough for his eyes to start stinging again. "Can you call her in?"

"You need help! *Artemisia, Garrett is awake.*"

Too late to spare his ears from the stentorian announcement out of speakers that the whole block must have heard.

And suddenly she was there, teleported into his room, her thinner face lined with concern. She'd lost weight, too, but she didn't look grim. Nope, she looked gorgeous.

"You're awake," she said.

"Yes, and hungry."

"Of course." She went into the sitting room and got two bowls of clucker and noodle soup.

While she was gone, he'd struggled into a nightshirt and had wiped his face with a wet cloth that had been next to a basin on the bedside table.

She put a tray on his lap, then took her bowl. His mouth watered and the kitten, who'd teleported into the room, hurried up to sniff at Garrett's meal.

He pulled it closer. "Mine." A word cats understood very well.

"You just had some food, kitten." Artemisia frowned.

Not enough, some milk from My dam, and other food was DRY. His stubby tail lashed.

"This clucker soup is imbued with Healing Flair and energy." *Want some.*

Artemisia lifted her brows at Garrett. "It shouldn't harm him. I have a dish in the dressing room. Do you want to give him some broth?"

The cat sat expectantly, ears forward. *Of course he does.*

Garrett didn't, but also didn't want to appear churlish. "Sure," he said, eating fast. He felt the zing of energy, the soothing as the broth slid down his rough throat and into his stomach.

He was glad he got noodles this time.

But she didn't tip any soup from her bowl or his; instead she got some more from the no-time. Made Garrett wonder what might be in there. Probably not steak.

Still, he was stronger when he was done, and as soon as she removed the tray, he set his jaw and struggled into pants, then used his Flair to help him stand, more, to walk the length of the room.

She hurried back and offered her shoulder.

"No, thanks," he said. "I've done this before." He didn't want to recall waking alone and walking through the mountain clinic littered with the dead. Better to remember the whole place going up in flames a week later, cleansed.

He made several circuits of the rooms. Artemisia's bedroom smelled more of her than Healing chemicals—secrets . . . a hidden garden? He didn't know. But by the time he returned to bed, he thought he'd gotten his strength and balance back. When he woke again, he'd be fine, he was sure.

He settled back against pillows. She didn't leave but took her chair, leaning back and closing her eyes as her lips moved in a prayer. When she opened her lashes, her emerald gaze met his and he saw a true smile from her. "We made it," she whispered.

His turn to raise his brows as he shifted, petted the kitten on his lap. "You didn't think we would?"

"Yes, I really did."

"It wasn't easy." He didn't want to think of the days and nights past, the memories, the old and new suffering.

"No."

Dragging in a deep breath, he said, "It's over. Finally." He wouldn't let the idea that nightmares might return bother him.

She nodded solemnly. "I hope so." Her jaw firmed. "We should learn from this and the whole epidemic will finally be ended."

"Artemisia, please join Garrett on the bedsponge," TQ said.

"What!" she asked.

"I wish to suction all of the Iasc microbes from these rooms into the sitting room and seal it. The spell is much like a whirlwind spell. You will need to hold on to each other."

Garrett's pulse picked up. When she sat next to him and he wrapped his arm around her waist, he vaguely remembered them touching, body to body. When? And why? Medical necessity, he supposed. Too damn bad.

"What about the food in the sitting room no-time?" he asked.

"I am having specialties delivered tomorrow morning for our celebration," TQ said, then, "Kitten, are you anchored?"

YES! All the cat's claws were hooked in the cover. Garrett curved his fingers around the kitten's middle.

The wind started. Artemisia grabbed Garrett with both arms. He liked that.

"Focus on the mural," TQ said.

The scene of the sacred grove flashed on the opposite wall.

Whee! the kitten cried.

For an instant Garrett could have sworn that there was no air in the room. All went freezing for half a second, then unbearably hot, then freezing again. The door to the sitting room slammed, and when he glanced that way, foam filled the cracks around the door.

Sealed for sure.

Artemisia gasped, then coughed. She tugged against his hold and he let her loose. She got up to pour some water for herself and Garrett. He missed her presence in his bed, but drank gratefully.

Tilting his head at the grove mural, he said, "A very beautiful spot."

"Yes, it is," she said, and he got the idea she knew it. He wouldn't ask. Instead, he translocated two silver slivers from his duffle at the end of the bed and sent them rolling with skill, not Flair, over his knuckles.

She smiled. "Wonderful."

"Getting back to normal," he said.

"Yes." She sighed.

He forced words from his throat. "I haven't thanked you for being here and helping me. So, thanks."

Her eyes rounded. "Just doing my job."

He grunted. "Not a nice job." He sucked in a breath all the way to his gut; some muscles still ached. "Thanks again."

She inclined her head. "You are quite welcome."

Good, courtesy was done, but he wanted to give her more. He took her hand and slipped the silver coins in it, curled her fingers over them. "Please, take these. A token of my . . . gratitude."

"Thank *you*." She smiled and it was the most carefree he'd seen. "I've never had magic coins before."

"Not really magic," he said.

She chuckled. "I'm sure I can't manipulate them like you do."

"If you want to appreciate my party tomorrow, you should sleep now," TQ said.

A mulish expression pouted Artemisia's face. "But we just got up and I wanted to spend a little time with Garrett."

"It's the first we've been alone and healthy in a few days. We should have a moment of quiet celebration right now," Garrett said. He couldn't deny her. Not this, weakened, minute. The simple pleasure of her presence enveloped him.

A pleasant fragrance swirled into the room and Artemisia gasped; her eyes went wide at the wafting scent.

Rusby gave a tiny mew and turned limp.

"The Healing and strengthening broth works best if you sleep after eating," TQ said. "You should be asleep in one and a half minutes, Artemisia. Two for you, Garrett."

She stared down at him wildly. "TQ drugged us."

"Dammit." Garrett put no force into the word. Only shallow breaths. He stroked the tiny body of the kitten with his finger. "Did you hurt him?"

"Absolutely not!" TQ said, then went on. "The kitten is fine, and both you and Artemisia are weary. You both have suffered disturbing dreams. The incense will calm you and is guaranteed to promote excellent sleep with pleasant dreams, as well as the Healing and strengthening."

"How could you!" Artemisia demanded.

"It is best for you."

She stiffened. "There are *rules*, you know. About sentient Residences and Houses drugging their people."

"I know the rules!"

Score one for the Healer, she'd irritated the House. Good, serve it right.

But when TQ spoke again, it was in his smooth and silky voice. "And the rules state that I cannot harm my occupants or release a drug that will have effects lasting longer than six point eight six septhours. This dosage will wear off no later than six point eight five septhours at the most, taking into consideration your masses and your state of health—"

"Fine line, there, TQ," Garrett said. Artemisia started to sway. Would she fall on his bed? He wanted her to.

No. He didn't. "Better get to your bed." He made a pushing motion. To keep his hands from yanking her down, he picked up the kitten and set him on a pillow on the far side of the bed.

"What?" she said, then her expression crumpled into hurt. "Go to my bed. Oh. Yes." She drew herself up, panting slightly, keeping her own breaths light. She headed toward her bedroom . . . weaving.

"This is wrong of you, Residence." Her voice was thick.

"*And* I cleared the use of this drug in this amount with Lark Holly," TQ said, quietly smug.

"Huh!" Artemisia flounced. To Garrett's riveted horror, she began to strip. Her tunic was first, thrown on the floor in the middle of his room. Then she said a Word and all the seams of her trous split and they fell. She paused to step out of them and he saw nicely rounded legs, then focused on her dimpled rear. His mouth dried. She wore beige pantlettes that looked flesh colored. Her ass was also round, good handfuls. Her waist was narrower than he'd thought under all that cloth.

He swallowed hard.

When she got to the doorway of the dressing room, she dropped her underwear. He couldn't tear his gaze away, hoping for more than a quick, silhouetted peek of full breasts tipped with rose-colored nipples.

Then she turned to face him and his gaze went to the joining of her thighs, whisked up the curve of her stomach to her breasts. His mouth might be hanging open, but since no thought was in his head, he wasn't sure. All his blood had gone to his groin and he was damn annoyed that he was wearing soft, loose trous. He wanted her, wanted her to know he wanted her.

"G'night, Garrett," she said and dove for her bed.

He caught a flash of tender, dark pink sex. His shaft strained.

Darkness clobbered him.

The next morning, Garrett woke and stretched and felt the best he had in a long time.

Even before he opened his eyes, he knew one of the reasons was that he felt the energy of his HeartMate fizzing toward him from the next room. Soon he and Artemisia would be released to leave . . . after TQ's celebration. Garrett didn't want a celebration and he couldn't wait to leave, except he and Artemisia would part ways.

Fourteen

*G*arrett *was ready to return to his life, without Artemisia. Really.*
Meanwhile he could enjoy her energy, even the peacefulness of their
bond—the much larger bond between them. He was sure that it
would fade if he pinched it tight. As he had all the years before
except for those times of Passage to free his Flair when he couldn't
control the depth or breadth of the link.

Passage was the last thing he wanted to think of. Those dreamquests were as rough as the damn sickness he'd survived—for the
second time. Three Passages and two bouts of Iasc sickness. That
could make a man believe he'd suffered enough for the rest of his
life.

If he was lucky, the year he'd lost Dinni would be the worst of his
life and this time period would rank second. That was a cheerful
enough thought for him.

He lingered in bed because Artemisia still slept and he didn't
want to rise and wake her. When he got up, he'd have to accept the
fact their days together were over.

How did she look asleep? She was quiet, wasn't restless. He'd
known, somehow, even in the deepest part of the sickness, when she
was awake and near or asleep.

Now that he thought back, her sleep hadn't been easy.

Again he stretched, testing every tendon, every muscle, popping joints. He felt a little creaky, but one workout should put him back into good shape. His mind drifted to sex as exercise and he got up and headed straight for a cold waterfall.

As soon as he stepped back into the bedroom, wrapped in a large towel, Artemisia entered the dressing room from her door. She wore the pretty silkeen robe that Lark Holly had given her. For putting up with Garrett? Probably. The robe shimmered and clung to her curves, and he knew she was naked under it and had to swallow hard. The silver gray color accented her deep green eyes. Her thick black hair was caught up with sticks on the top of her head, showing her lovely neck. Her beauty took his breath.

When she nodded as she passed, he thought she must have forgotten how they'd said good night, but when he looked around, he saw her clothes had been tidied away.

Then the door to the dressing room, which had been open the whole time he'd been there, closed firmly.

His body had stirred again, but other, deeper feelings had fired through him, more than simple gratitude, bordering on affection, as unwelcome as the sickness. Hands clenched, he *willed* himself to calmness, using an image of Dinni—small and sprightly and athletic. And then he felt as if he'd besmirched her memory and his own honor and *dammit all*!

"How long will you fight your attraction to your HeartMate?" TQ asked, sounding merely curious.

"Forever. I don't want her."

"Because you lost a lover," TQ said. There was a pause and Garrett noticed a spritz of fresher air coming from the ceiling. Summer flowers, something that he might smell outside. Which reminded him of his so-called kitten Fam, whom he hadn't seen this morning.

"Where's Rusby?" Garrett folded the towel on the bed. Like all the linens, the cloth was prime, soft and absorbent. A pity it would be destroyed. But not a waste since he'd enjoyed the feel of it. Move on.

He dressed in clothes that had been sterilized—tunic and trous, boot liners and boots. Not nearly as luxurious as what he was surrounded by but they were his own, even if they didn't smell like him.

Garrett went to the window and looked out at the back grassyard. There were cats, but not a spotted kitten. "TQ?" Garrett prompted.

TQ stayed silent for a minute, then said, "I have consulted all my human psychological data and it states that a person holding strong to a grief—obsessing—is not mentally healthy."

"Stay out of my mind."

"I *could* report this to D'Sea, the FirstFamily GrandLady mind Healer. I have permission to do that for any of my occupants since I don't have a steady Family."

"As if the Families who live in the intelligent Residences aren't all crazy."

"They are the *FirstFamilies*! The descendants of the colonists who funded the trip to Celta, the ones with the greatest Flair!" TQ sounded shocked.

"That's what makes them odd. Four hundred years of privilege."

"All humans have problems." TQ was stiff.

"All sentient beings have problems," Garrett said. "From what I understand, there are some pretty strange Residences, too." He thumped the doorjamb. "Like a House-becoming-a-Residence seeming to grow emotionally like a human."

"If you are saying that I do not have the knowledge to speak to you about HeartMates and HeartBonding and love—"

Garrett heard the waterfall shut off. He didn't want Artemisia walking in. "That's my business, and so far I'm only hurting myself." A question prodded. "Has *she* spoken to you of HeartMates? We connected during our Passages." Much as he hadn't wanted to.

There was a creaking wood sound Garrett suspected was TQ laughing. "She has said nothing." The House continued politely, "Do you want me to ask?"

Heat crept up his face. "No." He lifted his voice, "Where's my Fam? My . . . clever . . . kitten?"

No answer, but there was a suspicious wiggle in his duffle bag at the end of the bed. "What's going to happen to my possessions, TQ?"

"The clothes you wore while you were ill have been deconstructed and sent to the Noble Death Grove."

"Ah-hmm."

"I have sterilized and decontaminated your sleight-of-hand tools in your bag and the bag itself."

"That's good." He nodded to Artemisia as she came in, her voluminous hair slicked down and falling to the middle of her back. He wanted to see it unconfined, so he distracted himself by asking, "And the Healer's pillow?"

She gave him a bland stare. Yeah, he was avoiding calling her by name again, so what? Did she think that just because they'd spent three miserable days together, they were close? He'd thanked her already. He shifted so his clothes settled better. They were a little large.

"Yes, TQ, what of my pillow?" Artemisia asked as she went into her bedroom and rustled around, packing. Garrett wanted to turn and watch her, so he didn't. Yes, he was *obsessive* in ignoring her. He accepted that and had no intention of changing.

"There are no signs of the illness in the pillow. I have a gentle decontamination cycle I will use to ensure you carry no contagion. And your new robe, of course, is pristine."

"No contagion at all this time, TQ?" asked Garrett. The past crowded in on him again. He'd been forced to take a lot of sick people up to a mountain quarantine clinic for fear of contagion, and the sickness had spread from the HealingHall that had turned them out. And the clinic. And the Smallage estate.

"No person carried *any* cell of the Iasc sickness from here!" Pride rang in TQ's tones.

Garrett heard Artemisia's relieved sigh . . . and her movements as she dressed. He stopped himself from visualizing.

"None of you have any microbe of sickness. Nor will you have when you leave."

"That *is* cause for celebration!" Artemisia grinned and squeezed her pillow. She was dressed in a tunic and top that was several years out of date, and held her scuffed bag. "Well done, TQ!"

"Thank you." If the House had been the actor whose voice he had, he would have bowed. "There is bubbly and juice and special breakfasts in my mainspace for you. Please leave and I will seal the rooms."

"Not sad to see the last of them." Garrett picked up his duffle and opened the door to the hallway. He sucked in a deep breath, but it didn't smell any different than the bedroom.

Artemisia followed him and he heard her soft sigh. "It's good you can redecorate, TQ."

As they got closer to the mainspace, Garrett's nose twitched as he scented food. He hurried in.

There were the camp chairs and a rickety table with a small bottle of bubbly and a carafe of orange juice. Eggs and porcine strips steamed gently beneath spellshields.

"I'm ravenous," he said, set down his bag instead of dropping it, and headed to the larger portion.

The Healer's bag thumped beside his and she joined him at the table, eyes gleaming. "Looks fabulous, TQ, thank you!"

"A toast, if you please!" TQ said.

Garrett poured juice into the goblets, leaving a small space for bubbly. Artemisia didn't contradict his portions. He didn't know about her, but he wasn't about to spend a lovely summer morning, the first morning of the rest of his life, buzzed.

"To life!" TQ's voice throbbed with passion.

Artemisia laughed and clinked her glass to Garrett's raised one. "To life!" Her lips curved, her lashes lowered as she sipped. "Such a vintage, TQ!"

"The best," the House agreed. "May you live long and fulfilled lives."

"Thank you," Artemisia said.

The bubbly was smoother than any Garrett had ever tasted;

effervescence seemed to slip straight into his blood. He didn't care that TQ had added advice to him.

They ate in companionable silence, Artemisia looking out the window as often as he. When they were done, TQ said, "I have instructions from the Healers. One set if you return to Primary HealingHall—"

"No," Garrett and Artemisia said in unison.

"Very well," TQ said. "Viz starting."

Light flashed on the long wall, then Lark Holly smiled at them. "Greetyou. Our preliminary data is favorable that this difficult experiment was successful. The top medical researcher has been analyzing GentleSir Primross's blood and Flair and is hopeful we might duplicate several components."

"Wonderful!" Artemisia said.

Lark continued, "We have studied the most recent data on your health from this morning and release you to return home. However"—Lark's image raised a finger—"if you do so, we request that neither of you use any great Flair. Including no teleportation today or tomorrow until we meet at Primary HealingHall tomorrow at MidMorningBell. We want you to rest completely. Merry meet and merry part and merry meet again. Good job!" The viz faded.

Artemisia huffed. "I suppose I'm not allowed to Heal."

"Correct," TQ said. "I have forwarded such instructions to your home."

A shade in TQ's tone caught Garrett's attention. The House hadn't said, "Family." Where *did* Artemisia live? With whom? For one second of dread, his gut clenched as he thought she might be married.

Stup! She wore no marriage arm bands.

She could have a lover.

She didn't. No matter how tiny their thread, he'd known she'd had few lovers. He would have known if she presently had one. He was a trained observer and she didn't act like a woman who had a lover. She seemed available physically and emotionally and had given unconscious signals to him as a man that she was interested in him—physically and emotionally.

Though he might be physically available, he wasn't emotionally. He ignored that he was lying to himself.

He stood and put his softleaf on his clean plate. "We can make the next public carrier on the street outside if we hurry."

Artemisia smiled with a polite and empty curve of lips. He told himself he wasn't disappointed. "Of course." She went and picked up her bag.

Garrett looked at his duffle. Something definitely moved inside. Careful to leave the tab strips open on one end, he lifted the bag. Rusby didn't weigh enough for Garrett to feel.

Artemisia strode past him to the front room and threw open the main door to the sunshine and the warmth of the day.

They left the House and stood in the courtyard. Being outside for the first time in days, feeling good, was simply great.

"Farewell to you!" TQ projected through the open door. "Visit anytime."

And Garrett *saw* the mural in TQ's HouseHeart. His image was there, dressed in leathers, his face somber, and he stood near tall trees. Artemisia sat on a rock near the waterfall, dipping bare legs into the pool, wearing her silvery robe.

The surprise of the visualization—from TQ to his mind?—had Garrett stumbling a step.

Artemisia steadied him, hand wrapped around his upper arm. "Are you all right?"

He pulled away, shaking his head, straining to remember more of the HouseHeart. "Yeah." His vision was still muddy, focused inward on a dim room lit by a large fire.

"I don't know . . ." She sounded worried, so he let memory wisp away and blinked. Managed a half smile.

Her brow was lined, her gaze concerned.

"TQ attempted to speak to me mentally. It didn't exactly work."

"Oh." Her lips folded down. "Perhaps we should go to Primary HealingHall."

"No."

They stood in silence, studying each other. Her round chin set stubbornly. He didn't change his pleasant, revealing-nothing expression and knew he'd win.

The public carrier swished by on the street outside the courtyard. "Dammit, we missed the transport."

"TQ, when does the next public carrier come?" she asked.

"In half a septhour," TQ lilted. His tone tipped Garrett off. TQ had distracted them so they were stuck together for another few minutes. Though half a septhour with Artemisia wasn't a lot if he planned on ignoring her for the rest of his life.

She walked toward the gate.

"Where are you going?"

"To the public carrier hub less than a kilometer north."

"I can call a glider." Laev T'Hawthorn would do him that favor.

"It's a beautiful day and I've been cooped up." She shrugged her bag over her shoulder. It didn't appear heavy, as if it contained only the robe and her pillow and his two silver coins.

"I'll walk with you," he found himself saying. Ever since he'd awakened, he'd been torn. His body wanted his HeartMate, but his emotions still hurt from the loss of Dinni; yet it had been over three years. Experiencing the horror again made him yearn to put it behind him. Keep it in the past and not let it affect the present.

He wearied of hurting.

Losing a HeartMate would be the *worst*.

He wasn't ready for anything like that.

Artemisia pushed against the tall gates enclosing the courtyard. He caught up and put muscle into opening them; that felt good. They exited and he closed the gates. They turned north and stayed in step. His fingers brushed hers, and he liked the tingle and kept it up. She didn't draw away.

They hadn't gone four blocks before his bag wiggled. *Are we there yet?*

Fifteen

Garrett snorted a laugh. "That you, Rusby?"
A hesitation. *Maybe.*

Garrett let the laugh roar from his gut into the early-summer afternoon. Let it loosen his muscles, his tense shoulders. For the first time in days, he felt like himself.

Artemisia's lighter laugh rang. It rounded and flushed her cheeks, added sparkle to her eyes . . . they went from deep emerald to a green like grass shadowed by trees in a sacred grove. Strands of hair escaped her braid. What appeared black or dark brown indoors was a blend of brown and a deep auburn. She was simply beautiful.

Warmth suffused him, pleasure in being alive and healthy. And in the company of a lovely woman who laughed at the same things he did.

He opened his duffle enough for the kitten to poke his spotted head out.

I am leaving the Turquoise House! Rusby sounded thrilled. *I am going home with MY FAMMAN!* The little cat glanced up at Garrett with love in his eyes and Garrett missed a step. He'd never seen that expression for him from a cat. Had rarely seen it at all.

Rusby was very young. Soon he'd don the arrogant cat manner.

In the meantime Garrett would enjoy the kitten. He curled his fingers around Rusby's middle, lifted him to stare into yellow eyes.

"We're heading to MidClass Lodge." Garrett put the kitten on his shoulder and said a simple spell so the young one couldn't fall.

The foxes speak of that place, Rusby said.

"There were a few foxes once, but now their families are larger, they like more space."

MidClass is close to the beach of the ocean. I have never seen a beach or an ocean.

With his sandy brown coat and dark spots, Rusby could easily be lost on the beach. Garrett put on a mild expression. "The beach can be dangerous. You must promise not to go there by yourself."

I promise, Rusby said easily.

Garrett figured that like all young things faced with irresistible temptation, Rusby would break his promise.

"There are new collars with a recall teleportation spell," Artemisia said.

"Good idea." His fingers stroked fur softer than most things he'd touched in his life. So soft. So young. So vulnerable and needing protection. "We should consult with Danith D'Ash, the animal Healer, and make sure you are top-of-the-pyramid fine," he said.

Cats do not get Iasc sickness, Rusby said.

"No, you don't," Artemisia agreed.

A gasp from the kitten. *I will get to see the great D'Ash?*

"The sooner the better," Garrett said. He provided Healing for his feral informants if they got wounded or sick and asked for it. Not all of them did. He was accustomed to sending creatures by translocation to Danith D'Ash and her son for Healing, along with a spell informing them of any data he might have.

Rusby should spend time with more civilized, domesticated Fams. Garrett frowned. What might he lose if the kitten became domesticated? He wasn't much domesticated, either. But he'd feel better if D'Ash checked Rusby out. Closing his hand around his Fam, Garrett released the attachment spell. "I'm sending you to D'Ash's right now." He tried a guileless expression.

Artemisia arched her brows. "Using Flair?"

"Minor Flair. Rusby, I don't know your dam's or sire's name or lineage. D'Ash likes to note that."

I am the first Cat in My Family to be a Fam, Rusby said proudly.

"D'Ash will be interested."

Rusby grinned, showing pointy baby teeth. *I will tell her all about My life.*

Artemisia chuckled. "All five weeks of it."

"Yesss," Rusby articulated. *I will tell her of My dam.*

"She'll be fascinated." Artemisia laughed again. Garrett liked listening to that.

"Of course." Garrett stroked Rusby's tiny head, scratched under his chin, and felt his purr. Nice.

Cupping Rusby in both hands, Garrett muttered the data spell and attached it to Rusby's ear, which flicked. "Translocating Rusby to D'Ash's number four intake room in three seconds." His voice would be heard in D'Ash's office, and that teleportation pad was free. "One, Rusby cat. Two, Garrett's Fam. *Three!*"

Rusby's squeal cut off midsound as he vanished.

A few seconds later, a blue tag plinked onto the ground and Garrett picked it up.

"What's that?" asked Artemisia.

He flicked it into the air, caught it, made it disappear. "Receipt tag from Gwydion Ash."

"Oh." She stared at him with admiration. The warmth of being with her heated to lust. His cock hardened. Though he was glad to know it worked well, he wouldn't follow up on the attraction to his HeartMate. No. Absolutely not.

He tucked the tag in his pocket.

"You're a caring man," she said.

"Not so much."

Disappointment crossed her features before she masked them. She shrugged. He walked on; a breeze fluttered the leaves and cooled him.

They strolled together, Artemisia wasn't sure why. Outside was significantly warmer than TQ. She wanted to hold hands with Garrett, had enjoyed the touching of their fingers before as they'd walked. And she was having more feelings than she should for a patient . . . but he hadn't been patientlike from the first time she'd met him.

They'd struggled through a nightmare together, was all. When he'd thanked her, she'd thought he might be mellowing toward her. Now she was disappointed he'd reverted back to ignoring her. Her lips tightened against words—she didn't feel pleasant and didn't want to sound whiny. But she got conflicting signals from him. She didn't need an escort in this part of town, was perfectly safe. Why didn't he just leave?

Yet she was Healer enough to observe body language and she hadn't missed his physical attraction to her.

A puzzle. Unlike him, she didn't need to figure out puzzles. They were rocks in a path she wanted smooth.

So she was torn. She liked him beside her, the scent of his skin warmed in the sun. But if he wasn't going to act on the attraction, if he was more tied to his dead lady than living in the present, Artemisia was asking for trouble if she stayed with him.

Then his fingers feathered hers again as they walked and all her thoughts faded as she let the pleasure of his touch rule. And she sensed that he, too, both fought and wanted their connection.

"What's that?" Garrett said sharply.

She followed his gaze—across the green grass of Apollopa Park to the flat reflecting pool and a splashing center fountain of highly polished glisten metal cubes. She pulled her gaze back to a bundle of clothes.

Nasty odors whiffed to her. The bundle became a fallen person, lying on his side. She raced to him, refusing to admit she smelled death. Garrett pulled at her sleeve, her arm, but she flung his grasp away.

Kneeling, she reached out to touch the crumpled man, then stopped. More than her nose told her he was dead. His eyes stared, a pale brown in a soft-sag middle-aged face. Flies crawled on the long, deep slice in his wrist over a vein where he'd lost blood.

"Don't touch him!" Garrett ordered.

"I haven't." She had to swallow. Tears hovered behind her eyes.

Garrett sucked in a deep breath. "There's an odd smell."

She recognized the odor of the drug pylor, simply froze.

Memory rose and smacked her. Angry yelling voices in the night. The windows of her home breaking with exploding smoke bombs releasing pylor clouds. She'd breathed them in and coughed, coughed, coughed. Her Family rushing together, teleporting away from the mob attacking their home, wrecking it.

Her own nightmares threatened. She couldn't speak. Her hands fisted and she shoved them in her opposite sleeves. She focused on the dead man. He had a laceration on his head.

"Looks like someone hit him from behind," Garrett said. "Then fliggering carved him up." He gestured to the dark-stained earth and clothing.

Artemisia flinched. The man's veins had been opened and he'd bled out.

"Not a natural death." Garrett was grim. "You're a Healer, what are your conclusions?"

The breeze picked up and pylor hit her nose. She couldn't speak, held still and forced down bile.

"You know that smell?"

All of her shook inside, so it was easy to shake her head.

Garrett was scanning the park and she looked around, too, so she wouldn't concentrate on the pylor or the body. The fountain cubes reflected in the pool and soft falling water sounded. There was a small, columned round Temple on the far side of the park with no door, showing sunlight inside from a broken roof.

As broken as the body at her feet.

"The killer wanted this body found. He didn't hide him in the Temple," Garrett said. "I'd better call the guards." His gaze came back to her. "Murder."

She managed one word only. "Yes." Reverberations of the past, that cataclysmic change in her life, pounded in her skull. Those deadly threats to her mother. Artemisia's breath came fast. Could this threaten her mother, too? *Breathe!* Get control and act normally.

He'd taken out his perscry, a small glass pebble with a scryspell, and activated it, was talking to a guardsman. "I'll wait here by the body."

Discreetly, she drew in a breath, readied herself so her movements would be smooth. She shifted her balance and rose to her feet. Keeping her face set in the shocked and pitying expression she'd had when she'd first looked at the man wasn't too hard.

Garrett's gaze cut to her. "Do you know him?"

"No."

He nodded and went back to speaking with the guard, listing all the man's particulars—his height and weight, the plump body shape, his callused hands . . . detailing his shabby clothes. "We'll wait here."

She shrank inside. She didn't want to stay here but had no choice. Arms crossed in front of her, she cupped her hands around her opposite elbows. She wanted to wrap her arms around herself and rock, and cry out for her mother. But she was an adult now, and the Family would rally around to protect her mother.

No. She'd let her imagination run away. Her Family had lost everything because her mother was cross-folk and incense with the drug pylor had been found in their home. Pylor that had been used in the Black Magic Cult deaths. The misconceptions about cross-folk religion and pylor had been enough to destroy them.

Just because she smelled pylor on the man, knew he'd been drugged with it, probably after the blow to his head, didn't mean that her Family would be persecuted or the scandal would be raked up again. No. Breathe easier, steadier, relax muscles. Look concerned—and she was!—but don't appear afraid.

No one could touch her mother and father now. They were safe in the secret sanctuary. They'd already lost their titles and the respect of their peers and their careers. They'd moved on and made a good life for themselves.

That dreadful time was over. As Garrett's was. She'd survived and she wouldn't have to live through it again.

She opened her mouth to tell him of the pylor, what she thought might have happened, but couldn't. Couldn't force the words out.

The Mugworts had been driven from their home during a hideously cold and snowy winter. They'd hung on in lodgings for a year before they'd been hounded from the city, then had been offered the benediction of being caretakers for the old FirstGrove, BalmHeal estate.

She shivered in remembered cold and despair. Garrett wasn't the only one who equated cold with despair.

He signed off of his scry and pocketed the pebble, then glanced upward and frowned. "Clouds are rolling in. TQ should have told us the weather report."

Artemisia looked. The sun was shrouded by gray clouds with bruised bellies. Good enough reason to shiver.

Garrett squatted by the body. Obviously his ordeal had been wiped from his mind by this new situation. His frown grooved his forehead. "I don't know this smell."

Artemisia wet her lips. She should force her conclusion into the open, into the freshening breeze that spun the scent of pylor around them.

There were a couple of slight *pops* and two guards, one male and one female, strode from the Temple and up to them, moving together like longtime partners.

The female guard scrutinized her. Her brows came down and her mouth formed "Mugwort," and Artemisia trembled.

The guards joined Garrett and only then Artemisia realized she'd drawn away from the body and the scent of devastation.

Her perscry in her sleeve pocket lilted a tune. "That's Primary HealingHall," she said. "I work there."

"We know," the male guard said. "All guards are treated at Primary HealingHall and we recognize your tunic and insignia."

She cupped her marble and Ura Heather's irritated face looked out at her. "Well, where are you?"

"I was told not to report today," she said.

"T'Heather wants you here for a debriefing. Come now." She signed off.

Garrett grimaced. "I can inform the guards of our discovery."

She grabbed at the chance to get away, flexed a smile at the guards. "Artemisia Panax. You can reach me at Primary Healing-Hall. I must catch the next public carrier." She gestured to it a few blocks away.

"Fine," the male guard said. "We'll contact you later."

With a last inclination of her head, she walked at an even pace to the public carrier plinth. She wanted one last, long glance at Garrett but she didn't want to see the body.

She didn't turn and welcomed the carrier's cool air as she stepped into it and rode away from the past—recent and long-ago—and to her career that would ground her in the present.

The time with the other Healers, FirstLevel Heather and Holly and the great T'Heather himself, and their discussion of the experiment eased Artemisia until she was as involved as they in the final conclusions. Garrett's blood should provide them with excellent information to use against Iasc sickness.

The guards contemplated the body, then the guy held out his hand to Garrett. "Fol Berberis."

Garrett clasped arms with him. "Garrett Primross."

The guard smiled. "I know."

Garrett turned to the woman, who offered her arm. "Rosa Milkweed," she said.

He clasped her arm.

When they finished recording the scene and had sent the body to Druida Guards' Death Grove, he accompanied Berberis and Milkweed to the main guard station, under the command of Black Ilex Winterberry, Captain of all the Druida guardsmen.

While Garrett waited for Winterberry to end a scry, he rolled a couple of new coins on the backs of his fingers. The guards were intrigued at the sleight of hand.

"Can you do something with a softleaf? I love softleaf tricks," Rosa said.

Agreeable, Garrett asked, "Do you have a softleaf?" He had a scarlet silkeen one precisely folded and tucked in a front belt pocket for an impressive appearance, but the trick he was thinking of could be done with any.

Fol grunted and pulled a large square softleaf from his pocket and handed it to Garrett. He folded the thing into a little dancing-lady poppet, sang a jingle as he made her perform, and ended with a final "Hey!" as she did a high kick.

Rosa laughed—she'd watched every movement intently—and the men chuckled. Garrett presented the softleaf back to Fol with a flourish. The man's brows came down as he looked at the unfurling folds as if trying to see the pattern.

"Poppets were a way I used to track and find the Black Magic Cultists," Winterberry said. "But poppets made with and infused with Flair." He smiled but the topic had returned to the serious study of murder.

It wasn't a hardship to spend time at the guard station discussing a mystery. A whole lot better than suffering through sickness and nightmares and at the mercy of a bunch of female Healers. Now Garrett was in control and part of a project with like-minded men and women. Relief swept through him with enough force to nearly blow the top of his head off.

Nothing he liked more than a puzzle, and no one seemed to recognize the dead man. None of the local guards near Apollopa Park knew him. From the labels on his clothes, they were made in Gael City, and the man looked as if he'd done hard work for most of his life.

The Death Grove Healer stated that he'd been struck on his head and drugged with pylor, then his wrists had been slit so he'd bleed out. Things that *almost* made sense. It looked like the killing was *almost* part of a ritual. The man's features were *almost* like someone Garrett—and others—recalled.

After a couple of septhours, Garrett got an exasperated scry from

Danith D'Ash to come pick up his new Fam, and waved a hand at the guards as he left. The case wasn't his, but he'd found the body and made himself agreeable and had a good enough rep as an investigator that they'd keep him informed.

When he hopped on one of the infrequent public carriers to Noble Country, his muscles felt looser, he had more energy, and he resented only a little that he'd lost weight and was out of shape.

He'd never appreciated a day more. The streets of Druida widened and the trees lining them grew larger, the buildings opened to vistas. The sky was deep blue, and the dark clouds had transformed into high, white crystal-glitter scarves. The sun was the usual tiny blue white.

He was alive.

Some poor guy was dead.

Garrett was more interested in the mystery than in the man himself, accepted that and said an absent blessing for the dead. He, himself, was alive and life was fine. As he exited the carrier, he stretched and popped some muscles. Yeah, he felt good. He jogged past the sign "Danith and A. Gwydion Ash, Animal Healers" and through the arched stone tunnel. The corridor was pretty, with climbing plants, but Garrett wasn't fooled, it was a security measure—and for Commoners who took the public carrier. He let the annoyance burn off.

The door was open when he reached it, a small woman with brown hair standing on the threshold, arms crossed: GreatLady Danith D'Ash. "Garrett Primross!"

He winced.

She turned and he followed. She had such an aura of nobility, it was hard for him to recall she'd been born a Commoner. She led him past her office reception rooms to a small white room reminding him of TQ's sterile walls, then pointed to a cage behind the examination table.

His Fam sat in it, looking pitiful.

Sixteen

*J*ail for you, huh? Poor cat," Garrett said.

"He's too young to be away from his mother," Danith D'Ash said.

Am NOT! Rusby shouted telepathically.

"His choice," Garrett said.

Danith D'Ash narrowed her eyes. "He's small. He got into the housefluff burrows and scared some mothers and kits."

Housefluffs hop fast! Rusby said gleefully. *They ran and ran!*

Garrett bit the inside of his cheek, hoping he looked properly serious.

Danith showed her teeth in a smile. "That's two hundred gilt."

That sobered him up. Garrett nearly yipped in pain.

"For all the time I'll need to soothe the housefluffs and their babies, make sure they took no harm physically or emotionally. I must keep them longer and ensure they'll go to homes that won't make them nervous after this incident—place them in homes without cats."

Garrett looked at his Fam behind bars. The kitten tried to appear pitiful, but there was still a gleam in Rusby's eyes; the tip of his tail flicked with joy.

"You cost me more than three months' worth of feral animal

injuries," Garrett grumbled to Rusby. Concentrating, he translocated two one-hundred gilt pieces from his home safe, plunked them into Danith's outstretched palm.

She slipped the gilt into her tunic pocket, opened the cage, and set Rusby on the firm permamoss bedsponge on the table. "He's small for his age, and will remain a small cat." She placed a holo orb next to the kitten and sheets of papyrus with instructions. "The care and feeding of a kitten," she said, plopping large tubes of milk on the table. "Some initial feedings. Every two septhours."

An appalled expression stretched Garrett's face. He'd been anticipating a good, long, and uninterrupted night's sleep. He looked at his kitten with a jaundiced eye.

Rusby drooped, curled into a small ball.

Danith was right: The kitten ball was too small. But Garrett was stuck with the little guy. He picked Rusby up and held the softness of him, the fur caressing his palm. Soft as Artemisia's hair.

No, he wasn't thinking of her.

He put the kitten on his shoulder, attached him with a spell. "That will keep you out of trouble." As he thought of Rusby tearing through the housefluff burrows, he had to keep a straight face again. "Good to see you again, Danith."

She gave an exasperated sigh. "Males."

Garrett grinned.

"Also, I'm handing over your regular account—your stream of feral informants who get sick or wounded—to Gwydion. He'll be Healing them." She put her hands on her hips. "And if they want to become adopted Fams, they stay with us."

"Always the deal," Garrett muttered.

"I expect you to get more of them off the streets."

"Some like the freedom of the parks and the estates . . . and the streets." He smiled his slow and charming smile that he knew she liked. "I might have a raccoon for you."

Her eyes widened. "A raccoon! They're almost extinct."

"One's been hanging around MidClass Lodge. It might want to be a Fam."

"They always had the potential," she agreed.

Garrett stroked Rusby. "I'll need a recall collar for this guy."

"Of course." She turned and opened a drawer, displaying collars of all sizes.

I want the sparkly one! Rusby demanded.

"Sparkly is for girls," Garrett said.

"This is a temporary collar," Danith said, whisking out the white one with bits of glitter. "A recall collar if you get in trouble. It will activate to bring you here."

Garrett sucked in a breath between his teeth and eyed Rusby. Surely soon he'd grow so he couldn't fit into housefluff burrows. Garrett would stuff the little one with food.

Every two septhours.

Danith addressed Rusby. "As all Fams know, a *real* collar is given to the Fam in three months if the Fam is *good*."

Garrett figured Danith meant if the kitten didn't chase housefluffs. "The Fam's companion decides whether the Fam is good. That means no adventures on the beach," he said.

"Oh." Danith pursed her lips. "I'd forgotten you lived in Mid-Class Lodge." Her gaze slid toward him. "I'd heard you spent some time in the Turquoise House."

"Didn't agree with me," he said. Then, reluctantly, "I wasn't asked to stay."

"Maybe *you* should have asked the Turquoise House. Mitchella D'Blackthorn will start redecorating tomorrow and TQ should be ready for occupancy the day after."

He wondered what the rent would be. TQ was in a middle-Noble-class neighborhood. Probably too rich for his blood and his gilt.

"TQ is farther from my office than MidClass Lodge."

"Can't lose anything if you don't ask to stay." Danith muttered cleansing spells and a slight wind picked up . . . and carried the fragrance of disinfectant herbs that made Garrett's stomach squeeze hard. He took the three paces to the door and opened it to regular animal smells in the hall. The walls of the examination room swirled with color and Rusby squealed, hid his head in Garrett's neck, and dug his claws into his shoulder.

Garrett yelped.

Danith snorted. "Your Fam has only been within *white* walls of a House. He demanded white."

Looking at the sweeps of pastel, Garrett didn't blame him.

The animal Healer's lips compressed. "Already at five weeks, he's set in his ways." Her gaze drilled Garrett. "As you are. You should live in more upscale lodgings if you want to grow your business."

That flicked a nerve. "I like MidClass Lodge. I do get some business from the residents."

Danith grimaced. "You want Noble clients or middle-class clients?"

Despite his Fam's fear of pastels, Garrett moved back into the room, leaned closer to Danith. "Both. I don't want to be exclusive to the Nobles, to only people who can pay me a lot of gilt." If Dinni had been Noble or had had a lot of gilt, they wouldn't have turned her away from the clinic. He'd never base his services only on price.

Danith's eyes widened.

"Mama, you all right?" asked a rough voice from the door.

Garrett turned and saw that Gwydion Ash, at fourteen, had grown since the last time they'd met. He was already centimeters taller than his mother, and Garrett judged he'd be taller than his father, and with as heavy a build as the blacksmith. Still a boy, though.

"GentleSir Primross and I just disagreed about living with a lot of people." Her smile was reassuring for Gwydion and the boy relaxed. Garrett noted he was like his mother and didn't have an up-front killer instinct like his father . . . or Garrett himself. Though there was no doubt that Gwydion would have had the best fighting training possible.

The youngster was an Animal Healer. No matter how much he grew to look like T'Ash, he'd have a soft spot inside if life didn't harden him. Gwydion was a second son accepted by his mother into her practice. Blessed and didn't know it.

For some reason Garrett wanted the boy-man to keep that soft spot.

Danith continued, "GentleSir Primross is happy at MidClass Lodge."

A dimple creased Gwydion's cheek as he smiled back at his mother with easy love. "And you wouldn't be," he teased.

Lifting her small nose, Danith said, "That's what happens when you grow up in Saille House for Orphans."

Garrett stiffened. He hadn't known that part of her past. Both mother and son remained casual, so it wasn't a touchy topic. He relaxed with an easy smile. "So if you were in my shoes, GreatLady, you'd ask to stay at the Turquoise House."

Gwydion laughed. "She wouldn't be able to take a step in your shoes."

He joined Garrett, measured feet. "Thought so. Mine are almost as big as yours and she can't walk in mine."

Danith sniffed but still smiled. "I told GentleSir—"

Garrett offered his arm to Gwydion to clasp. "Call me Garrett."

Nodding, Gwydion squeezed Garrett's arm with just enough firmness. "I heard that I'll be taking over any Healing of your motley ferals." He beamed.

"And he might have a raccoon for us!" Danith said.

"Great." Gwydion rubbed his hands.

All this 'coon, 'coon, 'coon, Rusby grumbled, stretched along Garrett's shoulder. *You woke Me and didn't even admire My collar.*

"Sparkles," Gwydion said, hiding a grimace.

Past time for Us to go home! Rusby said.

"That's right."

Rusby licked Garrett's ear and he flinched. "Don't do that. I'll feed you when we get home."

We need glider. The cat twitched whiskers at Danith D'Ash.

"I'll arrange that," Gwydion said.

"Thanks, Danith," Garrett said, though he was feeling considerably less flush in the pocket.

"You're welcome. And teleport next time!"

Garrett moved tense shoulders. "Was under orders not to do that."

"Oh." She looked like she wanted to talk about the experiment. He reckoned everyone in the FirstFamilies knew what was going on. But Danith wasn't as close to the Healers as others. "Scry and we'll send a glider whenever you need it," she said.

He wouldn't be doing that. Wouldn't do that now except weariness insidiously seeped through him. "Later." He walked with careful steps to the office exit and into the sunlight. The adrenaline push he'd gotten with the discovery of the body had definitely crashed.

The glider door lifted. He frowned as he saw T'Ash's coat of arms painted on the thing, something people at MidClass Lodge would note. But he didn't have much time to worry about that because when he slid into the vehicle, he passed out.

More than one of his neighbors helped him into the building and to his door. Vaguely he heard someone ask if it was true that he'd been on a top-secret mission for the FirstFamilies. Whispers about the experiment were getting out. He wondered how soon the news about the murder would surface.

To his surprise, Rusby was able to manipulate the spellshield and lock to open his door, then hissed with mental threats—which Garrett didn't think anyone could hear—as Garrett was shoved on his couch.

His body sank into depressions he'd previously made in the permamoss cushion. Wonderful.

*G*arrett *woke at twilight. His body was fine, but in his muzzy state,* his mind *reached* for his HeartMate. Unlike the previous few nights, she wasn't with him and a quick, sharp fear spurred him awake.

A couple of seconds passed in disorientation, then his stomach rumbled and firmly grounded him. Of course his HeartMate wasn't near. She'd gone to her own home, wherever that was. Instinctively he tested their bond. It was wider than usual and he narrowed it.

He did sense she was disturbed. Without thought, he sent calm and affection down the bond, realized what he was doing, and shut it down. Not before he noticed that her anxiety had eased.

He was hungry. The apartment had a small kitchen with three no-times stuffed with food . . . another result of the most miserable days of his life, he realized. He always kept a lot of unspoiling food on hand.

By the time he'd taken a few paces toward the kitchen, his body was moving all right and he became aware of the *scritch, scritch, scritch* sound that had awakened him. Glancing at the wall timer, he saw it was NightBell. He sighed and rubbed his face. At least it wasn't TransitionBell. He hated waking then. And at least he was home tonight.

Scritch, scritch, rripp.

His chin angled and he abandoned the thought of food for now. His kitten was up to something! Crossing to the bedroom, he saw a dark kitten shadow on the windowsill, claws out. The spellshield was thin there, as if Rusby had already worked on it. Garrett had left the window slightly open, enough for a small kitten to flatten himself through if he could get through the reinforced screen. That Rusby was working on shredding.

Garrett scooped up the cat and got a snarl and scratches on his hand for the effort. He ignored the pain. "Time for food. You look hungry. I am, too. I'll program access for you to a no-time." He'd have to limit the portions.

Rusby eyed him, gave a big smile, revealing his baby teeth. *D'Ash says I can have little furrabeast steak bites.*

Garrett wasn't even sure where the sphere and the papyrus with instructions were. He put his Fam on the top of the small round kitchen table. "Stay there and I'll get you some furrabeast and milk formula for you."

Formula is for babies, I am not a baby! I am a FamCat!

"Yeah." But Garrett's neck was burning with the guilt Rusby wanted—he'd missed at least two feedings. He stepped to the no-time food storage unit and looked at the feastday meal section and opened it for Samhain—New Year's. The scent of prime furrabeast drifted out and his mouth watered. He heard little mouth-smacking noises from his Fam.

They both *wanted* that feastday meat, and, hell, they both deserved it. The meal was blessed, of course, by the cooks who'd made it and transferred it to his apartment. Garrett cut off a portion of steak and put it on a small dish, set a knife on the meat, and said a spellword. There was a loud grinding noise, then the meat was in tiny bits. He shoved the plate at Rusby, sat down, and cut his first bite, popped it into his mouth, and nearly moaned at the taste.

"Our first meal together." Garrett cut his next bite. "Enjoy."

You are the BEST FamMan.

They ate quickly and in silence. As he saw the kitten's belly stretch, Garrett decided he'd given the cat too much and Rusby wouldn't have enough room to squeeze in formula milk. The kitten burped, then curled up on the table.

Garrett programmed the lowest no-time to open at the tap of a tiny paw and stocked it with the smallest portions he had. Then he set his wrist timer to remind him to wake the cat in two septhours, tidied the kitchen, found D'Ash's stuff, and put the formula tubes in the no-time and the instructions on the table.

He took Rusby into the bedroom and deposited him on a pillow on the floor near the waterfall room—he needed a litter box—and went to the window. Long black shadows of the tall trees swayed in the courtyard. He preferred the courtyard view to the ocean, more fun to observe people.

As he tinkered with the screen, and Artemisia's image rose again in his mind, something tugged at his brain that he couldn't pin down. Finally he gave up trying to prod the damn bit out and returned to bed. It wasn't as comfortable as the couch, and dreams and warped memories slithered in to chomp on him.

*A*rtemisia reported the good news that there was hope for a cure of the Iasc sickness to her Family and BalmHeal Residence at dinner. After the meal she spoke of the murder and the pylor. Her parents were

interested but not concerned. Her sister, Tiana, recommended a soak
in the Healing pools and Artemisia withdrew from the pressure of
Family with a little relief. Tiana followed, carrying a couple of huge
towels.

"We don't have anyone in the sanctuary?" Artemisia asked. The
time away felt odd—like she'd been gone for years but had returned
to find all was the same.

"No," Tiana said.

"Just Family, then." Artemisia smiled, took the thick towel, and
hugged it to her, liking the feel of the plush fabric, the smoothness
under her fingers—and the fragrance of herbs and not the dreadful
remembered scent of pylor.

Tiana's gaze lingered on her face. "You seem a little different."

"The circumstances were tense." Artemisia's muscles twinged at
the recollection. "I was afraid," she admitted.

"Of what?"

"Losing Garrett." There! She'd said it.

Seventeen

As Artemisia wished, her sister, Tiana, took the revelation at face value.

"Watching a patient die of Iasc would have been horrible," Tiana said.

"Yes." Artemisia squeezed the towel harder. It reminded her that her pillow was in her duffle. A pillow that would smell of TQ and decontamination and the ozone of tech forcefields and maybe even a trace of Garrett. She should never have taken her own pillow. Why had she done that?

Because she'd wanted something of comfort from home and hadn't realized it would soak up new memories.

She'd already put the silver coins Garrett had given her in her jewelry box. At least they'd be out of sight.

Then the main Healing pool was before them, huge with curving bays. Sparkling blue, even in the late evening. A sigh sifted from her lips as relief trickled through her. Another true blessing at the end of the day.

She and Tiana shucked their clothes and slipped into the indentation of the pool that faced the gate to the northeast. Most desperate people found that gate into the sanctuary. If anyone came tonight, it would probably be from that direction.

The Family had cleared a path to the Healing pool and a few shelters they'd made near it.

Tiana moved to an underwater seat and Artemisia joined her. The hot liquid of the pool, infused with natural herbs and minerals, slid silkily across her skin in the most comforting reminder of home. Again her breath sighed from her. They wouldn't lose this home, this sanctuary. They were the caretakers. The shields melded with illusion spells on the stone walls around the estate were the strongest in the city, and so the strongest on Celta itself. And an intelligent Residence was a formidable being.

No one could get in to hurt them.

She said, "Not many people know we're here. Only those the estate have sheltered."

Tiana's usually serious expression lightened. "Yes, our parents are safe. If worse comes to worst and Father's pseudonym were revealed, he would only lose the publication aspect of his new life. He'd still continue to write legal theses and philosophy, but not see them in print. That would be fine with him. And some of those people we—and this estate and BalmHeal Residence—helped have great influence, are in the FirstFamilies."

Artemisia said, "None of those people can come back, but they do know of the sanctuary and us."

"Why do you think this strange murder would have anything to do with us?" Tiana asked.

Artemisia would have said she'd felt it in her bones, but now her bones soaked up heat and seemed almost pliable. She shook her head and her nape was caressed by water, lovely, so she tilted her chin up and saw the thick, bright spangles of stars flaming into view as the sky deepened into night black. "The smell of pylor brought the whole nasty situation back to me." She waved a languid hand on the top of the pool, sending ripples to the center. "The fear and cold and hopelessness."

"Yes, that time was bad for us. But perhaps you thought the worst because you had recently endured a dangerous situation."

"The Iasc project? Perhaps."

"That and seeing your patient fight for his life in another dreadful situation," Tiana continued. "The Turquoise House kept Balm-Heal Residence—and us—briefed.

"He must have gone into detail."

"Yes. BalmHeal Residence missed you dreadfully."

"I'm sorry."

"You felt you had to do this project because you were asked?"

"Because FirstLevel Healer Ura Heather asked and thinks me expendable." That shot out with more force and bitterness than Artemisia had expected.

Reaching over, Tiana tugged at a wet tail of Artemisia's hair. "Let it out. It scares me that you think you must always be serene."

"I *like* a serene life. And being calm around patients reassures them." Artemisia couldn't just sit there. She floated to her feet, then marched back and forth against the pressure of the water, splashing her discontent. "I *hated* that time in our lives when everyone was against us. When we begged our distant cuzes to take us in and were rejected. When we sold everything for tiny and cold and uncomfortable rooms. People treated us like pariahs, like criminals, and we did *nothing* to deserve that." She aimed an index finger at Tiana. "Don't tell me that Mother doesn't still have scars. She would rather be working in a busy HealingHall." Artemisia threw her arms wide, above the level of the pool. "Instead she is here, tending to the few utterly desperate who find the sanctuary despite themselves."

Tiana nodded. "Is that why you want to work in a HealingHall, so you can tell Mother about it and the gossip?"

"Maybe I do it for her, but I do it for myself, too," Artemisia replied. The short exercise had stimulated her blood and she wanted to swim.

"And FirstLevel Healer Ura Heather reminded you that you were at Primary HealingHall on sufferance."

Artemisia pushed out her lower lip and huffed a breath to get a strand of wet hair away from her eyes. "She didn't treat me well."

Garrett Primross had been irritated with her, too, but she'd thought that had been *personal*. He didn't like her for some reason— but he was aware of her as a person and an individual.

Ura Heather didn't even seem to notice Artemisia—as if the woman had taken one look at her when they'd met two months back, determined Artemisia was a daughter of the disgraced Mugwort Family, and, therefore, was beneath Heather's august notice.

After another huff of breath, Artemisia said, "Well, I can let my bitterness boil out here, but must watch my step at Primary Healing-Hall, before Heather and the others."

"Your career is so important to you?" Tiana probed softly.

Artemisia grinned. "Not as important to me as yours is to you. But my people are more snobbish. You can use our true surname and still rise to the top of the pyramid. That won't happen to me. I am only SecondLevel in Healing. You have the ambition in the Family." She began to swim to the far end and back, and found her sister gone by the time she reached the seats.

Artemisia had regained her serenity. She'd always have the pool and the estate and grouchy BalmHeal Residence and her Family to help her keep that inner calm, which, in turn, she could share with her patients.

She'd cleared out the scent of pylor from her nostrils and banished through a vigorous summer night's swim all past cold and scary winters.

She'd overreacted. The murder would have nothing to do with her or her Family.

*S*creaming filled *fiis restless sleep, dragging fim to the surface of wake-*fulness. Where he didn't want to go, because something terrible was there.

He jerked up, covered in cold and clammy sweat, blinked against the bright white walls and the horrible smell. The quiet. Soon he'd walk the halls of the clinic and find everyone dead and decomposing. Soon he'd see Dinni. He retched but nothing came out of his mouth.

But it wasn't light. Night painted black and gray shadows in the room. No smell of his own piss or shit or worse, rotting humans, slammed into his lungs. No, it was memory that hit like a hammer.

Dinni was dead. Everyone in the clinic was dead. Years ago and he didn't need to remember her like that. The last he'd seen of her had been only the shell of her body that she'd left. Her sunny and sparkling spirit had moved on to the wheel of stars and her next life.

No, no, no!

The damn nightmares were worse than suffering through the whole incident with Dinni and her baby and driving the quarantine bus to the clinic again. At the time . . . even reliving it . . . he'd had hope. He had fought his hardest to do his job, save his girl.

Now, in the aftermath, bitter memories shuddered through him. No hope. He'd fought and lost.

And with the night, the scars in his memory had ripped open and throbbed and bled anew.

Mind scrabbling to find something else to think about, disparate facts fell into place and he had a clear idea of Artemisia and how she'd lied to him.

Anger sizzled through him, his fingers fisted until his knuckles showed white.

Artemisia used the last name of Panax, a distant relation of the Healer Family, the Ginsengs. But her true surname was *Mugwort.* As in the Mugworts who had been implicated in the Black Magic Cult murders. Murders that had used *pylor.*

She must have recognized the scent, and she was a good enough Healer to know what had happened to the man—the blow to the head, the drugging, the blood loss that killed him. She hadn't said a word about that to Garrett.

For three days and nights he'd trusted her. With his body. With his life. Trusted her to be there, close, when he struggled through memories and dreams. Grew to depend upon her, had respected her.

She hadn't trusted him.

She'd *lied* to him. Hurt and rage roared through him, scouring him.

She'd lied to him!

Wha'? Wha's wrong? Artemisia's telepathic words slipped into his head, stunning him. He'd projected strongly enough to rouse her.

He shouldn't answer, should reduce the bond between them, not let it expand with emotions, with anger. *You lied to me.*

About what?

That made him grit his teeth. *More than one thing, obviously. First item, your name. Your true surname isn't Panax, it's Mugwort. As in the Mugworts who were tied to pylor and the Black Magic Cult murders.*

Yes. Her words crackled with her own anger down their link. *As in the Mugworts who had a lady whose religion was different, and because of that, because she had incense that most households in Druida had, containing a small amount of pylor, we were scourged by the newssheets.*

"Lady," he sneered. *You were also Nobles.* He flipped through the information in his brain about NobleHouses. *You were a GraceHouse. You would have been GraceMistrys Mugwort.*

He kept his mental tone smooth as a sharp blade. *And you, as a Mugwort and a Healer, knew the scent of pylor, probably understood what had happened to that murdered man as soon as I examined him.*

YOU examined the body.

I asked if you knew the smell. You said no.

I . . . shook my head.

I asked your opinion, you said NOTHING.

Her silence went on a beat too long, twisting unbearable hurt within him. *My mistake*—he made sure his tone was mocking—*thinking you were honorable enough to help without being asked.*

Thinking I was too stupid to understand what I saw, more like, she shot back.

Had she tossed her head? Maybe.

And it took you long enough to think everything through. And when you did, you anger and rage like a man, blaming me. Waking me. I'm tired of that and of YOU and your own self-righteousness.

Self-righteous! *Haven't you wondered why I was able to contact you mentally?*

She snorted this time. *A bond often forms between a Healer and a patient in such shared circumstances. Don't worry about it. It will fade. The sooner, the better.*

He laughed and made sure she heard it through their bond. *No, it won't. Not a link between HeartMates, DEAREST.*

Complete shock vibrated through their connection. Gasping, maybe. Heart thundering—he could feel how her pulse raced.

NO! IT CAN'T BE.

Yeah. It is. He sensed her thoughts fluttering.

You can't tell me! It's against all our laws to tell me that I am your HeartMate. It takes away my free will!

His turn to snort. *Yeah, let's call the guards. We can tell them all about Artemisia Mugwort who helped discover the body of a murdered man. A Healer who kept her mouth shut as to how he died. Do you know who he was? Are you hiding that, too?*

No! I said nothing . . . for my own reasons. It has nothing to do with you.

We're HeartMates. Most would say that whatever one does would affect the other. He paused. *Just because you're my Heart-Mate doesn't mean I want you.*

Of course it doesn't. Her tones were frigid. *You want your lost Dinni.*

What!

You didn't think that I would know that? It's obvious.

There was a pause, and when she spoke mentally again, it was like she'd sent icicles down their link. Cold enough that he shivered inside. *And I figured out a long time ago that you didn't want me.*

He could envision her now, chin up, gaze straight, green eyes lit with anger of her own. *I understood that when the years went by and you never came for me. You're older, you must have felt the HeartMate connection earlier when you had your Passages. You're a man who likes to solve puzzles. You must have looked until you knew who I was.*

That wasn't a question, but he answered it anyway. *Yes.*

But she was continuing, *I thought that since you knew who I was, you didn't want me because of the scandal, that claiming me might besmirch your own name or reputation.*

He *heard* her bitter laugh.

But you really didn't care enough about me to see under the surface, did you? Well, now I know why you've treated me like you have. Enjoy your life, Garrett Primross. I won't bother you. Ever.

The link between them didn't snap, not between HeartMates, but it squeezed so narrowly he couldn't feel it—nothing of the emotions that might be churning through her. So he had to shout his last words. *I WILL SEE YOU MIDMORNINGBELL AT THE HEALINGHALL!*

He couldn't feel her emotions; as for his own—relief that he didn't need to hide anything of himself from her again, that she understood about Dinni.

Rusby jumped up to the bedsponge. *You woke Me up.* Tilting his head at Garrett, he said, *You were mean.*

Garrett winced.

The kitten licked his forepaw. *But you have always been mean to her.*

Garrett's gut knotted. He'd been wrong in not controlling his anger, wrong in speaking with Artemisia at all. His emotions had been too damn scrambled.

Trust was an iffy thing. He had trusted her and she had lied, but she'd nursed him and been there with him, went through a lot to take care of him.

He tasted the bitter ashes of self-anger. He must apologize tomorrow.

Eighteen

$\mathcal{G}$arrett Primross was her HeartMate! As soon as she choked off the bond between them, Artemisia sobbed. Shock, initial joy, anger, and then pain at his words rejecting her. Oh, Lady and Lord, how she *hurt*. She folded up into a ball and pulled the linen cover over her head.

How wonderfully horrible. She wept until the throbbing emotions drained and she was left with a stuffy nose and a headache.

And a heart ache.

In the deepest reaches of her being, she'd had hoped that her HeartMate just hadn't found her. That he hadn't looked for her or discovered who she was. That he hadn't made a decision to avoid her.

She hadn't pursued him. At seventeen, when she'd had her Passage dreams, the Family had still been in flux. She hadn't been at her childhood home, nor had she been here, in BalmHeal Residence. They'd been in rooms rented to them by lower-class people who would be suspicious of the Panaxes if one of the Family had had a strong Passage to free equally great Flair.

Artemisia and her mother had agreed to bring on her Passage with drugs and make it proceed at a quicker pace. They'd gambled that Artemisia wouldn't have more Flair than her parents. If she had, the drugs would cripple that Flair. Artemisia had accepted it all. Anything that would ease the lot of her Family. So she'd suffered through a fast Passage. Not over weeks or days, but in septhours, less than half a day. There had been a quick sexual connection with her HeartMate—and a quick release—but she hadn't had the time or the luxury to experience long dreams or deep connections with him.

Now she knew that he would never want her—he'd been so cutting.

She rose from bed and went to the waterfall, washed, then threw the sheets in the cleanser. Staring at her favorite pillow, she saw it was stained with tears. It was feathers and she'd have to use a special spell to clean it.

The other pillow on the bed was the one she'd taken to the Turquoise House. All right, looking at that hurt. The best way to get rid of the scents that would remind her of the slight time she'd had with her HeartMate was to air it in the herb stillroom. Then she'd re-cover it with a different fabric.

Everything would be all right. She had to get through only a few days. One final meeting at the HealingHall this morning.

At least now she knew her HeartMate didn't want her. Because he was in love with a dead woman. Because of the scandal. Because she'd once been Noble. Because she *worked* with Nobles and respected them. Was that all? Too much? Too *little*?

Didn't matter. She didn't want the narrow-minded, self-righteous man, either.

And now that she knew no HeartMate was coming for her, she'd get on with her life. She was a pretty enough woman, and a Healer, and had a good career, and maybe, Lady and Lord bless, a few good connections. She'd find a man and be content. Have children.

She would choose carefully, a man who wouldn't demand to live outside the walls of the sanctuary, who'd live in her home. She'd like children . . .

Bleakly, she sat on the window seat and waited for the dawn, watched the sun rise through a bright and clear sky. Then she moved through the early morning with forced calm, staying busy with housekeeping spells and work in the conservatory. Her home.

She hadn't let despair win before—she wouldn't now.

She dressed very carefully to meet Garrett again, in her most pristine and professional SecondLevel deep green tunic with silver embroidery on the long sleeves, around the hem and side slits of her tunic and her trouser cuffs. The outfit wasn't good for messy Healing, even with all the spells to keep off various bodily fluids. But she needed the confidence boost.

Fine for a meeting with the FirstLevel Healers and Garrett—GentleSir Primross—though. And it made her feel good. As did the approval of her Family. With a gleam in her eyes, Tiana said that since Artemisia looked so good, she'd invite her to lunch after the meeting at Darjeeling's HouseHeart and Artemisia agreed. They walked through the estate to the gate together.

"So, what are you hiding?" asked Tiana.

Artemisia gritted her teeth; her sister knew her too well. "Nothing I can tell you of."

"I'm a priestess, I know how to help with psychological and emotional problems, and something has you stirred up beyond what we discussed last night."

"I don't want to talk about it." When had her steps turned to stomping? She slowed them, knew her sister and raised a palm out. "I need to mull this over first." And she couldn't tell her sister, or her father, the ex-judge. They would be disturbed that Garrett had broken a cardinal Celtan law by telling Artemisia that he was her HeartMate. Upset enough that they might take action.

Her mother would be hurt.

And none of them would approve of the fact that Artemisia intended to do *nothing* about the situation. They all saw her as the most softhearted of them, perhaps the weakest. Just because she didn't like risk or confrontation.

That she wanted to ignore the man wasn't weak. He didn't want her, so what? She would get on and find a man to love and marry, have children. She wouldn't let Garrett Primross put a rocky boulder in

the path of her life. She let out a quiet breath. "I'm thinking that
with the successful end of this experiment, my career is on the right
path and I should consider marriage."

"Really!"

"Yes."

"What of your HeartMate?"

Since Artemisia had been sure Tiana would ask, she was ready
with an offhand comment. "Oh, since he hasn't shown up by now,
I don't think he will."

"And you don't want to go looking," Tiana said with a note in
her voice that meant she was equivocal about her own feelings to her
own HeartMate.

"Not my style," Artemisia continued lightly, let her true wistfulness show. "I'd like children soon."

"You'll be a wonderful mother." Tiana beamed a sincere smile.
"Our parents and BalmHeal Residence want children sooner rather
than later, too." She said the low chant that dropped the layered-for-
centuries spellshields and opened the door into the illusion of a
thicket. As usual, the abandoned warehouse district in the northeast
corner of Druida was empty.

Tiana turned and hugged Artemisia, then said, "I love you. I'll
meet you at NoonBell at Darjeeling's HouseHeart restaurant!" Her
elfin smile flashed. "And I'll start considering men for you!" She
teleported away.

Even for Family, teleportation was discouraged into and out of
BalmHeal estate and Residence—for the rest of Celta it was impossible. Artemisia said the rhyme that locked the door and raised the
shields—blocking the image of Garrett Primross from her mind.
She'd find other men attractive, she was sure.

Yes, all she had to do was to get through this one final meeting.

*O*nce again Garrett was in the main den of Primary HealingHall.
Rusby hadn't wanted to go to another place with *harsh-nose Healer
smells* and had stayed snoozing in the apartment.

Just as well, Fams weren't encouraged in HealingHalls unless they were providing comfort and Healing aid for their people.

FirstLevel Healer Ura Heather sat arrogantly behind her carved antique and massive desk, and FirstLevel Healer Lark Holly was next to him in one of the two plush chairs before the desk. Artemisia *Mugwort* sat in a straight-backed chair against the wall near the door. Ready to leave.

Her face looked more stern than he'd thought was possible, nearly expressionless. Her body was stiff with watchfulness.

"GentleSir Primross, I am pleased to confirm that we should be able to manage the Iasc sickness due to the successful experiment we conducted," FirstLevel Healer Ura Heather said.

"Heard that yesterday. Don't know why I had to come in today," Garrett said. He needed to get Artemisia alone to apologize.

Heather's nostrils quivered. "With the measurements that the Turquoise House took and the blood we drew, we have found an anomaly that might explain, among other factors, why you survived the sickness."

That focused his attention on her. "Twice. I survived the sickness *twice*."

"Yes."

"We are all too conscious of your altruism in this matter," Lark Holly said smoothly. "The FirstFamilies Council met, and upon recommendation of T'Heather, have authorized an annual gilt to be paid to you for the rest of your life."

Garrett whipped his head around to stare at her. Smiling, she named a figure that was triple the annual income from his business. He opened his mouth, shut it, said gruffly, "I didn't do it for the money." Then he looked back at Heather; faint disapproving lines bracketed her lips. "And I didn't do it out of any sense of guilt or for fame."

Heather's eyes flashed like the stream of a blazer shot.

"We understand that," Lark continued smoothly. "It is our thanks for allowing us to put you through such an ordeal to better the life of Celta's citizens."

He wanted to grunt. Instead he inclined his head. "Thank you." He wasn't too proud to take the gilt, especially since it ensured he'd be financially stable for the rest of his life. He glanced at Artemisia. She looked the same. He'd have liked some show of cheer on his behalf.

Not that he deserved it from her. But he hadn't thought she was the type who could hold on to anger or a grudge. He was disappointed in both of them.

So he looked back to Heather. "What about this anomaly you found in my blood?" The thing more important than his guilt or Artemisia's hurt feelings, the way to save people.

"Neither this HealingHall nor T'Heather's or Culpeper's research laboratories have been able to isolate the anomaly. We do know that something about your blood reacts with your Flair in a significant manner that shields you from the Iasc sickness and apparently even combats it. We know that the more you succumbed to the illness, the more Flair infused your blood and worked with the anomaly."

"But you don't know as much as you wanted," he said.

"We know a great deal more than we did before. Our labs will continue to work with your samples—"

"You took enough of them."

"A good thing we did, too," Heather snapped. "However, to continue, we have also couriered some of your blood to the laboratories of the starship *Nuada's Sword* to be analyzed. Ancient Earthan technology works differently." She sniffed in a superior sort of way and her voice fell with dissatisfaction. "The starship might possibly shed some light on the sample. In any event, we should still be able to manufacture a panacea that acts like your blood to save any future cases of those infected with the sickness."

"Good to know."

"SecondLevel Healer Panax will continue to be our liaison with regard to this matter," Heather said.

"I was assigned a full caseload of patients this morning and am expected on full shift tomorrow morning," Artemisia said. "I can't handle the time out of the HealingHall that this matter might consume."

Heather's brows snapped down. "What?"

Lark Holly moved and he understood what had happened. Lark had given Artemisia enough work—or Artemisia had asked Lark for enough work—to avoid him.

Heather swiveled in her chair to the data screen on her wall. "Show Artemisia Panax's patient roll."

The screen blinked on and pics and stats of patients scrolled along it. Enough that Garrett couldn't keep count, more files than he was working, that was for sure. More files than he would ever need to work again.

"I will reassign some of your cases," Heather grumped.

Garrett almost caught a flicker of reaction from Artemisia, but she was sturdier than he'd thought. "I am a better Healer than liaison," she said.

"Nevertheless, I'd like you to continue with this matter," Heather said. "Thank you for coming to this debriefing, GentleSir Primross."

So they were being dismissed. He and Lark Holly stood.

Heather said, "You are cleared to teleport and use whatever amount of Flair you need for your work."

"FirstLevel Healer, I would like to request that I not be the contact between—" Artemisia said.

Heather glared at Artemisia, who still sat. "I am in charge. Tell me, do you value your job here, SecondLevel Healer *Panax?*"

Artemisia went white. "Yes."

"I tolerate you, no more. I've allowed you to stay in my HealingHall and you've been adequately competent. But I do not forget your background or your bad blood. If you wish to keep your position here, you will accept the duties I give you."

"Yes, FirstLevel Healer Heather."

"Already I have been tasked with rumors about a murder that included your name in the report."

Artemisia turned wide staring eyes at Garrett, as if he'd talked to the flitch behind the desk about finding the body. He could read his HeartMate now. Betrayal.

After wetting her lips, Artemisia said, "Of course it will be my pleasure to be a liaison between Primary HealingHall and the research laboratories of T'Heather and Culpeper to GentleSir Primross." She stood and took a step to the door.

"Indeed," Heather said.

The scry panel lit with a buzz. "Yes?" demanded Heather.

Her assistant said, "Captain Winterberry of the Druida guards to see GentleSir Primross and SecondLevel Healer Artemisia Mugwort Panax. He is in the small conference room."

Anticipation suffused Garrett. Dealing with the Captain and murder was so much easier than Healers.

"Inform the guard that the pair of them will be there momentarily," Heather said.

"Yes, FirstLevel Healer."

"SecondLevel Healer Mugwort, I will remind you that your probationary period at this institution has not expired and you will be up for review in a week."

"Yes, FirstLevel Healer Heather," Artemisia said. When she met Garrett's gaze, her pupils were so dilated that he could see only the tiniest rim of green. "GentleSir Primross, please come with me to the small conference room." She turned her straight-spined back and walked away from him.

Nineteen

Garrett followed Artemisia from FirstLevel Healer Heather's office, at a loss for words. He'd had no idea that Artemisia's job was in jeopardy, that she wasn't as solid in her career as it seemed. That her whole life wasn't set . . . though he should have gotten a clue since she hadn't trusted him with information about the murder, shouldn't he have? Maybe.

Before he pulled the door shut, he heard Lark Holly say, "A moment of your time, Aunt." Garrett frowned. If Holly was going to fight a battle on behalf of Artemisia, the woman's timing was off. Anything Lark Holly could say just now would make Heather more entrenched in her dislike of Artemisia. He hesitated but saw his HeartMate take a fast corner and he had to catch up.

With her face still smooth of expression and not meeting his eyes, Artemisia stopped in the hallway before a door. She opened it and held it for him to proceed. Irritation rumbled through him and he said what was on the top of his mind rather than what he'd planned. "I am sorry you are in the power of such a FirstFamily Noblewoman as FirstLevel Healer Heather."

Artemisia's gaze flashed to his. "She's . . . not her father or niece." Artemisia stood even taller. "I have options in work . . ."

A faint smile he didn't like curved her lips. "And options in my personal life." She hesitated. "This is not the time or place to speak, but it will do since I never intend to broach the subject again." She wet her lips. "Thank you for stating your position last night. Now I can move on with my life."

A shadow darkened the door and Garrett saw Captain of the Druida guards, Ilex Winterberry, face as impassive as Garrett's own, but eyes glinting with curiosity. Garrett had no doubt that the guardsman had heard Garrett and Artemisia's exchange and filed it away in his memory in case it became pertinent to any case he was working or would work on in the future.

But the current case was murder. Garrett wanted to put his arm around Artemisia, indicate more than with body language that she was under his protection. She wouldn't allow that, and he'd forfeited the right, and that gnawed on him as much as guilt.

"You wished to see us about the murdered man we found in Apollopa Park yesterday, Captain Winterberry?" Artemisia asked.

Winterberry frowned. But if he'd wanted to keep the whole mess more confidential, he shouldn't have come to the HealingHall, shouldn't have spoken with Heather's assistant, and definitely shouldn't have blocked the way into the conference room. He stepped back.

Artemisia inclined her head to Garrett, as if he were of higher status than she and she had to be wary around him. Another thing he deserved but didn't like.

"Yes, I have some questions for you, SecondLevel Healer," Winterberry said. "Glad to have you here, too, Garrett." The guard waited until the door was closed and Artemisia and Garrett sat. Winterberry pulled up his own chair across from theirs. He wasn't as solidly built as Garrett, nor as tall, and looked younger than his white hair indicated. Prematurely grayed, then, though he was significantly older than Garrett.

"My first question is for you, SecondLevel Healer Mugwort."

"Yes?" Artemisia asked.

"You don't use your birth surname."

This time her smile was quick and bitter. "No. Healers tend to be status conscious. Either extremely proud of their nobility or flaunting their common origins and emphasizing their accomplishments in the field. As a woman born Noble, then stripped of the title, I am . . . looked at askance by all."

"I see," Winterberry said.

Earlier than Garrett had, but then Garrett had been trying to ignore Artemisia when they'd met.

"The guards didn't take your detailed statement yesterday?" Winterberry asked her.

"I was called here. I would have stayed had I been asked and had they informed FirstLevel Healer Heather or FirstFamily GrandLord T'Heather."

"But you weren't forthcoming otherwise."

She lifted and dropped a shoulder.

Winterberry sighed. "I'm not here to hurt you in any way."

"Too late for that," she said and Garrett heard a hint of rancor there, too. He leaned toward her. Winterberry noticed but Artemisia didn't.

"My apologies." The guard sounded sincere. His voice lowered, gentled. "Would you please tell me in your own words of the discovery of the murdered man?"

"You still haven't determined who he is?" Artemisia asked, innate sympathy shadowing her expression.

"No."

"That's sad."

"Yes, and why we need everyone's help."

"All right." She didn't relax. In a calm, uninflected voice, she reported the discovery of the body—and didn't omit that she'd recognized the scent of pylor, that she'd guessed that the man had been hit on the head, then drugged into a stupor and his veins slit.

Winterberry didn't comment that she'd failed to inform the guards of her observations.

"You didn't notice anything else?" Winterberry asked.

"Only what the others did." Another shrug. "His general age,

weight, state of health, and I agreed with the guards in those particulars."

There was a small and awkward silence, an interrogation technique. Artemisia didn't hurry to fill it, merely sat with a serene
expression as if her mind was somewhere else. Garrett began to realize how little he knew or had learned of her. He'd felt her presence
to the depth of his bones, in the depth of his sickness, had trusted
her, but hadn't spent time getting to know her. But then, he hadn't
been at his best.

Artemisia rose. "If you'll excuse me, I have patients I must
attend to."

"One moment." Winterberry stood, too.

Garrett got to his feet.

"This isn't the first time your Family has been linked to murder,"
Winterberry commented.

A quiver went through Artemisia. Garrett stepped closer.

"No," she said. "This isn't the first time."

"But the link was previously false," Winterberry said mildly.

Artemisia blinked, took a step back from him. "What?"

"Rather it was true in only one aspect. Strong evidence *did* connect
you Mugworts to the Black Magic Cult murders," Winterberry said.

"What?" She sounded stunned. Garrett took her arm to steady
her and she didn't appear to notice.

"Long after the case was over, after your Family had disappeared,
we guards eventually determined the evidence against you was planted
by Modoc Eryngo, one of the Black Magic Cult conspirators."

A low buzzing started in Artemisia's ears, a reaction to shock.
She didn't want to ask "What?" again. "I didn't know that," she said
in a voice that sounded too thready.

"Modoc Eryngo also anonymously informed the newssheets of
the 'proof' that your Family, and perhaps the cross-folk, were implicated in the murders. This was at the height of the scare, and the
newssheets' frenzy."

"Oh." After the mob took their house, when they were in hiding.
Irreparable damage had already been done.

"Modoc Eryngo," Garrett said.

"What?" This time Winterberry asked the question.

"Modoc Eryngo," Garrett repeated slowly, patiently. "The missing man."

Winterberry's mouth twisted, his eyes slitted. "You mean the culprit who escaped me, who got away. None of us guards who worked that case were unaffected by it. All of us recall the bodies of the sacrificed teenagers and their nearly dead Fams. We've all been haunted by that case."

Garrett said, "I studied the Black Magic Cult murders. Every detective worth his spit did. Modoc Eryngo's face was splashed all over the newssheets, sent by the guards over every scry in Druida, circulated in Gael City and the other towns when he was discovered to be a member of the Cult and after he ran. The man we found yesterday looks like an older version of Eryngo's holo."

"*What!*" Artemisia and Winterberry said at the same time.

Garrett nodded. Excitement ran to her from him. From his hand on her arm. She pulled away and he let his hand drop from her.

"I'm sure of it. The murdered man is Modoc Eryngo."

"Fligger," Winterberry said, glanced at her. "I beg your pardon."

"A lot of people would like him dead," Garrett said. To her horror, his gaze rested on her thoughtfully. Her stomach lurched. She took another couple of paces aside. He didn't reach for her again and she told herself that was good. She shouldn't be wanting his touch, as angry and hurt as she was.

"Yes, there are now a lot of suspects," Winterberry said with suppressed feeling. "All the relatives of the people he murdered." His gray brows lowered and he looked at Artemisia. "The Mugworts were greatly affected by Modoc Eryngo's actions. They were ruined."

She caught her breath, lifted her hands. "No. We had nothing to do with his death. We didn't even know he was here. How could we? We are a law-abiding Family, a judge and Healers and a priestess. We would never kill anyone. It is against our most basic nature." She sucked in a breath. "It is against the Lady's and Lord's tenets, and cross-folk spiritual law, too."

Once again she felt betrayed, as she had in Heather's office when she believed Garrett had been talking about the rumors of murder. She grabbed hard on her control, vanquished incipient fear. "I don't know what you're speaking of. I didn't recognize the man, didn't know he'd hurt my Family."

"But you found him, didn't you?" Winterberry said. "And you might have led GentleSir Primross to the body to find him."

"No." She was firm.

Garrett watched them as if at a play, cynicism in his eyes. The man had a wide streak of that. She was better off without him. He angled his head. "As you said, a lot of people would have a motive to kill Modoc Eryngo. Including you, Winterberry."

Winterberry's eyes flashed fury. Garrett sank a little into a fighter's balance, challenged, "Can you deny that you'd want someone who'd tortured and attempted to kill your HeartMate dead? And also nearly killed your cuz?"

"No. I can't. And if you're right, the FirstFamilies Council needs to be informed of this immediately." Without another word, Winterberry teleported away.

Garrett pivoted toward Artemisia. "Are you going to flounce away, too?"

Her mind boggled at the thought of Winterberry's teleportation being called a flounce, but she only murmured, "I wonder to which FirstFamily he teleported to. Or perhaps the FirstFamilies Council is in session and he teleported there."

Garrett stared at her as she babbled, but replied, "Don't know about the Council. Probably 'ported to the Hollys. He's a distant relative to them."

Artemisia headed toward the door. "And I'm not flouncing out. I have work." She gave Garrett a steely smile. "I'll need to see how my caseload has been revised." With an inclination of her head, she continued, "I'll let you know when the HealingHall has any word back from the starship *Nuada's Sword* or Culpeper's labs."

He nodded, his expression searching. His gaze went to the corner of the conference room where a viz camera was. He opened his mouth, shut it, then said, "I'll check in with you daily. And we can make a trip to *Nuada's Sword* together. But I wish to speak with you privately."

Anger sizzled in her brain, frying thoughts. "I believe you wanted to ignore me. Why are you doing this?"

"Because I'm contrary?" he said. "Because I want to apol—"

She opened the door . . . saw a lot of Healers lingering in the hallway, heard the buzz of curious conversation. No, she would *not* talk to him about anything here in the HealingHall. She needed fresh air and open space, so headed fast for the back door to the Healing Grove and yanked it open.

Garrett couldn't let Artemisia go. Not before he'd had a few more apologetic words with her. "One moment," he snagged her arm as she whisked through the door to the Healing Grove.

She stopped, her jaw flexed, and she stared down at his fingers around her elbow. He took his hand off her.

"You said you didn't want to speak of what was between us—"

Pain flashed across her face. She glanced at him and away. "I don't." Her shoulders straightened and she put her hands in her opposite sleeves, began to stroll with deceptive casualness down the path to the shade in the center of the grove. "I don't care for cruel people. You made yourself perfectly clear." Her voice was clipped.

He winced. "What if I have something to say?" he asked.

"You said quite enough last night," she answered.

"Too much." And he was too sharp now, too. "Please, I wish to apologize."

That didn't relax her back, stance, or entire manner, which was stiffer than he'd seen before. She met his eyes, then her glance slid away. Lifting her chin, she turned her gaze to meet his squarely. Her round chin quivered, then she set it. "You were cruel last night."

He winced—thought of the hideous nightmares of sweat and sickness and bloodred and wet and rotting people. Still, no defense for what he'd done. He jerked a nod. "You're right. Unnecessarily cruel. I apologize again."

With a tilted head she studied him. "Probably a bad night."

He grunted.

Her lips compressed and brows came down; she touched above her full breasts. "You hurt me."

No use, he had to say it until she understood he was sincere. "I apologize for being cruel."

"But you meant what you said," she said quietly. "You don't want me as a HeartMate."

He scraped the answer from his throat. "No." After a cough, he jerked his head up. "So you get some free shots."

Her lower lip curled and she settled into her stance. "All right, then. But since it was an emotional hurt, I get to inflict the same on you."

He shifted his shoulders; he'd rather have a few jabs in the gut. But she wouldn't want to injure her hands.

"You love Dinni."

"Yes." The words came automatically. "I did. I don't know—"

"And she was . . ."

Easy answer, "My childhood girlfriend and first lover."

"But not your only."

That was a blow. He kept anger from his tone. "I was true to her while we were together."

Looking sad and determined, Artemisia said, "Dinni had a son."

He would *not* remember his last sight of the baby. Better to let his mind fog with the grayness of old despair. "Yes."

Artemisia said, "Do you realize that you always speak of Dinni as a girl, Garrett? But Dinni was a woman. One who married and had a child. And I'm not a girl, Garrett. I'm a woman, with a woman's heart and feelings and needs."

Needs. He couldn't catch his breath, dreading what was coming. Artemisia and her needs that he didn't want to think about.

"And since you can't provide what I need—love and partnership and children—I'll find someone who can. So now we understand each other."

He watched her sweet backside as she walked away.

And without her, the day dimmed and he became aware of an awful ache and a terrible hollowness, and the idea that he'd made a hideous mistake.

Twenty

Garrett teleported back to his office, hoping there would be cases to take his mind off this latest disaster, his emotions that were even more tangled this morning than the night before. Stuff he couldn't wrap his mind around.

He knew only that he had to figure out his life, and he had to keep Artemisia in it. At least she was still stuck with her liaison job with him.

When he got to his office, the first message in his scrycache was from the guards confirming the murdered man was Modoc Eryngo. The second was a notice from his bank that an incredible amount of gilt had been deposited into his account. Enough to make him thump down into his chair.

His creaky chair with the hard cushion.

That would go.

And cats were warbling demands outside his shut door. He had to feed his feral brigade, and soon.

Easier to deal with details, do minor things, than to acknowledge a deep truth. His life had changed, wrenched into a new shape. Completely and irrevocably.

Not just having the gilt to do whatever he wanted. That was so secondary to meeting his HeartMate, learning about her, and his revelation to Artemisia of their HeartMate bond.

And her words that had cut into revealing *stuff* that he didn't want to think about, either. Insights that would work on him—awake and asleep.

The cat yowling was getting fierce, so he stopped the playback of his messages, rose stiffly—he'd need some workout time soon; a good bout of fighter training would sweat crap out of him—and went to the door.

As he opened it, Black-and-White trotted in and Sleek Black waited with the other five cats outside the door in the hallway. Garrett didn't ask how they'd gotten in . . . the building didn't have a Fam door so they all must have teleported. Better not to ask or know. Asking would mean he'd have to pay for the info, and, besides, Fams were not allowed in the building.

We have been very good. We have much information. And We need food, Black-and-White said.

"All right, follow me. I'll check out the food trough." Still, he glanced at the color of the next message on the flat scry panel and wasn't too surprised to see that it was from Laev T'Hawthorn. Garrett raised his brows a little when he saw the call had come in late that morning. Must be about the murder.

He moved to the threshold and the line of cats opened for him. Black-and-White trotted after him.

In the back courtyard, he filled the trough with dry cat food, then sat on a greeniron bench that was bolted to the back wall. It was almost too hot, but he appreciated being outdoors. He stretched luxuriously, rotating his shoulders, extending his legs, even flexing his feet.

Alive and outside.

And rich.

The fact that he was financially free began to filter though his consciousness. Pure relief. His business was occasionally dangerous and he'd worried that he'd take a disabling wound that the Healers couldn't mend.

Now he could select the cases he wanted to work. More like, he could turn down those cases that didn't appeal.

When final belches signaled the cats were done with their food, Garrett sent them telepathically, *I am most interested in what went on in Apollopa Park the night before last.*

One of the younger female cats squeaked, "Eeeee," and bolted under the bench to shiver behind Garrett's legs. *Mean and angry one walks at night. Hunting, hunting.*

Garrett's heart thumped. *Did you see this mean and angry one?*

Not good. Felt a lot. Was stalking the man who was killed, heard the mean scary one went after raccoons this morning.

Stalking? Garrett pounced on the word. Stalking implied that the murderer had known who Modoc Eryngo was, which confirmed the theory that the man's own murderous past had caught up with him.

Yes, stood in shadows, prowl after. She pressed against the backs of Garrett's calves.

Where did you first see the killer and the murdered man?

Late, late at old airship park. Bright lights. Prey left old ship. Killer saw and followed. I watched, but soon close to Turquoise House and did not want to be near the big red anger. You were at Turquoise House and food and the soft Healer to feed us and pet us and was much nicer than scary killer.

He imagined so. *You didn't go to Apollopa Park?*

Park with pretty mirrors stuck in stupid water and old Temple full of smells? Raccoon den? No. She snuck back out from under the bench, stayed close, but began grooming her whiskers.

Garrett grunted. One of his talents was the ability to meld minds with a Fam, but he didn't do it often, and this cat was skittish enough to harm them both if he tried. He mulled over her words. "Why would he go after the raccoons this morning?"

Because they are ugly and nasty, said Sleek Black, not even bothering to look up from cleaning his stomach.

The newest cat, a gray tabby tom with big eyes and ratty ears crept closer to Garrett but stayed out of kicking range. Garrett had gotten the idea that this one had been abused. The cat's voice was no more than a whisper in Garrett's mind. *Because raccoons took something the killer left by the prey.*

And killer went back to park this morning to search, said Sleek Black between licks on his stomach hair.

So there were three cats who'd seen something of the murder and aftermath. The young female cat, who'd seen Modoc Eryngo arrive in Druida and be stalked by his killer; the abused gray tabby, who had seen something of the killer and his prey; and Sleek Black, who had been in the area that morning, a full day and night after the murder.

First things first, the most important item, the murder itself. Garrett stared at the new gray tabby tom. He shrank back a few steps, huddled in on himself.

You were near Apollopa Park when the murder happened?

No!

But soon after?

Maybe.

How soon after?

The cat's glance slid away, but not enough that he didn't keep an eye on Garrett's feet.

Maybe I saw a strange bundle in park that looked like prey. Maybe there was a shadow dancing around the fountain, admiring self in mirrors.

The image of a capering killer sent a chill down Garrett's spine.

Do you think the bundle was dead? he asked.

Another shift away a few centimeters, one whisk of his gray-and-black-ringed tail. *Maybe. Not moving.*

Though tension had tightened his muscles, Garrett strove to seem relaxed, easy. He couldn't afford to scare the cat away.

Tell me exactly what you saw.

The cat hunched into a crouch, watching Garrett, ready to shoot out of the courtyard and into the alleys. All the other ferals moved closer, ears rotating, curious. They were all nearly as curious as Garrett.

Gray Tabby swept his glance around the rest of the cats, probably hoping that they might protect him from Garrett. The cat had joined the band only a couple of weeks past, and Garrett thought it had watched for an eightday or two before that.

Garrett had never hurt a cat deliberately—trod on a tail that he hadn't seen, little incidents like that, but never had hurt one, or any animal. Would never hurt an animal. Well, would never hurt any sane animal . . . a mad cat or something, that was a different situation.

Gray Tabby's claws flexed, scraped against the flagstones. Again he gazed at Garrett, then his eyes focused on the food trough—yet holding enough for several meals—and back at Garrett.

Apollopa Park is a common area for many animals, the cat sent telepathically, this time with a cool and precise accent of Noble Druidan, though the Flair power behind the thought remained slight. Very interesting.

I was trotting to the park to sniff the scents of those who den there. A quick flick of eyes at the rest of the band. *I do not sleep with these others. I was looking for a nice hollow. Cool and dry and something that smells good. I prefer a burrow near herbs, chamomile or even lavender. A hardy fragrance herb garden was once planted around the old Temple.*

Black-and-White snorted.

"Go on." Garrett flipped a hand at Gray Tabby and he cringed. Garrett couldn't link deeply with this cat's mind, either.

The cat continued. *I went by way of the main street in the front of the park. The path you and Healer Artemisia took yesterday morning. There was a small family of intelligent raccoons, a sire and dam and two kits, who were living at the park, but I thought that they might be moving.*

"Um-hmm." Garrett encouraged.

I did not want to interrupt. A raccoon mother is fierce.

"Most mothers are fierce."

I saw the bundle on the ground. Hesitation now. *I do not think the prey was dead. But the dancing shadow was a threat. There was nothing I could do.*

The cat could have yowled and summoned help, or run for help.

Perhaps if you had been available, I would have told you. But you were sick and Healer Artemisia was watching you and is too soft to deal with such a fellow.

Chills slid through Garrett at the thought of Artemisia confronting a crazed killer. She'd have immediately gone to the fallen man, would have Healed him. And been new prey for the killer.

Nausea burned up his throat, bittering his mouth. He dragged a breath through his nose. "You did right," he said, since the gray tabby trusted only him and Artemisia.

A shrug rippled through the cat, as if it didn't care for Garrett's approval, or, more likely, the tabby had already accepted that what was past was past and he couldn't change it.

Something the cat—all cats—could teach Garrett. Something he'd have to learn.

The hunter danced until the prey died, then went back to him and gloated. Then the killer put a man-claw that was shiny and nasty and sharp—next to the dead prey. Did not eat the prey.

Garrett frowned. "I don't recall seeing a man-claw—a knife?— by the body."

I do not know a knife that shape, said the cat stiffly. He rocked back to his haunches, licked a forepaw in arrogance, still watching Garrett. *There was no man-claw by the body because a raccoon took it.*

"Ah."

Sleek Black, now done cleaning himself, ambled to the toes of Garrett's boots and stared up at him. With a cock of his ear, he indicated the gray tabby. *Gray Tabby ran from the green place and back to TQ and has slept there since.* A sniff. *Before sunrise this morning, he tells of hunter and prey. I went to see.* A pause and a shiver. *Killer was there. Fury. Search for the man-claw. Found den of 'coons. Found man-claw. Kicked and kicked the burrow and all the 'coons ran. Waved the man-claw. I did not want to stay. Returned to TQ for food.*

"I understand," Garrett said.

The gray tabby scratched cobbles again and Garrett looked toward him.

His big eyes got bigger; the whispery telepathic voice was back. *I talked to you for a long time and gave you big news, yes?*

Yes. Garrett nodded.

Then big news means big treats. A small pink tongue slipped over his muzzle. *I haven't had furrabeast steak in a long time.* A pause with intent scrutiny. *They say you have nip.*

"That's right." Garrett stood, stretched again. When he moved, his tunic released a slight herbal odor. He'd sweated and his bespelled shirt was sending his perspiration into the air.

The gray tabby smiled.

Garrett liked the fresh odor, too. It occurred to him that he could now buy a wardrobe of bespelled clothes. Of course, when he was sneaking around on his job, he would like the odor absorbed.

Come inside and I'll give you your treats, Garrett said.

Me, too! said the young female. *I gave news of stalker and prey.*

Also true, Garrett said.

Sleek Black watched Garrett with narrowed eyes. *I should have a treat for data about the raccoons. I also ranged the dens of the rich in Noble Country.*

Anything regarding the murder around there?

Saw, smelled, felt no angry hunter, Sleek Black conceded.

The slightest tension in Garrett relaxed. Nothing worse than setting himself against a FirstFamily Noble.

With a draft of cool air, the back door of the building opened and a fashionable woman came out. Gray Tabby and another cat scattered. A couple went back to the trough and slurped more food. The rest gathered near Garrett.

The woman, a mind counselor who officed in the building, tsked and frowned. "Really, Garrett, how often have I asked you not to hold your little meetings—" She broke off as her eyes widened and she took in the sight of him. Obviously noticing his appearance had changed a bit—he'd lost weight. He'd hoped the lines in his face hadn't gotten deeper, but since she stared, the grooves must be more noticeable. A hint of slyness slipped into her eyes, and when she walked toward him, it wasn't her usual professional stride, but one that had her hips swaying. "I'd heard that you had helped out Primary HealingHall . . . and gotten a grant from the FirstFamilies. I hadn't quite thought—"

Sleek Black rubbed against her bloused trous.

"What! Get away from me, you filthy—" With a scowl and a short exhalation of breath, she abandoned her flirting and hurried away.

Garrett glanced at Sleek Black. "Nice going."

Sleek Black purred. *Thank you. I get good treats, too?*

"For sure," Garrett agreed. He opened the back door and Gray Tabby zoomed from the alley and inside, followed by the female cat who'd seen the murderer stalk Eryngo, and Sleek Black. The fat brown female tabby wedged through the door opening, too.

"You want a treat, too?"

She revved a purr. *I have been following your lady for you. I hopped on the public carrier and We went to Primary HealingHall. I napped in the sun in the trees until she came out. Then she went home last night and ate with her Family.*

Garrett stood motionless, hand on the door latch to the storage room. Sleek Black swiped at his ankle to get him moving again. Garrett should have stopped the plump female from her report on Artemisia but couldn't find it in himself to do so.

The cat wrinkled her nose. *It was a long walk. They put out food for Me. Food was good but not as good as yours. And then she and sister walked to the Healing pool and sat and swam. Then they went back home and went to sleep. This morning I ate there, too, and went to HealingHall and watched you both.*

Sounded like the cat had missed the most stupid things Garrett had done. Just as well. And he was learning information. Artemisia lived with her Family near a Healing pool. Her home must be close to a HealingHall. Which one?

Whap! Sleek Black's paw hit Garrett's ankle hard. *TREATS!*

He pulled out some dried furrabeast steak bites on three plates.

Gray Tabby wrinkled his nose, but when the others gobbled with an eye on his plate, crunched the bites down. After they were done, Garrett led the little parade back to the courtyard and put a pinch of catnip in front of each of the three.

The plump female licked it up, then fell on it, wriggled, and went to sleep, paws up. Gray Tabby snorted it in, then gamboled about the yard. Sleek Black rolled and rubbed on his, then ran away on his own cat business, tail waving.

In the distance a Temple rang NoonBell and Garrett's stomach grumbled. He didn't want one of the casual meals he kept here. A hearty lunch would be good. He wondered if Rusby had had his feedings and checked on the bond with his FamCat, felt a low-level hunger in the kitten, too. Have to find a place that would welcome Fams. Laev's wife, Camellia D'Hawthorn, had Fams . . . and two tearooms/restaurants that served food. He didn't want to go back to the original, where he'd inadvertently killed a guy, but Darjeeling's HouseHeart had substantial enough meals for a man.

Rusby? he projected mentally. Got back an image of his kitten stretching hind end up and yawning.

Yes, FamMan? Food soon?

That's what I was going to tell you. Stay there and I'll teleport, then we'll go to Darjeeling's HouseHeart.

We will?

It serves Fams.

He sensed his kitten cocking his head, purring. *I would like to be served.*

Garrett gave a short laugh. Thing was, he'd never admit it, but he'd like to be served this meal, too. No pulling something from the no-time. *I'll be there in ten minutes.*

All right.

Garrett wanted to list a lot of *don't goes* but didn't want to put ideas into his Fam's small head. But before he went to lunch, he wanted to take the call from Laev.

He strode back to his office and hitched a hip on his desk, scried Laev T'Hawthorn.

The GreatLord answered, "Here."

"You called? And I hope you took some messages about new cases for me."

A smug expression settled on Laev's face. "I negotiated fees for a few."

"What!"

Laev lifted his brows. "You were grossly undercharging for your services."

Garrett narrowed his eyes. "Tell me you didn't soak any lower- or middle-class people."

"I didn't soak any lower- or middle-class people." Laev smiled. "But they were impressed when I told them you were on a secret mission for the FirstFamilies. You have two cases from that strata." A throbbing pause. "Four from the Noble class, one GraceLord, two GrandLords . . ." Another pause where Laev turned serious and his mouth hardened. "And a vital commission from the FirstFamilies Council I was requested to present to you."

"Ah. I don't mind charging the FirstFamilies Council a lot, soaking them."

A short nod from Laev, but strain around his eyes.

"It's about the Modoc Eryngo murder, right?" Garrett said. "The FirstFamilies Council is accustomed to using Captain Winterberry as an investigator in high-Noble, high-profile cases, and he's got a big conflict of interest in this one."

"You are a detective," Laev said drily.

Garrett lifted and dropped a shoulder. "Not difficult to deduce."

One side of Laev's mouth tilted in a half smile, then, in a habitual gesture, he tapped his fingers together. "As a matter of fact, the FirstFamilies Council likes the idea of not using an official Druida guardsman as an investigator."

Garrett's scalp prickled.

Twenty-one

Warning buzzed in the back of Garrett's mind as he stared at his friend GreatLord Laev T'Hawthorn. "I can't be bought by the First-Families." Garrett's mouth flattened, then he smiled and crossed his arms. "Especially now I have enough gilt that I never need to work again."

Another tap of Laev's fingertips and upraised brows. "Very good. I'm sure you will have to meet with a contingent of us"—he meant the younger generation of lords and ladies on the FirstFamilies Council—"and define your concerns and boundaries, but we know you to be a man of honor."

That statement flicked Garrett straight on the raw. He hadn't acted with honor toward Artemisia. He kept his face impassive but saw a considering weight in Laev's eyes. But whatever Laev thought, he was Garrett's friend.

"I'm glad the FirstFamilies Council approves of me." Garrett's turn to use a dry tone.

"We want you to make finding this murderer your first priority. Captain Winterberry will be in charge of the guards as they do their standard investigation, but he will report to you. We expect you to ensure that Winterberry's feelings do not cloud his judgement on this. We would prefer not to officially remove him. He is a good man and handled the original case, so has vital information." Laev's expression soured. "And several of the FirstFamilies believe the fligger Eryngo got what he deserved."

"Murder is not necessarily a good answer. Should have let the councils take care of the man," Garrett said.

"You sound more like Captain of the Guards Winterberry than I'd anticipated," Laev said.

Garrett recalled the greatest Nobles also had a habit of duels and feuding to settle problems. Well, he didn't care about that and sure wouldn't interfere.

"I'll take this case, since I'm already involved, but don't think I'll be the FirstFamilies' pet."

Laev's face went bland. "Of course not. Later." He ended the scry.

Garrett rubbed at his face. Had he insulted his best friend? Maybe. But since he meant what he'd said, he couldn't really take it back. His stomach rumbled again.

There was a quick *pop* and Gray Tabby was there, staring up at Garrett and licking tiny shreds of furrabeast from his paw.

"Yes?" Garrett asked.

Gray Tabby looked away. *Garrett . . .* Gray Tabby whispered.

Yes?

As if reluctant to go on, the cat flexed his claws once or twice. Finally he said, *The hunter was happy and proud. I do not like people who are happy and proud and kill for fun and not for food.*

"I hear you," he replied. "What—"

But Gray Tabby teleported away to someplace safe.

I am WAITING, Rusby yelled down their bond.

And I'm coming now.

Good, I am hungry!

Garrett's gut emitted another sound. *I am, too.*

*F*or a while, Artemisia wandered through the trees of the Healing Grove next to Primary HealingHall, letting the greenness soothe her and the heat of the sun allay her pain.

Garrett hadn't followed her. Her smile was small and tight as she considered that she'd given as good as she got. She shouldn't be glad of that, of inflicting pain, but she wasn't a priestess or a saint or a doormat.

He was gone from the grove and the building when she returned. Organizing her caseload soothed her even more, and visiting her new patients took her mind off anything else.

Soon it was time to meet her sister for the midday meal at Darjeeling's HouseHeart. Artemisia took the public carrier. She arrived first and was glad, since she wanted to use a private room. Camellia Darjeeling D'Hawthorn, the owner, was one of Tiana's best friends so Artemisia's request was granted.

She'd just opened the door to a small room that held three booths and a couple of tables when her sister hurried in. Tiana gave an absent wave to her friend Camellia behind the cashier counter.

As Artemisia was sinking into a chair at a table for two, Tiana grabbed her hand and moved them to a booth for four.

Artemisia raised her brows. "Who else is coming?"

Tiana beamed. "One of my colleagues. You've met him before, Leger Cinchona. I think you'd be a good couple."

"All right." But Artemisia felt twitchy. She had to bring up the murder. She said a Word to close the door and added a chiming alert when it opened. "I forgot to ask where you were the night before last and early the next morning. At home?" That could be tricky to explain.

Tiana stared at her, and sat, smoothing her priestess robe around her. "Why does it matter? Surely no one could suspect me of the murder." She narrowed her eyes. "Or you."

"The victim's name is Modoc Eryngo. He was the last Black Magic Cultist who sacrificed those people years ago."

"What!"

"Yes."

"But . . . but that has nothing to do with us!"

"Apparently he was the one who made the trail connecting us—

our Family as cross-folk—to the crimes. That trail was more threatening than we thought; I believe Father spared us that knowledge."

"He would." Tiana frowned, then nodded as she worked out the ramifications of the information Artemisia had given her. Her eyes, as green as Artemisia's, searched her expression. "You have a solid alibi. You were watching Garrett Primross. And in the sentient Turquoise House."

"Yes, I should be all right."

Her sister didn't seem to hear Artemisia's doubts. Again Tiana nodded. "I attended a long spiritual vigil with *the* priest and priestess of GreatCircle Temple. The highest spiritual people in the land." Tiana's lip curled. "Let anyone try and contradict that."

Artemisia's breath whooshed out of her. She sat. "Good."

The door dinged as someone tried to open it. Tiana gestured the spell gone. "Come in, Leger!" she called with enthusiasm.

A man about their age with long blond brown hair and a welcoming smile walked in. When his gaze lingered on Artemisia, she knew her sister had begun her matchmaking plans. Good.

Artemisia studied him, too. He was slender, with a narrow and interesting face engraved with a few lines—a thoughtful man, all to the good. She would *not* compare him physically to Garrett. Not make the same stupid mistake her HeartMate was in holding on to the past.

Leger came over to them. Before he could slide in next to Tiana, she rose. "I'll be leaving early." She winked at both of them. "So you can talk and get to know each other." She gestured and a laughing Leger took the inside booth seat.

Artemisia found herself smiling. It was refreshing to be with a man who wasn't brooding, someone open. Someone who frankly liked the way she looked and was disposed to like her.

Their conversation was casual and they ordered—Tiana no more than a sandwich—and Artemisia understood why her sister thought Leger might be a good match. All three of them had a common point of view on life.

From what he said, she understood that he knew her Family lived in the secret sanctuary of Druida, so she was comfortable being with him. One secret she didn't have to hide.

But . . . he was too comfortable. He reminded her of her father. Not even an incipient tickle of attraction.

And after Tiana left, there was a short silence as they studied each other. Leger seemed to acknowledge the fact that she wasn't flirting—and maybe that he found her too comfortable also—with a lopsided smile. They began to speak of Tiana and a career in the Temple.

Leger grimaced in dissatisfaction that he had not received his own Temple assignment yet.

Under her lashes, Artemisia considered him. Though his robes were the simple ones of a minor priest of the Lady and Lord, they were of expensive fabric and tailored for the man. He had gilt to use for his career.

"It has been my experience," she said in a low voice as she lifted her wineglass, "that refurbishing an ancient place is extremely rewarding."

His gaze pinned on her. "Yes?"

She sipped her wine, and it was good and tart on her tongue. "Yes, indeed. And, you know, some Temples are in a sorry state. Such as the one at Apollopa Park."

His gaze sharpened. "That was the park where the body of a murdered man was discovered, right?"

"Yes."

She saw calculation come to his gaze and continued, "It is a place that won't be forgotten soon. And the Temple is small and beautiful . . . and in disrepair. A wonderful challenge for someone. It could be exciting to bring back as a sacred space."

His lips curved, and misty blue eyes lit with the first excitement she'd seen from him. "Yes. It would be." He rose, and she did, too.

He offered his arm courteously and she thought that touch might confirm that there could be nothing between them. She was right, but the muscle in his arm was stronger than she'd thought.

He opened the door and let her lead, his fingers touching the small of her back. Leaning his head down toward her, he said, "I understand that the victim has been identified." In silhouette his face hardened and nostrils flared. "As the last Black Magic Cultist."

"That's right."

Leger's forehead wrinkled. "The park will have to be cleansed and rededicated. As you said, a challenge."

A sizzle zipped up her spine. Slowly she tilted her head until she could glance around the room from the corner of her eye. Garrett stared at her. Even across the chamber, she could feel his intensity, the tug on the bond between them.

Drawing in a breath with her diaphragm, she imagined the tiny tendril that linked her with the private investigator icing over. She *would not* allow it to interfere with her future.

He didn't want her. Fine.

Her spine stiffened. She was proving she was getting on with her life and that included a man other than him.

She smiled up at Leger. "Yes, a challenge—on three levels, physical, mental, spiritual."

And he shared a slow smile she hadn't seen. "Sold. Do you know when the guards will release the area—"

HEALER ARTEMISIA! YOU ARE HERE! *I AM HERE, TOO.* The shrill mental comment from the kitten nearly pierced her head.

Rusby bounded—using Flair—across several tables to land on her shoulder. *THIS IS FUN! AND THE FOOD IS GOOD, TOO!*

Thanks to spells, not one hair or bit of pollen or dust flew from the kitten. Most people smiled; some looked confused, as if they weren't quite sure what had happened.

Leger grinned, scratched the kitten on his head with a forefinger. "Greetyou. Who may you be?"

I am RUSBY PRIMROSS, the kitten shouted mentally.

Nodding, Leger said, "I'm pleased to make your acquaintance. I am Priest Leger Cinchona."

Garrett was there, plucking Rusby off Artemisia's shoulder.

Leger inclined his torso to him. "And you must be GentleSir Primross himself. I've heard that all of Celta owes you thanks for a great service."

"It's done," Garrett answered.

"And I'm sure you're glad of it," Leger said in a smooth priest's tone. Then he straightened and looked down at Artemisia. "And you were one who discovered the . . . unfortunate's . . . body yesterday." Leger took her fingers and kissed them, eyeing Garrett. "I did not commiserate."

"I'm fine," Artemisia said; the odor of male hormones swirled around her.

A quick smile from Leger as he met her eyes, then switched his glance to Garrett. "I was going to ask you if you had any notion if the guards were done processing Apollopa Park for clues, and whether they would release it to Temple authorities."

"I don't know. I'm not involved—" she began.

"I think they've gathered all the evidence they can," Garrett said.

"Wonderful!" Leger enthused. "Artemisia told me of the Temple." He squeezed her fingers, then apparently enthusiasm got the best of him and he dropped her hand to rub his own together. "Sounds like rehabilitating the Temple is an ace project for me."

She noted that Garrett flinched at the same time she did when Leger said the word *project*.

With more roughness in his voice than Artemisia expected, Garrett said, "There's an herb garden that needs to be tended that was planted around the Temple."

Leger nodded, took Artemisia's hand again. "Artemisia can help me with that, too. You must excuse us, we have plans to make." With a last half bow, Leger tugged Artemisia from the restaurant.

She heard Rusby's mental comment, *Back to our food, FamMan*, before the heavy door closed behind her and Leger.

"Good meeting you." Leger whisked her fingers to his lips. "I'll contact you and Tiana about rehab ideas." He bowed to her with a distracted air and teleported away, eager to talk to his superiors about claiming Apollopa Park and the Temple.

Artemisia shook off her own distraction—the sharp pain of seeing, being with Garrett a little, *smelling* him—and started moving her feet before he and Rusby finished their lunch.

*G*arrett watched *A*rtemisia walk out with the priest. <u>*Good to see Healer outside TQ*</u>, Rusby said from his perch on Garrett's shoulder. Garrett could hear the small slurping sounds of the kitten grooming. *She remembered ME!*

"Yes," Garrett said.

And I liked her man.

Garrett's mind had screeched a loud warning. She'd meant it; she was cutting her losses with him and moving on.

So soon. He didn't change easily. That Artemisia could slide so soon into change, accept his words and not fight against the circumstances, not fight to change his mind . . . was inconceivable.

Zoom. Right to another guy.

Options in her life, she'd said.

He'd been discarded as a viable option. His own damn fault. He wasn't going to have the time he needed to process this. He sat back down at his table, and when Rusby saw that Garrett wasn't eating, the kitten marched over to the grilled clucker strips.

Garrett had no appetite.

*A*rtemisia decided to walk home through a series of parks—and burn some energy to offset the heavy meal.

For some reason her memory flashed on an image of a slender and active Dinni that she'd gotten from Garrett's mind. The peek at the woman he'd loved and lost haunted Artemisia, making her less self-confident about her body than she usually was.

If he liked slender pixie women, Artemisia would never be a fit. She got her curves from her mother, and they weren't sleek.

Finding that she was grinding her teeth, she stopped. No help for it, the man was her HeartMate and they would have bonded well.

But that didn't mean there wasn't another man out there she could love and have children with.

A short scream pulled her from her thoughts; hurt-panic swept over her. She turned to see a woman staring at her hand, which was turning red and swelling alarmingly. Her gaze fastened on Artemisia and she stumbled toward her. "Healer, help me!"

Artemisia plunged toward her. "What is it?"

"A stingsect. I'm allergic."

Artemisia could see that, could almost sense the poison pumping through the woman's body. No time to get her to the HealingHall. Grasping the woman's hand in both of hers, Artemisia drew in a deep breath, concentrated, and sent her Flair from herself into the woman's body, making it magnetic to the venom. The woman's system was already reacting and Artemisia braced her patient against her as she worked.

Not difficult. Tiring, but also satisfying as she used her talent to help. She held her patient as she vomited, sent much of the venom out that way, as well as pulling it from the wound.

Soon they were both sitting down on the grass, her patient's skin skimmed with perspiration as she panted.

Artemisia handed her a few softleaves.

"Thank . . . thank you."

Satisfaction infused Artemisia. "You're quite welcome."

"And thank the Lady and Lord you were here."

Artemisia nodded. "Yes." She leaned close and wrapped her arm around the other's waist, feeling more than one set of eyes on them. "Let's get you to a HealingHall to be checked out. I work at Primary HealingHall—"

The woman clutched Artemisia's arm. "No! My council health care is through MidClass HealingHall."

Artemisia frowned, shaking her head. "I'm sorry. I don't know the teleportation pads there, and you aren't in any shape to 'port us both. I do know those at AllClass HealingHall—and I know First-Level Healer Lark Holly, who works there."

Leaning against her, the woman said, "That's fine."

A few minutes later, Artemisia left her unexpected patient in good hands with Healers at AllClass HealingHall and walked out with a spring in her step.

She *was* a good Healer. She *did* have skills to benefit to the community. All the time with Garrett when she could only sit by and alleviate pain, not fully cure him, was an anomaly in her life. Past and done.

She was a better Healer, a better woman than most gave her credit for. Because she was quiet and didn't like risk or confrontation. Because she wasn't ambitious and only wanted a good and stable—and fulfilling—job.

And previous to Garrett, she'd helped the Turquoise House, who valued her for what she was.

She wouldn't settle for a man who didn't respect and value her as she deserved. She didn't have to. And she tripped over a gnarly root that extruded from under the wall encasing BalmHeal estate because she couldn't see it. Her vision was blurred from the tears in her eyes that dribbled down her cheeks.

Help! Help me, Healer!

This time the voice was telepathic, small and squeaky. Artemisia jolted to a stop. "What? Who's there?"

A whimpering cry had her moving again, searching. Her Family kept the brush heavy along the walls so they were obscured. But there had always been an animal path. She scanned the area to fix her position along the long concave wall that faced the city.

She was closest to the door that led to the Healing pools, fine. Backtracking a few steps, she pushed through a light illusion spell that led her behind the dense bushes.

I . . . am . . . here . . . There was a ragged gasp.

Artemisia trotted along the path, ducking, weaving. Keeping her senses open to find the injured . . . someone. If not a person, a child, it must be a Fam. Breathing in liquid gulps, tears falling more at the hurt that throbbed through her from *someone* else, she followed the weak mental pattern. Easier to sense the hurt and follow it. Biting her lip, she did.

And found a young and bloody animal—Fam animal.

Pain filled its dark eyes. She wasn't sure exactly what it was—its fur was thick and mostly matched the brown of the dead leaves it was in.

Help . . .

Twenty-two

She wet her lips and stooped—seeing enough of its muzzle to know it had sharp teeth. "I'm picking you up now." Sliding her hands under the thing that was about the size of a cat, she lifted it. Again it cried out in pain. And she felt an object sticking from it, something she couldn't take care of now because her arms were full of animal.

It closed its eyes and went limp, though she believed it was still conscious. *Saw you. Earlier. Saw you help. Saw you touch nice. Felt your Healing energy. Safe . . . now.*

"I'm not an animal—Fam—Healer. Let me take you to D'Ash."

It screamed—aloud and mentally, pain filled her head. *No. No. No, no, no!*

Drawing in a shaky breath and the animal's musky scent, Artemisia soothed, "Very well. You'll be all right with me, with my Family." She felt, *smelled* blood and urine trickle onto her sleeves. Wouldn't be the first tunic she'd ruined that way. As she brought the animal closer, angled to cradle it in the crook of her arm, she saw its muzzle was very pointed and its fur was black around its eyes, like it wore a mask. Then she knew she should be able to name the animal—an *Earthan* animal—but it escaped her.

I am a raccoon. A female raccoon, it—she—said.

Artemisia swallowed. "All right, then. We're close to the door and will be inside BalmHeal soon. I'll take you to a Healing pool."

Bad person threw knife. I 'ported AWAY fast, then rested and 'ported again. I was drawn here, whisper in mind. Came. Hurt for a long time.

"This is a good place for the desperate. I know you're hurt." Now she was able to feel the wound. Not to mention seeing the object still stuck in the raccoon—a hilt?—sticking out. A knife?

The spit in her mouth dried as she studied the weapon, the handle wasn't long, equal to the cross-piece arms. She didn't think the blade was very long, either, but it was plunged completely into the animal—who had rallied a little.

But the internal wound was bad. Artemisia must get to a safe spot quickly, remove the knife, cleanse, and Heal the wound.

Fast. Fast. Fast! In a stumbling run, she hurried to the door. The Word opening the door to BalmHeal trembled off her lips, and the arched wood swung open. Artemisia picked up the pace on the well-kept path—most of the desperate came this way—straight to the Healing pool.

Then she was there and putting the unconscious raccoon on the soft moss near the edge of the pool—moss that would comfort and help Heal. She wiped her face, her tears and her own snot, with her ruined sleeve, sucked in a breath, and reached for the knife.

She pulled it out quickly; the hilt seemed to burn her hands with negative energy and she flung it away, heard it splash in the large Healing pool. She didn't think it would harm the pool, but—*Mom, Dad, come quick to the big pool!*

Artemisia put her hand over the raccoon's wound and *saw* the injuries with an inner vision. She summoned her Healing Flair and concentrated on suctioning any internal bleeding or hurtful fluids from the knife wound, pulling them from the cavity of the raccoon's body through the wound to the creature's skin and into the thick underfur. Then she began mending—drawing the sliced tissue together, sending Flair to weave, to meld the hurt.

She sighed, sucked in a breath. Not so bad, really. Didn't take too much Flair. The raccoon's organs weren't too different than a human's.

There was a *swoosh* of air and the comforting scent of her mother was there. "What's . . . Oh. What's that?"

"I believe it's a female raccoon." Her father's calm voice settled Artemisia and her energy became less spiky, stronger, quicker. She was too used to working in a HealingHall, always knowing she might face an emergency there. Her mother usually handled the urgent problems here in the sanctuary.

"I threw the knife into the pool." She spared a glance for her father and his raised brows. "It was in the raccoon and it looks a little familiar, but I couldn't place it."

Curiosity lit his eyes.

Another deep breath. "It had very bad energy." She swallowed. "I think it might have been used to commit that murder yesterday."

"And it's in the pool!" her mother cried. She stared into the water with a scanning gaze.

"Clothes off," Artemisia's father said and dove in.

Ignoring her parents, Artemisia finished her work on the raccoon. Its—her—eyes opened and she snuffled at Artemisia. *Thank you, big human person. There are not many of us and we have been afraid of humans, but I would like to be a Fam animal.*

The affection and acceptance radiating from the Fam who'd rolled over and cuddled in Artemisia's arms sheathed the cutting edge of the pain of Garrett's, her HeartMate's, rejection.

She cradled the animal—surely it wasn't full grown?—and answered, "I'd like that. But first we must wash."

Fur is sticky and we smell bad.

Artemisia figured that wasn't the royal *we* that cats used. Her new Fam was making a comment on her person's odor. The raccoon's urine was feral and gamey. "Healing is like that. So we'll head into the pool." Looking around she saw her parents sitting on the far side of the large multicurved Healing pool, staring at an object. Her father was dressed and dry, which meant he'd said a spell.

"First we bathe. I'll hold you."

I can swim.

"That's wonderful. And then I'll make an appointment with Danith D'Ash to see us."

She is SCARY.

Artemisia blinked. She hadn't met the small GreatLady very often, but even as powerful as D'Ash was, since she was one of the highest Nobles of the land, Artemisia didn't consider her frightening. She *did* tend to trust the highest Nobles, especially of the younger generation, thought they were honorable people. There was nothing wrong with that.

"Who told you D'Ash is scary?" Artemisia asked the raccoon, and muttered a Word to take her boots and liners off.

Cats told us. Cats said D'Ash TORTURED.

"The cats probably wanted to keep Danith D'Ash to themselves so they scared you."

A small gasp, then a growly mutter. *Cats cannot always be trusted.*

"You have that right. We're going in now." Artemisia jumped over the rim of the pool and landed in warm, churning water up to her waist. Her new Fam squealed in delight and Artemisia let out a small sigh of relief.

Carefully she washed the raccoon's fur; the animal wriggled in her grip, surged up to swipe a rough tongue on her chin. *Thank you.*

"You're welcome. You know you are in the city's secret sanctuary?"

All are safe here, even raccoons.

"That's true. And if you want to be my Fam"—another little spurt of love between them as Artemisia said the words—"you will have to keep the location secret."

All animals know about this place, but not all animals can remember how to get here until hurt.

"Only hurt humans can find this, too," Artemisia said.

The creature shivered and Artemisia slogged to the steps and out of the pool. The early-afternoon air was warm, edging into hot, so her wet and heavy clothes stuck against her skin didn't cool her much. Carefully, she set the animal on its paws. "No telling any humans of the sanctuary or where it is."

Raccoons don't talk to humans much.

"I saw a raccoon at the Turquoise House and know that many of the animals that Garrett Primross uses as informants were there." Yes, it hurt to say his name. She'd have to practice it aloud—when alone—until that reflexive stab no longer came.

We have never spoken to him. The raccoon sniffed in disdain. *We keep ourselves to ourselves.* Artemisia's new Fam patted her foot. *Not all humans are bad.*

"No. And not all animals are good."

Again the animal shuddered. *Bad person hurt me! Kicked our den open and took knife. Big red anger and threw it at me and hit me and hurt me!*

"Yes, we need to talk about that." Artemisia's father crouched by the animal, his large hands soft and relaxed. Yet the raccoon skittered to the other side of Artemisia.

I am not YOURS; I am HERS.

Her father stood and inclined his torso in a half bow. "I understand, Lady Raccoon. But Artemisia is my daughter and we are close. I heard most of your story. If you live here, you may wish to stay with Artemisia in the Residence, especially in the winter. The Residence is an intelligent House."

A Fam House? Like TQ?

Artemisia's father's smile was quick and crooked and charming. "Yes. It is grumpy, though, and it loves Artemisia best, too. So she will have to soothe it and you will have to take care around doors and hanging objects."

The raccoon whimpered and rose to her back feet to set her claws in Artemisia's trous. Despite the sodden fabric, it ripped nicely.

"That outfit is definitely ruined," Artemisia's mother said as she joined them. A softleaf floated beside her on an anti-grav spell, and Artemisia realized that it covered the knife.

The raccoon stared at the shrouded knife and squealed.

"Why don't you teleport to your room with your new Fam and change clothes?" Artemisia's father said. "We'll join you shortly to discuss this matter."

Artemisia's mother's lips tightened. "This problem you've brought into our home."

"Quina, my love," her father said. "BalmHeal estate is a magnet for problems."

Her nostrils pinching, Artemisia's mother said, "I suppose so. And we wouldn't be here if I hadn't caused some of those with my religious preferences."

"Quina," Artemisia's father said even more gently. He put his arm around her mother's waist. "You are guilty of nothing, and what's past is past and should remain there. We have a very good life now."

She leaned against him. "I know."

But her eyes were haunted and Artemisia understood that the murder had brought all the circumstances of their ruin back to her mother. That hurt Artemisia's heart, too, in a different way than Garrett's rejection. Scandal and disgrace, something she lived with every day outside the estate. "Is Tiana still at the Temple?"

"Yes, her afternoon sessions."

"Ah." Artemisia bent down to pick up her Fam and her combs gave way and her heavy hair flopped in a long sheet around her head, hiding her face. Just as well. Her parents didn't need to hear or see the new burden on her heart. "Raccoon, I'm going to pick you up now and we will teleport home."

I HAVE NEVER TELEPORTED WITH A PERSON BEFORE. IT WILL BE FUN!

Artemisia managed a chuckle. "I'm glad you think so. We will go on three. One, raccoon Fam. Two, new home now, and *three*."

They alit in the corner of the sitting room/study attached to her bedroom that Artemisia had designated a teleportation area.

"What do you have there!" demanded BalmHeal Residence, then added, "It is a raccoon. Hrrmph. Long time since a raccoon was here."

"You know of them?" Artemisia asked.

"Of course. I was built not long after all the FirstFamily Residences by the colonists. They had some domesticated pets, cats and dogs, on the ships. They also revived the DNA and bred some of the more hardy of their Earthan animals, like llamas and horses and rabbits and raccoons, to make themselves feel more at home."

"Oh," Artemisia said.

This is a beautiful place. The raccoon wiggled in her arms and she put the animal down.

"What did it say?" the Residence asked.

"She is female and complimented you on your beauty."

"Of course. If she is well behaved, she may stay."

That was a great concession. Artemisia wasn't sure why the Residence was giving it to her but didn't question it. As she stripped and threw her wet and ruined clothes into the deconstructor, she asked the raccoon, "What is your name?"

I need a Fam name from a human, the raccoon said, discovering the line of Artemisia's shoes in the open closet and snuffling from one to the next.

"I would like to give you a BalmHeal name. Perhaps the Residence can suggest one?" Artemisia asked.

"I'm honored," the Residence said but made no suggestion while Artemisia stood under a waterfall foaming with cleansing herbs, dried, dressed, and cleaned up the mess of her ruined clothes.

Finally, the Residence said, "I would like to offer Diceranda as a wonderful Fam name."

The raccoon chittered. *Randa Raccoon, I LIKE it.*

"Randa loves the name Randa, Residence," Artemisia said.

There was a little creak. "That will do. And the raccoon isn't as big as that dog was," the House muttered.

"I'm sure all our mental and emotional connections will progress quickly so we can speak telepathically with each other," Artemisia said. "Residence, could you contact Danith D'Ash's office and request an appointment with the animal Healer for Randa?"

Randa whimpered. Artemisia gave her a stern Healer look. "I will feel much better if an animal Healer checks your health."

"Scrying T'Ash Residence," BalmHeal said.

"Good."

We are in the conservatory, her mother projected mentally and Artemisia relayed that to Randa. She took off in a back-hunched lope, ears straight out. She didn't move like any cat or dog Artemisia had seen.

When they reached the conservatory, her parents were sitting in greeniron chairs with plush brown cushions. Caff and cocoa carafes were on the glass-topped table, along with an object draped lightly in a softleaf. The knife.

Artemisia went straight for the cocoa.

"I thought so," her mother murmured, sharing a glance with her father. "What's bothering you, Artie?"

Just that easily, she recalled Garrett and his words. Her hand shook and a stream of milky brown liquid splashed on the table and ran off to the flagstone floor. Randa lapped it up.

"I can—can't." Artemisia's voice broke. "Can't talk about it. Not now. Maybe not ever, and espec-specially not to Tiana."

Her father gave her a straight look. "That's not like you, and not healthy."

She inhaled a deep breath. "I will speak to someone. A priestess, maybe. But not right now. Now I only have to get through it." And if she told her father that Garrett had revealed they were Heart-Mates, it would deeply trouble the older man. Her Family had had enough problems in the past and it appeared that controversy would be spinning around Artemisia and Tiana some more. Artemisia wouldn't add to that.

As for her, she didn't care about the law since she hadn't been hurt by it. Garrett wasn't claiming her illegally. He'd set her free.

A slow breath sifted from her father. "Very well."

Her mother had said a short housekeeping spell and all traces of the cocoa spill disappeared.

Randa burped. Artemisia's mother waved a hand in the direction of flagstones near the dry sink. "We can finally use the Fam feeding area there." Randa's head swiveled, then she scampered off to the small square and a bowl of dry dog food.

"Now, about this knife . . ." Artemisia's father started.

She told them how she found Randa, had pulled the knife from her and thrown it into the pool.

Randa's crunching of the food stopped and she padded close to them, hunched down.

There were interesting smells in the park where we denned. Then there was death. My dam took the knife and hid it in our burrow. Then the bad human came and kicked our den apart and found the evil knife and threw it and it hit me and hurt! We all ran away in different directions.

"You nearly died," Artemisia's mother said, obviously now able to hear the raccoon's telepathy, though her mother's face remained haunted. "This is another wrong against me and my religion."

"What?" Artemisia asked.

Her mother gestured to the knife under the softleaf. "That is a cross-folk ritual knife, but with edges and point sharpened enough to become a weapon."

Artemisia's father cleared his throat, but his gaze stayed on Artemisia. "You and Randa must tell the authorities this story."

"I know," Artemisia said.

He nodded to the softleaf folded over the knife. "And give them the knife. It may have trace amounts of evidence on it. And someone with Flair might be able to sense the murderer from it." He lifted his elegant hands, let them drop. He wasn't a judge, a man of legal authority, anymore. Her heart twinged. It wasn't often she saw regret for his lost career, but it peeked out of his eyes now. "I can provide you with a sterile vacuum box for the weapon." He still had that skill.

"Thank you."

"But your mother's softleaf might have also left traces, and might identify her. You will have to be more careful than usual to guard our secrets."

The dreadful feeling that neither of her parents would survive being cast from the sanctuary welled inside Artemisia and clogged her throat. She coughed. "I'll be very careful."

His gentle smile was back. "I know you will. You are often too careful. Both my daughters are."

His gaze searched hers. "It is a cross-folk altar knife, and your mother—and I—might know more about such than the authorities." Skin tightened around his eyes. "Will you grant me a little time to research the knife? I think I might be able to determine the artist who crafted it. You could take it in to the guards tomorrow with more information."

"Of course."

"We are breaking laws keeping it." He shifted in his seat. "But something of the energy surrounding the knife also feels a bit familiar."

"The murdered man was Modoc Eryngo."

Her father's face solidified into a stony judge's expression. Her mother gasped.

"He did great harm to us, implicating us and the cross-folk in the Black Magic Cult murders." Her father's tone was harsh and his lips tightened. "It seems this new murderer wants to do the same." He let out a deep breath. "But your mother and I were here, and you at a Healing vigil in the Turquoise House with Garrett Primross, and Tiana at a spiritual vigil at GreatCircle Temple. In this particular case, the murderer was unlucky."

"Will you researching the knife add traces?"

"I don't intend to touch it."

Artemisia eyed the lump under the softleaf. She hadn't gotten a good look at it. But she really didn't want to. Though her father had it shielded so they couldn't feel its negativity, she recalled the evil of it. She made herself smile. "I can take it in tomorrow, with an expert opinion."

"Artemisia," BalmHeal Residence said aloud, "the first appointment Danith D'Ash has to examine a new Fam is tomorrow morning

at WorkBell. I accepted that as your schedule shows your first shift
at Primary HealingHall begins at NoonBell."

"Thank you, Residence."

"I'll have the weapon and my report on the knife ready then,"
Artemisia's father said.

Her mother closed her eyes, murmured a prayer to her god, then
opened her lashes. "We will be all right. Everyone except those who
granted us this sinecure believes that we left Druida City after suffering a year of disgrace and scandal." Her mother's mouth was
turned down with bitterness, again something Artemisia didn't
often see.

Her father reached out and took both of his HeartMate's hands.
"This should lead to a final ending of the matter."

"I hope so," her mother said. "But it will stir everything up like
dirt in well water first. Don't let the *authorities* fall into the trap of
thinking I had anything to do with this, again."

"I promise you that," Artemisia said.

We will not, Randa said. She stood on her hind paws and put her
front ones on the edge of Artemisia's mother's chair. *I will say I
found the softleaf. It has my blood on it, too. I can lie,* she ended
proudly.

Artemisia's father chuckled. "Not really a quality that should be
encouraged."

His wife raised her elbow to nudge him in the ribs. "Little lies
make life smoother."

He leaned over to kiss her on the lips. "As always, we will agree
to disagree on that point."

The cocoa that had made it into Artemisia's mug had cooled and
she drank the half cup down. "I'll scry Guard Captain Winterberry
from Danith D'Ash's office after Randa is checked out. That may give
the guards some pause, being called from a FirstFamily Residence."

"Very true," Artemisia's mother said. "A good idea."

Randa had hurried back to her bowl and was crunching again,
as if eating would help her forget the upcoming ordeal.

The Residence made a sound like a clearing of a throat. "I have a scry from Barton Clover, who wishes to invite Artemisia to dinner tonight."

Artemisia's mother sat up straight, eyes gleaming. "Oh, today is not without blessings!"

"I hadn't thought to go out into the city again today. I wanted to spend more time with my Fam," Artemisia said, even as she knew her mother would insist.

But Artemisia's battered heart had picked up its beat and determination washed through her. She would find a husband.

Twenty-three

Garrett spent some time at the guardhouse with Winterberry, Berberis, and Milkweed, telling the guards what his informants had relayed. Naturally he protected the secret source of his data.

Suppressed emotions swarmed through the station. Every guard who worked there knew that a smear on their honor—the escape of the last Black Magic Cultist murderer—was finally over. Winterberry, of course, was outwardly calm, but his eyes glittered. He'd been the main investigator at the time. Berberis must have been on the team, also, and maybe even Milkweed, though she was younger than her partner.

When Berberis and Milkweed went to question people at the old airship landing port, Garrett couldn't resist the itching at the back of his mind to ensure Artemisia was safe.

The guards had offhandedly told him that the Turquoise House had confirmed her alibi, but the team didn't seem too impressed. Time to talk to the House itself and see what kind of hard data the place had that might clear her.

This he could do for her, easily and right now. He could protect her.

Rusby had stretched out on Garrett's shoulder to snooze, attached by a "stay" spell. Garrett was taking no chances with his Fam.

He was taking no chances with his woman.

That wisp of thought/emotion twined through him, as if the bond between them had already infiltrated his nerves, wrapped around his bones in tight spirals.

She'd gotten to him. Not just to his body, which would be attracted to her because of the bond, but her quiet serenity, her grace, her compassion.

Her sharp insight into him that made him so uncomfortable.

He left the public carrier before Apollopa Park. As he walked by, he found the gray aura that he associated with the miasma of murder had already dissipated. Near the Temple, he saw the man Artemisia had lunched with, Leger Cinchona, and Garrett's gut knotted, his shoulder muscles stiffened. Threat.

The man was hunkered down, looking at pink yarrow blossoms. Gawky, intellectual. A priest, so probably even sensitive. And was still a threat to Garrett, taking his woman.

His whole body tensed as he stared at the guy. Who didn't seem to know he was being watched by an enemy.

Messing around in Apollopa Park looked suspicious to Garrett. He pulled his glare away from the man and shook out his limbs. He needed a good workout in the worst way, would have to take some time at a gym. Or maybe even darken the door of The Green Knight Fencing and Fighting Salon. His friend Laev T'Hawthorn had put Garrett's name in as a guest for a temporary membership. Garrett had never followed through on that.

Maybe it was time. Good networking for his business and the best training in fighting and weapons a man could get—if he could afford it. And he could afford it now.

As he could afford to stay at the Turquoise House, no matter what that being charged, something Danith D'Ash had put into his head. Though he wasn't sure it was a move he should make. Since he'd actually have to ask . . . or hint heavily that he might want to be the House's tenant. Would the House allow that?

The shells he'd encased around himself since Dinni's rejection—and especially since the hideous trip to the clinic and the aftermath, the continuing struggle against the sickness—were cracking, letting more emotions in.

Tenderness and love for a kitten.

Yearning and attraction and lust for a woman.

Now an unexpected ambivalence about wanting a special place, a home.

So he thought of *home* as he approached the Turquoise House. He'd been in the HouseHeart and recalled being amazed and touched, though not at what. Yet he doubted if TQ was the right home for him. Garrett liked MidClass Lodge, but he was worried about Rusby and the nearby ocean, all the threats from people and animals that could harm a youngster.

The Turquoise House would be safer, and Garrett's band of ferals liked it. He rolled his shoulders. The resonance, the feeling didn't seem right. And would he ever forget suffering through the Iasc and reliving the worst days of his life there? He didn't think so. Bound to be memory smudges.

For some reason, the fever dream where he looked through gates at a garden rose. Dream home. Lush garden, serenity, turquoise pools—Healing pools. Didn't Artemisia live near . . .

Hello, Garrett. Sleek Black paced him.

Rusby awoke, shook himself out, and stared down. *Hello, feral Cat.*

Sleek Black growled.

"Enough of that." Garrett glanced at Sleek Black. "You have information?"

I want a treat.

Of course he did.

"All right, once we get to the Turquoise House." As far as Garrett knew, the House still had someone delivering food for the ferals it fed. And if there wasn't a stash of treats, he could translocate them from his office or his home.

Then he was there, and gleaming, recently tinted greeniron gates opened. He glanced up at the scrystone embedded in the pillar. "Good control, TQ."

The green blue crystal pulsed in response, but TQ didn't have the power to talk much outside its walls and Garrett saw no front speaker.

It was probably contrary of Garrett to prefer the rusty gates he'd seen in his dream, and a tangled green garden, to TQ's tended grassyard and flower beds and, now, polished flagstones in the glider courtyard before the House.

Neither the shiny walls of the House itself nor the pristine door appeared any different than when he'd walked through a few days ago. But all *was* different, for Garrett himself, Artemisia, TQ—whose HouseHeart had changed—and the fliggering bastard who'd been killed.

Who'd deserved to be killed after his own actions with the Black Magic Cult torture murders. Garrett was pretty sure that everyone on Celta would think of the death as justice.

Sleek Black gave a small throaty whine and Rusby sniffed in Garrett's ear and he turned aside from the front and walked around to the back grassyard.

The flowers exploded with even more color and abandon. He eyed them. No doubt TQ was very proud of them, as he was with everything that pertained to himself. Garrett didn't think he could live with such a summer view. Too darn groomed . . . and there wasn't as much land as he liked—a nice-sized yard for a middle-class Noble, but the courtyard in MidClass Lodge was larger and close to the beach.

Garrett stretched. Yeah, he wanted more room. Who could have known? He wouldn't be asking TQ about renter's rates. Garrett's tight breathing eased. No, he wasn't ready to have TQ as a home. A blessing, he supposed.

But they were in the back area where the bowls for ferals were. He lounged on a bench, letting Rusby hop down to sit on his thigh, and petted his kitten as Sleek Black munched a few bites. Just for form, Garrett thought.

The cat came and sat in front of Garrett, slicked his whiskers, and wrapped his tail around his paws. He gave a small belch and lifted his gaze to Garrett's. *The raccoons from the park have definitely moved. They have not returned.* His back gave a ripple cat shrug. *But raccoons usually move very often.*

Garrett crossed his ankles, let his lids droop over his eyes. Bright with flowers, the garden smelled really great, and even in the shade, the heat was settling into his bones. Nice to be able to take a break and not worry about a case or gilt or responsibility or . . . personal problems. "I don't think that's enough information for a treat."

Rusby snorted and smiled, showing baby teeth. Garrett tapped his small head with his forefinger. "Don't tease. You're with me now, you're a Fam. You have more dignity."

The tip of Rusby's tail twitched and he wriggled on Garrett's leg, then subsided.

Sleek Black's ears angled, nearly flattened. His eyes narrowed. *I am sure that at least one of the raccoons would have seen the big red anger well. You just must find them.*

"Um-hmm." Garrett rubbed his chin, put Rusby back on his shoulder with a "stay" spell, and stood, popping his joints. Felt good. "Come on inside and I'll get you a treat."

Sleek Black hissed. *Do not want to go into bad-smelling House.*

Garrett thought of all the House's plans. He supposed he was surprised that there weren't workmen or furniture movers or something, that the yard and House seemed empty.

"So, Sleek Black, how many winters have you lived through?"

The cat shuddered. *One. Icy paws.*

"Maybe you should consider an inside job."

He lifted his muzzle, wrinkled his nose. *Do not want to be a tame FamCat.*

Rusby snorted. *I will have pets and food and warms all of My life. And love.*

Garrett swallowed as emotion rose through him. *That's right.*

As he approached the back door, it opened. There was a very small room with a bench and hooks. One of the shelves—new oak shelves on a sage-tinted wall—held several bags of dry pet food in various flavors. And a couple of small bags of moist treats.

"How'd you like some fishy moist treats?"

Sleek Black's tongue came out and licked his muzzle. "Yesss," he vocalized.

"You've gotta come in," Garrett said, stooping down to pour out some of the fish-shaped bits into a little bowl.

"Welcome back, Garrett," TQ said. "It is good to see you and Rusby. You must have a tour!"

Garrett supposed so. Sleek Black inched through the open door, sniffed. *Smells much better.*

"Yes," Garrett answered. He could only pick up traces of herbal housekeeping spells but knew the cats' noses were more sensitive.

While Sleek Black ate, Garrett said to him, "Tell all the others that I want a background check on a man." When he'd first started gathering his little troupe, he'd explained the term. As new ferals joined, they got the info from the others. Garrett had never asked his informants to trace a priest before, wasn't sure how to describe him, fell back on location. "He ate lunch with Artemisia Mugwort this afternoon at Darjeeling's HouseHeart and left with her. He was just in the park."

The altar man from the biggest round, Sleek Black said mentally, licking the bowl clean. *I saw him.* He glanced up at Garrett, and Garrett made sure from his expression that the cat knew begging for more was useless.

"Tell everyone to keep an eye, ear, and nose out for the raccoons."

I will go now, Sleek Black said and flipped his tail, running from the House and back toward Apollopa Park.

"Altar man?"

He is a man who stands at the altar in outside holiday human circles for other humans, Rusby said.

Though any man could perform the duties of a priest and act as a manifestation of the Lord, a priest would do it more often. Garrett had already figured out *the biggest round* meant GreatCircle Temple.

He closed the back door and kept Rusby on his shoulder. Since the kitten was sitting up, Garrett touched him to make sure all was well.

Stepping into the main hallway, he found the color of the walls a pale, warm gold, and golden oak molding around the ceiling and for baseboards. "Very nice, TQ," he said.

"Thank you."

The more he went through it, the more he was impressed, though his heart was settled now that he knew it wasn't the home for him. The tinting throughout the House was something either a man or a woman could live with.

"I only have furniture in my MasterSuite," TQ said.

Garrett's steps lagged as he approached the place of his suffering. He glanced in. The walls and ceiling were a pale blue. Tinted wisps of clouds drifted across the ceiling. Sort of charming.

The furniture was a deep cherry, with a bedsponge platform in a rounded rectangle and smooth curved sides. The headboard was a simple half circle. There were tables on each side of the bed and simple white lamps.

"Looks great." Garrett put enthusiasm in his voice.

"Thank you."

Rusby mewed impatiently. *I want to jump on the bedsponge.*

"No," Garrett said. He reached into his pocket and took out a chewy treat that would keep the kitten occupied for a while.

An idea occurred to him. "Say, TQ," he began casually. "Do you still have that mural on the wall? I liked it." The only thing besides Artemisia he remembered with fondness. And he felt a buzzing hesitation from TQ.

"No," the actor's voice said aloud, with a hint of regret. "It was decommissioned, as requested by the artist and the provider of the images." A more cheerful tone. "It was made especially for you."

"And I thank you for it again," Garrett said, though his ears pricked up at TQ's wording. "You have the artist's name?"

"The mural was also an experiment by GreatMistrys Avellana

Hazel. Though we did not activate the option, it could have been three-dimensional."

Garrett grunted, disappointed. No way he could afford a mural by Avellana Hazel, an artist from the FirstFamilies.

"TQ." Now his own tones were soft. "Did you provide enough data to give Artemisia an alibi for the murder?"

"They question *me*!" TQ thundered. "If they question me, they will question the honor and verity of every Residence."

"I guess so."

"I will speak to my . . . colleagues."

"They *are* colleagues, TQ."

"I am still almost the youngest. But the other Residences will not be pleased. As I understand the time of the death of the Black Magic Cultist, you and Artemisia had been drugged and were sleeping."

"That's true."

"I monitored your sleep patterns because she objected to the soporific."

"Monitored?"

"I have minute-by-minute graphs of your breathing and REM cycles."

"That should do it." His breath eased out. Artemisia was safe. Since he didn't know where or from what TQ was watching him, Garrett bowed in a circle to the House. "Thank you."

"Are you going to claim your HeartMate?" TQ asked, again in weighty tones.

"I think so."

TQ sighed. "It is good that you came to your senses."

Garrett found his jaw clenching, his contrary nature irritated at all the trouble this whole HeartMate thing had caused him, his own roiling emotions on the subject.

And TQ continued on, "Though I have witnessed the fact that the bond between HeartMates—even before the sexual HeartBond is in place—remains intact despite the avoidance of one of the participants. You would have all your lives to claim her."

Garrett's eyes widened. He wouldn't. Artemisia had made it clear she wanted a husband and children, and soon.

Made him think—and feel—more. Fear and dread of what he had done mixed confusingly with a hopeful image of making those children with her.

Yes, he'd wanted children. Yes, he'd be terrified for their fates.

"Your respiration has increased and your body is perspiring. Is something wrong?" asked TQ.

"No," Garrett denied.

"You are not truthful, but I will not press."

"Thank you for reassuring me about Artemisia's alibi." Garrett changed the subject. "I have appointments I must keep. I wish you well."

Garrett and Rusby had reached the public carrier plinth when he received a scry from the guard station. Since there was no one waiting with them, he took the call.

"We checked out the old airship landing area," Berberis said.

Milkweed took up the story. "Spoke to a couple of pilots. One recalls bringing a passenger up from Gael City. Guy approached him, saying he was an old guildman and needed a lift. Offered a little gilt, but our pilot was feeling generous, and the man helped him with the checklist and knew what he was doing."

Berberis said, "So the pilot let the man travel up. Said he'd thought there was something familiar about him, but couldn't figure it out, and the guy didn't talk much on the flight."

Milkweed grimaced. "Turns out the pilot had worked for Eryngo a while back before he started his own courier service. He said that now that he thought about it, the man looked like old Eryngo."

"And if he'd known it was Modoc, he'd have pushed the fligger out of the ship," Berberis ended.

"Thank you, that confirms my info."

Berberis grunted, eyes keen. "You've got good informants. I'd heard you had that—but now you've proven it."

"Thanks again," Garrett said and ended the scry.

Rusby swallowed his chew and said conversationally, *I did not see My mother at the Turquoise House.*

Garrett hadn't even thought of that.

"Does that bother you?"

She is a good dam for a Cat. But My life is with humans now. My FamMan and FamWoman.

Another deep breath for Garrett as he contemplated the fact that Artemisia would be a wonderful mother.

And he couldn't get over that it seemed she had already moved on from him.

Evening was finally falling and his feet—and heart—itched. He didn't want to return to MidClass Lodge. Or his office. He was too unsettled—hadn't been like this since—well, maybe never.

So he went to a friend, Laev T'Hawthorn.

They sat in Laev's study and discussed the murder case, Laev watching him with a penetrating gaze. Rusby was stretched out on the arched back of Garrett's wing chair, and Laev's FamCat, a long-haired black named Brazos, slept on a pillowed cat tree.

Finally the GreatLord said, "What's bothering you?"

Garrett stood, walked to the bare fireplace, then to windows looking out on a grassyard that had been tended for centuries. He turned to his friend with a grimace. "I made a bad mistake."

He heard Laev's breath. The man tapped his fingertips together. "I can probably fix any mistake that you've made. Run through all your gilt already?"

"No!"

"Falsify any data in the Iasc experiment?"

Garrett's face set in the new lines he'd developed with the ordeal. "Of course not. Sick. Nothing during that whole fliggering project was within my control."

"Tough. Commit any crimes?"

His shoulders tensed. "No crime, but I broke a big law."

Laev's brows went high as if in disbelief. "Which law?"

"I told my HeartMate we were HeartMates."

"You finally found your HeartMate—" Laev began to grin, then frowned as he processed the rest of Garrett's sentence.

"You did *what*?" Laev asked.

Garrett didn't think he'd ever seen the man so surprised. His mouth had fallen open. "You heard me," Garrett grumbled.

Laev's sucked-in breath was easily heard. "Who?" he rasped.

"Artemisia Mugwort."

Again Laev's jaw dropped. His Adam's apple bobbed as he swallowed, then snapped his teeth shut. "Fliggering Cave of the Dark Goddess," Laev said.

Garrett didn't think he'd heard the man curse before. Not something a sophisticated GreatLord did. Garrett's insides tensed as his nose whiffed danger. Looking at the man from under lowered eyelids, Garrett slid into a chair and kept his lounge casual.

Laev straightened in his own chair, not looking cool at all, as if Artemisia Mugwort was someone special to him. But Laev was HeartBonded to his wife, Camellia. Garrett searched his memory for anything that Laev might have said and remembered that Laev had indicated that he knew her. Mistake on Garrett's part, talking about her. "Didn't know you were such a stickler for the rules."

"It's a pretty big law you broke," Laev said crisply.

Garrett stretched his muscles. He was bigger than Laev, could move as fast, and was a better fighter than the lord with everything other than blazers. "What's Artemisia Mugwort to you?"

Twenty-four

❦

Artemisia Mugwort saved my woman's life," Laev T'Hawthorn said, scowling at Garrett.

Uh-oh.

Reaching out to a blue green perscry on the table next to the chair, Laev took it and ordered, "Scry Artemisia Mugwort."

Worse and worse.

"Artemisia here," she said.

Garrett's heart gave a hard thud in his chest at the sight of her. She wore fancy braids and a black evening dress of the latest style with a square neckline that showed the tops of her full breasts. His cock stirred. Dammit!

"Greetyou, T'Hawthorn," Artemisia said politely. She seemed to be sitting in a booth in an expensive club. The wallpaper appeared to be silkeen, the cushion behind her blue leather. "What can I do for you?" she asked.

That was Artemisia, always offering to help without thinking of the cost.

"Are you alone?" Laev asked.

Her pretty arched brows rose. "For the moment, but I'm not sure how long I will be."

"End the call when necessary," Laev said. "Garrett Primross just told me that he broke the law by informing you that you and he are HeartMates."

She flushed . . . all the way down to her neckline and Garrett noted that her breasts rose and fell with ragged breaths.

"What do you want me to do to him?" Laev asked.

"You're friends. I don't want you to hurt your friend."

Laev smiled over the scry at Garrett, an arrogant FirstFamily GreatLord smile. Garrett sat straight.

"I take some things very seriously," Laev said, then, "Your father can't be happy with this."

Which had Garrett thinking about the puzzle he wouldn't let nag at him again, Artemisia's Family and her home—though the information that her father was an ex-judge spurted through his brain. The elder Mugwort would not approve of Garrett's actions.

Artemisia's lips firmed. She lifted her chin. "My father doesn't know about this. I prefer he doesn't find out."

"What do you want me to do to Garrett?" Laev repeated.

Garrett was beginning to sweat. He'd misjudged the Noble. Stup to think Laev was his friend first, would stand by him no matter what, even if Garrett was in the wrong. Stup!

Artemisia's eyes went distant for a moment. "My . . . gallant . . . has arrived. I thank you for your interest, GreatLord T'Hawthorn, but I want you to do nothing to GentleSir Primross. Let this matter go."

"I'm not sure—" Laev began but stopped as a big man entered the picture, walking like a fighter.

"Barton Clover," said the guy. "Very pleased to meet you, Gentle-Lady Mugwort."

Artemisia waved her fingers and Laev's perscry went dark.

Garrett found himself on his feet as he'd strained to look at the couple. Now he forced his hands from fisting, and his breathing regular. Anger burned in his belly and hurt pulsed in his heart.

He bowed formally to Laev, as a Commoner would to a Great-Lord. "I am sorry that I have inflicted my presence upon you."

"Don't look now, but you have that reverse prejudice attitude running again," Laev said.

Garrett flexed his jaw to keep words from spurting out.

"I understand you want my support," Laev said. "But the fact is, you're tough and you can take care of yourself. You're set for life." He raised a hand. "Due to your own generosity, compassion, and efforts."

Garrett snarled.

"But Artemisia Mugwort's place at Primary HealingHall is shaky. Furthermore, I don't believe in hurting women."

That was a damn insult, and stung all the more because Garrett *had* hurt Artemisia. But he couldn't let the slur pass. "Is that so? You hurt Camellia plenty." Garrett wasn't going to point out that Laev had also hurt his first wife. Though that woman had brought any hurt from Laev down on herself with her dishonorable behavior. "Not to mention the fact that you, of all people, know what it is to make a damn mistake."

Laev's face set. "I can't believe you brought that up. And I'm just doing you a favor here, handling this myself and discreetly, instead of reporting you to the guards or judges or any of the councils." He stood before the door. Garrett bumped him out of the way, was glad when he saw the return push and evaded and turned to work off some of his irritation.

FIGHT! Rusby shrieked in glee and launched himself off the top of the chair onto Brazos, who was sleeping on the plush stand.

Foolish of the kitten. Like a Commoner attacking a GreatLord.

Yowls split the air.

Garrett dodged a fist to his face, hit Laev's gut with his shoulder, and took the lord down, rolled with him.

Laev nearly slipped from his hold when the door slammed open and Camellia D'Hawthorn and her FamCat, Mica, rushed through. From the corner of his eye, Laev saw the female cat wallop Rusby with a paw and send him rolling.

Water came out of nowhere and dumped on him and Laev,

caught all three of the cats, who shrieked so that Garrett thought he'd go deaf.

"Quiet! And stop everything!" Camellia shouted.

Laev grabbed his HeartMate and, with glinting eyes and a wide grin, yanked her against his sopping form.

"You stup!" she cried.

Garrett took a squishy step toward Laev, got his temper under control, and halted.

Camellia glared at him. "I didn't expect this of you."

He shrugged.

She looked at her husband. "I suppose you won't tell me what you're fighting about."

Laev looked innocent. He didn't do too badly.

After sniffing loudly, Camellia kissed the side of Laev's jaw and said a drying spell on herself as she walked to the door. As she went out, she threw a glance over her shoulder at Garrett. "You're invited to dinner."

"Thanks."

As she closed the door, Laev said an intricate verse of a house-keeping spell that sucked the water from the room, his and Garrett's clothes, and even their hair. Garrett was still annoyed, but said, "Good job."

"Getting better at it," Laev said. He smiled, cheeks creasing. "Artemisia looked incredible, didn't she?" He raised his brows.

"Didn't notice."

"Liar."

Yes, he was, but the anger and guilt at himself for hurting her and irritation at her for being with another man sizzled back through him. The scuffle with Laev had relieved his feelings a little, but had been all too brief.

They were no sooner seated at the table with a bowl of chilled soup and a large salad and thick slices of bread than Laev shot Garrett a bland look and remarked to his HeartMate, "I understand one of your friends has seriously begun looking for a good husband."

Camellia D'Hawthorn, whose thoughts had appeared to be distant, perked up and straightened in her chair. "Who?" Without awaiting an answer, she continued, "Not Tiana—she still has hopes of her HeartMate looking for her—and Glyssa will be heading out to find *hers* soon enough, I think."

"Artemisia," Laev said, lifting his glass of wine and sipping.

"Oh, that's good!" Camellia said.

Though the cushion was plump under his ass, Garrett shifted in his seat. "Gossip at the dinner table?" he grated.

Camellia laughed. "What, you expected more of Nobles? I'll have you know that one of the main topics of conversation with the FirstFamilies is rampant rumor, like for everyone else."

Laev looked at Garrett. "Just garnering information."

"Nope." Camellia shook her head. "Gossip. Hmm." She crunched on a bit of raw vegetable. "I'll think about who might be a good man for her. Someone gentle and thoughtful, with a good sense of humor, like her father."

Laev laughed.

And Garrett tried not to wonder if Artemisia was enjoying Barton Clover's company.

*A*rtemisia *smiled brilliantly at Barton Clover.*

He blinked, appearing a little stunned, then leaned forward and clasped her hands. "You know, lady, we Clovers do not have a Healer in the Family yet, and I assure you, we value those."

His hands were warm, his blue gaze intent, and he was charming enough that she was able to push the other man to the back of her mind.

She was pleasantly surprised and attracted to the man . . . probably because he was the same general type as her Heart—as Garrett Primross. A big man, working in a very physical profession as the chief of security for the Clovers. He seemed much more easygoing than Garrett, but, like that other man, there were shadows of secrets in his eyes. That appealed, too, where it might not have before . . .

She had secrets of her own and she now viewed those who had them as having hidden depths. A completely open man—a man like she'd wanted before—no longer seemed to be enough.

Their conversation was easy, and after dinner, as she teleported to the nearest pad to BalmHeal estate, she assured herself that his brief kiss *had* given her a tingle. Maybe two.

Though the evening with Barton had been good, she knew they couldn't get serious about marrying. He was the head of security for the Clover Family and their compound. He wouldn't be available to live where she wanted.

But it wouldn't hurt to make a friend of him; he'd flirted but she thought he'd already come to the same conclusion—that she would be a good friend, maybe a sometime lover, but not a wife. She didn't know if he had a HeartMate and wouldn't ask.

Still, as emotionally injured as she was, he'd be a good man to accept as a gallant and lover. *He'd* looked at her with appreciation, *he* wouldn't reject her—not for what she wanted. A solid man, a shrewd man, like Garrett. But a man with an easier surface manner and not one interested in a deeper relationship with her. That would ease her pain until she found a man she could forge a strong life with.

That night she let Randa out to roam the estate. Her FamRaccoon was excited to range her new home. And while her Fam was gone, Artemisia decided to do something none of the Mugworts had ever contemplated—ask BalmHeal Residence directly about future mates for herself and Tiana. A daring move, and she didn't like risk, but she needed the information to craft her plans.

She waited until deep in the night, near the dreaded hour of TransitionBell, and she knew that the rest of her Family was asleep and would not wake. She drew in a large breath. "BalmHeal Residence?"

"Yes, Artemisia?" it asked, as it always did. But she heard the smugness in its tone, as always. The Residence liked their dark night chats. She wouldn't let it know that she'd had nightly conversations with the Turquoise House. Her Residence was touchy, with oversensitized feelings.

"I've decided it's time I wed." She held her breath but didn't think the Residence would ask about HeartMates.

"That's good. You are in your best childbearing years."

Her breath expelled on a hiss and a wince, but she couldn't contradict. "Yes," she said steadily. "I thought I'd ask what sort of man you would like to live here with us."

There was a loud creak of surprise from the rafters. "Another inhabitant for me?"

"My parents would not like to be separated." She swallowed. "And I am determined to have a good marriage, as they do. That means my husband will need to live here."

The low-level humming vibration that came when the Residence was in deep thought permeated the room. She scooted around on her bedsponge, plumping up her pillows and arranging them and the comforter until she had her regular little nest. The smell of her pillow that TQ had decontaminated wasn't quite right. Not that she'd ever tell the Turquoise House that.

She didn't hurry BalmHeal; patience was always a boon with the entity. Instead she looked up at the ceiling and whispered the spell that made the roof transparent so she could see the stars. It was an old, old spell and one she had to funnel energy into every month—and it worked only on this particular room, which is why she'd chosen the chamber so many years ago. She loved the night sky, and she especially loved this view. It seemed as if a spiral galaxy was right overhead, glittering white and red and blue and black when the twinmoons were new.

The sky had been beautiful at the Turquoise House, too, but she hadn't dared leave Garrett during TransitionBell—the time when most souls left their bodies to die and cycle on the wheel of stars for the next reincarnation. And she shunted that thought—the image of his tortured and sweating body—aside. Just as well that she'd known him longer as a patient than not.

"I missed the sky," she murmured, soothing herself as well as the Residence. "The Turquoise House is surrounded by city and there is too much light around to see all the stars I can view from here."

"Mmm." The vibration had risen to a small hum, signaling that the Residence would talk . . . in the next few minutes.

Artemisia watched as the faint light from the crescent twinmoon Eire silvered the edge of the roof. The depth of the sky, the brilliance of the galaxies, the sliver of moonlight eased the tightness of her body. This was unchanging, unwavering, something she could count on forever.

The stars had been the same when title and home and wealth had been stripped from her Family. The stars hadn't moved when she suffered through Passage in the rental rooms, suppressing it as much as she could, trying to hurry through it, trying to be quiet. And when her Family had accepted being caretakers of the secret sanctuary, the stars had been there, this room with the panorama had been here, to comfort her.

She would survive the huge and horrible ache in her life right now, and the night sky would help by its pure and stable infinity.

"I have thought on your question, dear," said BalmHeal Residence. "And I would like a big, athletic man."

Artemisia's heart twinged and her eyes overflowed with sudden tears. She rubbed them away on her pillow, yanked a softleaf from a packet on the table and blew her nose, then blinked hard to clear the smears of stars back to white diamonds. "Why?"

"He should be a gardener and a landscaper, able to work outside. A builder would be good. And a FirstFamily Nobleman."

Her breath stuck in her throat as she gasped a laugh. "All of that."

"Yes. I will review the FirstFamilies for the proper person. I like your father's gentleness. A quiet man would also be good."

Obviously she'd asked the wrong question of the wrong person. On the other hand, she foresaw that BalmHeal Residence would spend much time on the matter. She only hoped that it wouldn't insist on her marrying its choice.

Clearing her throat, she said, "When we have a candidate, we should bring him here so you could check him out."

"We must ensure he will not give away our secret!" The Residence sounded upset.

"That's true. You might have to do some background research on the men before they visit." She blew her nose again, wiggled around until her pillows were right, and began to sink into a pre-sleep meditation.

"They must be honorable!" the Residence insisted.

Her lips curved. "Like we are," she said, closing her eyes.

"Yes." There was a thump. "My Mugwort Family is honorable."

Wistfulness rose like a mist within her. Not many people she knew truly believed that the Mugworts were honorable.

She was tugged from falling into the softness of sleep by a twist of anxiety at what she had to do in the morning—revisit the past that she wanted to leave behind. Get involved in the mess of retribution and murder. She had no doubt that in the days to come, she'd have to defend her Family's honor.

And she'd probably see Garrett in the morning regarding the case, but she'd already decided to shield herself from him. She could do that, pretend he was nothing to her . . . until it was true, until the thread between them withered from lack of use. Until she found someone else to love and wed and have children with.

Her face was cool from the dampness of tears when she finally fell asleep.

As usual, *Garrett walked around the long rectangular inner courtyard* of MidClass Lodge. The heat of the day was fading and there were others strolling, or sitting on benches—those who liked people in the conversational groupings of chairs or people more solitary like him, sitting alone on benches in the garden.

And walking with Rusby on his shoulder was a pain. Everyone who passed had to comment and speak to Garrett or try to talk to the Fam. Rusby's mental shout gave Garrett a headache. The women cooed.

When dark had fallen and most folk had retreated into the building, leaving those whose cycles better fit the night, Garrett stopped by the gate to the beach. He noted that the greeniron would be use-less in keeping Rusby in the yard. The kitten could slip under the thing, or between the simple, upright spears. Garrett idly confirmed that this wasn't the gate in his dreams.

"Ssst!" came from the dark beyond the gate, along with, *It is Black-and-White and I have news of your altar man.*

Garrett's heart jumped. He scrutinized the shadows beyond the gate but didn't see the cat, only smelled fish and fur-with-a-hint-of-salt-spray.

Not news of the raccoons? he asked.

The kits were ready to wean and all scattered. Not a group any-more.

That was a little sad . . . no, disappointing.

We are all looking for each of them, Black-and-White added vir-tuously. Garrett thought he might be cleaning grains of sand from between his pads.

All right, Garrett projected. He turned and propped his shoul-ders against the redbrick wall next to the gate. Rusby jumped down and went to sniff at the portal. He gave Garrett a dirty look when he realized Garrett had bespelled all openings of the gate against the kitten. Though Rusby could and did touch noses with Black-and-White, who had slipped through the bars.

Tail waving, Black-and-White sauntered up the flagstone path to one of the doors. Narrowing his eyes, Garrett saw bowls there, a new deal. Huh. Someone must have figured out that feral animals with Fam potential were frequenting the courtyard. He wondered if whoever put the bowls out was looking for a Fam. And whether management knew and/or approved.

What of the background check on the altar man? Garrett called mentally.

All ferals have talked. Even dogs. Even foxes. The cat sniffed. *Even housefluffs. We have agreed. No bad stuff. We give the altar man a rating of Very Good Man.*

Garrett wanted to cuss, but didn't. Of course that was nice to know. Artemisia deserved a very good man. She didn't deserve Garrett and his problems, his stupidity in hanging on to the past. His cowardice.

Rusby nipped him on the ankle. Since Garrett wasn't wearing boots, that hurt.

"Dammit!" At least he could swear at that. He flung out a hand and pulled the kitten into his palm fast with Flair.

Wheeee! Rusby said.

"Let's head on in," Garrett said.

*G*arrett *needed his woman. Deep and dark in sleep, he knew if she* wasn't near, he'd have wrenching nightmares again. And he knew pain awaited when he woke . . . some sort of emotional pain that was worse than the physical. In his experience, physical pain didn't last as long as heart hurts.

She'd been comfortingly close lately, but now when he reached for her through their bond, it was tiny. He didn't like that. He had to stretch more to find her, search.

She should not be so far away; why had he allowed it?

But he would always be able to find her. She lived in the back of his mind, had since he was seventeen, even when he'd had Dinni.

Dinni was the past and long gone, had not fit him as well as this woman. His HeartMate. He, the primal man, knew her.

So he broke free from the mind's constraints and *reached* for her.

Twenty-five

Garrett gave a satisfied hum when he found his HeartMate. Not sleeping in his bed, pity. But sleeping.

Heat flooded him and he was hard and hungry for her. He didn't remember making love to her in his Passage Flair-freeing quests and he *needed*.

He flung the coverlet off her, slipped next to her. He sensed more than saw her pearly skin, and as he curved his hand around her full breast, felt the weight, he recalled her nipple was light pink until it puckered and flushed with his touch—there!

She rolled to him, wrapped her arms around him. So good! Being held filled his inner heart-canyons of deep need. Her hands ran along his back and he shuddered at the tactile memory.

Yes, they'd danced this coming together before, long, long ago.

And her scent rose to him . . . the fragrance of her skin, and even better, the blossoming scent of her arousal. To speed things up—he was so hard he was hurting and he yearned to slide into wet warmth—he set his fingers on her sex. Another thing so easily remembered, how she liked to be touched, the form of her. The dampness.

Her small moaning whimpers of passion that had his breath coming uneven.

She nibbled along his jaw.

He stroked her, teasing her. Teasing himself until need became unbearable.

Until her hands bit into his shoulders and she drew him over her and her body was soft and cradling under him and her hips tilted and he slid into her—so gooood!—and then they were rushing, groaning, her muscles tensile under her soft skin where his hands curved over her bottom—fine, *fine* ass. And they rose together and spun into the universe of sparkling stars and endless night and he exploded with her like stars.

And they settled down together, sparks from fireworks, and he became aware of night birds calling outside an open window and the smell of verdant greenness and secrets.

So soft under him. Long tendrils of her silky hair clinging to his face. Her heart beat hard and in tune with his. Made for him. His.

Wonderful, the best.

What the hell do you think you are doing! Her angry voice shattered his peace. His heart shrank and his mind struggled to understand.

He was flung back into his own bed, his own room. The smell of kitten and sound of soft snoring was sensed, then lost as her fury thundered along their bond—their luscious bond that was shrinking to a taut, minuscule fiber.

Wha'? Wha'? Artemisia.

HOW DARE YOU. YOU ARE THE LOWEST OF THE LOW. HAVE YOU NO HONOR?

"What!"

But she wasn't listening. His head pounded as he heard the gigantic echo of a door slamming shut.

Panting raggedly, he sat up and put his head in his hands. Then became aware of his own odor. Physically, he hadn't been with the woman, despite all the sensations.

Rusby snuffled. Garrett could imagine kitten comments on the smell of sexual release and the state of the linens. Discretion wasn't cowardly. Not in the middle of the night. So, he whispered a tiny spell to keep the kitten asleep while he stripped and remade the bed.

When he stood, he moved like an old man, muscles creaking worse than after he'd survived the Iasc sickness for the second time . . . a couple of nights ago.

He knew the reason. His heart—and his body—wanted Artemisia, despite the thorns of the past embedded in his brain, and the fear of loss screaming inside him. He'd never thought that he'd been a man who gave in to fear. He was wrong. He'd let fear eat him alive.

He'd let his fear rule his thoughts enough that he'd been a complete idiot and had made a terrible mistake.

He *did* want Artemisia.

Lifting Rusby to an empty space atop his bureau, he grabbed the sheets and yanked them from the bed, stalked to the cleanser in the waterfall room, and shoved them in. Got clean ones. Not as smooth as those he'd slept on at TQ or sensed at Artemisia's. Harsh in comparison.

He could afford better, now. The past was truly past.

Time to also acknowledge that Dinni had been right in not wedding him because he had a HeartMate—and Artemisia had been right when she spoke of the *girl* that he'd loved. Childhood sweethearts, first lovers. All that was good and real and right.

He had a HeartMate who would fit him better, who he'd ignored because he'd wanted what *he* wanted, not what was best for him. Dinni had been wise and he'd refused to see that. Just because she'd ended their relationship first? Before he was ready to let go?

All right. Dinni's timing had sucked, and as a practitioner of sleight of hand, he knew excellent timing was essential.

His own timing had sucked, too. Namely discovering that he truly, mind deep, heart deep, bone deep, wanted his HeartMate, Artemisia Mugwort—a courageous and compassionate and *strong* woman. After he'd already rejected her.

He wondered how soon she'd forgive him. What he'd have to do. He couldn't sit back and wait, the woman—*his* woman—was meeting other men to check them out as a husband and father!

Oh, yeah, that hurt. That idea damn well sliced him in two. Pain enough for him to stagger as if the linens he held were massive boulders.

He'd have to figure out how to prove himself to Artemisia, but he'd make sure he was a part of her life as much as he possibly could. At least the liaison job would keep them together, and give him time to plan how to court her.

He made the fliggering bed, took a damn shower, and slipped under a sheet. Then he chewed a sleep-inducing pill and let sleep drag him under. The herbs worked. An image came of the sacred grove, then the rusty gates behind which his dream garden beckoned with lush growth and a Healing pool.

He recalled that Artemisia lived near Healing pools. His last thoughts were idle wonderings about Artemisia's home and the itch of curiosity settled under his skin. He would find out.

*A*rtemisia *awoke a septhour before WorkBell at the sound of dawn* songbirds singing outside her window. She wanted to sleep more, lounge in bed after the intense few days . . . and, all right, pull the covers over her head and forget the deep wound inside her. Forget that her HeartMate had visited her in her dreams. She *would not* let him spoil her for someone else.

But more than anger and the sensations of sex with Garrett weighed on her emotions. There was lost hope of a true HeartMate marriage. Not to mention murder, and the discovery of the murder weapon, and how her Family was being implicated again.

She had to take the knife to the guards. And she and Randa had an appointment with Danith D'Ash.

Whoosh. Flop.

Rising to sit, she followed the sound . . . and her mouth opened in surprise as she watched a Fam opening swish back and forth in the bedroom door. Randa waddled toward her, and she let out a sigh. She had a Fam, another blessing.

Randa hooked her claws on the long comforter that draped over the elevated bedsponge and climbed up. *Greetyou, FamWoman.* The raccoon's muzzle lifted and her mouth stretched in a smile, showing little pointy teeth. She hurried over to Artemisia, stopped to sit and clasp her paws together as she stared at Artemisia's body under the covers.

Artemisia patted her lap. "Come on."

Randa ran up her body and snuffled under Artemisia's chin, leaving a slight wet smear. *Love you, FamWoman!*

"I love you, too."

"I am pleased that you are here, Randa," said the Residence.

Yes! I am! And I will be a good Fam. I will no longer be a feral 'coon. I will stay on the estate. There is no reason to go outside the walls. I am home.

Artemisia smiled, and looking into Randa's eyes, she said, "Yes, you are. But we're still going to D'Ash to make sure all is well with you." Artemisia dressed quickly in one of her best work tunics and tops.

Her father knocked at her door, then opened it. He held a simple square wooden box. His face was pale, his expression weary. "I studied the knife. It is definitely a cross-folk altar knife, crafted by one of their more famous artists."

"Valuable?"

"Valuable enough for me to extrapolate that it came from a private chapel of a Noble cross-folk Family."

One that had been luckier than the Mugworts.

Her father continued, "Or one of the chapels in their main church." He shrugged, offered her the box.

Though he'd shielded it to keep the vitriolic negativity within, she still took it gingerly.

"And, Artemisia"—his green gaze, the same color eyes as her

own, met hers in a heavy, straight look—"the knife was created after the Black Magic Cult murders, so it is unlikely that the murdered man had it in his possession."

"You mean that he used such cross-folk objects to point the authorities at us long ago, but didn't have this knife then."

Her father smiled slightly. "I've always been proud of your intellect."

She didn't feel so smart for letting her HeartMate have dream sex with her, letting him hurt her. She refrained from rubbing her chest over her heart. "Thank you." She concentrated on the murder weapon, not really recalling what a regular altar knife looked like. "Randa and I are leaving now for Danith D'Ash's office."

Randa whimpered.

"You'll be fine," Artemisia said. She kissed her father's cheek and accepted his hug before walking into the corridor and checking to see that Randa followed.

Artemisia sensed that her sister, Tiana, had left for the day, and a small *pop* told her that her father had teleported away.

At the northeast side door, she paused. "I'll see you later, Residence," she said.

"Yes. I am studying the rosters of the FirstFamilies for a good man for you."

Artemisia's mouth dried, then she swallowed. "All those First-Family Nobles are extremely powerful; do you think they'd be satisfied here—and being bespelled never to speak of you?"

"All FirstFamilies keep secrets," BalmHeal said absently.

"Uh-huh."

"Anyone would be honored to live here with us," the Residence said. "Preliminary research is favorable for the Blackthorn men, sons of a cadet branch who were brought into the Family and took that name."

Artemisia figured she wouldn't be able to talk the Residence out of his newest plan right now. "I *do* insist that the man I marry be someone I can love."

"You can love a man who is Noble as much as one who is not," the Residence retorted.

"See you later," Artemisia grumbled.

"I love you, Artemisia," BalmHeal Residence said.

"I love you, too." But it didn't stop her from being exasperated with the Residence. She and Randa walked to the area that held the secondary Healing pools. The estate had two sets of natural Healing hot springs and a trio of warm swimming pools. Near the secondary pools were the chapels—the small round Temples, one open-air and one enclosed, and a small building that Artemisia's mother used for her worship. It was an equal-armed cross with a tiny dome in the center painted yellow on the outside and deep blue and silver on the inside.

About once a year, the whole Family celebrated a ritual with her . . . but for a long time, Tiana and their father had crafted more spiritual and less Lady-and-Lord-centric rituals that the whole Family would participate in. Occasionally, they included both the cross-folk quadri-spirited god and the Lady and Lord in overlapping rituals.

Theirs was an eclectic household, and the flexibility of spirituality and religion had helped Tiana in her career since she became accustomed to crafting unique and creative rituals. As for Artemisia, she took great comfort in the old rituals of Celta, in the belief of a dual and loving Pair—a Lady and Lord.

Randa walked with her but occasionally coursed into the underbrush. They didn't speak to each other mentally, were quiet together, but the bond between them hummed with affection and that was nice.

Yet when she reached the door of her mother's chapel, she experienced the serenity that permeated this equally sacred place. Her ruffled emotions—from sex with Garrett and the whole throbbing hurt of the last few days—were soothed.

Until she thought of the prejudice and intolerance of people for those who were different. Like Garrett's distrust of Nobles.

She had to stand and breathe deeply as she marshaled her feelings before she entered the holy place.

Hadn't their ancestors left Earth because they were persecuted for their psi power? Why couldn't people learn from history?

She stood and let the sounds of nature, the sun filtering through the tall trees, soothe her spirit. Then she left the knife box outside the building, put her hands together, fingers upright, and bowed to the door.

Once in, she bowed again at the huge sculpture of a square cross edged in gold and filled with mosaic and grouted in gold in the center of the chapel.

Again she let her breath filter from her as she soaked up the peace. There was the lingering scent of incense, but no pylor—the type that had played such a large role in the Black Magic Cult murders and was found in their home. As if most other Nobles, cross-folk or not, didn't have pylor incense. The sticks and cones had been standard once. No more.

There were four large square windows set high in the walls, all stained glass and showing a child to aged man in a boat on a journey. The rich colors always made her catch her breath. Right now the sun was illuminating the man-in-his-prime's terror as the boat rushed to the waterfall.

No, she wouldn't feel that, the uneasiness that had settled along her nerves. Another big breath, and it was good to recall that everyone in this voyage of life had terrible times. Life was not smooth . . . though she also wished that she was in a round Celtan Temple that suited her more than this chapel. But she'd wanted to check out the knife on the altar.

So she walked up to the draped rectangular table and studied the implements set upon it. Celtan altars usually had two knives, a blunt one for use spiritually and a sharp one used for cutting candles, trimming wicks, and any other sort of necessary mundane actions. The cross-folk used only one knife for everything.

Artemisia stared a moment before she recalled the knife was part of one of the four equal-armed square crosses. Three of the crosses were solid, but when she peered closely at the second on the left, she could see a joint where one arm of the cross could be removed to reveal a blade. The opposite arm would be the hilt, and the other two arms perpendicular, like a rough hand guard. This was made of rounded dowel-like wood with Celtic knot carving.

Staring at it and comparing it to the knife she'd left outside the chapel, she understood something else.

There was a sheath for the murder knife that would match the other arms of the cross.

It was missing, but when it was found, it would point to the murderer.

*G*arrett walked, with Rusby on his shoulder, from his apartment in MidClass Lodge to his office. He half listened to the kitten's mental chatter-comments on the world around them.

He'd made things worse with Artemisia. Now he'd have to work hard to insert himself into her life.

He recalled intimately how her body fit his, how their hearts pulsed together when they made love. No way he'd forget that. It was ingrained in every molecule of his being, and particularly settled in his cock. Damned hard to ignore.

Unwillingly, he stopped in front of a jewelry shop that had a display of marriage armbands. He liked the glisten metal ones that were shiny and shot off rainbow-colored light. They also had a subtle and intricate engraving of lines that flowed into each other in a never-ending pattern, symbolizing the HeartMate bond. And each band had a ring of small cabochon emeralds, the color of Artemisia's eyes when she was in a passion, around the wrist. They both had a large oval stone also of dark green crystal, though he didn't know what the jewel was.

Then he realized exactly what he was doing. Sweat trickled down his spine and his vision blurred.

Yeah, he was a coward. He didn't want to lose another woman. Didn't want to have to see another child dead.

Yet if something bad happened to Artemisia, Lord and Lady forefend, he would lose her anyway, even if she were wed to another man.

And that idea made his gut clamp.

He had little idea on how to court her. He grumped a sigh. Might have to visit his good friend Laev again. Must be a glutton for punishment in the friendship field as well as the arena of HeartMates.

First he had to check on his office—he'd had no new business scrys forwarded to his perscry pebble, but his feral informants would expect to be fed.

He'd sent the word out that he wanted to meet all of them—all species—in Apollopa Park at NoonBell. With everyone looking for them, the small familial group of raccoons would be found.

Garrett had heard from Captain Winterberry that the councils of Celta had put pressure on the Eryngo Family to hold a memorial for their murdered son that afternoon.

The Captain of the guard had been tight-lipped. No matter how much Winterberry had disliked being *the* guardsman the FirstFamilies requested when they were involved in any kind of case, he wasn't happy at handing Garrett the lead on this one. Garrett couldn't blame him and didn't hold it against the guy.

And here We are at the office! Rusby nipped Garrett's ear. *Let Me down!*

"You don't want to lord it over all the other cats from my shoulder?"

I will sit on the back stoop.

Garrett didn't think that was the right strategic move in showing a tiny FamCat's superiority over tough feral informants, but shrugged and placed Rusby on the small back porch.

Black-and-White greeted Garrett. *We have told some dogs and the foxes and others that you wish a meeting at Apollopa Park at NoonBell.*

"Thank you." Garrett undid the spellshields, went through the back door, the hallway, and into the storage room. The building smelled like mildew again. He wondered if he should let the landlord know or move to somewhere a little more upscale.

As he poured food into the trough, he sent a mental comment to Black-and-White. *I am thinking about moving my office.*

As he munched, Black-and-White said telepathically, *We would like the Turquoise House fine.*

Not going to be the Turquoise House; that is for a home. And not his.

Now Black-and-White stared at him. *We do not like the alleys as much as we like brush and greenways. Perhaps you could make the old Temple at Apollopa Park an office.* The last was said slyly, as if the cat was aware that the priest, Leger Cinchona, seemed to be restoring it.

"No," Garrett said aloud. He put away the supplies and locked up again. "But I'll take your preferences under advisement."

You are not working today?

"Not inside."

Black-and-White wiggled his whiskers to rid himself of some stray bits of kibble. *We will see you later.*

"Sure," Garrett said. Of course he wouldn't tell the cat that everything other than his HeartMate could wait.

He had to *do something* for Artemisia. Had to prove he wanted and needed her. For more than sex. Would do whatever it took to show her he'd been mistaken.

For the first time in his life, his relationship with a woman was his first priority.

*G*reat*Lady Danith D'Ash*, <u>the</u> animal and *Fam Healer*, cooed and complimented Randa until she preened and allowed the woman to scan and study her as a prime example of a raccoon.

When the examination was done, Artemisia asked to use a private scry cubicle. Randa accompanied Artemisia on her own four paws, stating that the feel of the energy in the floor sparkled on her pads.

The cubicle had a simple counter with an equally simple metal scrybowl that Artemisia wanted to use instead of her own perscry.

With Randa sitting on her lap, she stiffened her spine and scried the main Druida guardhouse and asked for Captain Winterberry, the head of all the guards and the man she and Garrett had spoken with before. Winterberry liaised with the FirstFamilies—and the FirstFamilies would, of course, meddle in this, the case was so scandalous.

He answered her call at once. "What can I do for you, Second-Level Healer?"

"I am scrying about the Black Magic Cultist murder." She took a steadying breath. "I have more information."

His eyes gleamed, then he shook his head. "I'm sorry, but I'm not able to help you." He paused a few seconds. "My HeartMate and my cuz were the only victims who survived, so I am not allowed to work that case." He bared his teeth in a grin and the fire of fury showed in the back of his eyes. Despite the fact that it had been sixteen years, the man looked as if he could be a suspect himself.

Artemisia was afraid that all the other Families who'd lost loved ones would feel the same.

"You should contact Garrett Primross, as he is coordinating the investigation," Winterberry said.

Twenty-six

$\mathcal{G}$ *arrett Primross is the head of the murder investigation!" Artemisia* bit her lip. "But he's a private investigator, not a guard."

Winterberry's gray gaze flattened and he replied with exquisite courtesy, as if his feelings were ruffled, too. "Very true. But the FirstFamilies have confidence in GentleSir Primross and requested he be put in charge of this matter."

And, like always, the FirstFamilies got what they wanted. Had it been less than a week ago that she'd defended those Nobles to Garrett? But that was before she'd been so intimately entangled in their interest in the murder. Now her and Garrett's positions had switched. He was the one the highest Nobles had confidence in and she was the one who didn't trust their motives or actions—reactions—to this matter.

"Do you need GentleSir Primross's personal scry image?"

"Yes, thank you," she said automatically through cold lips. She had hoped to avoid her HeartMate until her feelings were less tender.

Randa cheeped and Winterberry's glance focused on the Fam and his masklike face softened. "Who is that?"

"She is Randa, my FamRaccoon."

Winterberry dipped his head. "A pleasure. Here's Primross's business image." The icon of a golden pyramid appeared.

"Thank you."

The guardsman's mouth thinned and he nodded once more. "I wish I could handle this." His shoulders shifted. "I'll have to wait to get word through official channels. Merry meet."

"No, wait." Artemisia swallowed. "I, uh, have an object that I must bring in. At once. I'll be right there. You can scry GentleSir Primross." She ended the call and leaned her head on her hands, rubbing her scalp for a while.

A knock came at the scry room door. "SecondLevel Healer, are you all right?" asked Gwydion Ash.

She *had* been in the cubicle longer than she'd expected and now she noticed it was stifling. She opened the door with a smile. "Yes, I'm fine."

"Good." The large teen, slightly clumsy in his body, smiled back at her.

"Can you tell me where the main guardhouse of Druida is in relation to here?"

His brows went up and he shook his head. "No, I don't know. But I'll have one of our gliders take you there." Before she could disagree, he hustled away.

She petted Randa, liking her chirruping sound. It was very tempting to keep Randa with her, but Artemisia had no illusions about how the guards would treat a person bringing in a murder weapon a couple of days after the killing.

The whole situation would be tense. She rocked with Randa before speaking mentally to her, *Danith D'Ash wasn't scary.*

No. Randa snuggled.

But the guard station may be.

We will not go. Randa sat up and patted Artemisia's face.

Artemisia sighed. *I must, but you don't need to. Hold still and I will translocate you home.*

I love you. I will help with the 'porting.

Artemisia fixed the image of the teleportation area in her sitting room in her head, the faded colorful pattern of the rug, the cream-colored walls of old silkeen that showed trailing pastel flowers, and projected the scene to Randa.

Randa added her mental image—similar enough that Artemisia was sure that the Fam would have no trouble.

"On three," Artemisia whispered.

"One, Randa 'coon, two, BalmHeal home, and *three*." She pushed her Flair to send Randa to their room, felt her Fam's Flair meld with her own.

I am here!

Another sigh, this of relief, broke from Artemisia's lips. She stood, lifted her chin, and strode with a false smile to the glider outside.

The guards would suspect her, of course. So might Garrett.

*G*arrett found *Artemisia sitting on the edge of a carved wooden bench,* back completely straight and hands folded in her lap. When she saw him, she flinched, then her expressive face went stiff. He didn't like either reaction. He sat down next to her—close—and she tensed.

His teeth hurt from clenching them. She could affect him faster and more than anyone else in his entire life.

Several other guards he'd met previously were there, including Fol Berberis, Rosa Milkweed, and Captain Ilex Winterberry. The Captain sat behind a desk angled across a corner.

"I understand that FirstLevel Healer Ura Heather reported a missing knife from the cross-folk altar in Primary HealingHall right before GentleLady Panax arrived with the item?" Garrett asked.

"My name is Mugwort," his HeartMate said without looking at him.

"That's right," said Rosa Milkweed. Her forehead wrinkled as she glanced at Artemisia and away. Garrett got the gist of that look. Her boss would have stood behind her; the guard respected Artemisia and wasn't sure why Artemisia's superior wasn't supporting her.

Winterberry may have seemed casual, but his penetrating gaze was on Artemisia. "A little odd that of all the places that the knife could have come from, it was the Primary HealingHall chapel."

Artemisia swallowed, wet her lips, then answered. "Unlike many cross-folk chapels, the one at Primary HealingHall is not secured."

Winterberry nodded slowly. "And most cross-folk chapels *are* secured. Especially since the accusations that they were in a conspiracy with the Black Magic Cultists sixteen years ago. Odd how things circle round."

Artemisia's deep breath wasn't audible, but Garrett noted it. She said, "The cross-folk were wrongly implicated sixteen years ago by the press and your current victim. I'm sure they aren't involved now."

"You sound as if you are still angry," Winterberry said. "But then your Family was the one that suffered the most—your home was mobbed, your parents lost their careers. How is your mother, by the way? Is she concerned about this—and how you now seem to be the main . . . target?"

Hopping to her feet, Artemisia went to Winterberry's desk and planted her hands on the gleaming wooden surface. "Naturally my parents are concerned about me. But I have an alibi. I was in quarantine with GentleSir Primross. The Turquoise House has vouched for me."

"And your mother?" Winterberry pressed.

"My mother has not stepped onto the streets of Druida City for many years."

"Interesting phrasing," Winterberry said as Garrett thought the same.

Artemisia stepped back. "My mother isn't in Druida."

But there was a shadow of a lie in Artemisia's voice, and Garrett thought every guard in the room heard it.

Her lips pursed, then flattened, and she swept the room with a glance. "The press whipped up a scared mob, and the Nobles of our rank who envied us our . . . our happy Family life and the status of our careers were the ones who savaged us before. That's far past. As for now, FirstLevel Healer Ura Heather would be concerned about anything missing from Primary HealingHall. It is her purview. Has she accused me of anything?"

"No," Winterberry said.

Artemisia jerked a nod. "As a Family, years ago, we Mugworts didn't appeal to the FirstFamilies Council for an investigation." This time her breath sucked in. "But I have an alibi for the murder and so does my sister, Tiana. She was participating in a vigil in GreatCircle Temple. Neither Mother nor Father were anywhere near Apollopa Park. We will fight this time." She lifted her chin. "I don't know what FirstLevel Healer Ura Heather will say about me, but she is not the only FirstFamily Lady or Lord that we know." Now the truth in her words rang.

Winterberry's lips curved, but his eyes remained steady and serious. "I hear you."

Garrett wasn't lulled. The man was acting pleasantly to Artemisia but didn't believe in her.

Garrett would protect her and keep her close. He said, "The FirstFamilies have their own ideas and ideals, their own viewpoint on matters, and their own standards of behavior."

Rosa Milkweed nodded and snorted, relaxed a bit, as if trying to lessen the tension in the room. "That they do."

Fol Berberis shot a glance at his Captain, then looked down into Artemisia's eyes. "Nobody wants the FirstFamilies meddling in this."

Garrett slid his gaze to Artemisia. "Someone once told me that those greatest Nobles do the best they can for everyone."

Artemisia stiffened even more as the guardswoman laughed. Captain Winterberry raised a brow. At that gesture, Garrett turned to him.

"You have an optimistic friend," Winterberry said. "Though, in general, I have found the highest Nobles to be . . . odd but honorable."

"Uh-huh," Garrett said.

"Really?" Fol Berberis asked.

Winterberry inclined his head. "Yes."

A shrug from both Garrett and Rosa. "Well, you should know."

This time a faint smile passed across the Captain's lips. "I have been on more cases regarding them than I care to think about." The corners of Winterberry's mouth turned up even as his eyes narrowed—evidently he had mixed feelings about something and Garrett figured he'd hear about it.

"I think in the future, they may be considering having a more private consultant than me. Guards have rules that we don't care to bend," Winterberry said.

Icy chill slithered along Garrett's spine. He was all too afraid that Winterberry was right and the new liaison between the guardsmen and the FirstFamilies would be himself. He stood. "Just because they might pay me"—and he'd make sure that he got a good rate from whichever FirstFamily Lord or Lady needed his services—"doesn't mean that I will break laws and bend my own rules, betray my own honor." Though laws were sometimes less important to him than his own rules.

"I didn't mean to imply that you would act less than honorably," Winterberry said.

Garrett noted that the man didn't say anything about lawful behavior. Good thing, since Garrett was painfully aware that he would break quite a number of laws to protect the woman standing near him. A woman he'd already deeply hurt.

But if there was anything he was certain of, it was that Artemisia was as honorable as he, had her own code, and was definitely more compassionate and optimistic.

A woman worth protecting and defending.

He turned his head to meet her eyes, but she wasn't looking at him. Her stare was fixed on the notice board crowded with papyrus on the wall opposite them.

Suppressing a sigh and loosening his jaw *again*, he stood and moved in front of her.

She didn't look up.

"Artemisia," he said as softly as Winterberry had done.

Another flinch, and Garrett could feel the observant interest of every guard in the room as they watched. "Did you take the knife from the altar of the cross-folk chapel in Primary Healing-Hall?"

She lifted and dropped a shoulder. "No." It was flat, as if she resented him even asking the question. He wanted to tell her it was more for the guards' benefit than his own—that he trusted her. But would she believe him?

Gesturing to one of the recordspheres on Fol Berberis's desk, she said, "I've already reported how I came to have the knife." Her lips firmed. "And I've answered all the questions from all three of these guards."

Garrett inclined his head, picked up a copy of the sphere, and tucked it in a belt pouch. He and Rusby had been in Noble Country, on his way to see Laev T'Hawthorn, when Garrett had gotten the scry from Captain Winterberry. Rusby had not been pleased with the change of plans, and Garrett had teleported the kitten to the T'Hawthorn breakfast room pad so Rusby could play with the Hawthorn Fams.

Though Garrett had spent some time in this guardhouse, it wasn't enough that he could safely teleport to the place. It had taken him a while to get here after Winterberry's scry.

The bond between himself and Artemisia was narrow and he got nothing from it—though it took no special Flair to feel the hint of despair radiating from her.

He was concentrating on her so much he didn't much notice the other items on the desk—a scattering of several equal-armed crosses—until Fol Berberis stepped up, chose one, and handed it to Garrett.

He looked at the wooden cross in his hand, made the deduction. "This is an altar knife?"

"Yes," Rosa Milkweed said.

Garrett turned it over in his hand. The arms were rounded and carved with what he now saw were elongated faces. He grimaced, not to his taste. He saw the crack around the bottom of one of the arms where it joined the rest in the middle.

He pulled it apart, saw a narrow pointed blade with sharp edges, and raised his brows. "Hmm." He didn't look at Artemisia, who was probably the only one familiar with such a weapon.

"It's an *altar* knife. Used as we would use a bolline, a white-handled knife in our rituals. A tool," Artemisia said.

"It's a concealed weapon," Fol Berberis said.

Garrett sheathed the thing and put it in another belt pocket. "The murder weapon was like this?"

"Bigger, prettier." Berberis shrugged. "Our weapons specialist is still studying the actual knife."

"And it came from Primary HealingHall," Garrett stated. His gaze skipped across those of the three guards in the room. "We'll go check out the chapel ourselves."

Again Winterberry's brows went up when he looked at Artemisia. "Sounds good."

Garrett held out a hand to Artemisia. "Shall we go?"

Her round chin turned stubborn. Her emerald eyes were cool. "Why do you think I should go with you?"

"Are you familiar with the cross-folk chapel in Primary Healing-Hall?"

"Yes." Her mouth turned down. "There will be traces of my presence." She looked at Winterberry. "I occasionally visit the chapel. It's a sacred place and usually empty, unlike the Lady's and Lord's Temple. A good place to relax."

"And your mother is cross-folk, so you are used to the vibrations of such a religion," Winterberry said.

"Yes."

Winterberry waved a hand. "Then you will notice if there is anything unusual about the chapel."

"The altar missing the knife is unusual," Artemisia said.

"Beyond that." Winterberry was unruffled at her irritation.

"I suppose," she said. She took a pace so she was outside Garrett's reach—an action that made the back of his neck heat. She glanced at him, then at Winterberry. "I don't know the chapel well enough in all light to be able to teleport there now, but I can teleport to the pad outside my office cubicle."

Garrett stepped up and took her hand. Warm and soft and feeling right in his. She frowned. He ignored that. "We'll head out, then." He nodded to Winterberry. "I'll give you a report in a septhour or so."

"Fine," Winterberry said. "I prefer you take a guard also."

Guardswoman Milkweed inclined her head at Winterberry. "I'll accompany them."

"A lot of time and effort's going into this investigation," Fol Berberis said.

Rosa Milkweed nodded. "Yes. If we'd caught the guy with the others, all those years ago, he'd have been dead like his cohorts. You—we—all missed him for years."

"Every guard in Druida regretted that, wanted to close the case," Winterberry said stiffly.

"Guy who killed him should get a medal," Berberis said.

"For *murder*?" Artemisia asked.

"Justice, not murder," Milkweed said. "Justice has finally been done." The rest of the guards nodded, then the guardswoman continued, "Let's head to the HealingHall and get on with it."

Garrett nodded. "Right."

"On three." Artemisia began the teleportation countdown, lacing her fingers with the guardswoman's. "One, GentleSir, two, Guard Milkweed, *three*."

And they arrived in the corner of one of the most miserable working spaces Garrett had ever seen, including at the beginning of his own career. The room was large but depressingly filled with rickety-walled partitions around desks. Bright, harsh light emanating from Flair-tech panel squares showed every flaw in the furniture, and there were many. The ceiling was only a few inches above his head and there were no windows. His nostrils stung with the odor of astringent cleansers.

He was nearly shocked. He'd have never considered such a place would exist in Primary HealingHall, known for its luxury.

The guardswoman pulled her hand from theirs and took a stride from the teleportation pad before setting her hands on her hips and looking around. "Not inspiring."

Artemisia did a hunched-shoulder shrug and went to a counter in one of the few tiny spaces that appeared occupied. "This is for the temporary staff. There are only three of us up here."

Milkweed sniffed. "The rest of Primary HealingHall is lavish enough. I have friends who work in AllClass HealingHall who have better offices than this."

"Yes, well, I don't anticipate staying here very much longer. Hopefully, I will share an office on the administrative floor." She glanced at an old-fashioned scry bowl. "I have no messages in my cache that I need to deal with."

She said nothing but crossed to an opening between the cubes that Garrett realized was a main thoroughfare between them. Milkweed followed Artemisia, and he fell in last. As they walked to the stairwell, he understood that they were on the top floor, the third, of the HealingHall.

The wide stairs were equally vacant as if they weren't much used. When they reached the doors to the main floor, he saw Artemisia take a big breath and glance at the guardswoman and himself. He couldn't help but smile back at her. She shouldn't worry so much. True, she was escorting a Druida guard, but Garrett himself was with Artemisia. And he was sure by now that he was the talk of all the Healers in Druida. Him being seen with her would remind everyone how Artemisia had taken part in the project that would stop the Iasc sickness.

But when they walked through the richly appointed hallways, more gazes went to the guardswoman's uniform than to Garrett and no one greeted Artemisia. His jaw clenched. Even when he was a guard for merchant traders, he'd never let anyone treat him like that—as if he didn't matter.

It irritated him that she accepted the slights.

After a couple of long corridors, they reached a double door with a sign over it that read, "Sacred Spaces." Artemisia pushed through, and the fragrance of incense tanged the air.

There were only three doors, two on either side of the short hall and one set in a curved wall ahead of them that was obviously a regular round Temple. To the right there was a square cross over the door, and to the left, a series of symbols of religions that Garrett didn't quite recognize. Most people of Celta were comfortable with the culture that their colonist ancestors had established. He understood that the cross-folk beliefs spun off from other Earthan religions. There were a few other faiths that had followers. And some folk didn't believe in any sort of religion at all.

Artemisia automatically swung to the right.

The voice of the HealingHall came. "One moment, please, SecondLevel Healer Panax. FirstLevel Healer Ura Heather noted that you arrived with a guard and requests you await her. The door to the cross-folk sacred space has been spellshielded against all entry." The HealingHall wasn't so much a sentient entity as an automatic monitoring system. Garrett wondered how close Primary HealingHall was to becoming an intelligent being, but decided no one would answer the question if he asked.

Artemisia's face had hardened. "Has anyone needed the chapel?" she asked.

"The shield has not been disturbed since it was placed," answered the system.

The doors behind them opened and FirstLevel Healer Ura Heather swept in. Garrett noted that she was wearing elaborate Noble robes with long pocket sleeves, a long tunic, and heavily bloused trous billowing over the ankle cuffs. All in a lush purple-and-gold-patterned silk.

He bowed a little short of what the woman should have received. "Greetyou, FirstLevel Healer," he said.

"Primross? I thought Winterberry was handling this mess."

Garrett angled his head. "As he handles all FirstFamily messes?"

The woman's mouth turned down.

Garrett continued, "It appears that this mess is connected with the murder of the last Black Magic Cultist." He aimed a smile meant to irritate at her. "You must have forgotten that his wife was a victim of that cult."

Heather's lips soured more and she set her hands in her opposite sleeve pockets. "So?"

"So, it was thought by the FirstFamilies Council that he should not be the primary investigator on this case."

"And you should?"

He made his smile more patently charming. "The FirstFamilies Council has faith in my skills."

"Do you often work for the Druida guards?" Heather asked.

"Occasionally," he lied. "And I must tell you that this project is much more to my liking than the previous one I was involved in."

Artemisia made a small sound. "A man has been murdered."

FirstLevel Ura Heather's brows lowered. "Why are you here at the HealingHall so soon before your shift, SecondLevel Healer?"

"She has been requested by the guards to help with the investigation," Garrett said smoothly. Another way to keep close to her.

The Healer pivoted to glare at Rosa Milkweed. "Is that so?"

With an arch of her brows, the guardswoman said, "Yes."

A slow smile showing teeth appeared on Heather's face.

"The guards have requested you, Artemisia Mugwort, as a consultant in this matter," Ura Heather said with a satisfied smile. "So you are released from the staff of Primary HealingHall to fulfill that position."

Twenty-seven

Shock. The death of her career echoed in Artemisia's mind, as did Ura Heather's words. *You are released from the staff of Primary Healing Hall to fulfill that position.*

Artemisia had never known why the FirstLevel Healer didn't care for her, and lately the woman's malice had gotten worse. A wave of cold nausea washed through Artemisia and she locked her knees to stay upright, opened her mouth to gulp more air.

"Temporarily," Garrett insisted, his voice sounding too loud to Artemisia. He'd moved very close. Supposed to be supportive?

FirstLevel Healer Ura Heather bridled. "I don't think—"

"If SecondLevel Healer Panax's consultation will impact her career poorly, the guards will, of course, understand and forego her help on this matter," Garrett said.

Anger, accompanied by vicious threat—toward the FirstLevel Healer—throbbed along the bond between Garrett and Artemisia.

A too strong bond. Artemisia would have to do something—she didn't know what, but soon—about that.

When she looked up at him with eyes that had dilated due to the emotional blow, she saw he was projecting an easy manner. Not even the guardswoman seemed to notice how furious he was. That Artemisia had was a warning sign.

Then she blinked as *his* words repeated in her mind. He was keeping her career as safe as he could. Her head went a little light. Would the guards have requested her help, like he had? Yes. And Ura Heather would have used that for dismissal, as she did.

Sounded like Artemisia was hanging on to her place here at Primary HealingHall with her fingertips. She let a breath sift out. Life as usual with the FirstLevel Healer.

"Very well," Ura Heather snapped. "The SecondLevel Healer can *consult* with the guards and keep her position here."

"Good," Garrett said.

"That's good," the guardswoman said. "We should proceed into the Temple."

"Yes," Garrett agreed. "Who discovered the altar knife was missing?"

"Our FirstLevel Housekeeper, who personally checks these rooms every eightday." Heather stared at Artemisia. "She's been on our permanent staff for thirty years."

"Is she cross-folk?" Garrett asked.

"No, but she knows the inventory of each room," Heather said.

Artemisia winced at the word *inventory* but said, "Then you don't need me to tell you what might be missing."

All of them looked at her.

"Please, stay with us," Milkweed said and gestured for Artemisia to open the door. She turned the knob and went in first. Milkweed followed, looking around. Garrett held open the door for FirstLevel Healer Ura Heather, but she shook her head and marched back to the main doors at the end of the hallway and through them.

Garrett entered and scrutinized the room with a glance. Definitely religious, with the heavy fragrance of candles and incense; tiny tiles made up a mosaic on four sides of a plinth. He scraped his grovestudy memory for something on the cross-folk and finally recalled they had a four-spirited god. He still didn't know what that meant.

He didn't like the ambiance of the chapel . . . It felt graver, less joyful than what he experienced when he went to Temples of the Lady and Lord.

Artemisia stopped a pace away from the altar, and Milkweed, who was close behind her, came up short and off-balance. Taller than Artemisia, she fell forward and had to grab the edge of the velvet-draped altar table to steady herself.

The cloth skewed, and with a couple of smooth pulls, she made it straight.

A flushed Milkweed moved to face them and nodded. "My Flair includes an excellent memory for faces, and a small aspect of a talent like Captain Winterberry's. I can tell how many and who have been in this room." She looked at Artemisia. "You have been in the room before?"

"Of course," Artemisia said. Her lips hardened, as if she were tired of the questions. But investigation was checking every detail from every aspect. "Like I said, I sometimes come here to relax or meditate."

Milkweed's brow furrowed. "It seems like your vibration has been here for a long time."

"My mother worked here for years. Also, when I was hired on, she wished that I light a candle of thanks to her god here in the chapel. She asked me to check on the chapel every other eightday or so since there is no cross-folk priest on staff."

"When was the last time you were here?" asked the guardswoman.

Artemisia frowned and her gaze went blank as if calculating. "It would have been two eightdays ago on TwinMoonsday." Her smile was faint, then she gestured to the Celtan Temple. "The last couple of days, I spent more time in the Lady's and Lord's Temple here."

"Did you touch anything on the altar?"

"Of course not. The pieces are consecrated by a priest of the cross-folk and not to be handled by unbelievers. I would not do such a thing!"

"Didn't light the candelabra on the altar?" Garrett asked. The wicks of the sixteen candles in the stand were burnt.

"No, I used those candles." Artemisia gestured to a small alcove in the side wall and an iron stand holding three rows of small tapers. Only three melted stubs showed use. "Those candles are for anyone who has a prayer."

"Huh," Garrett said. The more he stayed in this place, the less he liked it. As if eyes watched and judged.

Milkweed stared at the altar that showed a large empty space in a row of three crosses, where the missing knife would have stood. Her gaze swung back to Artemisia. "But you've been in here several times?

"Yes."

"And you found the murder knife, which is a blade and three arms of a square cross, but didn't recognize it as coming from here?"

Artemisia's eyes had deepened to forest green and again Garrett was aware of secrets—but not lies, not this time. Nor did her tone waver when she answered. "I didn't pay much attention to the altar or the knife upon it." She shrugged. "And it looked ordinary to me. A cross that would be used in a public place like this, not one in a dedicated cross-folk chapel. I didn't realize that it was a work of art."

That was news to Garrett since he hadn't had time to review Artemisia's statements to the guards.

"I *do* feel your presence in this room before today," Milkweed continued to press.

Chin lifting, Artemisia tilted it in the direction of the Celtan round Temple. "And if you go into the Lady's and Lord's Temple, you will find my presence there, later and more often."

Milkweed nodded. "I'll check that out." She pursed her lips. "Too bad Winterberry isn't considered reliable in this matter. His Flair for that is better than mine." She turned to Garrett. "What of your Flair?"

Before he could form an answer that revealed very little about himself and his Flair—how he could speak with all Fams, and even meld minds with them—the door opened and the FirstFamily GrandLord Straif T'Blackthorn entered the room.

Either FirstLevel Healer Ura Heather or Garrett's own friend

Laev T'Hawthorn must have asked him to come. He was the best tracker on Celta.

"Greetyou, guardswoman, greetyou, GentleSir Primross. And SecondLevel Healer Mugwort Panax." The GrandLord bowed.

Artemisia curtsied deeply. Milkweed angled her body in a short bow. Garrett nodded.

Straif T'Blackthorn said, "I was briefed by a few members of the FirstFamily Council on the death of Modoc Eryngo and was asked to look at this chapel for tracks of the one who disposed of him."

Garrett itched to ask who'd spoken with him and whether it was Laev—who was nearly a generation younger than T'Blackthorn—but kept his mouth shut. He'd find out later.

T'Blackthorn scanned the room with a penetrating stare, particularly the floor, which Garrett had heard would show the Grand-Lord the trails of each individual who'd been in the room. "I can tell you that I see nothing unusual here."

Then he crossed his arms. "And that's all I will tell you. As far as I'm concerned, the flig—" His gaze seemed to snag on the altar and the image of the four-spirited god and he stopped the curse word. "Modoc Eryngo got what he deserved. I've fulfilled my annual NobleGilt public service and if the guards wish to request the councils hire me, be aware that my fee for this matter is high." He quoted a figure that had Garrett's mouth dropping at the sheer size of it.

Milkweed choked.

The FirstFamily GrandLord nodded to them all again and vanished.

Artemisia expelled a breath that was loud in the silence, then murmured, "Well, I suppose that isn't surprising."

"No?" asked Milkweed.

Artemisia shrugged. "He's married to a Clover, after all, like Winterberry."

The guardswoman shook her head. "I can't always keep the tangles of FirstFamily relationships straight."

Garrett frowned. "How, exactly, is he related?"

Pressing her lips together as if in thought, Artemisia replied, "I think T'Blackthorn's wife is cousin to Trif Clover, who is wed to Winterberry and was one of the two surviving Black Magic Cult victims. But the other who lived and is close to Winterberry is of his blood. Another FirstFamily Lady, wed to Saille T'Willow."

"Crap," Garrett said, and didn't like the ripple of disapproval that even that mild oath provoked in the atmosphere. Nope, he didn't think he liked this cross-folk god.

He rubbed the back of his neck. His senses and Flair were clogged here. He'd have to sort through his impressions later.

Milkweed completed a prowl through the room. "I think we've seen everything we need?" She held the door open. "I want to do a quick check of the Lord's and Lady's Temple, then speak with the housekeeper and"—she grimaced—"GrandMistrys FirstLevel Healer Ura Heather." The guardswoman ended with a low mutter under her breath, "Sure wish her father, GrandLord T'Heather, was still in charge here."

Artemisia exited first, saying, "You won't need me for that." She glanced at a pretty timer on the wall. "And my shift starts in about twenty minutes."

"You're with me now," Garrett rumbled. "And we have things to do."

"No!"

"I'll be in the Lord's and Lady's Temple." Guardswoman Milkweed hurried away.

"Do you really think that FirstLevel Healer Heather hasn't already reassigned your cases?" Garrett asked.

"Again?"

He didn't want to disillusion her, but she should face reality. "Ura Heather probably flexed your work time the minute the knife was discovered missing."

Artemisia's face stilled in that way women have when they are fighting tears. He *hated* to see that, held out his hand.

She dodged around him. "I still must check my shifts," she said in a choked voice.

She had to turn away from him, from all the hurt pounding

through her. Nothing had gone right lately, so many things had tested her inner calm, her strength. She knew she was strong, she didn't need to prove that to herself or anyone else. "I'll join you in a few minutes," Artemisia said, insides wavery. "I also need to program my scrybowl to forward to my perscry." She strode away and wound through the building to her sorry cubicle.

One glimpse of the "Amended Work Schedule, Artemisia Panax" posted on the inside partition showed that Garrett was right. She was slated to start work in a couple of septhours and her shift was truncated enough to give her the minimal amount of work time— and gilt.

She unfolded a temp-sit chair from the wall of the partition and sat. Options must be considered—for her job, first, then her personal life. How much did she want to work in this HealingHall? A great deal. The energy felt *right*, but Ura Heather would rule for a long time. Artemisia grounded herself, let her tumbled feelings drain. Maybe she could hang on to her position here. She was a good Healer and if Lark Holly would be her advocate . . . if all this mess passed without more irritation of Heather, and Artemisia sank below her notice again, she had a chance. If, if, if. She wouldn't give up yet, but one more incident and she'd have to walk away.

The smooth surface of the water in the scrybowl caught her eye. As for her personal life, she had to get beyond her own hurt and pain to do that, which meant she had to follow up on her promise to her relatives. She needed a counselor and at least one session. She thought of the priests and priestesses she'd met through Tiana over the years. Some were too high to call on. Some were so close to Tiana that advising her sister would put a strain on the friendship.

Artemisia sighed. There was something easy about Leger Cinchona that she liked. So she put the call through.

His mobile face fell when he understood that she wanted to consult him as a priest, then he smiled and waved the slight regret aside, accepted her as a client. She took his next free appointment which was at EveningBell.

Now to find her spine and face Garrett.

Her perscry lilted a dance measure. Her parents were calling. She pulled the pebble out of her sleeve pocket and put it on the counter. "Here," she said.

When she saw their serious faces, her stomach jittered. This wouldn't be good news, either.

"We have discussed the matter," her father said, with his implacable judge face on. Whatever decision they'd come to, there would be no appeal. "We can only believe this murder situation will become increasingly unstable and affect your career. We want you to go to T'Hawthorn Residence and speak with Laev T'Hawthorn, call in the favor he owes us to exert influence regarding your position there."

Artemisia's voice was high. "We saved his HeartMate's life, we'd have done so for anyone, but Camellia is our friend."

"Yes," her mother said.

"But he offered the favor," her father continued inexorably, "and we accepted on your behalf."

She remembered and resentment spiked. They'd always thought she was softer, less a fighter than her younger sister.

"It's not that you're gentler than Tiana," her mother said.

"That's exactly what it is," Artemisia said.

"You helped save Camellia's life," her father pointed out, "so the favor was also for you. Tiana did not. And Tiana's colleagues accept her. Yours do not."

"When the scandal broke sixteen years ago, FirstLevel Healer Ura Heather at Primary HealingHall was quick enough to tell me my services were not needed," Artemisia's mother said. "And GrandLord T'Heather did not overturn her decision."

Artemisia's father ran a hand up and down her mother's tense back. "It was not a battle he could have won."

"So he didn't fight it."

Artemisia frowned. Her mother brought the steely will to fight to the Family—that of a Healer battling for life and death. Artemisia was more of her father's contemplative temperament, unless she was engaged in that Healing struggle. And, like him, she understood not fighting battles she couldn't win outside Healing. "I'll go see Laev." Tomorrow. Maybe.

"Thank you." Her father dipped his head in understanding that she'd do this because they asked.

Her mother smiled her usual serene smile. "Thank you."

They didn't fear for themselves, though Artemisia was beginning to think that they should. They worried about her. That was Family. "I love you," she said.

Her parents answered in unison, "We love you." Her mother blew her a kiss that made Artemisia smile and the scry ended.

Artemisia let her shoulders slump and wallowed in self-pity for a few seconds before she stood, returned her perscry to her pocket, and walked down to meet Garrett.

To her relief, he and the guardswoman were speaking with the housekeeper. Artemisia thought from the simmering irritation through her narrowed bond with Garrett that Ura Heather had given them a perfunctory interview.

The Healing Grove was crowded and Artemisia didn't want to stay in the Hall when she couldn't work. She didn't know who took care of her patients—people she'd almost begun to know—but it was disheartening to be there and not allowed to help. So she waited outside, sitting on a smoothly sculpted bench, soaking in sunshine, until Garrett reappeared. Alone.

Her hope of keeping the guard and a professional attitude between herself and Garrett was futile. "Where's Guardswoman Milkweed?"

"She was called to duty at another venue." He glanced at his wrist timer. "Same place we need to go. A viewing of Modoc Eryngo's body."

"A *viewing* of the body!" Artemisia was shocked. That wasn't a usual part of death rites in their culture, though some cross-folk practiced such.

Garrett slanted her an ironic look. "Apparently the Family—and the All Councils—agreed a viewing to show everyone the last Black Magic Cultist is truly dead was necessary."

Artemisia swallowed. "I don't like this."

"I don't think anyone does." Garrett gestured to the public carrier plinth and offered his elbow.

She ignored it.

He scowled. "Better get used to being with me today outside your work schedule at the HealingHall, Artemisia." The guards had wanted her at the memorial, and had requested he keep an eye on her. If her being there would fix in their minds that she was innocent, he'd get her there. But with regard to the murder, he had a nagging feeling in the back of his mind that he'd missed some simple clue that he'd seen or heard.

She looked him straight in the eyes. "I have an appointment to speak with a counselor at EveningBell." How she wished she could walk away from Garrett. But her Family was too entwined in the murder, and now she had a source of inside information.

She swallowed, felt her mouth turn down. "Even if I was working my full shift, I'd be allowed to take the time to see him."

"Him?" Garrett pounced.

She blinked. "Leger Cinchona."

"I thought you were seeing him socially, like a gallant."

She made her voice icy. "As I believe I said before, I have options for my personal life." Staring at the beautiful Garrett, she kept her tone and heart hard. "I will not cancel my appointment with Priest Cinchona for you, and if you object, I will notify Captain Winterberry of the appointment and ask his permission." However hideously embarrassing that would be for all of them.

Garrett strangled a sigh. Not difficult to understand Artemisia was trying to distance herself from him. Their bond had thinned again. He was *not* making her feel safe, as he'd thought to do, to protect her, to cherish her. And he would protect and cherish to the end of his strength and life. Hadn't he proved that previously in his life during the Iasc sickness?

But he'd only hurt Artemisia.

When he'd met with Ura Heather, he'd wanted to threaten the old flitch with political ramifications of her dislike of Artemisia—reports to Laev and the FirstFamilies—but this was not the time.

Gentling his voice, he said, "Of course you must meet the priest. I truly believe you will be of help in this matter." Thankfully she didn't ask how.

"Shall we go?" He gestured to the upcoming public carrier.

She grimaced. "Oh, very well." But her eyes went stark before she said with a shake of her head, "It's not going to be pleasant. Despite everything, too many people believe the cross-folk and we Mugworts were involved in the Black Magic Cult murders."

Garrett was afraid she was right.

Twenty-eight

$\mathcal{A}$rtemisia made sure to hop down from the public carrier glider before Garrett so he wouldn't attempt to help her.

Nevertheless, when he caught up with her in a couple of strides, he wrapped his fingers around her upper arm. Sensation sizzled between them, lovely, deep—heart wrenching.

She didn't want to go to the body viewing, but Garrett gave her no choice—unless she wanted to stop in her tracks and argue in public with the man.

Nor did she expect the ambiance of the whole situation to be at all nice. Having a body available for public view wasn't common.

The viewing wasn't at a round Temple. Garrett told her that the highest priestess and priest of the Lady and Lord had stated that since the man had defiled their faith and he could not possibly have remained a believer in the duality, they would not house his shell in their Temple. Nor would they offer him any rituals for the dead. So the body was in an outbuilding of the Southern Temple, a rectangular building.

There were guardsmen at the door who questioned their presence. Fingers firm on her elbow, Garrett told them their names, that he was investigating for the FirstFamilies, and that he and Artemisia had discovered the murder.

Loud enough that some of the crowd lingering near could hear—and so could those in the anteroom.

They stepped from hot summer sun into a cool, tile-floored and walled room that held odd echoes as they crossed to the arched opening of the main room.

The body lay on a platform under a stasis spell, Eryngo appearing cleaner and more prepossessing than he had in crumpled death.

There were people in a short line filing by the body. Neither the sight of death nor the shell of the soul and spirit bothered Artemisia, though this event was distasteful.

Guards were stationed around the room, including Rosa Milkweed and her partner, Fol Berberis.

Next to the dais sat a tense-jawed woman with the same features as Modoc Eryngo, probably his sister. She looked as if she did bitter Family duty and seemed to be the only Family member present.

To Artemisia's fascinated horror, a viz recorder sending images was positioned in the ceiling over the body.

"People have always been morbid," Garrett murmured, then made a disapproving noise. "And the councils want to prove to the public that the last of the Black Magic Cultists is dead."

His quiet words were loud enough to be heard in a moment of awkward silence. "Is that true, do you think?" an elderly man asked. His face was lined and he hunched over a cane—a man worn down more by emotional ills than physical. His embroidered cuffs showed him to be GraceLord Sorrell, the father of the last victim killed. He scuttled to Garrett, raised a hooked nose to stare him in the eyes. "So much is still unknown."

"I don't think so, sir," Garrett said. "I believe everything was straightforward except for the capture of this guy. Now he's dead."

Sorrell's lower lip curled. "Good riddance. Still had plenty of more years than my Calla. There's a lot of speculation about the cultists, that one or two might have been missed."

"No. The guards accounted for everyone except Modoc sixteen years ago. And there are stories because time has passed and rumor and myths spring up like weeds. A lot of odd and just plain wrong theories," Garrett said.

Artemisia hadn't known that.

GraceLord Sorrell stared at the corpse with contempt, swept a glance around the room, and said loudly, "I'm glad he's dead and I bless the one who did it." He marched to a corner where other people—Families of those who had been sacrificed by the cult members—had gathered.

Garrett had winced at Sorrell's words. He gazed at the corner. "There are quite a few people from the Families of the victims present."

Modoc's sister's face tightened with gray lines. "They were the first to arrive and will no doubt be the last to leave." She angled her head at the body of her brother. "A barbaric custom. A cross-folk custom. He meddled with other religions like cross-folk before he joined the Cult." She swallowed as if acrid anger had coated her mouth, took a drink from the wineglass set on a table beside her.

"You don't mourn him?" Garrett asked.

She glared at him, jutted her chin at Artemisia. "About as much as GraceMistrys Mugwort—sorry, that was your old title, was it not?—about as much as GentleLady Mugwort does. He ruined my life. He was the heir; when he disgraced us, our business faltered and has never quite recovered. Furthermore, I had my life planned, then I became heir. He upset all that."

"I'm so sorry," Artemisia murmured and withdrew, and Garrett came with her.

"I suppose we should add some Eryngo Family members to the suspect list," he said.

"How long do we have to stay?" she asked. She sure didn't like this aspect of his work.

"A while," he muttered. "To see who might come. The killer might like to gloat, to get a feel of the approval from people like Sorrell. All the suspects are gathering."

She glared at him.

"You're not a suspect. You have a solid alibi. You're just with me." She rolled her eyes.

Artemisia flexed her knees a little to steady her emotional balance. Her next surprise was when Barton Clover entered the room, along with GrandLord Walker Clover and his lady. Barton scanned the room and acted completely like the household security guard he was. Captain Winterberry accompanied the three.

Holding her body tight, GrandLady Clover crossed to the body and Modoc's sister. "I'm sorry for your . . . difficulties," she said to the woman. Glancing at the body and away, she turned to face Winterberry and said in a calm, clear voice, "I did not know the man. He was not one of my friends in that time long ago. As I've stated, I only knew three of the Cult."

"Only the three highest in the Cult *used* my lady as a resource," Walker Clover's mellow voice said. "We will leave now." He looked as forbidding and unhappy as Winterberry, who sent a narrow-eyed scathing glance at the body.

Artemisia blinked. More and more people were involved in the case than she'd ever anticipated.

Barton Clover's gaze met hers and his face relaxed into a brief smile. As he passed, he murmured, "You should not be here, Artemisia." Another quick scan of the room, then his eyes met hers again. "Not a fit place for any sensitive lady."

Garrett stepped in front of her, and when she moved from behind him, she saw Barton's brows had raised and his smile had turned wry. He nodded and left after Walker Clover and his wife.

She didn't think Barton would scry her again. Anger flickered through her at the masculine posturing.

Gasps came and people went motionless around her. Slowly she turned toward the door—to see that some of the greatest people in the land had arrived, FirstFamily Lords and Ladies.

Like most, she knew them from newssheets images. First was a pale but determined GreatLady D'Willow, Dufleur Thyme, who had nearly died on the altar of the Black Magic Cult . . . and when the

GreatLady moved, Artemisia saw a small cat—and recalled that while most of the human victims of the Black Magic Cult had died, there had also been Fam animals involved who had lived.

Would the Fams come?

GreatLord T'Willow set his hand on his lady's lower back. He wore a long sword on one hip and a blazer on the other. No one said a word and the atmosphere thrummed with tension.

"I don't recall much," GreatLady D'Willow said steadily. "I don't remember this man specifically. But I'm glad he's dead." She put a hand on her chest. "It's a relief there will be no more threat from him." She and her HeartMate crossed to the other victims' Families.

Before the door swung shut, another couple entered. And everyone remained silent, shrank against the walls like Rosa Milkweed, or huddled in their seat like GraceLord Sorrell. No one wanted to call the attention of Vinni T'Vine, the prophet of Celta, to himself or herself. Not many cared to casually hear their future.

Garrett stiffened beside Artemisia.

Walking beside T'Vine was GreatMistrys Avellana Hazel. T'Vine carried a housefluff, and Hazel a tomcat. Cuddling the Earthan rabbit–Celtan mocyn mixture, T'Vine showed the Fam the body. "Flora, this is the last of the people who hurt you. He is dead and circling the wheel of stars until his next reincarnation." He paused and his eyes changed colors as he saw what others couldn't. "Which won't be pleasant."

A ripple of motion went around the room as people felt the powerful Flair of prophecy in T'Vine's announcement.

Bad time, Flora projected loudly. *Bad, bad people.*

The tom leapt from Avellana Hazel's arms onto the thin shield surrounding Modoc's body, and the stench of cat urine rose.

"Oh, Rhyz," Avellana said.

But Artemisia stepped forward, along with D'Willow and Great-Mistrys Hazel, and they said a common chant for cleaning cat pee.

The atmosphere relaxed. Artemisia went back to where Garrett stood, though she kept a longer pace between them. The Nobles said something to Eryngo's sister, then went over and spoke briefly to the other Families.

On their way out, T'Vine paused by Garrett, his gaze warm as he looked at Garrett, then Artemisia. "Good job," he said in a low voice that no one else could have heard. "And you should leave now. You will learn no more here today, and you are overdue for an appointment."

Garrett's face went blank, then his eyes widened. He nodded to the guards and took Artemisia's elbow and they followed the Nobles out. By the time they reached the fresh air outside, the Nobles had all teleported away, and Artemisia relaxed.

She shouldn't enjoy being with Garrett, and when she thought of how he'd hurt her, she didn't . . . but her body knew they were HeartMates.

Garrett wiped an arm across his forehead. "Glad to be out of there."

"It wasn't pleasant," Artemisia agreed. She glanced at her timer. "I'm due to start work in a septhour, I should return to Primary HealingHall."

Garrett's gut clutched even as his brain sought to juggle a few thoughts: T'Vine knew who Garrett's HeartMate was and was pleased. Garrett had followed the prophet's advice and T'Vine was pleased at that, too. How much had Garrett and T'Vine changed the future? How bad had the alternative been? Not that he would have refused the Healers . . .

And what of the viewing? There had been plenty of suspects; who was important to the case?

"See you . . . sometime," Artemisia said not really cheerfully.

"Please, Artemisia, walk with me," the words were out of his mouth before he realized how pleading they sounded.

"I don't think—"

Sleek Black shot from the bushes, trotted beside them. *There you are!* he scolded Garrett loudly. *You called the ferals together and did not come.*

"I'm late," Garrett agreed between his teeth. *Go to the park and tell them I am on my way and those who stay will have extra good food. So will those who have left and return.*

The cat's tail thrashed. *And I get treats, nip.*

"Go," Garrett said.

Sleek Black narrowed his eyes, twitched his whiskers, and bounded away.

"Gathered the ferals together?" Artemisia asked.

"Yes, my informants that I use in my business."

She blinked.

"You must have figured that out."

Color came to her cheeks. She jerked her arm from his grasp. "Yes, but I didn't consider all the details because I'm just a gentle, naive soul."

"Why are you angry? And why do you say that?" It was true, but he wasn't foolish enough to admit it.

"Everyone seems to think that I am not a strong person. That I should be sheltered. Because I like a peaceful life." She stomped a few steps. "I *don't* like confrontation, but I can fight if I need to."

"You're very strong." That was the truth. "And I'm sure you fight." Battled against sickness, at least. He wouldn't have trusted her in old Downwind that had been demolished.

"I don't need to be protected." She tossed her head and some of her hair escaped her braid. "Barton Clover said I shouldn't have been at the viewing. As if I haven't seen more corpses than he ever has, haven't seen more blood and wounds and sickness."

Guilt twinged through Garrett. He *shouldn't* have taken her to the event. "The atmosphere was bad."

"True." Her lips firmed, she shook her head. "I doubt Barton Clover will scry me again, the way you acted."

A surge of satisfaction was chased by incipient panic at the thought of her wedding—or even having sex—with someone else. He was in a terrible mess. His own damn fault.

She slid him a look. "T'Vine seemed to know you."

At least she was curious. He matched step with her and slid his hand around her arm again. He'd like to hold hands with her, even link fingers, but was sure she wouldn't allow that.

Oh, yeah, he was doomed, all right, unless he did something right. Soon.

"Didn't I tell you?" he kept his tone light. "T'Vine paid me a visit the morning that I met you at Primary HealingHall. He recommended that I do everything the FirstLevel Healers requested."

"Oh!" Her lovely emerald eyes widened and she looked up at him, fascinated, stroking his ego.

"Yes. And I did." He linked elbows at that.

"I wonder . . ." But Artemisia shook her head and sighed. And though she was gentle and naive in some areas, Garrett believed she had enough imagination to visualize another epidemic of the Iasc sickness.

"It's a pretty day," he said.

"Yes."

Great, he was so smooth he had to talk about the weather to his HeartMate. They were in step, the link between them had naturally widened. The rhythm of their breathing and hearts were the same.

Apollopa Park came into view, already looking more tended from Leger Cinchona's efforts. Garrett's shoulders tightened. He *had* faced the fact that Artemisia wouldn't wait for him. Gentle she might be, naive, but he was sure she had a stubborn streak. She wasn't going to change her mind about him, about waiting for him because he was her HeartMate. She planned on loving someone else, making a life, having children, with another man.

He ripped inside, bled.

But why *should* she wait? He hadn't searched for her, claimed her, offered her a HeartGift. He'd even resisted making a HeartGift during the dreamquest Passages that freed his Flair.

Had she made *him* a HeartGift? He was afraid to ask.

He couldn't go on like this. Couldn't. There was no way around it, he'd have to make more of an effort to win her trust.

If he accompanied her to the appointment with the priest, offered to be counseled with her—or even spill his guts, accept whatever the man had to say—that might help. Show he would work with her to fix his mistakes.

When he reached the park, none of the ferals waited in the open, though he could sense them hiding in the shadows or the bushes or a burrow.

The mirrored cubes of the fountain glittered with shiny surfaces, reflecting rainbows, throwing colorful sparkling water droplets into the air. The splashing water sounded cheerful. Garrett didn't know what the priest had done to the park, but the layer of negativity laid by the murder had been erased.

Yet he led Artemisia to the opposite side of the park from where they'd found the body, closer to the round Temple and flowers that released equally pretty fragrance into the summer afternoon. Reluctantly he withdrew his arm from Artemisia's, holding his breath to see if she'd run.

"Oh, Leger Cinchona has done so much work in such a short time!" she said.

Garrett had wanted her focused on him. "Will you sit with me as I summon the ferals?" No need to say they were already near. He rocked back, heel to toe, sensing the energy of the earth and the area. Again, cheerful. "Place seems acceptable for a light meditative trance."

Once more her gaze slid to him, along him. Did she wonder whether she was safe with him?

"I will always protect you," he said.

She snorted, shrugged, her lip curled. She trod around a small area, using her own Flair, then settled in the short grass, legs crossed.

Keeping an eye out, he moved close to her, only stopping when he saw a line form between her brows, then slid into the same position. Not quite as near as he'd wanted, of course, their bodies didn't touch—though as he breathed deeply, he became aware of the energies cycling between them.

She dropped immediately into a deep trance and he stared. She could do that—would do that—in a public place?

He was torn between calling her back with a sharp lecture and the fact that she must really trust him, innately, to defend her.

So he didn't go deep, only let his body and thoughts relax into the hum of nature. He drew more ferals that way, the more skittish came to talk—or be a part of the circle—or partake in the energy or whatever. He figured Artemisia's serenity and the feral Fams' curiosity would lure them all.

His eyelids lowered, and he remained lightly in trance but alert. The area had an unexpected feeling of blessing about it, obviously was still sacred ground. He was aware enough to feel the auras of the feral Fams as they crossed into the open. Sleek Black came and sat before them, beyond Garrett's reach. Garrett let the Fams ring him until he thought they were all there . . . eight cats, two dogs, and three foxes. Despite the word he'd sent out, there were no raccoons.

One last deep breath and release and he opened his eyes fully and scanned the crowd. As usual they were quiet . . . pride was involved and not one of them wanted to show any uneasiness before members of their own species, let alone any other.

At his movement the leader of the fox contingent barked. *You have an interesting quest?*

More than one. Garrett smiled; some of the animals rustled in anticipation. Before a cat could ask, Garrett said, *I will provide a feast for you all in the courtyard behind my office building, but I wanted to speak to you here first.*

Because a man was killed here, said another fox.

Yes.

Black-and-White sniffed. *There are many human smells here of people who looked for data about the man and the one who killed him.*

And it has been long since, the smallest cat added.

Sift everything with all your special senses, especially anything that might pertain to the murder. Each of you who comes to me with an individual report will be given a treat.

Mouths smacked. Drool spilled from one of the dogs' muzzles.

That is the first request, said the fox. *What else?*

I want to track each of the raccoons who lived here, learn their whereabouts, and speak with them. Garrett gestured to the raw opened earth where the den had been. *I believe there was an adult male, female, and two kits. They are smart, like you, potential Fam animals.*

Artemisia jerked awake beside him. Garrett examined his band for clues that one of them knew something more.

A dog with gray around his nose yipped. *I heard the male 'coon likes beach more than forest. I heard one kit was hurt by the bad one who killed the man, heard a raccoon male said so.*

Fam murder! someone yelled. *We are looking for Fam murderer!*

Shudders rippled through the Fams, some of the youngest bolted. Garrett treasured each and every informant, never knew which qualities he might need for a job. He hoped they returned, if not now, then later.

Cats hunched down, ears flattened, gazes darting, hissing. Dogs and foxes hopped to their feet. Fear.

Should he use Flair to *reach* and *sweep* and *hold* many Fam minds?

Twenty-nine

❦

No. He watched young ones dash away.

An instant, clear memory flashed of Artemisia sending *love* to a . . . to a Fam in TQ's HouseHeart? He let his shoulders fall from the high line of tension and gathered concern . . . affection . . . for these colleagues.

He took Artemisia's hand—it was unexpectedly cool—and on a long puff of exhalation, he imagined a silver stream from himself to the feral Fams. Artemisia eased beside him and bolstered his sending with affection and power. They worked together, a good sign.

Purring rumbled from the cats. All the foxes sat straight and the muscles of their muzzles pulled back, showing their tongues as if they were smiling. The dogs trotted close to Garrett, then flopped in front of him and rolled over so he could rub their bellies—their tongues had been lolling, too.

Garrett grinned himself as he sent more affection out, enjoyed the rough hair under his fingers as he petted the dogs and the dampness of their tongues on his hand as they wriggled to lick him. Surprise and pleasure filled him when a wave of love came back to him from the group.

Black-and-White leaned against his knee, even Sleek Black purred loud enough that Garrett could hear him. With a last stroke on each of the dogs, he addressed his friends. *Are we calmer about the murder now?*

"Yesss," vocalized Black-and-White.

"Good," Garrett answered aloud. "Because I'm not done."

What else? asked the head fox.

Garrett took the simple square cross he'd picked up at the guardhouse from his belt pocket and unsheathed it, revealing the knife. He didn't like the way it felt in his hands, poorly balanced and not a good weapon. Of course, it wasn't supposed to be a weapon. Even as he frowned down on it, he knew it wasn't a tool he'd have felt comfortable using in a ritual.

That, too, surprised him. He didn't consider himself a spiritual man . . . and knew more about the Dark Goddess who claimed those ready to transition to another life than the more benevolent Lady and Lord. He shrugged the idea aside as the ferals crowded around him to examine the object.

Odd knife. One of the foxes shook his head. Then he sneezed. *Smells of smoke stuff, but not blood or hurt 'coon.*

"That's right," Garrett said. "The weapon that killed the man and hurt the raccoon looked like this." He angled the blade so sunlight gleamed off the edges. "The knife was found, but not the sheath." Opening his hand, he showed the sheath to his informers. "It would look something like this."

Again there was some shifting, mental images flying between those animals of the same species so quickly Garrett caught only flickers of the speech.

Black-and-White mewed, then broadcasted, *We have not seen this knife.*

None of us foxes have noticed such a thing in our travels, said the leader.

The dogs shook their heads. *No, no, no. Nothing like that, no.*

Garrett nodded. "Very well, you will all look for the sheath?"

He got various types of assents, then the cat yowled. *It is now time for Our feast food.*

Garrett went back to telepathy for the whole group. *Yes, raw and cooked meat will be dispersed in the troughs of the courtyard behind my building.*

Sleek Black shot from Apollopa Park and down the street, a black blur. The dogs followed fast, the foxes were a bit more dignified, but it wasn't more than a minute before Garrett was alone with Artemisia in the greenery.

He scanned the grasses, the flowers, but saw nothing, *sensed* nothing he'd missed before.

"That was very interesting." Artemisia stood and shook out her tunic, brushed it, then actually smiled at him. "It's obvious you have a bond with those Fams." Then she glanced away and wet her lips. "I—"

"What?"

"It's hard to say."

"I've heard a lot of hard things from you. Don't stop now," Garrett said.

Her gaze flashed to his. Her brows dipped. "You haven't always been kind, either."

Gray Tabby slunk from the shadow of a big-boled tree. He darted up to Artemisia and sniffed around her feet and legs. Smiling, she bent down to pet him. He followed his nose up the line of her braid. Her eyes were wide, but there was no fear running through her connection with Garrett.

I thought so, the cat said smugly. *She smells of the raccoon family who denned here and specifically of the she-kit the bad one wounded.*

"What!" Garrett said.

Artemisia straightened, calm and reserved. She crossed her arms. "Yes, that's what I wanted to tell you. I found, or rather, Randa found me when she was wounded yesterday."

"Randa?"

"My new Fam."

Not only had Artemisia kept information from him, she had won the trust of the raccoons when he had not. It grated. "I need to speak with her."

Artemisia glanced at her wrist timer. "And I need to go to work. I'm late enough that I'll have to teleport."

And he, Garrett, damn well needed to send this new irritation away and treat her right. He couldn't afford any more screwups with her. So he sucked in a big breath and shook out his arms and legs. Noted that the cat ran toward the direction of his office.

"I'm sorry. My pride was hurt that . . . Randa . . . came to you instead of me." He gave her a rueful smile. "I've been trying to woo them."

"Unlike me," she said.

Stup! "Do I need to apologize again?"

"No. But I must go."

"I'll see you later."

She shrugged. "You have the recordsphere of my interviews with the guards regarding the altar knife and how it was found." She swallowed. "In Randa. She's fine, by the way."

Artemisia teleported away.

FAMMAN! yelled Rusby. *I am at Our office. There are A LOT of FAMS here and they all want FOOD.*

Gritting his teeth, Garrett teleported to the pad in the corner of his office. The smell of mildew was even stronger. He had no doubt that the other tenants had reported the problem the day before, but the landlord hadn't taken care of it.

Yep, he had to leave this place.

He noted a couple of calls in his scry panel cache, but fed the feral Fams prime soft kibble and some actual furrabeast shreds that he pulled from the no-time—the last of the batch.

While they ate, he and Rusby went back to the office and Garrett watched the scrys. One was from Laev and was brief and nearly angry. "The Mugworts don't have anything to do with the murder. Leave them alone."

Garrett stared at the fading image of his friend on the scry panel.

Oddly enough, in the second scry, Winterberry said almost the same thing in a more courteous manner and with a puzzled expression on his face. "I have been informed by several people—including Tinne Holly, the owner of The Green Knight Fencing and Fighting Salon, and Captain Ruis Elder of the starship *Nuada's Sword*—that the older Mugworts, the once GraceLord and Lady, have unshakeable alibis." His mouth twisted. "I have not been given proof of that." He ran his fingers through his cap of white hair, then smiled. "I trust that you will receive proof." The Captain of the guards shifted his shoulders. "I must admit I am beginning to like the idea that someone else will have to deal with the higher Nobles, the FirstFamilies, and the FirstFamilies Council." His grin spread. "Good luck."

Garrett sat in his comfortchair, leaned back, and contemplated the now dark screen of his scry panel. "Huh." He let notions flow through his mind, pulled out some coins, and exercised his fingers, rolling the coins across his knuckles. "Must be nice to have high-ranking friends." That didn't come out as bitterly as it would have a year ago.

Rusby, who was on Garrett's desk, stopped grooming and looked at Garrett with yellow eyes. "Yesss," he said.

"Don't need to think about the Mugworts right now. There are other threads to pull." Lounging, he scried Winterberry back and spoke at length about Modoc Eryngo's viewing. There were several copies of the viz camera recordings and one arrived in Garrett's office mail cache.

They discussed the Eryngo Family members who had rotated the duty of sitting next to the body—his sister and father and nephew and niece. All of them were angry and on the suspects list.

Garrett kept his face straight as Winterberry finally relayed in a dry voice the alibis for the murder for himself—at the guardhouse catching up on reports—and his wife, Trif Clover Winterberry—in bed and vouched for by her Fam, Greyku. Garrett had commented that if Fams' words were being taken, especially cat Fams, then the Turquoise House's reports should be good.

Having the man's knowledge available to him was priceless. Garrett shifted uncomfortably when he recalled that Winterberry had perfected the skill of interacting with the FirstFamilies . . . something that Garrett supposed he'd have to learn. Lord and Lady knew, the FirstFamilies would want a guy to report to them at regular intervals, too.

"My wife's Fam, Greyku, did attend the viewing." Winterberry's gaze went to the left of his panel as if staring at the cat. "Despite our requests that she would not go."

There was a loud cat sniff from Winterberry's vicinity. Since the FamCat wasn't projecting telepathically to Garrett, he didn't hear her comment but knew there had to be one. No doubt the cat was disguising her curiosity as duty or something.

"As for the rest of the alibis, we are continuing to tabulate the whereabouts of each of the victims' Families: the Gingers, Sedums, Dills, and Sorrells." Winterberry's voice went carefully colorless. "FirstFamily GreatLord Saille T'Willow was in bed with his HeartMate."

Despite the fact that Willow had worn weapons to the viewing, Garrett knew firsthand that the man was one of the least capable fighters of the FirstFamilies, not a man accustomed to violence. Not a man who would think of killing someone as a first option of revenge.

"I suggest that we take Willow's word for his wife's whereabouts, at least for now," Winterberry said. "Her presence in T'Willow Residence is also confirmed by that entity, her FamCat, Fairyfoot, and T'Willow's FamCat, Myx."

There was something Winterberry wasn't spelling out. Garrett narrowed his eyes at the Captain.

A corner of the guard's mouth kicked up. His voice remained soft and polite, though there was the hint of a gleam in his eyes. "As you work with the FirstFamilies, Primross, you will have to become accustomed to each particular Flair. You do recall that GreatLady D'Willow is also D'Thyme and she can move through time."

Garrett shuddered. "I'd forgotten."

"The way I understand how her Flair works, she can move through time, but not space." Winterberry stated it flatly, as if he was sure the Willow-Thyme Family was keeping secrets, as, of course, every FirstFamily would. "There is no indication D'Willow-Thyme was outside of her Residence, her estate, or Noble Country."

"Thank you," Garrett said. "Is that all?"

"Our weapons expert is still examining the knife. She should have something within two days."

"That's good."

"We have discovered that the reason Modoc Eryngo was in Druida City was to manage and retrieve some money he had under an alternate identity. This was not the first time he had returned."

"But someone recognized him this time," Garrett said.

"Sounds right." Winterberry's steady gaze met Garrett's. "And that's all the information I have for you today. Our shifts will, of course, continue to work the case around the clock."

Garrett nodded. "I have some leads of my own."

"Good. No doubt the FirstFamilies will be in touch."

"No doubt." He straightened. "We're missing something."

"What?" asked Winterberry.

"Not sure, but something simple. We've gone over everything."

"That's right."

There were a few heartbeats of silence. "I can't read your mind," the Captain said. He dipped his head. "If that's all, *I* have other cases."

Garrett wanted to wince, but didn't. "See you tomorrow."

Winterberry nodded. "Been a hard day; glad I'm going home to my wife. Later." He ended the scry.

Garrett himself had discussed his other cases by scry, or, in the case of the lord, set an appointment for tomorrow evening at the man's social club. He wasn't sure whether the guy wanted to intimidate or impress him.

Garrett looked at the old wall timer. Artemisia would be ending her short workday now, too. And heading for her appointment with the priest.

Time to man up.

He paced the short length of his office, then prodded his kitten awake. Rusby had fallen asleep on the one cushy client chair.

He didn't want to talk to anyone about the damn meeting with the priest, but if he was going with Artemisia, best if Rusby understood some rules. He wrapped both hands around his Fam's middle and held the kitten in front of his face out of paw range. "This is a very . . . touchy . . . time between my lady and me."

You've been mean to her.

That hurt, but if he couldn't admit it again to his Fam, he had a feeling that he wouldn't get anywhere in a damn counseling session with Artemisia and the priest.

"That's right, and Artemisia and I and you are going to see someone to help us with the mistakes."

The man whose Flair smelled nice. The one We met when We ate and who was in the park later.

"That's right," Garrett repeated.

The man who wasn't mean to her. He will listen to your apologies.

Garrett ground his teeth only once before he answered again, "That's right. I want you to be as quiet as you can." One more half grind. "Please."

Rusby nodded somberly. *Yes, I will, so you can say again that you are sorry for being mean and making her cry and hurt.*

Garrett closed his eyes and parroted, "That's right."

I will be quiet, Rusby said.

One last request for the Fam. "And I'd like to take you in a hip bag, so . . ."

I like sitting on your shoulder; I can see everything.

"I worry about you on my shoulder." True enough. He translocated a small bag that he'd purchased from Gwydion Ash and had sent to his cache box.

It was an oblong bag with a long flap over the top that could be folded up to show a mesh where Rusby could see out. The Fam carrier was several times longer than the kitten. And if Garrett had to fight, the pouch had a loop that would break free with a yank of his thumb. If it fell, it turned hard, into a small fortress. Rusby would be protected unless he teleported out. The bag and the spells had cost more than Garrett had once made in a month, but he considered it worth it.

"This is yours."

Mine! My first present from My FamMan! The kitten squealed and pounced on it. The bag didn't seem to roll like Rusby expected and he fought it with tooth and claws, leaving raw scrapes on the leather. Garrett winced. But it was stupid to think that something made for a kitten would remain pristine—even for two minutes.

Rusby pawed the flap open and wiggled inside. The bag rocked, then took a slight shape around the kitten. Garrett folded up the flap but couldn't see through the mesh. Smiling, he crouched, "You in there, Rusby?"

You can't see Me?

"No." Though he could see plenty of here-and-gone bulges as Rusby squirmed.

A secret! A secret ride for Me.

"That's right." And hopefully it would be an added reason for Rusby to stay quiet. There was so much Garrett wanted to tell Artemisia—even before a priest—that he was afraid he'd stutter, and if his Fam distracted him, Garrett might not get everything out.

I will be your secret informer.

The identities of his informers were secret . . . except both TQ and Artemisia knew, since they'd taken care of the ferals when he was sick.

Garrett shrugged. If Artemisia was still speaking to him after this—and he prayed that things would go well—she would give her word not to talk about his irregulars.

He stewed about the appointment on the glider ride all the way to GreatCircle Temple, but when Artemisia stood outside the huge doors, he joined her.

She flinched. He hoped because she'd been lost in thought and hadn't seen him, not because the sight of him hurt her.

"What are you doing here?" she asked in less than serene tones.

He dipped his head in an inclination of respect and held out his hand, trying not to notice it was a few shades darker than her skin and rough with calluses. She'd never looked so Noble to him, standing here where the Nobles worshiped.

And never looked so dear.

"I think the reason you are troubled in your mind—" he started.

"In my *heart*." She put her hand between her breasts, shaping her tunic to them, lush and full. His palm tingled as he remembered how her nipple, tight with passion, felt against the hollow of his hand, how softness overflowed his fingers.

He cleared his throat, tried again. "I think the reason you are troubled in your heart is because of me." How could his throat have clogged up again so soon? "That I caused this, and that we . . . we should . . . we should speak to the . . . the priest . . ." Suck it up and get it out, Primross! "We should speak to the priest together."

She stared at him, as if she were amazed.

Not appalled, like he was.

She looked down at his hand, then back into his eyes, then stared at him, and he suffered, for far too long. He had to set into his balance, meet her eyes, accept her skepticism, and not look away. He *had* to stick this out.

After a long two minutes, her answer was whispery soft and gentle. "You really think we should go to Cinchona together?"

No, he didn't want to speak to the priest. Not with Artemisia, and not without her. But he'd already learned when she could be talked out of doing something, and this was not one of those times.

"Yeah. Yes," he said.

Her head tilted. "You *think* so? Or do you *believe* so? Or do you *feel* so?"

None of the above. Or, maybe feel, so he went with that. "I feel so."

She nodded and her fingers slipped into his. Seemed like he'd found the right answer for her.

"All right," she said, and pushed open the door.

The place smelled good. And looked rich and elegant. And felt wonderful, with incredible uplifting energy. Lady and Lord, if he'd known the place had felt this good, he might have come before.

Not really, but so far it wasn't a hardship to be here. Maybe he'd—they'd—get through this damne—*difficult*—session.

This south entrance was tinted in filmy streaks of gold and yellow and touches of orange, all melding together. The entry room was about four meters square, with another set of double doors—open—before them. Garrett's feet sank into the rug and he looked down to see it was white—not practical for an entryway.

Artemisia let out a sigh, her lips curved. "I always forget how lovely it is here."

She looked at him, as if weighing his commitment. He straightened his shoulders and squeezed her hand. "Yeah."

They walked together from the foyer into the wide corridor that circled the building. This time the doors ahead of them, leading into the main Temple, were closed.

The walls of the hallway were another pale color but had the fuzziness showing they held several mural spells, for different rituals, he presumed. Rusby shifted in Garrett's hip pack and Garrett sensed pleasure and excitement from his Fam.

Artemisia glanced down the left curving hallway almost furtively, then tugged on his hand and began to walk fast down the right side of the circular corridor. He slowed his steps. "We're in good time." He was in no hurry to do this.

She scowled up at him. "You *do* recall that I have a sister who is a priestess, don't you? Who works here? As a counselor?"

"Now that you prompt me, I do." Sounded as if Artemisia hadn't shared her troubled heart with her sister. Garrett matched Artemisia's pace. He was in no hurry to meet that woman, either.

Artemisia stopped at a door halfway between the south and east entryway with Leger Cinchona's name on it. Garrett wasn't sure whether the position indicated the status the priest had attained or whether the placement was spiritual in nature—Cinchona liked the energy of the southeast.

Garrett would inwardly admit that the man had good Flair.

The priest opened his door and Garrett noticed that his office was generally four meters by four meters, the outer wall curved, of course. There was a slight odor of incense and herbs but nothing that would bother Garrett any more than being here.

Cinchona nodded to Artemisia—good, the man didn't reach for her hand—and looked past her to Garrett.

Feeling exposed enough to check that the hall was still empty, Garrett also kept his voice low. "I requested that since much of the reason Artemisia wishes to speak with you involves me, I be included in the meeting."

The priest's eyebrows went up. He met Artemisia's eyes. "Is this what you want, Artemisia?"

Thirty

Garrett felt her palm go damp in his hand. Or maybe that was his. He closed his fingers tighter.

She sniffed and the priest seemed to take that as a good sign that Garrett wasn't intimidating her. "It's true, we have a tangled relationship."

"I wouldn't have thought that you'd have lunch or dinner with a man interested in pursuing his own relationship with you if you were entangled with another," Cinchona said gently.

Artemisia tugged on her fingers and Garrett reluctantly let them go. She raised her chin. "We weren't in a relationship, then."

"Yesterday noon," Cinchona said.

"It's complicated," Garrett growled. "Are you going to see us or not?"

"That depends." Cinchona didn't move. "On Artemisia's wishes—and on yours. Do you trust me as a priest, Artemisia?"

She smiled. "Of course."

"Good to know, but still a small pity that's all you see."

The guy was being too good. Garrett grunted.

"And you?" He switched his blue gray gaze to Garrett.

"Yeah, yeah," he said.

Cinchona cocked his head. "I sense that you don't trust many people." He raised a palm. "And you don't want to talk about your relationship with Artemisia."

"You got that right, but if it's something that Artemisia needs, I'll do it. I'll always give her what she needs."

Artemisia bumped into the doorjamb as she stepped back and looked up at him. Heat came to his cheeks, but he nodded to her. "I've been a stup."

"Come in." Cinchona stepped back and opened the door wide.

The room was comfortably furnished, and not as if the priest catered mostly to females. Rust and gold and dark brown chairs and cushions, well used but not shabby. Everything about the man indicated he was a lesser Noble, a second son or something, and had never had to worry about gilt.

But the data from Garrett's informants had stated Cinchona was a very good man. No doubt kind, compassionate, and caring, like Artemisia.

Too much like Artemisia. She needed someone, like Garrett, a little rougher in her life.

"Please, sit," the priest said.

There was a long couch with one side that angled up. Garrett nearly shuddered. Since he was the first in, he took one of the three chairs near a wedge-shaped outside corner, obviously set up for couples counseling. He stiffened his spine. He *was* part of a couple. He leaned against the back cushion, stretched his legs out.

Artemisia sat in the chair on his right, a little beyond his reach. Cinchona sat in the butterscotch brown fine-grained leather chair. Garrett's own chair wasn't as comfortable.

"I'm Leger Cinchona," the priest said.

"I know. I'm Garrett Primross."

"Ah, I have heard of you," Cinchona said. He blinked as if accessing his memories and Garrett let quiet sift into the room.

Artemisia sighed and settled into her own chair, her face in its usual, sincerely serene expression. Which was good, as was the priest and the atmosphere, but Garrett didn't have any expectation she'd remain serene long. Not when they started digging into the events of the night before last and the snarled bonds between them.

Before the man said the blessing that would start the session, Garrett added, "I saw you at Apollopa Park."

Cinchona smiled slowly. "I know."

"Yeah?" Garrett couldn't help himself, he angled his body to ruin the line between Artemisia and the priest.

"You don't think I could feel such an inimical glare?" Cinchona's brows rose. He was enjoying this, dammit. Garrett felt his face heat.

The priest went on, with a hint of a smirk. "You didn't like my interest in Artemisia. Or rather, you don't, even now, when it must be obvious that she considers me more of a priest, and perhaps a friend, rather than a gallant to woo her."

"What I need to know," Artemisia said crisply, "is if whatever is between the two of you will impede this counseling session."

Crap. Just that easily her mood had been broken. Garrett not only retreated a mental step, but ratcheted down his attitude. "No," he said.

"Of course not," the priest said in a smooth and professionally gentle tone.

Rusby flung back the flap of his carry case and hopped out to the large, rolled arm of Garrett's chair. The rust brown weave was loose enough that it didn't show any pinpricks made by small claws. *I am Rusby Primross and I have been very good.* He sat straight.

"You brought Rusby!" Artemisia said.

At her tone, Rusby huddled in on himself and gave Artemisia big eyes. Garrett could tell the kitten's feelings weren't hurt, that the Fam was curious more than anything else, but Garrett kept his mouth shut.

You don't want Me here?

She pursed her lips, looked at the priest.

"There are no rules against Fams," Cinchona said. "On the contrary, I've found they can be helpful."

"Hmm," Artemisia said, then shrugged. "Very well."

"Thank you, Artemisia," Garrett said.

Thank you, FamWoman, Rusby said, and revved his thin purr. The comforting sound lasted through the standard blessing for truth and gentleness and guidance.

Garrett's nerves tightened.

Artemisia began to talk. She was unexpectedly generous when she told of the experiment, touched on his ordeal, then revealed the circumstances of Garrett telling her that she was his HeartMate and that he didn't want her. Her words still made Garrett writhe inside.

The priest asked penetrating questions about the exact circumstances of the when and why Garrett had spewed so, and when Garrett was slow to answer, Rusby wriggled on his lap. Garrett figured the kitten wouldn't keep quiet about the nightmares, so he reluctantly answered each and every question, delving further into his feelings, more than he'd ever wanted.

And as he explained, he felt the bond between himself and Artemisia opening, flowing with emotion, her inherent compassion that tugged on his feelings, his very mixed feelings, in return. He stopped his instinctual squeezing shut of the bond.

He couldn't do that anymore.

Not if he wanted Artemisia.

At the end of all the questions, the priest studied Garrett, then Artemisia, then the both of them. "I have heard of your experience with the Iasc sickness, of course," Cinchona said slowly. "Three years ago when it was discovered you survived and were willing to help fight the epidemic with your blood donations. Also when the most recent experiment was proposed and successfully concluded." He slanted a look at Artemisia. "Your sister, Tiana, has duties to lead rituals here, and is required to report any other claims upon her energy and Flair. She told us—her peer group and our teachers— that she'd conducted a couple of Family rituals with regard to the experiment."

"Yes," Artemisia said.

Garrett hadn't known that.

She turned and met his gaze. "It was very helpful."

Again the priest studied them both, and Garrett felt the man's Flair brushing him.

"You have never seen a priest or mind Healer about your experiences? Your loss and grief?" Cinchona asked him.

"No," Garrett gritted out.

The priest sighed. His brows went up and down as he studied Garrett. "I'd recommend that."

When Garrett's jaw clamped shut, the priest amended, "When you're ready." He paused. "Since you and Artemisia came to me for counseling, and such is held to be completely confidential, I will not report your breaking of the law about informing your HeartMate that she *was* your HeartMate. Especially since I can see that you are both being punished by the knowledge." He drew in an audible breath. "Though I might recommend following the requirements of the law in circumstances such as yours, when one HeartMate informs the other who is unknowing of the link. You violated Artemisia's free will."

"It was a good thing," Artemisia said and her voice wasn't even unsteady. "I'd been . . . unconsciously waiting for him. When Garrett informed me that he wouldn't claim me, it gave me the freedom—"

"Stop," the priest ordered, pushed a little Flair behind the word. Artemisia did.

"I see no reason to go over this particular event again since it hurts you both. You will Heal well enough from the emotional pain if it is left alone."

Thank the Lord and Lady, this priest might be an okay guy after all. But Garrett hadn't looked up the consequences of breaking that law. His face hardened into a mask. "If that means staying away from Artemisia . . ." He held out his hand to her. Once again she stared at his fingers, then met his gaze with a troubled one of her own. "I can't do that. I've already stayed away from her too much."

He sucked in a breath and inclined his head to her. "I'm all right with having to prove myself to her. That's fair for all that I've put her through. But . . . but . . ."

He couldn't bring himself to say it.

Artemisia's took his hand again and tenderness—tenderness!—swirled along their bond. "You're afraid."

Only one side of his mouth twisted up in a raw smile. He kept his eyes meeting hers. "Yeah. Afraid I'll lose you. To another man . . . or worse."

"An understandable fear," the priest murmured.

"I want a husband and children," Artemisia said.

"I know." He drew all the intensity he had around him. "I can't say that I am ready for children." More deep breathing, and no one hurried him. "But I will protect and cherish you to my last breath," Garrett said. Since he already had a history of doing that with another woman, he figured they'd believe him.

The priest considered him; this time the man's pupils were dilated and the guy's Flair enveloped Garrett.

Cinchona said, "What if protecting and cherishing Artemisia means you must rid yourself of these negative feelings by piercing the wound of your fear and grief and letting them drain? I believe that's the best option at this point."

Garrett jerked. He'd never thought that he'd carried around an infected sore seething with pus—or worse.

The priest still looked at him, using Flair that slithered along Garrett's exposed skin, raising the little hairs on his body. "You sure about that wound business?" Garrett managed.

"I'm afraid so."

"And how am I supposed to do that?" Garrett scowled.

Artemisia dropped his hand, and he missed her touch.

"By telling us about your experience," Cinchona said.

"I've lived through it again recently, isn't that enough?" Garrett snarled.

"Have you ever told anyone every detail of that fateful trip, or has it only been as dry and factual a report as you could get away with?"

Bull's-eye.

"Once you say it, it should be done," Cinchona offered.

"You think so?" Garrett didn't believe that.

Cinchona's own smile was wry. "You think we haven't counseled warriors such as yourself before? Yes, this procedure often works."

Garrett made a disbelieving noise, added, "I can get a guarantee?"

Now Cinchona stiffened. "I have given you my best recommendations in this matter, the conclusions I came to through experience and the use of my Flair. However, if you don't wish to take my advice, that is certainly your prerogative. As is deciding whether or when to do this and whether with a different counselor."

Oh, yeah, he'd want to lay the whole damn stupidity out for someone else, sure.

"Such as the best mind Healer, FirstFamily GrandLady D'Sea. I'm sure that under the circumstances, with the service you've given to Celta, she would waive her fee."

Canny priest. Of course Garrett wouldn't want to talk to a female mind Healer, especially not one of the highest Nobles.

Artemisia stood up, straightened her tunic, looked down at him. Her gaze lingered on his arms across his chest, his closed-off body. Dammit, their bond had narrowed and he knew he'd reduced it automatically.

He didn't want to do this. He'd *never* wanted to talk about it, relive it. Hadn't he already done that enough?

But he understood from the expression in her eyes that Artemisia doubted him. That if he didn't go through this now, she might think he wasn't worth having. He'd lose her. And somehow she'd become too dear to do that.

He'd meant what he'd said previously, to the marrow of his bones. He'd do what he'd have to, to win her, to keep her safe and cherish her.

His tense shoulders lifted, dropped as his breath nearly groaned out of him. "Yeah, I'll do it, right now."

Surprise and pleasure flowed through their bond from Artemisia, and her smile at him took his breath.

"Here's something to make it easier." Cinchona had gone to the no-time food storage unit and Garrett hadn't noticed. The priest held out a tube.

The liquid really didn't look like blood. Sure, it was red, but it fizzed with bubbles, was a whole lot thinner and lighter than blood. Pomegranate. Or cranberry. And that reminded Garrett of Opul Cranberry, and the boy's courage in fighting the sickness. Garrett was supposed to have courage, too, even if everything inside him cringed at doing this.

He stood and crossed to the priest and grabbed the tube—cool to his touch—and swallowed it down before he asked, "What is it?"

Cinchona's smile was wide and gently teasing. "Like I said, you aren't the first man who doesn't like to speak of his . . . concerns. We'll call it a tongue loosener."

"Great," Garrett said. The stuff hadn't tasted too bad.

Cinchona waved Garrett to his chair, and he obeyed. He turned his head at Artemisia. His tongue was beginning to feel thick, maybe he wouldn't talk after all. Not his problem if the potion didn't work on him.

Artemisia came to him, curved her hands around his face and bent and kissed his forehead. Memory swam of the time when he was sick. She'd been tender then, too. He was surprised she'd offer the gesture, though. "Thanks."

"She's your HeartMate, who else would be so much of a comfort?" asked Cinchona softly.

And I am his Fam, Rusby said.

"Yes."

"You *have* been a good kitten, keeping quiet," Garrett said.

Human problems pretty boring, the kitten replied. *Even Fam-Man's and FamWoman's. I fell asleep.*

Cinchona's eyes twinkled. "Kittens do."

"Yesss," Rusby said.

Then the three of them sat and watched Garrett. His body tightened with wariness. Artemisia scooted her chair closer and took his hand in both of hers. He *saw* the golden bond between them pulse with emotion—compassion and, affection?—from her. She had affection for him? After all that he'd done?

He could feel the drink working on him, too, cracking him wide open like he was some crusty shellfish, his outer protective cover gone, the tender, vulnerable meat of him exposed and throbbing anxiety.

Cinchona said, "The Iasc sickness was traced to an unknown fish with an unknown infection that washed ashore on the beach of the Smallage estate near Gael City. You received a scry from Dinni Spurge Flixweed, who lived on the estate, to meet her at a Gael City health clinic." The priest's tone was smooth, nearly hypnotic. He repeated the words Garrett had always used when giving his report of the events.

"Yes," and Garrett went on. And told everything, every detail, every feeling, every fliggering twitch of his gut. Like he'd told no one before, from the first person he'd scried from the mountain quarantine clinic after the disaster to the self-righteous and arrogant First-Level Healer Ura Heather.

After an eternity, he came to consciousness as a tiny rough tongue swiped at his wet face. Garrett was curled up on the floor of the office. His throat felt raw, his eyes grimy. Oh, Lord and Lady, he'd spilled his guts, hadn't he?

FamMan is awake, Rusby said, with one last lick. Garrett's face had dried with sweat. Maybe drool, too.

Cautiously he inhaled. Nope, didn't smell like he'd soiled himself again, like in real life, and a couple of nightmares since. Thank the Lady and Lord he'd been spared that.

He became aware of a soft body cradling his back. His neck cricked when he looked down. Artemisia's arms were around him, clasped as if she wouldn't let him go. The last of his breath soughed out. His spine felt . . . protected.

He wouldn't have to clean himself up and walk through a horribly echoing, smelly clinic . . . Had he told them that, too?

Yes, of course. The damn drink had loosened his tongue to a babble of every fliggering particular.

He turned his head, with another creak he felt more than heard, and saw the priest in his chair. Cinchona's face remained professionally serious, but he swallowed convulsively and sweat beaded his hairline, making the dirty blond widow's peak darker. Guy had long hair pulled back and tied in a tail, and Garrett thought some of those strands were darker, too. He was perversely pleased he'd shaken the priest.

There was a quiet cough and Garrett jerked to sit, his head wrenching around to see the newcomer. His stomach clenched as he recognized the highest priest of the planet, T'Sandalwood.

Thirty-one

*G*arrett *stared at* High *Priest Sandalwood as the great man scruti-*nized him. Garrett opened his mouth to speak, but it was too damn dry. Artemisia moved, withdrew herself, and he felt chilled. A moment later she was back, next to him, putting an arm around his waist, leaning against him. Snuffling. She rubbed her head against his shoulder and he realized she was crying.

Garrett glared at Cinchona.

The man shrugged bony shoulders. "I'm sorry, I didn't realize that I was out of my depth with you and the multiple deaths of close friends in such a manner and the horror of the trip and awakening, such grief . . ." He gulped and sweat was along his top lip, too. Guy looked wrung out.

Grunting, Garrett shifted his eyes back to the high priest in a formal robe. Now that he examined the man, a man who had an incredibly intense *presence*, he didn't appear very calm, either. Garrett sniffed again and smelled the herbs that absorbed sweat and released a nicer fragrance. Rich herbs, from the high priest's robe.

T'Sandalwood bowed. "You have my assurance and my sworn oath as a spiritual leader that I will keep this session confidential, as usual."

Finally Garrett gave in to the urge to cough and racked a few seconds until his throat was clear. "You can't tell me that you won't write everything down that you heard for your records." He nodded to Cinchona. "And that you won't have him write everything down, either."

Artemisia said, "Priests and priestesses are trained to have excellent memories."

The high priest sighed and met Garrett's eyes with a sober gaze of his own. "That is true. But I vow to you that I will speak to no one about this"—he shot a command at Cinchona—"nor will First-Level Priest Cinchona, unless lives are at stake." His attention returned to Garrett. "And our recordspheres, memoryspheres, and any journals we keep of this incident will be spellshielded and not available, except in extreme need, to be opened for two centuries."

"Huh," Garrett said. He rubbed his neck and sweat and skin flaked into his palm. "I guess that's the best that I can get." He didn't like it, though.

He felt hollowed out, scoured by emotions. Feelings he hoped never to live through again. Done with them. Done with all the people he'd known who he'd watched die. Done with Dinni and her child, who'd had no chance. Done. Done. Done.

The high priest paused. "I do not usually advocate premarriage counseling for HeartMates, but under the circumstances . . ."

Hot irritation streamed through Garrett's blood as he understood that Cinchona had revealed the whole HeartMate mess to T'Sandalwood.

Garrett glared at the high priest, looked again at the pale younger priest. "I thought once I talked this out, I would lance that wound you said I had and be all right. Good enough to woo my HeartMate, my Artemisia." She still quivered against his side.

Cinchona's mouth turned down, then he said, "No guarantees, remember?"

"Ah, hmm." T'Sandalwood shot a frown at his subordinate. "You said something like that?"

Holding his body with dignity, Cinchona said, "I did. My Flair indicated that GentleSir Primross would be better for such a catharsis."

T'Sandalwood's heavy salt-and-pepper brows dipped in near his eyes. "Better?" He turned his examination from the younger priest to Garrett.

"Much better," Cinchona added firmly. He cleared his throat. "And the man's fear of losing loved ones and his grief that such horrific experiences engendered in him *have* been *much* relieved."

T'Sandalwood's nostrils widened as he examined Garrett and Artemisia. He turned his palm over toward the ceiling, and curled his fingers. Garrett found himself rising to his feet, no muscles involved, as the priest's Flair lifted him. He had to brace his knees to stand steady, and took a little of Artemisia's weight, too.

She pulled a large softleaf from her sleeve and mopped her face, drew out another one, and lifted it to his face, murmuring a spell that made it sweetly fragrant and like it had a little lotion to soothe. Since it felt so good, he didn't complain about it being girly.

"I have an alternative to the prenuptial counseling," T'Sandalwood said in a soft tone that made Garrett flinch, knowing it would be nearly as bad as what he'd already gone through.

"What?" His voice rumbled all the way from his gut.

"We have rituals for survivors of catastrophic events."

"No!" Artemisia stepped away from Garrett's side. "Hasn't he gone through enough? Two fliggering bouts of Iasc sickness and telling Cinchona and me and you and Rusby about the whole dreadful thing?"

Garrett stared; he'd never heard her curse before.

"Artemisia, your natural compassion is wonder—" T'Sandalwood began.

"No." She stamped her foot. "I won't have it. He's been through enough." She drew herself to her fullest height and her gaze matched the high priest's. Garrett was impressed.

"And so have I." She pounded a fist once on her chest over her heart. "I tended him through his second Iasc sickness, and I just listened to his words of that terrible time in his life. As far as I am concerned, Garrett is far more stable than either of *you* priests. And far more heroic."

"A HeartMate would say—" T'Sandalwood once again was interrupted by Artemisia.

"Oh, let's go," she said, tugging on Garrett's hand. "We're done here. I'll transfer gilt from my account."

"I can do that," Garrett croaked. Making sure his hand was steady, he scooped up Rusby and put him on his shoulder. He sank a little into his balance to ground himself, get his legs. He didn't think anyone noticed. When he felt strong again, he straightened his knees, then stretched long—shoulders, arms, hands, then thighs, calves; arched and flexed his feet.

He turned and bowed to the high priest, who was having a stare off with Artemisia. Then he turned back to Cinchona and bowed. Much as he didn't want to, he said the courteous word. "Thanks."

"My apologies for . . ." The younger priest raised and dropped his hands.

Garrett snagged Artemisia with an arm around her waist. "Come on, woman, we have things to do." He met the high priest's eyes. "Interesting to meet you."

"I'll expect a clean mental and spiritual bill of health from you, T'Sandalwood, on my HeartMate," Artemisia said.

"And may I officiate at your wedding?" he asked.

Garrett's sweat turned cold. Artemisia noted his slight hesitation, before he lied as well as he could, "Sure." He met the older priest's gaze with a straight one of his own.

He left arm in arm with Artemisia, but she knew he'd withdrawn a bit. Wasn't really ready for marriage. Not. Quite. Yet.

He wondered how much slack she'd give him. A week, maybe two? Not nearly as much as she would have if he hadn't screwed up the whole thing.

They leaned on each other as they exited the Temple and into the evening. Garrett winced. His story had taken a lot longer than he'd realized. But here he was, hand in hand with his HeartMate. All to the good, he supposed. He really didn't feel that much better.

But if the nightmares would go away, it was also worth it. And thinking of dreams, the image of the turquoise Healing pool slid into his brain. "I could use a good soak."

He glanced at her from the corners of his eyes. She hadn't reacted, thinking of something else. Not thinking of him.

"Best in a Healing pool. You live near one, don't you?"

That had her stiffening against him.

"How do you know that?" she asked.

Rusby spoke up from his place on Garrett's shoulder. *The ferals told him.*

Her stare was accusatory.

"I didn't ask them to spy on you," he said, aggrieved.

True, Rusby said. *I am hungry. I have missed TWO feedings.*

How could that be? But when Garrett counted the minutes, he found the kitten was right.

"I can't go anywhere in this condition," Garrett said. He put a little distance between himself and Artemisia, squeezed her hand, but his voice was harsh when he said, "And you're still keeping secrets."

Her chin lifted, she didn't look at him . . . but she didn't pull her fingers away, either. Their bond had reduced a bit, and he thought she'd done that as much as he.

"There are things I can't—"

Hello, Garrett. Hello, Healer. Sleek Black trotted beside them. He looked up at Garrett and wrinkled his nose. *You smell, Garrett. You smell, Healer.* He snickered.

Rusby stared down at him. *You are not polite. I was being polite.*

Sleek Black ignored the kitten. *We have tracked all four of the raccoons. Two are with this Healer.*

Garrett stopped. "I understood that one is her Fam. Whom I need to speak with. Keeping more than one secret, it appears."

"Just because you let all your secrets out, I need to tell mine?" Her eyes had lightened from the dark green that he preferred.

"Of course. That's how HeartMates work." He was sure of *that.*

"Humph." She scowled at Sleek Black. *Thanks a lot, cat.*

You are welcome.

Artemisia's lips flattened, then she said, "You must have reviewed my interrogations. As you know, my Fam didn't see much, only experienced the"—she swallowed hard—"the hatred of the murderer. I don't know of the other raccoon."

A passerby grumbled as he walked around them. Garrett drew Artemisia into the deep doorway of a restaurant that served only breakfast and lunch and had already closed. Rusby sniffed deeply; Sleek Black sat and watched them with a smirk.

"All your secrets revolve around your home." He'd wanted her to tell him of it freely, but now it didn't look like that would happen, and it hurt.

She tilted her head up and looked him in the eyes. "I am sworn to secrecy."

Bad things happen if she tells, Sleek Black said.

"What bad things?" Garrett grabbed her shoulders. "How can I help?"

"I can't say." Artemisia formed each word coldly.

"Fligger." Garrett dropped his hands from her.

"Please don't curse at me." She shifted and he suddenly knew she was about to teleport away.

"Not you, never you, at the situation. *Our* situation."

Secret place. Sleek Black flicked his whiskers.

More synapses connected in Garrett's mind, until he was sure. "The hidden garden. The first HealingHall established by the colonists. BalmHeal estate, the secret sanctuary that lets in only the desperate."

Artemisia's eyes flickered. "I can't say." She slipped around him, back onto the sidewalk. "I'll go find Randa and the other raccoon so they can speak to you about the murder. I'll scry you later, when the raccoons are available."

"Wait, you must know that our . . . bond is more important. That I've had a change of heart—" Garrett said, but she disappeared anyway.

Sleek Black angled his head. *You are not good with females.*

"No." But he could be persistent. "Do you know where this secret garden is?"

Of course. All ferals know. A cat shrug rippled down his back. *Some go there sometimes and some don't. But all know.*

"Take me there."

We are going to THE sanctuary, Rusby whispered in his mind.

"That's right. Now."

Food! Rusby said.

"All right, food first."

Sleek Black stretched, back end up, tail swishing. *I could eat, too. It's a long walk.*

Didn't sound like the cat knew a better way. Damn.

*A*rtemisia 'ported directly to the empty pad set in a trellised area close to the main Healing pool in BalmHeal estate. She wasn't really surprised at the tears running down her face. She'd cried a lot during Garrett's tormented story.

She hurt for him and for herself so much she was tired and dizzy with it. She shucked her clothes and put them in a cleanser that would translocate them to BalmHeal Residence. Then she slid into the hot water and sat on the stone seat.

As had happened so often in the last eightday, jumbled emotions clashed through her.

Randa? she kept the mental call quiet, easy to ignore if her Fam wanted. And no matter what Artemisia had said to Garrett, she wanted the comfort of her Fam more than to convince Randa to speak to Garrett.

I am here. Randa moved in the almost graceful lumbering run toward her, stopped near her, and sniffed, held out her paws over the gently steaming water. *Nice.*

"Yes." Artemisia leaned back and closed her eyes but lifted her arm to pet Randa's thick pelt.

The raccoon made a pleased noise, nothing like a cat's purr, but Artemisia smiled. She had a prized raccoon Fam that Garrett had wanted. Small of her to enjoy that, but she did. Randa settled beside Artemisia, gently humming.

Artemisia sighed and simply enjoyed the heat of the pool soaking out the tension in her muscles and the soft rustling of leaves in the quiet breeze and the crickets beginning to chirp around her.

Such a wrenching day! The calmness of her time in the chapel this morning seemed months away. That her job was in jeopardy, her whole career, only merited a long and tired sigh. Then came a tiny jolt that she'd forgotten to speak with Laev T'Hawthorn as she'd told her parents she would. Well, she would do that tomorrow and she'd let them know that her meetings at D'Ash's and the guard-house, and work, and the appointment with Leger Cinchona had eaten up all her time today.

Of course she thought of her HeartMate. Poor Garrett, the time he'd driven to the clinic and his experiences there had been harrowing. But he'd let the memories of it control his life, and that had affected Artemisia, too.

After a few minutes, she let Garrett's words filter back into her ears. *I've had a change of heart.*

He seemed honest when he'd said that, a hint of desperation in his tone.

Change of heart.

What a phrase. Could he have had a change of heart? Had he truly allowed himself to put away his grief for Dinni, for those he'd known who had died? Turned his heart from an old love to a new?

Of course he couldn't love her.

Not the way she already had come to love him. More fool she!

She'd realized that she loved him when he'd fallen to the floor during his retelling of his ordeal and she'd curled around him. And what a time for such an insight! What a very sick time to understand that. To understand that her own heart had managed to forgive him his hurtful words.

Again, so many events and feelings had happened since the night before last that it seemed like a long time ago. And she'd changed.

She wasn't sure how, and didn't want to scrutinize herself in that much detail now, but she hoped she'd grown.

She'd respected him from their first meeting, had probably fallen in love with him—as prompted by the HeartMate bond—somewhere during the time they'd spent in TQ's HouseHeart or in that peaceful walk after the project was over, before they found the body.

They certainly hadn't had much normal time together. So she supposed they should take it slow. But for once she didn't *want* to take it slow. She'd put her life on hold for him long enough.

You are thinking of The Man Who Feeds, Randa said.

"Yes, how do you know?"

His image is very strong in your thoughts.

He is my HeartMate. She didn't say it aloud, not here, in her home that she shared with her Family.

I have heard of mates, but it makes little sense.

"That's all right." Artemisia petted Randa; her fingers went to the place where her Fam had been wounded, but there wasn't even a scar. Randa flinched.

"He's a good man." Artemisia reluctantly began to don responsibility again. "Since he's my mate, you will be able to speak to him mentally." She was pretty sure that was standard for Fams. Garrett's Fam, Rusby, had called her FamWoman. She hadn't had any trouble hearing him telepathically.

We watched him a long time. He fed us. He liked us, we could tell.

That was the very best thing Artemisia knew about Garrett, his love for feral Fams.

She wet her lips. She had to proceed carefully. "I've heard that someone else from your Family is here in the estate." She opened her eyes and turned her head to meet Randa's black ones.

The young raccoon had rolled to a sitting position and was grooming her tail, but stopped. *Yes, my dam is here, denning for a while. But I am not hers anymore. I belong to myself and you.*

"I would like to meet her, and to thank her for making such a wonderful daughter." That was true at least.

Randa grinned.

We can go see her. The raccoon tilted her head. *She will be stirring soon, and perhaps exploring the estate. It is a good place.*

"Yes." Artemisia exited the pool and took a thick, fluffy robe from a nearby storage shelf they used in the summer. Wrapping it around herself, she lifted Randa. "We'll go home and get dressed and eat in my rooms." That way she wouldn't have to confront her parents right now about not following their advice, and wouldn't have to talk to them about her miserable day. "Then we'll go find your mother."

Randa licked Artemisia's face. *Yes.*

*T*he walk to the abandoned warehouse district in the northeastern corner of Druida City *was* long. Garrett had passed from nicely kept city blocks to rubble-strewn pathways between decrepit and tilting buildings. The colonists had laid out Druida City and built most of it with their machines, but the Celtans hadn't been as prolific as their ancestors, and there was still plenty of free building space on the outskirts of the city. And the number of Celtans had declined even more due to the Iasc sickness.

Finally, Sleek Black had led him to a narrow path outside a tall tangle of thorny brush. *It is here,* the tom said. *Now I wish to join the hunt in south Druida. Be back tomorrow morning for food!* He popped out of sight.

Squinting, Garrett could see an old, old wall behind the vegetation. He forced his way through it and touched the wall.

And was shocked and flung back into the path three meters, landing hard.

Thirty-two

$\mathcal{A}$ long time later—Garrett couldn't tell how long, he'd lost track of time with every attempt at the walls—scaling, jumping with Flair, pounding against—he was still trying to get in.

The door is over here, Rusby chirped helpfully in his mind, laughing at Garrett, he could tell.

How come you can get in and I can't? He knew what was behind the wall, but it felt like he'd been thrashing through thorny bushes for septhours. His mind was dim as to exactly where in Druida City he was, though he *knew* he'd known that a few minutes before.

Because I am FamCat to the HeartMate of Artemisia who lives in here.

Garrett banged his shoulder against the wall with a jolting, singeing sizzle from the spellshields every time, trying to get through and climb. *Then I, as that HeartMate, should . . . be . . . able . . . to . . . get . . . in!* He moved a meter or so and thumped against something that wasn't as unforgiving as stone, might not leave a bruise. The door?

And you are a FamKITTEN, Garrett said. *I hope you're all right in there on your own. Almost everything is bigger than you.* No, he shouldn't be scaring his Fam, but, dammit, he knew Rusby was enjoying being somewhere his FamMan couldn't get into.

Since his left shoulder hurt, Garrett used his right to batter at the door, again and again. Rested.

Another sniff. *Something is burning!* Rusby said.

My clothes and me. His padded armor with the inbuilt shields were no match for those on this place . . . Why was he here again?

Artemisia! Rusby shouted telepathically.

Yeah, that was why. Garrett wanted to find his woman, his HeartMate.

I am calling her! Rusby cried.

The kitten was yelling loud, broadcasting to all in the area who could hear him. Garrett could always tell the shades of telepathic communication. He breathed heavily, his shoulders ached. His whole body. Why? What was that smell? He was caught in a forcefield? Leaning against something? He had to get out of here.

But Rusby was near, and not with Garrett. Trapped?

ARTEMISIA! Rusby shrieked in his mind along with a shrill yowl from his mouth.

Yes, Garrett's HeartMate was beyond the shield, too. Was *she* trapped? Is that why he fought so hard? Why he couldn't give up? He didn't know. But he'd fought and held on before in situations when he'd lost the sense of things.

Artemisia. Trapped. His heart picked up beat. He had to get to her.

Rusby whimpered.

Garrett was desperate to find them, protect them, save them. Fight. Throw himself against the block. Fight. Batter the shield. Fight! Desperation, it was all he knew.

What he was leaning against gave way.

He fell to the ground and rolled as he'd been trained. Hell, he had burns on his body, his tunic was in tatters. He could feel dirt and rocks under him.

But he wasn't caught in thorns anymore, and his head was clearing, even if his brain felt scrambled. He lay on a packed-soil path that smelled . . . okay. The bushes around him smelled good. He rolled to his back, which seemed the least hurting part of himself.

The stars were fabulous, thick and bright. The twinmoons hadn't risen yet, but maybe he'd lie here until they were up. The sky show was great.

He heard running and low female voices. Couldn't bring himself to care. He was in BalmHeal estate and so was Rusby and Artemisia. The safest place in Druida? Maybe.

He is over here; he is HURT! Rusby yelled, then he landed with a thump on Garrett's chest, propelled by his fear and his Flair.

Footsteps pattered fast and murmuring women loomed over him. No threat, he didn't think. If they were, he was a goner.

Disappointment raged through him. Neither of the women were Artemisia.

"Oh, dear," said the older one. She looked a little like Artemisia, but her hair was of a lighter color. Her hands went to his shoulders as she knelt next to him and he flinched. Then swore as his tunic was pulled from his burns. Her fingers touched raw muscle and blackness swarmed across his vision. Then he felt cool, Healing Flair. Rusby licked under Garrett's chin. That felt good, too.

"Odd," said the younger. Yes, she was near enough for him to see well. Not Artemisia. Had to be a close relative.

"He doesn't seem to have any other wounds than what the estate spellshields gave him. Why would he persist in trying to get through them?" the young woman asked in a cooler, more logical tone than he'd expected. Must be Artemisia's . . . sister. Younger sister, Tiana, the priestess.

"Desperate," Garrett said, and his dry lips cracked open and bled. How had that happened?

"A desperate person wouldn't have to fight the shields," Tiana said tartly.

"I did get in."

"Stubborn man," said the older woman in a rich voice the timbre of Artemisia's.

"He's Garrett Primross," Tiana said.

And then she was there, Artemisia; he smelled her fragrance and smiled and bled a little more. "HeartMate," he said.

"HeartMate!" The older Healer took her hands off him and he hurt, hurt, hurt. She looked at Artemisia.

"HeartMate!" Tiana pivoted and stared at her sister.

"Lady and Lord!" Artemisia sank next to him, framed his face with her delightful Healing palms.

"Artemisia." Garrett sighed, then, "Guess you didn't tell them, huh?"

"No!" the other women said far too loudly. Now his hearing was sensitized. Did the damn wall spellshields act on all his senses?

Her relatives frowned at Artemisia and she was displeased.

"Uh-oh," Garrett said, not sure if he meant the words for himself or his love. Blackness drove away the starry night sky, the edge of the rising moons, and swallowed him.

*A*rtemisia sat in the Family mainspace with her parents and sister. Everyone was trying to be quiet and kind, but she knew them; they seethed with questions.

Garrett was Healed and resting upstairs in one of the bedrooms they kept for the wounded and sick.

Randa was outside the House, exploring but near. The raccoon's mother had vanished back into a wilder portion of the estate when Artemisia had stopped to care for Garrett.

But now she faced her Family. She'd been with Garrett often enough to learn how to make a brief, factual report, so she did—reminding her Family of his experience with the Iasc sickness the first time around, touching on Dinni, whom none of them had heard about, recapping the experiment, and finally laying out his position with regard to the murder.

There were a few exclamations and murmurs from her mother and Tiana; her father lowered his brows as he did when he considered a legal problem. Nobody brought up that she hadn't gone to Laev T'Hawthorn to claim the favor.

Artemisia had *not* told them that Garrett had informed her that she was his HeartMate, but let them assume that they'd discovered each other. Her mother and Tiana seemed to believe that.

Artemisia had said her courtship with Garrett had been rocky, but they'd visited Leger Cinchona and T'Sandalwood that evening and she was hopeful. She wasn't sure whether that was a lie or not.

"I'll speak to Primross later," Artemisia's father said.

"I am unsure whether he is an acceptable suitor," the other male in her life—BalmHeal Residence—said.

"He's her HeartMate," Tiana stated in her that's-the-end-of-the-discussion priestess voice.

The Residence creaked and Artemisia knew he disagreed.

Garrett woke to a soft light that showed a room decorated in shades of blue, the scent of Healing herbs and more—the smell of antiquity. Really old furniture and spells that had been infused in the House for a long, long time. Maybe old spells that didn't quite use the same herbal components or combinations that modern ones did. Interesting.

Rusby was curled by his left shoulder. His Healed left shoulder. He glanced down at his bare chest: no burns.

It hadn't been easy, but he'd done it. He was in BalmHeal estate, the sanctuary where his HeartMate lived.

He sat and groaned at the twinges of lingering bruises. "You are awake; I will tell Quina Mugwort," a cranky male voice said.

Garrett stilled a moment. Slid his gaze around the room. No one was there. So . . . he must be in an intelligent House. That was unexpected, but explained a few things. "BalmHeal Residence?"

Yes, said Rusby mentally, mouth wide in a yawn, showing his baby teeth.

"Yess." It was the hiss of scratchy tree branches scraping against a window. Then the shutters to his own window slammed shut.

"You'll tell the elder Healer, not Artemisia?" Garrett asked and heard the near-plaintive note in his voice. Unattractive. He rolled from under the sheet and off the bedsponge to his feet and found himself nude.

"The Mugworts are having a Family meeting to question her about you," the Residence said.

Didn't sound good. "I need to go to her, to help." This time his voice was firm and he was relieved.

"There are stacks of tunics and trous in the wardrobe," the intelligent House said. "The extra large should fit you."

"Thank you." Best to be overly polite.

"*She* said you were her HeartMate," the House continued.

"Artemisia? Yes, I am." He was getting better about admitting that aloud to strangers.

YES, HE IS, yelled the kitten.

Garrett winced. "I don't think BalmHeal Residence can hear you yet, Rusby."

The kitten frowned or pouted, whatever, his muzzle scrunched and his whiskers flicking.

"I wanted Artemisia to marry one of the new Blackthorns," said the Residence with a creak of the windowsill sounding like a whine.

Rusby snorted. *Stup House. My FamMan is better than any Blackthorn.* The kitten hopped from the bedsponge to lick Garrett's ankle.

He gulped at the idea of Artemisia as one of the greatest ladies on the planet, figured his kitten had no clue who the Blackthorns were, then said, "Of course you'd want a FirstFamily Lord for Artemisia. You love her and want the best for her." He went to the wardrobe and opened it, took out a large tunic and trous that looked like training gear of a soft gray material.

They felt good on.

"You are right," the Residence said, the words not as irritated as previously. It sounded as if the sentient House was actually listening. Rusby had gone to the door and was sticking his paws under the crack at the bottom, playing with a stray scrap of cloth.

"I'm her HeartMate and will fit her best," Garrett said.

"Artemisia said that your courtship was rocky. You hurt her?" demanded the Residence.

Rusby stopped playing to hiss, "Yess," aloud.

Garrett could have done without the insert by his Fam. He answered, "We hurt each other. But that, I hope, is over. You must know that even couples who are HeartMates and have been Heart-Bound for a long time still have conflicts."

"Ye-es." The Residence paused and said, " 'The course of true love never did run smooth.' "

It sounded like a quote, in as vibrant a voice as the Turquoise House had. Garrett would have bet the actor who'd given TQ that voice would know the quote, but Garrett didn't.

He shut the wardrobe door, found his coins on a table with the items that had been in his trous pockets, his belt, and his blazer, and began rolling the silvers over his fingers.

"What are you doing?" asked the Residence.

That settled that. There was a viz or camera or scrystone in the room. Garrett didn't like it, but he *was* in one of the sickrooms, where the Healers would want to monitor people.

"My ancestors' name was Primrose."

"Theater folk!"

"Yes, but I don't recognize the quote."

"From Shakespeare's *A Midsummer Night's Dream*."

"Uh-huh." Garrett knew the ancient Earthan name, thought the play was a tragedy, and figured he wouldn't be watching it anytime soon. "Well, the—" There was a special name for Shakespeare, wasn't there? He had enough knowledge of his heritage he should be able to recall it. Ah, yeah. "The Bard was right. Our love hasn't been smooth."

He walked to the door and pushed through.

Food! Rusby said.

"I heard that," BalmHeal Residence said. "Yes. Kittens need food at short and regular intervals. I will inform the Family that GentleSir Primross is awake—"

"Call me Garrett," he said.

"—and you two will be going down to the Family mainspace."

"Thank you, Residence," Garrett said. Rusby turned left and darted down the hallway.

Garrett followed, thinking about true love. He swallowed. He didn't know much about HeartMate love, only knew his body yearned for Artemisia's, and they had a good connection that emotions flowed through.

No, their courtship and true love hadn't been smooth. But he hoped their in-person loving would be. Did he dare hope they could come together tonight?

*G*arrett settled Rusby in the kitchen slurping up special kitten food from the no-time there before being guided by the Residence to the mainspace.

He rapped on the door, then opened it on a Family scene. They all sat in a small circle of chairs arranged near a wall-long window. Artemisia looked comfortable, not as if she'd been grilled. That was good.

Now that he thought of it, he tried to recall the emotions pulsing through their open link and couldn't . . . so she hadn't been tense enough to alert him.

He nearly envied her the obvious closeness of her Family. His parents had been HeartMates, more involved in each other than their son, who'd been an afterthought of their relationship. They'd died when he was seventeen, just after he'd become an adult, and he'd missed them a little. Not as much as the others on the Smallage estate who'd been his extended Family.

The Family stood. "Greetyou," said Artemisia's mother, father, and sister in unison.

Garrett let a sigh whisper out. He gave them all a deep and formal bow, then said, "Greetyou, I'm Garrett Primross. Thank you for your Healing."

Artemisia's mother walked forward, a welcoming smile on her

face, but her gaze wary. "I am Quina Mugwort." She gestured to the man, must be a HeartMate the way they acted. "This is my husband and HeartMate, Sinjin, and my daughter Tiana."

The former judge and GraceLord Mugwort gave Garrett a short bow. He was nearly as tall as Garrett, but thin. His eyes were as sharp as any guard's, Noble's, or lawmaker's that Garrett had ever seen. Caution ran through his muscles.

But the former lord joined fingers with his wife and they raised their hands. Flair entered the atmosphere and one of the chairs from a different furniture grouping moved to the Family circle. The other chairs rearranged themselves, too.

Garrett was being included in the Family. His heart gave a jolt. His eyes met Artemisia's and she smiled.

"Thank you." He cleared his throat, met each of the others' gazes. "Thank you for the welcome."

Sinjin nodded with a slight smile. "You showed great determination in persisting against the spellshields of the estate. We will see if we can key them to you."

"Shall I contact the former occupant who does that?" asked the Residence.

This time the silence was longer than Garrett cared for.

"Yes!" Artemisia said and came to him, hands offered.

He accepted them gratefully, enjoyed the snap of connection between them, the way his body heated and a flush came to her cheeks.

"Ahem." Sinjin coughed.

When Artemisia turned to look at her father, Garrett slid an arm around her waist . . . and nearly went light-headed. He hadn't ever been so close to her while he was healthy.

Sinjin gestured to the chairs. "Artemisia told us you are in charge of the murder investigation of Modoc Eryngo. Shall we get a few things regarding that matter cleared up, first?"

First. That meant *he* would be grilled. This time Garrett suppressed a sigh. He nodded.

Artemisia stepped from his grasp and went to her chair.

Thirty-three

The elder Mugworts and Tiana also took their chairs, and Garrett sank into his—a deep maroon leather furrabeast deal with brass studs—not as faded as the others because it had been in a corner. Rusby trotted through the open door and jumped onto Garrett's knee and sat up.

I am Rusby Primross, he announced.

From the smiles on the others' faces, they'd all heard him.

"Artemisia told us about you," Quina Mugwort, Artemisia's mother, said. "Welcome."

Thank you. The little cat's head swiveled. *Where is the raccoon?*

"Randa is still primarily nocturnal," Artemisia said. "She's exploring the bushes around the House."

Garrett caught himself clearing his throat again. He didn't like the weakness. "I will have to speak with her about the case."

Artemisia's lips pressed together, then she said, "Very well."

"Now," Sinjin Mugwort, Artemisia's father, said, "we should formally offer Garrett our alibis."

"Thank you," Garrett said again. He hadn't said that phrase so often in years.

"I was at a spiritual vigil at GreatCircle Temple," Tiana offered, with a professionally serene expression on her face covering a turmoil of emotions Garrett sensed. Unlike her mother and her sister, the priestess didn't have a deep inner calm. She continued, "As Artemisia was on a vigil with you while you suffered from the Iasc sickness at the Turquoise House. That can be proven for us both."

"It has been," Garrett agreed.

The elder Mugworts relaxed.

"And my HeartMate and I were here," said Sinjin mildly.

Garrett knew instinctively that the man had told the truth. His whole manner was that of a person with great honor. Too bad the newssheets had smirched that.

"BalmHeal Residence," Sinjin raised his voice.

"Yes, Sinjin?"

"You can submit physical evidence that my HeartMate and I were here in your Residence at the time of the murder?"

"Of course. I have sent data regarding your—ah—activities, breathing rate and pulse and so on, for the time that the *experts* believe that the murder occurred to T'Hawthorn Residence for Laev T'Hawthorn, who is handling this matter for the FirstFamilies. He will share it with the guards if necessary."

"Activities?" Sinjin said blankly.

His wife chuckled but turned pink.

"Well, that's awkward," the former judge said.

Garrett kept his amusement from showing. "But very lucky."

Quina laughed, winked at her husband. "He often gets lucky."

"The data has been transferred to GentleSir Primross's office, too, since he is in charge of this investigation. I have confirmed with *all* the Residences of the FirstFamilies that they agree that the Turquoise House's information about Artemisia's alibi is true," the Residence said. "They have informed their lords and ladies."

It was evident to Garrett that the Residence loved Artemisia most.

I told everyone, too! Rusby said.

"Of course you did." Artemisia reached out and petted the kitten, who arched under her fingers. Garrett wished she'd put her hand on his thigh instead.

"And the highest priest and priestess in the land vouch for Tiana," Garrett said. He slanted a smile at Quina and Sinjin Mugwort, who were holding hands, then continued softly, "Neither of you have stepped foot on Druida streets for fifteen years."

Sinjin blinked as if in surprise, looked around the room and at his Family and out to the gardens, then inclined his head. "I hadn't quite realized, the estate is large with many pleasures." He squeezed his lady's hand. "But you are correct, Garrett. We have remained behind the walls except for a time or two when we have teleported to GreatCircle Temple to take part in a ritual Tiana was officiating." He swept a hand around him. "It is not easy to teleport into or out of the Residence and beyond the estate's shields, but with preparation it can be done."

An antique timer on the fireplace mantel bonged and they all looked at it.

"I didn't realize it was so late," Tiana murmured. "I should retire; I have a dawn ritual tomorrow." She rose.

Artemisia's mother and father stood, too. Artemisia followed and Garrett's pulse began to pump a little faster as he placed Rusby on his shoulder and got to his feet. It was night and he was here with his HeartMate. Everyone else was going to bed.

Artemisia's mother looked him up and down. "We will put you back into the second-floor sickroom and *talk* tomorrow." Garrett was pretty sure the room he'd been in was nowhere near Artemisia's. Her Family was very protective.

They must have seen her distress over the past couple of days and now understood he'd caused it. So they didn't want him near her tonight.

"I have requested all information regarding GentleSir Garrett Primross from all Residences and the Turquoise House," BalmHeal said.

Garrett winced. Despite his reassurances, the Residence wasn't on his side. Or, rather, the side of HeartMates. Damn.

But the bond between himself and Artemisia was wide open and fizzed with attraction and desire. He kept his expression serious.

"Fine with me." He let everyone precede him and stayed close to Artemisia. Her desire was mounting like his own.

"I'll feed Rusby another small meal." Anything to keep his kitten happy and maybe sleeping when he found Artemisia or she found him.

At the door Tiana stopped and looked at Artemisia and Garrett behind her. "Speaking of Leger Cinchona, he's proceeded quickly with regard to Apollopa Park. He'll be having a cleansing and recon-secration ceremony at twinmoonsrise a little after EveningBell tomorrow. He invited you." Tiana's smile was quick and sincere. "Both of you. He seemed to believe that you were together."

"We are," Garrett said.

"And Leger thought I would speak to you," Tiana said.

"You did," he added blandly.

"Um-hmm. Good night." A longer pause and a sly smile from her that matched her dancing eyes. "And sweet dreams." The priestess's glance lit on her hand in hand parents and her gaze softened. "You're invited, too, of course. It would be good for you to go into the city, do something other than teleport to GreatCircle Temple and back."

"We'll think about it," Quina said.

Tiana glanced aside, then back. "You always say that."

"We'll think about it," Sinjin said.

Tiana's expression lit with joy. "And you don't." She hugged them both solidly, kissed her father, then her mother on their cheeks. Garrett thought this was the usual nightly custom and felt another twinge of envy.

"Good night," called Tiana and went up the stairs, turning right at the top of the landing at the second floor.

Artemisia's parents lingered at the bottom of the stairs and stared at him—well, the guy watched him with resignation after he'd hugged and kissed Artemisia. Artemisia's mother did the same, then glared at Garrett until her older daughter went upstairs. Garrett listened and heard her footsteps continue to the third floor, then lost track of them.

Food! Rusby prompted.

"Sure." Garrett nodded to the older Mugworts and turned to take care of his Fam. "Good meeting you. I'll see you in the morning," he said.

*R*usby *was sleeping, splayed with kitten abandon in the middle of* Garrett's bedsponge. He stood at the window, staring out past the deep dark of the estate at the lights of the city and the distant hulk of the starship *Nuada's Sword*, body tight and yearning for his HeartMate.

She wasn't asleep, that he knew.

But it didn't appear as if she was coming to his bed, either. He wasn't sure what would happen if he prowled to her room. Would the Residence wake the elder Mugworts? Would the House give a running commentary of his actions? How private was Artemisia's room? Garrett didn't care for the idea of the House watching.

Recording pulse rates was bad enough. And how often did it do that, and why?

And he couldn't wait any longer.

No choice, he had to get out of the sentient House and lure Artemisia into his arms. He was real sure the Residence wouldn't keep him from leaving . . . or leaving the entire estate, either, though it shouldn't have control over the walls.

He shifted his shoulders. He didn't know what most Residences were capable of, let alone this one that had been the first Healing-Hall built by the Earthan colonists.

He found his boots and slipped them on. His trous were still being cleansed since they weren't around anywhere. He hesitated as he looked at his sword propped in the corner, but didn't take it. He *did* buckle his belt and slip his blazer into the holster.

Soft footed, he opened his door, closed it behind him. Again he paused, but he'd already decided not to bespell Rusby into a heavy sleep. That was wrong. He'd sense if Rusby came after him or was in danger from any animals that might roam the estate.

It wasn't right to spellshield the door, either, in this House that had welcomed him and wasn't his, on a room that was primarily for the sick.

And though the Residence didn't say anything, low-glowing spell-lights lit as he walked down the hall and the stairs, through the greatroom and to the wide front door.

He eased that door open and slipped into the night. When he was far enough away from the Residence that he didn't think it could feel him, he tugged on the ropelike link between himself and Artemisia, called to her, mind to mind. *HeartMate?*

There was a slight jerk of surprise on her part.

Garrett?

Who else? He put all the emotions he had for her in his words— desire, tenderness, respect, affection—and sent his need down their bond. *Come to me.*

She was silent.

Come to me. Come show me some of your home, he coaxed. He didn't hide his passion, didn't pretend he didn't want to make love with her. But he didn't overwhelm her with desire, didn't make it primary. *The night is wonderful, the stars and the sky.*

Somehow that tipped her decision. *I'll be there.*

He'd been correct in remembering her staring out the window at night. He allowed himself a satisfied smile, faded back into the grassy space that should have been a hard-packed gliderway, and looked up, trying to see a glow of light from her window. There wasn't one, which meant that her room probably was in the back of the House, with a view beyond the city.

Oh, yes, he knew where he was now. BalmHeal estate was tucked into the very northeast corner of the city, with its north and east walls the great city walls. He wasn't sure of the dimensions of the sanctuary, but he could learn that later. Maybe.

He didn't want to think about any more future than the next few minutes.

And then she opened the door and his heart beat faster. She wore the expensive shimmery silver robe that Lark Holly had given her. As she walked, it flowed against her body, showing the lush curve of her breasts or hips. She didn't appear to be wearing anything under the garment.

His mouth dried.

She moved to him and smiled and everything in the whole world got brighter—the galaxies of stars, the twinmoons silver bright, the very atmosphere around him.

"Garrett," she whispered.

"You're gorgeous," he said. He took her hand and his sex hardened, lust seared through him, and his movement was jerky as he drew her arm through his own. The fragrance of her own sexual readiness rose to him and he had to freeze so he wouldn't pounce. He must go slow so he wouldn't frighten her or disappoint her or make her wish that she'd never had a HeartMate. Most important, he had to ensure she wouldn't regret making love with him. Not tonight, not tomorrow morning, not ever.

"BalmHeal estate," he said in as much of a conversational tone as he could manage. "FirstGrove, the original Healing Grove and HealingHall." He stopped to draw a huge breath of air into his lungs. "The secret sanctuary of Druida that calls to the desperate. The hidden garden." He glanced around at the huge trees—Celtan and even Earthan and hybrids. Managed to get his feet going, one step after another, looked down to see her face tilted up to his, lovely, smiling, happy.

That was good. Good start. Keep going.

His side tingled where her arm was. They were linked together in the most innocent of ways, but *connected physically* enough to make him light-headed. "Did I tell you that I've been having dreams about a secret garden?"

Her smile widened into a beam. "No."

"It's a rusty iron gate, with curlicues, and a turquoise pool beyond. Lots of plants."

Her eyebrows peaked in question. "Hmm."

"Like this," he said, and sent her an image—then regretted it when he saw in his mind's eye that he wore his weapon harness with his sword and his holster with his blazer.

"Oh." It was a soft exclamation. "I know where that is, one of the enclosed gardens with a minor Healing pool. It's rectangular. We like the curved ones better, and the major pool is a series of curves."

"This garden and pool is on the estate?" If it wasn't often visited by the Mugwort Family, that was all to the good.

"Yes." She laughed quietly. "But it won't be the amber color of the sun. Not tonight."

"No." A thought occurred. "What of the sacred grove that was included in the mural on TQ's wall that I liked so much?"

She dipped her head. "Yes. We have several groves here, the main Healing Grove, of course, close to the primary Healing pools, and, um, three groves we use for rituals. The most sacred grove is the farthest from the House, near the southwest corner of the estate and the southern door."

He gave up the idea of making love with her there. Too damn far. He could barely think and talk and walk at the same time and was holding on to the threads of his control.

"What about the garden in my dreams? How, uh, close is it?" Again he thought of the vision, yeah, there was groomed grass there, good enough for nice loving. If the damn vision was true. He had no doubt he and Artemisia would make this place their own. He hurried the pace a little, hoping they were going in the right direction. They'd been walking diagonally from the House, southeast.

She tugged on his arm and he followed her turn to the north. "That hidden garden is between the House and the herbal stillroom building."

"Close?" He slowed his steps so he could bend his head to hers, brush his lips against her temple, breathe in the fragrance of her.

"Yes," she whispered.

Artemisia knew what would happen, that she and her Heart-Mate were heading toward sex. Quivers slipped along her nerves, her nipples tightened, her palms dampened, and so did her core.

He wanted her, probably as much as she wanted him. His need was a fire along their bond, a red orange ravaging hot passion.

She liked it and enjoyed knowing that the desire was for her and matched her own. She could see the faint sheen of perspiration on his cheek, on his neck, and his chest revealed by the V of his loose tunic-robe. He smelled good, the best male smell that she'd ever experienced.

She withdrew her arm from where he had it clamped against his side and took his hand. As she did she thought she heard a catch of his breath and maybe a small groan, which had her wetting her lips in anticipation.

Yes, she wanted this and wanted him.

He'd hurt his body to find her and come to her.

He'd bared his emotions earlier in the day to show his most inner self to her, reveal all his doubts and fears and faults.

She had plenty of those herself, but it was time to set the emotional aside and let the physical rule.

They paused at the gates of the garden, rusted open as he'd seen in his dream, and she squeezed his hand as she led him through, wondering why it was this place that he'd seen instead of anywhere else on the estate.

The pool gleamed in the twinmoonslight. She'd no sooner stepped on the thick turf than he dropped her hand and turned to her.

His face was taut with desire, his gaze intense, with dilated eyes. They stood looking at each other, then he touched the tabs at the top of her shoulders and her robe fell in silver waves at her feet. He stared at her, and his eyes fired, his chest rose and fell with ragged breathing. All combined to spin lust thick enough in the air to envelope them.

"I'm finally here," he said. "With you. And you are so beautiful."

Thirty-four

He reached out and touched her above her heart, and the brush of his fingers on her breast had her nipples aching. She couldn't bear it, needed more of his hands on her, and her hands on him.

She stepped toward him, swayed closer as his wide and callused palm pressed against her breast, slid her fingers down the front overlap of his tunic, and opened it. More of his scent came to her, musky, tempting. She swallowed and tasted sweet desire.

Her hands flattened on the hard musculature of his chest, his hair teasing her sensitive palms. "I'm not the only beautiful one here," she said and heard her voice low and panting. She touched the waistband of his trous and they fell away, too, revealing his thick sex hard and ready. Her core clenched, and this time she whimpered. "Yes," she managed to whisper.

And he stepped from his trous, lifted her easily, and she was spun and placed supine on the dense grass, and the fragrance of crushed herbs imbued the night.

He knelt beside her and she focused on the strong, angular lines of his face. Lifting a hand he stroked her cheek and his wide mouth smiled. "Artemisia." Her name sounded soft and lyrical, she'd never forget that, and no one else would say it as well as he. Her heart pounded.

Then his face came close and his mouth pressed against hers, his tongue feathered along her lips, and she opened her mouth to him. Opened all of herself to him, the bond between them wide, wide and nothing but need.

Her fingers went to his face, traced the angle of his jaw. Such a dear face, she hadn't known how much she'd wanted to touch it and kept her hands there.

His hands curved over her shoulders, then stroked down her, caressing her breasts, rubbing lightly over her muscles until all of her ached and strained. And his tongue plunged into her mouth, probed, tangled with hers until the taste of him dizzied her with yearning.

He spread his fingers around her hips, swept his thumbs up and down on her stomach, and again a whimper broke from her. She arched into his touch, pulled her mouth away to beg, "Please. Please."

Nodding seriously, he brushed her swollen lips with his thumb. "I will please you. You and myself."

His breath trembled out of him and she was glad to see that. Her body clenched as he moved his fingers to cup her butt and squeezed.

Thinking sieved away, replaced by sensation. She let her hands slide down his strong neck, along the utterly male broadness of his shoulders.

And he was moving over her and between her legs and was a dark shadow against the bright sky as if he were a black nebula himself, full of awesome power.

His hips moved as he found her entrance and steadily surged in. She gasped at the luscious friction, the feeling of fullness, of completion. *Yes!*

Her hands went to his back, her fingertips pressing into the deep ridge along his spine. So big. So muscled. Just wonderful. She wrapped her legs around his hips, moaned at the fabulous sensation. Heated sexuality bound them tight, their hearts beating fast together, their lungs pumping hard.

She strove for the orgasm, but it was just beyond her reach without one . . . more . . . movement. Her gaze went to his and locked.

The world fell away. There was only him and her, only the savoring of the keen edge of passion. Loving that would slice deep but bind them together, not cleave them apart.

He reached out with shaking fingers and slipped them into her hair. "Soft. All of you. Silky." He closed his eyes and his jaw clenched and his hips rocked and it was good enough for her to moan again, beg again, "Please."

His chest expanded and she heard his breath. She *needed*. She would *get*. His back was damp as her hands massaged up it. His nostrils pinched. She touched his nape and was rewarded with another stroking, another stoking of her lust. Almost, almost.

She moved her fingers to the front of his shoulders, and trailed her nails down the front of him, scraping at his nipples.

He yelled and his hips pistoned and she grabbed on for the ride, the heat, the spiraling pleasure surging, surging, bursting until she exploded like a sun herself.

He moaned long and low, breath rattling, and they rolled and him inside her was fabulous. She saw the curled golden bond, the HeartBond, stopped herself from reaching for it, from trying to tie them together forever. Her deepest self needed for him to offer the bond. She would not.

And he stopped groaning and his arms fell away from her and she rested on his chest, on his body, such a man's body that she'd never had before. Incredible, the strength of him.

She heard the rustle of sound as he reached for something, then felt the exquisite glide of silkeen on her skin as he draped her robe over her. He kissed her head. "Sleep." He sighed.

So she did.

*S*omething tugged his hair, and he opened his eyes to see two masked raccoons snuffling at him. A feeling of doom engulfed him. Only the fact that sharp wild animal teeth were near his face. Only that. Not another foreshadowing. He didn't want another forewarning.

He sat up and the larger raccoon squeaked and retreated under a bush. In the lightening sky of dawn, her bright eyes gleamed as she watched him.

The other, smaller one scampered around him to the far side of Artemisia. He and his lover—his lover! his HeartMate—had been sleeping side-by-side.

I AM RANDA MUGWORT AND I AM THE FAMRAC-COON TO MY FAMWOMAN, ARTEMISIA! she shouted mentally as if he were mind deaf. She sat back, her long forepaws clasped together.

"I hear you fine." His own voice rasped. He rubbed the back of his neck where the feeling of dread had lodged, ready to slither down his spine.

My FamWoman said my dam and I had to talk to you. Randa's glance darted to the larger one under the bush. *About the big red anger who killed the man and hurt me.* Randa trembled with fear.

Garrett wanted to stroke her but knew that wouldn't be allowed.

We are here. Also, my dam found a piece of the bad thing and hid it.

"The knife sheath?" He formed the image in his mind and projected it to both raccoons. The elder one yipped.

Artemisia snuffled beside him, rose to an elbow, and the movement attracted his gaze to her full breasts. His mouth watered and he suppressed the stirring of his body. Not right now. Dammit, he had to deal with skittish raccoons and murder right now, not sweet loving.

"Artemisia!" called Quina Mugwort.

Expression confused, Artemisia sat up, pushing her hair out of her face. "Wha'?"

"Artemisia! Primary HealingHall has scried and needs you there to start a shift ASAP!"

"Hell," she grumbled. She turned to Garrett, wrapped her arms

around him, and gave him a satisfying kiss that included sweeps of
her tongue and a good squeeze. "Later." She stood, bent, and picked
up her robe. "I'm 'porting to my room," she called to her mother,
then disappeared.

The rustling march of footsteps kept coming in his direction.
"Hell," he muttered himself, hopped to his feet. The older raccoon
shrieked and shot through the gate. Didn't want to be trapped. Garrett ran to the pool and dove in to clean off sex. It was cold. Colder
than any Healing pool had a right to be. More like a damn cold
plunge pool. He'd never liked those. But he didn't have a problem
with arousal anymore.

Artemisia's mother strode through the rusted gate and looked at
him in the pool, the heap of his clothes. She was carrying folded
cloth. "Artemisia isn't here," she said.

Pretty obvious, and, crap, he wasn't staying in the damn pool,
shriveling his balls. The grass and herbal groundcover might show
loving, but he wouldn't smell of it anymore.

"No, she teleported to her room when you yelled about the shift
at Primary HealingHall." He swam to the rounded steps in the corner and slogged up and out.

A triumphant smile lurked at the corners of the Healer's eyes. She
held out her arms with the bundle, saying, "Here are your trous and
a good, sturdy shirt."

She hadn't bothered to bring a towel. Good thing it was high
summer. He took the clothes from her and pulled them on. "Thanks."
He grabbed his liners and boots and put them on, too.

"You're welcome."

She didn't really mean that.

Randa loped up and pawed at his boots, leaving scratches; he
was glad he didn't mind that sort of thing, either.

"Oh." Quina stepped back. "I didn't see you, Randa."

Garrett picked the raccoon up; her fur was thicker, seemed more
layered than a cat's, and not as soft. He cradled her in the elbow of
his arm.

FamMan needs to talk to me about the big red anger, Randa

said, then hid her pointed nose and muzzle between his arm and side.

"She seems to trust you," Quina said thoughtfully.

"I'm a trustworthy guy."

"Hmm." Now she looked him up and down again. "Maybe." But her mouth pinched under lines.

My mother is running, running, running. We need to catch up! Randa said.

"I'll leave you to your business." He gave a half bow.

"You really are my Artemisia's HeartMate?"

"I really am."

Quina Mugwort swallowed. "She does not have a HeartGift to give you. Due to the extremities of our scandal, that was taken from her, her Passages were rushed." The woman looked at him, eyes tearful. "She should have been a FirstLevel Healer, but rushed Passages constrain that."

"What!"

Tears slid down Quina's face. She didn't wipe them away but gestured as if wiping the past away. "It's done and can't be undone, best not to brood on it."

As he had brooded on the past, and Artemisia hadn't. Ire lit within him. What had her parents been doing that they couldn't give Artemisia a good environment to experience her Passages? He'd find out.

He petted Randa. "I need to go now." Courtesy was pulled from him to this woman much like his HeartMate. "Merry meet."

"And merry part."

"And merry meet again." He walked from the hidden garden. *Is your dam still on the estate?* he asked Randa.

Yes, she doesn't want to go back out into the world.

The world was a fascinating place. He'd go mad if he stayed within these walls as the elder Mugworts had done.

Tell your dam to find a place she feels safe to talk. That was how he always proceeded when recruiting Fam ferals.

As he strode the path to the main Healing pool, the sun rose and a multilayered chorus of birdcall sounded. Night-blooming flowers closed as he walked, and others opened.

Sometimes paths twisted and turned into overgrowth or animal trails, sometimes they were well-worn. Occasionally he'd find himself on a rise with a panorama before him—the city walls, a glimpse of the large curvy pool set in rich moss and grass framed by trellises and arbors.

His body moved well, each strand of muscle, each tendon, felt healthy. A weight had lifted from his emotions. He'd accepted that he had a HeartMate, had joined with her, and was on the way to truly loving her for just who she was. Serene, strong, generous, courageous.

Then the simple fact about the murder that he'd missed slid into his mind on an arc of brilliance and he knew who the killer was . . . could even guess why.

He'd need proof: whatever he could glean from the raccoons, and the knife sheath.

Soon he sat on a bench under a tree, addressing the raccoon above him.

"I must know more about the person who killed the human in Apollopa Park where you denned, if you saw the murderer, or were there at the time."

Yess, came a mental hiss. *I was there. Watched prey killed, watched human dance, saw cat watch. We all did.*

"All your family?"

Yes. He I mated with has forgot. I remember.

"I'm sorry, but I do need you to tell me every detail." He stretched, loosening muscles that had tightened into near battle readiness.

Randa sat next to him on a wooden bench, warm in the sun. He stroked her, picked her up, and held her so she was level with his eyes. She had no fear of him.

"You saw, too?"

She bobbed her head, gave a little shudder in his hands. *Yes.*

Glancing up at the raccoon, he said, "Part of my Flair is being able to merge my mind with a Fam's." Not that he did it often. He much preferred speaking telepathically; often that was challenge enough.

"I am asking Randa to let me see and experience what she did when the murder took place."

Randa shuddered and he rumbled a soothing noise. "I will help her remember. Then I would like to try the same with you."

The mother raccoon stared at Garrett. *Will you hold me, too?*

He didn't know if she wanted or feared that. "It's best if I have a physical connection. I could hold you, or one of your paws, or you could put your paw on the back of my hand. You can run if you need to, I promise, and my word is good."

Talk to Randa, first.

"Very well." He put Randa on his lap, and his hand on her back. She met his eyes.

"Ready?"

Yes, FamMan.

Her trust made him smile. "All right."

Gently, gently, he linked minds with her. *Think of the big red anger.* She cried out. He petted her. "I am here with you, I will keep you safe."

I feel you!

Yes. I will keep you safe. Remember the time. He thought of night sky after midnight, imposed the image of Apollopa Park. With his Flair, he helped retrieve what was being lost.

His vision skewed and colors left . . . except a big red anger. He barely saw the killing, though Randa had watched. He caught glimpses of the murderer, the shape, the anger, the glee in the triumphant dancing in the fountain. Randa's mind zoomed to a different, later memory, one of thundering footsteps and yelling human and kicking at burrow-home. Dirt spurted, soil flew, Randa dropped the odd thing she held and ran. *Huge* pain stabbed her side. She teleported a few blocks away to an old den.

Randa's heart pounded too hard with fear. He drew away mentally. His shirt was damp. "Let the memory go."

The small raccoon slumped on his lap.

"Great Fam. Great job."

Randa snuffled and wiped her damp and pointy nose on his trous. He ignored the smear, though Rusby wouldn't like it.

Garrett petted her until she stepped from his lap to the bench. She looked at her dam.

Easy! Not bad.

The elder female chittered but dropped from the tree onto Garrett's shoulder, balanced, then hopped down next to him. She put both her paws on his leg, dug in a little with her claws, enough that he knew she could rip his trous and the skin under them to bloody shreds.

Thirty-five

You may pet, said *Randa's dam. He brushed her pelt with his palm. That is nice!*

"For me, also." He kept his body casual, his stroking soft, appreciated the sun and flowering bushes. This, too, was a hidden garden, a little hollow with only the bench and a birdbath. He sensed Sinjin Mugwort spent time here.

I am ready, the raccoon said mentally, in a calmer voice.

He linked with her, saw the events of the killing from a different angle. One person snuck up on another, raised an arm, and the first fell. Then they were both on the ground and the prey's neck was tilted back. A vial gleamed, liquid was poured into his mouth. His arms were slashed. The killer rose and held the knife high, then dropped it close to the body and went to dance in the fountain.

Time passed. Big red anger left. Left shiny strange thing. Felt bad but was a tool. Raccoons didn't often get tools, things left by humans, in a place where humans didn't come much. Tools humans wouldn't miss.

Randa's mother took the knife, but it felt terrible to her sensitive pads, and she hid it. The sheath didn't feel as bad, but she hid that, too, in a different place.

Later the big red anger came and kicked open the burrow and found the knife and threw it and hurt her kit and all the raccoons scattered. Run! Run! Run!

A moaning squeal knocked the link apart and the raccoon headed back up the tree.

Garrett flinched and his eyes refocused on the birdbath where sparrows splashed.

He stood and crossed to the birdbath, now moving like an old man, his Flair depleted. Bracing his arms on the round rim of the bath, he plunged his head in the bowl and welcomed the cool slap of the water.

His eyes hurt. Leaning over, he propped his arms on his thighs and did some energized breathing. A man was not supposed to stay in another creature's mind for long.

Then he turned back to the mother raccoon, saw her in the tree. "I need to find that sheath. Can you take me to it?" It had felt different to the raccoon, might have left traces of the perpetrator that the knife hadn't . . . since the knife had been stuck in Randa, then thrown into one of the best Healing pools in the land. Physical evidence had been disturbed, and the layers of psychic evidence were being difficult to excavate.

I will do this. And you will take me to meet the Fam Healer, Danith D'Ash.

"Done," Garrett said.

FAMMAN! Rusby yelled, then pranced into the glen a moment later, looking incredibly tiny. *I am here! I had breakfast.* He belched. *And I found you all by myself!* He grinned.

The mother raccoon said, *I will meet you in Apollopa Park when the big bell in the city rings again.*

Almost a full septhour, seventy minutes.

There was the rustle of leaves and she vanished. Teleported away? Or had she landed on the wall to the city and was running along it? Garrett still didn't know the exact dimensions of the estate, and wasn't quite sure where he was inside the sanctuary or in relation to the city, a situation that dissatisfied him. Being good with directions, knowing where he was, was part of his Flair. And where was the nearest teleportation pad outside the estate? Yet the raccoon seemed to think he had time to head home and reach the park.

I will go with you, Randa said.

"What?"

My FamWoman is at the Primary HealingHall, and I do not want to be here alone, even though I am getting sleepy. I will go with you.

"You have the Mugworts to look after you," Garrett pointed out.

Yes, they are my FamWoman's. But you are hers more.

That gave Garrett a funny feeling in his chest. He'd seen the HeartBond when they'd made love. But Artemisia had not offered the golden bond to him, as he'd expected.

It felt odd.

Being a HeartMate felt odd, too. He—they—were just getting used to it. The bond would happen in time when they were ready. Meanwhile, he didn't think Artemisia would be meeting or sleeping with any other men.

He wasn't sure how long this grace period would last, but he'd savor every moment of it. Maybe he could change faster now that the future beckoned with joy.

Garrett scooped up Rusby and forced himself into a fast walk, hoping he could grab a quick breakfast before he gathered his sword and the items for his trous pockets. He didn't look at the temptation of the Healing pool as he went by, much as he'd like to soak a long time and recharge.

He, Rusby, and Randa stopped off at MidClass Lodge for a waterfall and change—naturally the Fams didn't stand under the water, but ate. Randa had sniffed around his apartment before curling up on a chair and had looked a lot more like a wild animal than any cats or dogs he'd entertained.

He knew the public carrier schedules and stepped outside the main door of MidClass Lodge just in time to enter the glider that would pass Apollopa Park. Both Randa and Rusby sat on his lap.

The other riders stared at the Fams, particularly the raccoon, and he had a casual conversation.

When the bus stopped at the plinth near Apollopa Park, Rusby scrambled up to his shoulder and Randa perched on the small shelf of his forearm across his chest as they descended.

The public carrier trundled on and Garrett stared at the round park, obviously being groomed for Cinchona's ceremony that evening. Two gardeners worked on the landscape and a lower-level priestess stood in the basin of the fountain, hands raised, cleaning and polishing the mirrors.

A few people lingered to watch the activity, and there were some across the street, too.

Too many humans! Randa said telepathically. *My mother will be hiding.*

Garrett had figured that. It was a good thing he had Randa with him after all.

We are coming here for the ritual later? Rusby asked, head cocked as he observed the scene.

Since he was sure that Artemisia would attend, Garrett would be there, too, however reluctantly. "Yes."

Randa scuttled along the curving sidewalk and into the still ragged brush on the far side of the Temple. Though the small round columned building appeared to have had a layer or two of dirt vanquished, the roof still opened to the sky and cracks yet ran through the marble floor. On a closer look, one wall sagged badly. The priest might need an architect to handle the rehab. For some reason, the challenges Cinchona would face made Garrett smile. The man had certainly put him through the wringer the day before.

Thrashing and snuffling and chirping greetings came. Randa had found her mother. Both raccoons spurted from some low and thorny bushes, leaving a bit of fur on them. The older female continued along the back of the park and across the street that looked to divide an upper-middle-class neighborhood from lower.

Garrett followed as the raccoons threaded through unkempt

grassyards between homes and buildings until they came to a gulch with a trickle of stream running through the area.

The mother raccoon headed for a tiny cairn of rocks and some dried plants that hadn't survived the heat of the summer.

Garrett slid down the gentle meter of bank and went to where the mother raccoon indicated with a long-pawed gesture. She retreated a meter and sat back on her haunches, clasping her forepaws together.

Randa sniffed at it, then trotted to a large bush, wriggled under it, and curled up. *I want to see!* Rusby said.

"You can't disturb evidence."

I want to see this cut in the land.

Apparently his Fam had never been in a gully. Garrett detached the small kitten from his shoulder and placed him on the ground. With the dried straw-colored plants and light brown dirt and the dark water, his Fam nearly disappeared. "Be careful," he said.

Rusby took off running.

Garrett sighed and squatted down. He unstacked the rocks, brushed the dried plant stuff and dirt aside, saw the slight gleam of carved and polished wood. Pulling a collapsible Flaired-cloth evidence vacuum tube from a belt pocket, he flicked it out and into shape, then pried the knife sheath free from dried mud with a twig.

"You should give me that."

Garrett angled his head and saw the guardswoman Rosa Milk-weed standing at the top of the gulch, holding out her hand. She rested the fingertips of her other hand on the hilt of her blazer. She had a pleasant smile on her face, but her eyes appeared a little wild and her outstretched fingers trembled.

He thought fast, and as he straightened and turned, he used Flair to slip the sheath into the tube and seal it.

"Don't!" she said.

"Too late," he replied mildly, considering how to play this.

"I've been keeping an eye on Apollopa Park and I saw you and the raccoon—the one who took my knife and the sheath." She pulled her blazer and pointed it at him.

*   *   *

*A*rtemisia had finished tending to—and enjoyed talking with—her fourth case, but the relief in her chest remained huge. She'd been called back to work a full shift at Primary HealingHall. It seemed as if she could breathe again, as if there was still a good road to the future. She murmured a prayer of thanks to the Lady and Lord.

She sent a pulse of happiness down her link to Garrett and noticed he'd narrowed their bond to a filament. Puzzling, then the connection throbbed with his emotions . . . threat, danger.

She stopped in the middle of the corridor, blood draining from her head, heart pounding.

He was a trained warrior, a private investigator who must sometimes face danger. What should she do? She had the worst feeling that any action must be immediate.

FamWoman, FamMan is in trouble! The shrill mental voice was Rusby, Garrett's kitten, sounding terrified.

FamWoman, SEE! Randa called, and projected an odd vision of Garrett facing a blazer muzzle. The hand that held the weapon wasn't quite steady. Could the person be distracted?

"What is going on here?" barked FirstLevel Healer Ura Heather, and Artemisia realized she was leaning against the wall, eyes closed.

"My HeartMate's in trouble. I must go."

"WHAT!"

FirstLevel Healer Lark Holly was behind Ura Heather, and Artemisia focused on her compassionate face. "I must leave. Now."

"If you leave now, your job is forfeit, and I will ensure you will not work in any other Healing facility in Celta."

Artemisia's stomach coated with acid. "Nothing's as important as my HeartMate. I'm leaving. 'Porting. Step back," she said, feeling cold.

FAMS, HELP ME VISUALIZE, she sent to Randa and Rusby. Triangulating with the Fams, trusting their vision, she teleported.

And lost her balance on sloped ground and fell near Garrett's feet. She looked up and saw she'd made herself another target. Damn!

Rosa Milkweed laughed. "Lady and Lord, a Healer coming to save you."

Artemisia rocked to her hands and feet, turned her head to spit up some nauseating bile, then stood. "I'm sorry," she said to Garrett.

He nodded. His expression didn't change, but he sent a wave of love to her through the bond. And determination.

They were both determined.

"I know you were the one who killed Modoc," Garrett said.

Artemisia shivered. She'd made things a whole lot worse.

Trust me, said Garrett mentally.

She looked at his dear profile, started to link fingers, but he moved his.

No, I need my hands free.

Self-anger tears welled in Artemisia's throat. She'd screwed up. She wiped her sleeve across her mouth. Her Healing tunic was dirty and stained, her hair escaping her braid.

"Not hard to deduce that I executed Eryngo since I'm holding a blazer on you," Rosa said.

"You recognized Modoc Eryngo," Garrett stated.

Rosa nodded, tapped her temple. "Part of my Flair, personal identification. No matter how the criminal has changed his appearance or aged, I don't forget a face. One of the reasons I became a guard." She shook her head and gave a little snort. "His bad luck, really, that I happened to be at the old landing field talking to a friend." Her eyes glittered. "And I got him. Everyone else missed him, but I got him! Proved myself better than you all."

"Um-hmm." Garrett drew out the sound. Then Artemisia heard mentally, *Artemisia, Fams, all we need is a distraction.*

Artemisia didn't see either of their Fams, no other person or animal.

Rusby and Randa, go together to find some of my ferals.

Guardswoman Milkweed narrowed her eyes; how much was she sensing? Artemisia shifted her weight, scuffed her feet, and the woman's glance flickered to her. Let the guard think she was stupid and bumbling. She'd come up with something or help Garrett.

I must stay with you! Rusby said.

Go!

I go! Randa said.

Then his words really sank in. *A distraction! She could shoot you!* Artemisia sent back.

The blazer is not set on kill. I can take a shot and a shock and burn.

Oh, she didn't want that! She eyed the blazer, didn't know enough about them to figure out the settings. Though she *did* understand that even at the lowest setting, a shot could fry nerves, cripple a person beyond Healing.

She began to pray silently, and fastened her gaze on the woman, her enemy. Anger filled Artemisia. If she could act, she would.

And I have a Healer right here, Garrett added.

She supposed he thought that was amusing. But she caught the trace of his panic before he locked it down. She even smelled it.

Rosa isn't as good a guardswoman as I'd thought. She's talking. Artemisia tuned back in.

Rosa was saying, "Yes, I got him and I executed him and I'm proud of it. *I* was the guard to close the most abominable open case."

Not only had the case affected Milkweed for a long time, but ego had motivated the murder.

Garrett prompted, "You were at the landing port . . ."

"Yes, and I recognized Modoc as he got off the airship."

"And you followed him . . ."

"Yes."

Gotta keep her talking, Garrett said.

Artemisia couldn't think of anything to prompt the woman into more story and less action. The guard had killed before. Would she kill them? How easily did she kill?

"You acted pretty fast, taking care of Eryngo," Garrett said.

"Yes." Rosa hissed the word, and for the first time, Artemisia studied the woman's eyes. Unbalanced anger. "I didn't want to lose him, was due at the guardhouse shortly."

"But why did you implicate Artemisia—the cross-folk?" Garrett asked. His voice was smoother than Artemisia had ever heard, calm. Through their bond, she felt he was hyperalert, watching for any opening so he could pounce.

Rosa shrugged, but her blazer aim didn't waver much. Not enough that Artemisia could tell.

"I recalled that the fligger had used the cross-folk for misdirection and thought I might do the same. I knew the Primary Healing-Hall chapel was open and not many folk visited. I teleported to the HealingHall and got the altar knife, 'ported back to the landing strip, and followed the fligger."

"That's a lot of teleporting," Artemisia said.

She received a contemptuous glance of humor from the guardswoman. "I was wired."

"Where'd you get the pylor?" Garrett asked.

Rosa snorted. "The HealingHall, of course. Most Healers can put you to sleep with a touch." She tilted the blazer toward Artemisia. "But they aren't the only ones who work in the HealingHalls. The Halls have all sorts of drugs locked up in cases. Including a vial of pylor."

"FirstLevel Healer Ura Heather didn't report the loss of a vial of pylor," Garrett said.

"Who'd tell a bitch like her? Not if it was one little tube and easy to replace?"

"Enough to keep Modoc unconscious," Artemisia said.

"That's right. That's exactly right," Rosa said. She bared her teeth and her eyes fired. "Just like he and his filthy Cult did to their victims. He deserved it. He deserved *more*." Her ugly expression eased a bit . . . and back into triumph. "But I was there when the prophet said his next life would be miserable. It helps to believe that. Not as good as suffering in this one, but maybe good enough."

"You murdered him," Garrett said.

"I *executed* him." Her eyes narrowed. "You plan on taking me in, don't you?"

"You're a murderer."

She made a disgusted noise. "I'm an executioner. Eryngo was an evil, murdering man." Her lips tightened. "He'd be dead like all the rest by now. I executed justice." Her chin lifted, but her blazer hand remained steady. "And I'm proud of what I did."

"Not proud enough to turn yourself in."

"You just want some of my glory."

"No. I want to do this through the law, as I'd have wanted Modoc to suffer through the law." He jutted his chin. "And look what you're doing now—threatening innocent people."

Rosa shook her head. "I'm not going to hurt you, or Artemisia, either."

"You're pointing a blazer at us."

Artemisia didn't know how Garrett kept talking when his mind was working hard to get them out of this mess, scanning the area, testing his bonds with his ferals, sensing where all his informants were.

And Rosa kept talking. "You won't get hurt, much. Just enough for me to get away." She grimaced. "Suppose my days as a Druida guard are over."

Artemisia thought her mouth dropped open. She shivered with shocky cold. How would a blazer shot affect Garrett? Herself?

Garrett rolled his shoulders, ran his left hand along the front of his belt in a gesture that Artemisia had never seen before.

Get ready. Artemisia, hit the ground. Rusby, stay quiet. Garrett's calm mental voice seethed with underlying tension and excitement. "You keep using the word *executed*," Garrett said aloud with a hint of a sneer.

"You don't know anything! My very first case as a guard was Tern Sedum's murder by the Black Magic Cultists. I found him. He was so young, my age, and his life was *stolen*. I helped tell his parents that he was dead. I found his poor Fam, near death, Flair sucked from her. Since then I looked for him, watched faces all the time, and I got Eryngo when nobody else did. I did my job when everyone else forgot him. I am the best." Her lip curled. "That fliggering fligger Eryngo deserved everything he got. He got an *easy*—"

Garrett whipped out a huge, scarlet softleaf. Milkweed stopped, stared, fired at the drifting cloth. Garrett shot her.

Animals yelled battle cries. Artemisia was already lunging up the bank toward the woman. No more blazer sizzles, but the odor of fire and earth; she hit the woman . . . who was screaming and clutching her stomach, which showed the blackness of a blazer singe.

Blood bloomed on Milkweed's ear as Rusby yowled, jumping from her falling shoulder to the ground and shaking himself.

A wave of cats poured around them; scratches appeared on Rosa's cheeks, her scalp.

"That's enough!" Garrett ordered. "Let's finish this up. Rusby to my shoulder!" He hauled the guardswoman up, tumbling a few cats, and grabbed Artemisia, who was holding Randa, who'd jumped into her arms, and they all teleported away to land on the pad of the main Druida guardhouse.

Once Rosa was there, she couldn't stop bragging about how she was better than everyone in recognizing Eryngo and taking care of him. How she was proud that she'd closed the case. Keeping the secret of the execution to herself was good—but not as good as everyone knowing her triumph.

The vial with dregs of pylor was found in Rosa's apartment and her partner, Fol Berberis, just shook a sorrowful head, more that she'd been stupid than the fact she'd killed Eryngo.

And Winterberry followed up on that simple fact that Garrett and he had missed. In the Primary HealingHall cross-folk chapel, T'Blackthorn had stated that he'd seen nothing unusual.

Straif Blackthorn's Flair showed him *everyone* who had been there, and his or her trails. So he would have seen Rosa Milkweed's traces, seen her marks on the altar. So she'd fallen against it when she and Garrett and Artemisia had entered. She'd ensured her traces and tracks were there for any who had the Flair to see them.

Winterberry had scowled, scried his cousin-in-law Straif T'Blackthorn, and confirmed Garrett's deduction.

Then Laev T'Hawthorn showed up as a representative of the FirstFamilies—curious as always—and called in the best mind Healer, D'Sea. Who had taken one look at Rosa Milkweed and sighed. After a private consultation, D'Sea gave her opinion that she thought that with a long period of counseling, Rosa could be rehabilitated. Meanwhile a Flair tracking device would be inserted in her body, and, of course, she was dismissed from the Druida guards.

Anonymous donations had already shown up to care for her for the rest of her life.

The mind Healer firmly advised that Rosa's trial should be as private as possible. Then lawyers had gotten involved.

By that time, Garrett, Artemisia, some of his preening ferals, and the full gaze of raccoons had all been interviewed. A lively Danith D'Ash and her wide-eyed teenaged son had helped interpret for the feral Fams.

To Garrett's surprise, Sleek Black had taken a liking to Fol Berberis, and the feeling was mutual. Garrett figured that the feral wouldn't be hanging with his group in the future. And Garrett's secret about how he got info would soon be revealed. More people would pay attention to the animals around them.

Artemisia was completely calm, even though it came out that she'd been fired from her position at Primary HealingHall. At that, Garrett and Laev had shared a glance and Garrett had sent a mental sentence to his friend. *I will take care of this.* Laev had grinned and dipped his head.

For Garrett, being with Artemisia, even during all the tedious time it took to straighten everything out, was a wonder. She held his hand when they were together. Most often they sat on a wooden bench, waiting for everything to be wrapped up.

Wonderful. And he could tell from the bond that spun between them that her serenity was bone deep and natural, that during the previous time he'd spent with her she'd been off-balance.

I have found my HeartMate, she'd said simply, mind to mind, lifting their clasped hands to her lips and kissing his big fingers, her eyes meeting his. *Everything else can be finessed.*

He had grinned back at her. *We have plenty of options. You could even work with me in a partnership.*

She'd shuddered and he'd laughed aloud.

Finally they had been dismissed . . . and somehow the moment he'd known they were free—free and together and *safe*—he'd become unbearably aroused.

He needed her. Now.

So hand in hand, they teleported to the door of BalmHeal estate. Even before she'd melded her visualization of the spot with his, his mind had been clear enough to pinpoint the place. A good sign.

He could barely wait to love her.

Thirty-six

Artemisia frowned. *"How are we getting through the spellshields?"*

The Fams laughed and 'ported in, ran toward the Residence for food.

Garrett was touched at Artemisia's question. We. No doubt she could walk straight through the door, as always. But he'd already thought of a solution. He swung her easily into his arms.

She grinned up at him, locked her arms around his neck, and nibbled along his jawline. He panted with desire. "Let's try it this way. The wall shields know you and they should damn well know me since they got a lick of my blood and flesh."

Artemisia winced.

He said, "And they might even be able to sense the connection, the vibration, resonance, emotional ties, *whatever* between us. And my Flaired intention that I *will* be an inhabitant." As he strode the few paces to the door, she tensed, but though he felt stinging along his skin, he could ignore the sensation. "Open the door."

So she pressed the latch and the door swung open.

He could really feel the shields now, minor burning. He hurried through, released his held breath when he was past the wall, and kicked the door shut with a slam.

"We'll get the spellshields tuned for you," she promised.

"That would be good, but I think that if we shared a HeartBond, that would take care of the matter."

He *felt* her blood heat and pick up pace; she grew warmer in his arms and he liked it.

"There's a pretty glade to the left," she said.

"Good," he replied, though his own breath came a little faster since she'd opened the front of his shirt and was sliding her hands up and down his torso. His blood headed south to become sweet, edgy, urgent desire. His sex thickened.

He stepped from an arbor tunnel, turned left, followed her directions, and stood at the edge of a glen high with summer grasses and wildflowers.

So beautiful. Such a fitting place to love his Artemisia. He wished he had a blanket and a cooler of food and drink—wine and delicacies for his woman. His HeartMate.

Still, he walked to the center of the glade and slipped her down his body, enjoying the feel of her against his hard sex. Holding her hands, he stepped back to arm's length and said a couplet that had their clothes falling away.

Her gaze focused on his cock and he grew even harder, thicker, needier.

As for her—she was simply the most beautiful woman he'd ever seen—her breasts and hips full curves, her waist small, the tumble of her dark brown, black, deep red hair accenting the cream of her skin and the emerald of her eyes.

His. His. His. It was a chant of the pulsing of his blood, knowledge settling into the marrow of his bone.

"Love with me," he whispered.

"Yes."

"HeartBond with me," he said.

She stared at him with serious eyes. "We don't know each other well."

"Well enough." He stepped closer until his body touched hers, lifted one of her hands to his lips, then the other. "We will explore each other, and the future together."

Her smile bloomed bright and shining. "Yes."

So he took them down into the fragrant summer grass, the summer land, and their hands and mouths and tongues explored, producing sighs and quivers and a longing that only each other could assuage.

And when he couldn't wait anymore, he slid inside her and she tightened around him and they pounded the rhythm of love together. The HeartBond materialized and he threw it to her and she caught it and tied them together, and even as reality fell away, they were bound together forever.

He was whole and complete at last.

When he could, he opened his eyes, lazily noted her own dreamy gaze, the ruddiness of her lips. Beautiful.

Then her eyes cleared and he knew that the mundane would soon envelope them, the everyday. But wonder yet fizzed in his blood, a gentle serenity still stayed near, with him. Artemisia. HeartBonded HeartMate, a comfort even in the quiet moments of the day.

He pulled her close, until she was propped on his chest and he felt the soft weight of her breasts.

She sifted her fingers through his hair. "You're all right with living here with me?"

"Yes, of course. Living here will be great."

Her breath sighed out. "Good."

Yes, it was. A lovely place, a secret that he'd keep close. It, too, settled into his soul. But on to the everyday of things. "I'll need an office outside. And I think I can get your job back at Primary HealingHall."

"I don't know—"

"The newssheets are beginning to relate the results of the experiment. You are a heroine."

Her brows dipped. "I'm not."

He kissed her. "Oh, yes, you are. They've already told of your selflessness of staying at the bedside of a man suffering from the Iasc sickness for four days."

She blinked. "I did nothing out of the ordinary—"

"Not for a dedicated Healer," he said, lifted her fingers, and kissed them one by one. "But there wouldn't be many who would have done that, and most other Celtans would be scared down to their toenails at the thought. You're a heroine. And a heroine this morning, too. You'll be legendary. More than Ura Heather, who is a FirstFamily Lady who runs things, not acts." He smiled at her surprise. "And I think that lady will want to keep your fame tied directly to herself and Primary HealingHall."

"No, she doesn't like me."

Garrett shrugged. "That won't matter to her as much as the fame."

"You think?"

"I think. So now that we've got that settled." He ran a hand down to her lush hip, squeezed.

"We're HeartBound now," she said and her whole being seemed to glow to him. He'd done that, given her that glow.

And she'd given him peace and love like he'd never known.

HeartMates, HeartBound, they fit, were right for each other. He hadn't realized what that really had meant. "I love you. Marry me."

"Yes."

He grinned. "You're supposed to make me work harder for the answer."

She shook her head. "I don't think so."

Again he caught her hands, placed them over his heart so she could feel it beating—fast and for her. "The future is ours."

"Yes. The future is ours."

"And no more secrets," he said.

Her lips curved and she kissed him and he wanted more, but she withdrew. Her green gaze matched his. "Only those we keep together."

Robin D. Owens is a RITA Award–winning author. She lives in Denver, Colorado. Visit her website at www.robindowens.com.